Praise for Joseph Heywood and the Woods Cop Mystery series:

"Heywood has crafted an entertaining bunch of characters. An absorbing narrative twists and turns in a setting ripe for corruption."
—*Dallas Morning News*

"Crisp writing, great scenery, quirky characters and an absorbing plot add to the appeal. . . ."
—*Wall Street Journal*

"Heywood is a master of his form."
—*Detroit Free Press*

"Top-notch action scenes, engaging characters both major and minor, masterful dialogue, and a passionate sense of place make this a fine series."
—*Publishers Weekly*

"Joseph Heywood writes with a voice as unique and rugged as Michigan's Upper Peninsula itself."
—Steve Hamilton, Edgar® Award-winning author of *The Lock Artist*

"Well written, suspenseful, and bleakly humorous while moving as quickly as a wolf cutting through the winter woods. In addition to strong characters and . . . compelling romance, Heywood provides vivid, detailed descriptions of the wilderness and the various procedures and techniques of conservation officers and poachers. . . . Highly recommended."
—*Booklist*

"Taut and assured writing that hooked me from the start. Every word builds toward the ending, and along the way some of the writing took my breath away."
—Kirk Russell, author of *Dead Game* and *Redback*

"[A] tightly written mystery/crime novel . . . that offers a nice balance between belly laughs, head-scratching plot lines, and the real grit of modern police work."
—*Petersen's Hunting*

ALSO BY JOSEPH HEYWOOD

Woods Cop Mysteries
Ice Hunter
Blue Wolf in Green Fire
Chasing a Blond Moon
Running Dark
Strike Dog
Death Roe
Shadow of the Wolf Tree
Force of Blood
Killing a Cold One

Lute Bapcat Mysteries
Red Jacket
Mountains of the Misbegotten

Other Fiction
Taxi Dancer
The Berkut
The Domino Conspiracy
The Snowfly

Short Stories
Hard Ground
Harder Ground

Non-Fiction
Covered Waters: Tempests of a Nomadic Trouter

Cartoons
The ABCs of Snowmobiling

A WOODS COP MYSTERY

BUCKULAR DYSTROPHY

JOSEPH HEYWOOD

Guilford, Connecticut

An imprint of Rowman & Littlefield

Distributed by NATIONAL BOOK NETWORK

British Library Cataloguing-in-Publication Information available

Library of Congress Cataloging in Publication Data

Names: Heywood, Joseph, author.
Title: Buckular dystrophy : a woods cop mystery / Joseph Heywood.
Description: First edition. | Guilford, Connecticut : Lyons Press, [2016] |
   Series: Woods cop mystery series ; 10
Identifiers: LCCN 2015037238| ISBN 9781493018864 (hardcover : acid-free
   paper) | ISBN 9781493018871 (ebook)
Subjects: LCSH: Service, Grady (Fictitious character)—Fiction. | Game
   wardens—Michigan—Fiction. | Deer hunting—Michigan—Fiction. | Upper
   Peninsula (Mich.)—Fiction. | GSAFD: Mystery fiction.
Classification: LCC PS3558.E92 B83 2016 | DDC 813/.54—dc23 LC record available at
   http://lccn.loc.gov/2015037238

♾™ The paper used in this publication meets the minimum requirements of American
National Standard for Information Sciences—Permanence of Paper for Printed Library
Materials, ANSI/NISO Z39.48-1992.

For Lonnie

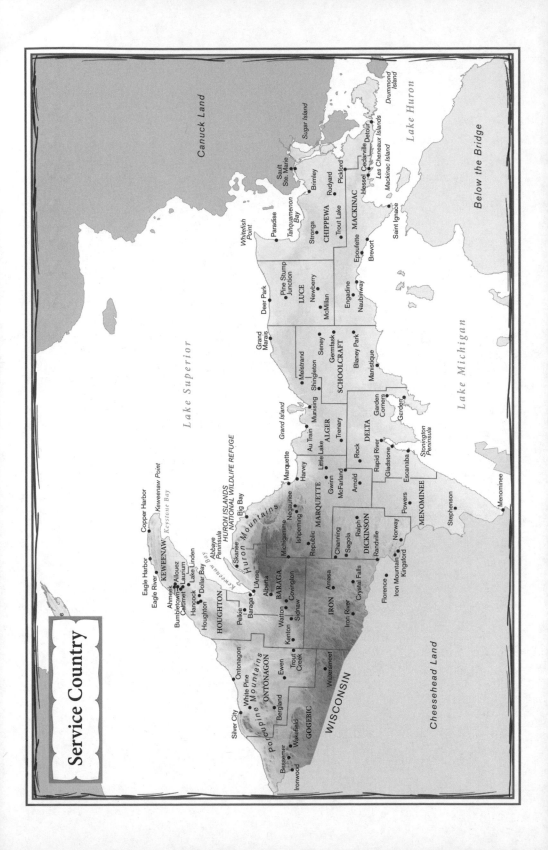

Service Country

Canuck Land

Lake Huron

Below the Bridge

Lake Superior

Lake Michigan

Cheesehead Land

MACKINAC
Sault Ste. Marie
Sugar Island
Drummond Island
Brimley
Rudyard
Pickford
Hessel Cedarville Detour
Les Cheneaux Islands
Mackinac Island
Saint Ignace
Strongs
CHIPPEWA
Trout Lake
Epoufette
Brevort
Paradise
Tahquamenon Bay
Whitefish Point

LUCE
Pine Stump Junction
Newberry
McMillan
Engadine
Naubinway
Deer Park

Grand Marais
SCHOOLCRAFT
Melstrand
Seney
Germfask
Blaney Park
Manistique
Shingleton

Grand Island
ALGER
Au Train
Munising
Trenary
DELTA
Garden Corners
Garden
Stonington Peninsula
Little Lake
Rock
Rapid River
Gladstone
Escanaba

Marquette
Harvey
MARQUETTE
Gwinn
McFarland
Arnold
MENOMINEE
Powers
Stephenson
Menominee

Big Bay
Negaunee
Ishpeming
Michigamme
Republic
Channing
Sagola
Ralph
DICKINSON
Randville
Norway
Iron Mountain
Kingsford

Huron Mountains
Skanee
L'Anse
BARAGA
Alberta
Covington
IRON
Amasa
Crystal Falls
Florence
Iron River

HURON ISLANDS NATIONAL WILDLIFE REFUGE
Abbaye Peninsula
Keweenaw Bay

Copper Harbor
Eagle Harbor
Eagle River
Keweenaw Point
Keystone Bay
Ahmeek
Allouez
Calumet
Laurium
KEWEENAW
Lake Linden
Hancock
Houghton
Dollar Bay
Bumbletown

HOUGHTON
Pelkie
Baraga
Watton
Sidnaw
Kenton

Ontonagon
Silver City
White Pine
Porcupine Mountains
ONTONAGON
Ewen
Trout Creek
Watersmeet
WISCONSIN

Bergland
Bessemer
Ironwood
Wakefield
GOGEBIC

ACT 1: PARTNER WITH A PAST

Today was good. Today was fun. Tomorrow is another one.
—Dr. Seuss, *One Fish Two Fish Red Fish Blue Fish*

CHAPTER 1

Harvey, Marquette County

FRIDAY, SEPTEMBER 11, 2009

Like Pavlov's pup to food, Grady Service was programmed to serve, not just during official duty hours but whenever and wherever needed. The veteran conservation officer had the sort of dedication to service almost never seen among the elected politician class but common among rank-and-file state employees. He answered calls and did what was needed, no exceptions. It was his commitment to something larger than a mere job.

Service debated answering the phone for a millisecond.

"What?" he mumbled into the cell phone. *Why the hell do they make this shit for Munchkins?* His fingers didn't fit the keys, never would. The crap seemed to be getting smaller while the human race was demonstratively growing larger.

"Grady, it's Linsenman. My deputies have just had a chase and found a miter saw in a field. There's hair and tissue."

Weasel Linsenman, a longtime Marquette County deputy, was now a sergeant. They had been friends for decades.

"Human?"

"Deer. Wake up."

"I'm trying. Where?"

"Al Quaal Trailhead."

Al Quaal was a cross-country trail in Ishpeming. "Your people still out there?"

"Affirmative."

"Twenty minutes max."

"I'll pass the word."

"More stupid deer?" Tuesday Friday asked sleepily, draping a leg over him.

"Maybe." The saw intrigued him. He'd found six deer carcasses over the past week, all bucks, each neatly shorn of antlers with a nice clean cut. He'd assumed some kind of battery-powered rig or electric saw, but a miter saw? Huh. All the remains had been dumped in locations he presumed were chosen to irritate the community's large and vocal tree-hugging, antihunting element. Or the drops could have been purely random. There was no way to know until he caught the perps.

"I won't ask when you'll be back," Friday whispered. "You want some breakfast?"

"No time. Stay in bed; you need sleep."

"I'm too tired to plumb all the implications of that statement."

"Thinking and sleeping don't mix," he said, pulling on a Danner boot.

Friday grabbed him, pulled him back, kissed him hard, and pushed him roughly away. "Tarzan, go!"

"*Bundolo*?"

"Ya think?" his woman mumbled.

No idea what the hell *bundolo* actually meant, if anything, but it had been prominent in every Tarzan comic book when he was growing up and made Tuesday chuckle when they bandied it about.

CHAPTER 2

Ishpeming, Marquette County

FRIDAY, SEPTEMBER 11

He saw only one vehicle on the drive westward to Ishpeming, an eastbound small red Toyota truck with two souls aboard. It wasn't speeding, and there were no visible problems to warrant a safety stop, yet his gut screamed he should pull them over. He had no probable cause other than instinct, so he pressed on, ignoring the red truck, the sense of a missed opportunity souring in his stomach.

There were two deputies waiting for him. Tristan Mach was called "Brandname" by other officers. His partner was Bettina "B.C." Cellini. Both looked like they were sixteen and were said to be sky high on enthusiasm and heart and somewhat lower on thoughtfulness, judgment, and investigative skills.

"You got a deer for me?" he asked Mach.

"Yessir." The young deputy held up an ancient looking miter saw. Barehanded, no sign of latex gloves. *Good-bye latent prints. Doofus, a saw wasn't a deer. Stay calm, talk them through this, harvest what information and clues you can.*

"Gloves?" Service said.

Mach said, "Cool old tool, James Turner, from Philly, cost you three fifty or four hundred for an antique like this. Been around a hundred years. What good will old prints do?"

"He knows the value of everything," his partner said, "and absolutely nothing." She wore blue latex gloves.

Service looked at Mach. No sense lecturing a fool. "Where'd you find it?"

"I found it, sir," Cellini said. "By that fence." She pointed. It was still dark. Service shone his light, saw a post and wire.

"We chased a dark-colored sedan from here, but we lost it," Mach offered.

"Take me through everything—from the start," Service told the deputies.

Mach deepened his voice. "We come up through the B Road on account of this place is frequented by dopers and couples getting it on. We got up there on that hill and looked down." The officer pointed where they had been on the hill above. "Us up there, dark as a butthole, and suddenly we see taillights about here and away they go."

B Road was a back way into the area. "That's all? Taillights?"

"Yes sir," Cellini said.

"Did they leave quickly?"

"Warp speed," Mach said.

"We closed on it at fifty max," Cellini added. "It was pegged on the speed limit."

"Did it accelerate when you got behind it, and did you light it up?"

"No, sir," Cellini said. "We broke off. No probable cause, no light problems, no anything. We can't stop every driver who parks in an obscure place, right?"

"They were probably done with the deed and dressed by the time we rolled up," Mach offered.

"He sees everything in the light of money or sex," Cellini said.

"They?" Service said. "You saw *two* people?"

"Negative," Cellini said. "Just the one, and that only after we closed on him."

"Male or female?"

"Male, for certain," Mach interrupted. "Had on a Gucci black leather baseball cap, retails at five Cs."

"Dark," Cellini said.

"Black," Mach corrected her. "Only color Gucci makes in that model."

"Where'd you break off the chase?" Service asked. *Gucci? Was this deputy for real?*

"County Four Ninety Two, Eagle Mills," Cellini said.

"You came right back here then?"

"Affirm," Mach said. "Found the saw. Look at the shit on it."

"Hair, tissue, probably brain," Cellini said.

"You think it's a deer?" Mach asked the female dep.

Cellini said, "Yes, and the gore seems fresh."

Service agreed. "Did you guys look for the deer?"

"Didn't want to screw up the scene," Mach said, this from he who wore no gloves while handling the evidence. The saw had no rust, had not been out in the elements long. "You get a plate number?" he asked the deps.

Both officers stared at the ground by their vehicle. "You got close enough to observe the brand of a hat but didn't get the *plate*? What's up with *that*?"

The deputies said, "Sorry, sir," in a pathetic chorus.

Mach recovered from shame first. "You wanna, like, for us to, like, help you search?"

"Like, no thanks. You guys can go on."

"Sorry we didn't get a plate," Cellini said. "Truth is, we never got *that* close to the vehicle."

"But you got a hat brand."

The young woman shrugged. "On that topic, I got nothing."

"It's not a total loss," Mach said. "How many dudes in this county wear five hundred–dollar ball caps?"

"What if hat-boy isn't *from* here or is a girl, not a boy?" Cellini shot back. "You fucked the prints, dude."

"It's an expensive antique," he offered.

Which explained nothing. Clearly the young partners had cooperation and trust issues to iron out—not exactly a partnership forged in paradise. "Thanks again," he told them. "I'm done talking now. Beat it."

The woman laughed and smiled, the man frowned, but the two got into their cruiser and slid silently away, the only sound their tires on cold night hardtop.

Grady Service cursed the absence of snow. The deps had shown him where the saw had been found, close to the sedan's alleged parking spot, though given how incomplete the officers' work had been, he couldn't assume any of it was accurate. For the moment, he decided to use the post where the saw was found as his base point for searching. He marched up and down the field, following a tight mental grid picture, until first light but found nothing, ending the night with a miter saw and low-level exasperation for young cops. He'd give the saw to Friday for the state police tech people to examine for print and fibers, anything, but he knew this amounted to nothing more than going through the motions.

Part of my six-deer case or not? No way to tell. Six carcasses dumped in very public locations, but this spot, while near a trailhead, is not nearly as prominent as at the other dump sites. Six with loped antlers, all the rest of the remains untouched, backstraps included. This was not about meat. It was about antlers—worthless, inedible bone.

Are they selling the antlers? Possibly, but six deer aren't enough. The market for such stuff tends to be largest in states with few deer, if such a place exists. Deer antlers were being sold as chew toys for dogs, and at exorbitant prices, but most of the stock for such products came from commercial deer farms. *Again, could this deal be about selling antlers? If so, it would be a first. Stop speculating. Stick to evidence. You don't have shit so far. But there'll be more. With hornophiles, there's always more. They can't help themselves. And you have the video.*

Service had promised Friday he'd stop smoking, but when he was on a case he found it impossible; he lit up now and sat back. They had gotten a surveillance video from a tractor store near the first dump site. The time stamp read 0300 and showed, in grainy black-and-white pictures, an older model dark pickup he was calling "the black" and a tricked-out light-colored Silverado extended cab they were calling "the white." The white truck had gone in with its cap cover raised and come back past the camera with the cap closed. Had the driver dumped something? He was theorizing and assuming it was three deer carcasses and that they had come from the white truck.

Now there may be an additional sedan, and does that have anything at all to do with the two trucks or the six deer carcasses? No plates on any of the vehicles, sedan included. A Gucci hat but no plates. He laughed out loud. Okay, stay focused. Is the sedan related to the trucks or not? If not, why the saw? There's more than one night cheat in this county. And what about the red Toyota I saw on the way to meet the deps? Should have stopped it, dammit. No evidence. You couldn't stop it legally. But that little red truck is something related to something. All I have to do now is define the somethings. Got six heads in the evidence freezer in Marquette. Maybe seven, if there is another deer here. So get off your butt and go look. You've got light coming on fast.

No, first get your blood-coffee titers up.

• • •

It wasn't until he was carving link sausages and eggs that he realized today was the anniversary of 9/11. He could no longer remember Pearl Harbor Day either. This was the reality of the world and history. Today always trumps yesterday.

CHAPTER 3

East Marquette County

MONDAY, SEPTEMBER 14

Marquette County officers had worked with Service on night-shiner patrols all weekend, seeing none and catching none, not even recreationalists operating after the statewide 11 p.m. curfew. He had seven deer in his case now, the latest a nice ten-point, a trophy buck by anyone's definition; he had found it a hundred yards from the saw the deps had recovered. His search that morning had taken an hour before he found the buck in a densely wooded fencerow. He had not seen it until he glimpsed a patch of color that seemed out of place, and then it was nearly underfoot. Lucky to find it at all. Horns intact, but the post where the saw was found was clearly visible from where the dead animal lay. Had to assume this was the same damn crew, but now they had no saw. What would they do about that?

He cut off the head, gutted the deer, and dropped the unprocessed carcass at a homeless shelter, where the director would cut it up and pack the meat in the freezer for future use.

Shining patrols back in the 1970s had been sure things, shining and shooting deer at night amounting to the state's rural sport of choice. Now, not so much. Violators these days were wiser, at least some of them were. The smart ones did their damage over lighted bait piles behind locked gates, killing silently with crossbows. The Natural Resource Commission had opened the way for increased crossbow use, which had immediately benefitted violators. It had only made law enforcement's job more difficult—exactly what the NRC had been warned about when its members made the decision. Sometimes it seemed like political appointees made decisions solely to interfere with law enforcement. They'd never admit to that, but there were times when no other reasonable read on their actions was possible.

Bottom line? Experienced jacklighters weren't willing to run the risks against Department of Natural Resources (DNR) patrols and overhead aircraft and had gone underground. Only the inexperienced and stupid took such risks now. The old days and old ways had been dangerous. But they also had been fun. He hated to see such times end.

"Gradysaurus," Friday sometimes called him, and it was too true to take umbrage.

He had himself in position at the back end of a camp property east of Skandia. Great spot, top of a nice hill looking at a north and east panorama, where he knew he'd see the faintest speck of light. The camp belonged to a U of M biology professor who encouraged him to use it whenever he wanted, including when she and her family were present, which was rarely during deer-whacking season. "Just ease on past the house and do your thing," she'd told him. One fall night, she'd brought him freshly baked chocolate chip cookies. He could still smell them in his memory.

His cell phone rang. The display said "Private." He didn't punch in the code to unblock the caller, knowing it was one of his partners.

The caller was CO Josh Spear, a fifteen-year veteran of the DNR who had just transferred up from Branch County. "Grady?"

"Yo."

"Josh here. You know that deer case you're working?"

"What about it?"

"I have another one, and I think it might be part of your deal. My daughter, Annakate, said today at lunch she knows some boys who drive a new white Chevy pickup . . . and an old black truck."

Seriously? It breaks like this? Annakate Spear was a junior at Negaunee High School, a scholar in the making and a social butterfly. "Friends of hers?"

"No, but she knows of them. The boy she actually knows is seventeen and a dropout. The others are older. The oldest is twenty-two, the others nineteen or twenty. Probably nothing to this, but I thought you should know."

"Thanks."

"If this connects, Deana and I don't want her name in the case, Grady."

"Done, she was just reborn as Confidential Informant Number One." Not being able to name an informant complicated an officer's work and changed the ground rules for obtaining search warrants to gather evidence.

"Deana and I thank you."

"No problem. Where's the deer, Josh?"

"County Road Four Sixty Two, near Gordon. I'm there now."

"Buck?"

"Hard to tell," Spear said jokingly.

Weird response. "I'm making my way toward you."

"Be right here. Deana made a tub of fried chicken."

• • •

The deer's skull had been smashed and split by a violent blow, the small antlers hanging askew, the rest of the animal untouched.

"Bit short of Boone and Crockett," Spear joked after they looked at the deer and got into his truck. "Chicken?"

The aroma overwhelmed. Service took a plump drumstick. Deer season had a host of victims—regular meals for COs, not to mention sex lives, or just having a glass of beer or wine.

"This one fit your case?" Spear asked with a full mouth.

"Don't know. You mind if I take the head, just in case?"

"Knock yourself out. I'm thinking it was shot today. Critters will be on it before sunrise. Got to admit, they do keep things clean around here."

"Too bad they don't eat violets," Service said. *Violets,* his word for violators and poachers.

Spear laughed and spit out a bite of chicken, which bounced off the laptop pedestal between the seats.

Eight now? Does this make eight? How many more before we can nail these jerks? An imponderable. I need a break. If those involved are young, there's always a chance for a break. Four boys, three vehicles, six trimmed bucks, one found with full antlers and a saw nearby, and now this one with the crushed head. Can't say it all fits, at least not yet. Need more. Got to find the boys named by Annakate, see what pops up on that front.

"What the hell is it about deer antlers that makes some people turn so stupid?" he asked Spear, who shrugged and tore into another chicken leg.

CHAPTER 4

West Ishpeming, Marquette County

FRIDAY, SEPTEMBER 18

They were at the DNR satellite office, Spear and Service and Simon del Olmo, who had popped up from Iron County on another matter and Service invited him to sit in with them. They had four names now, but none of the boys were living at the addresses on their operator's licenses, all of which came back to their parents. Typical young people, nomads searching aimlessly, moving on whims and such until they joined the military or headed for North Dakota, where there were jobs aplenty for those willing to work hard.

Grady's cell phone clicked like a cricket. It was Carrie Ericksen, the secretary-receptionist at the regional office near the prison in Marquette. "Grady, I have a young man on the line who wants to talk to a game warden about a poached bear."

"Can you transfer him?"

She was back quickly. "I guess he lost his nerve. He says he has to think more about it. I gave him your work cell."

"Did he give you a name?"

"No."

"Thanks, Carrie." He rubbed his head. *Break in the making or just a dumb interruption? Bear not deer, separate deal, don't get your hopes up.*

"Bad news?" del Olmo asked.

"Kid wanted to report an illegal bear whacking."

"Lost his cojones, eh?"

"Apparently. Told Carrie he's thinking on it, searching his soul, or whatever."

"Under-thirties have no souls," Spear said. "Only a long list of entitlements and parents circling a few feet over their heads, choreographing and micromanaging every detail of their lives."

"You included?" Service said.

"My wife, not me. But her chicken's damn good, eh?"

"The ledger balances," Service said, wondering what Friday's son, Shigun, and his granddaughter, Maridly, would grow up to become. Just as quickly he said. "Back to work, men. Eight deer, probably linked, and two hazy truck descriptions. One miter saw with the prints of one dumbass deputy on it. One sedan, which allegedly carried off the perps. Our deer-whacker apparently knew enough to wear gloves."

"But not the trained dep," del Olmo said.

"Some of his training must not have taken," Service said with a straight face.

Pressing on, "We have four names from Annakate Spear: Gardy Shintner, Josh Cair, Peter Basquell, and Belko Vaunt. As stated, all addresses come back to their parents, or guardians, or whatever, all except Cair, which came back to someone who was either an uncle or a grandfather. The retail sales file shows no DNR licenses ever for any of them and no hunter safety. LEIN shows clean, no wants or warrants, except for Vaunt, who has warrants and pick up and detain orders for both Marquette and Delta Counties. None of the four actually live at home, but we have no idea where they do live. We could make cold calls to daddies and such, but that might spook them if they're also part of this business. Violating is sometimes a family sport. Right now we don't know anything conclusive. All we have is a sort of alleged link to two vehicles, maybe three."

"Do vehicles come back to them?" del Olmo asked.

Service shook his head. "Loggerheads so far. We've got what look like bones, but no connecting tissue. For all we know, these four have no involvement other than vehicle similarities. Spear's daughter says she's never heard any rumors about any hunting, but she does say they run with younger girls, as in fourteen, fifteen."

"That opens the way to some ugly scenarios," del Olmo remarked.

"But no names for the girls," Spear threw out. "Annakate never heard any names, just that they had some sort of teenybop groupies, maybe looking to score drugs or booze."

"Turn it over to the drug team?" del Olmo suggested.

"Not until we know more," Service said. "We can always pull them in if we need them." *Funny how often drugs led to poaching cases or vice versa.*

"Big fat goose egg," the Cuba-born del Olmo grumbled. "*No tenemos nada*. We have nothing."

Service's phone clucked like a hen about to squeeze off an egg. "Conservation Officer Service."

The voice gushed. "I've had enough, eh. All them deer, then two nights ago those fuckers put a bear head in my truck and took it to a party! A bear! At a party! Enough is enough!"

"Who am I speaking to?" Service asked.

"Ain't gone say yet," the voice answered.

"No problem. All *what* deer?"

"Seven bucks and just for damn horns. What douche bags."

"Seven bucks *and* a bear?"

"I think this is all so bogus, but I want to be left out of it, man. I just want to do what's right."

If the caller was not a participant, why did he want to be left out? Test him; see if he's legit. "Tell me about the chase."

Long pause. "You know about *that*?"

"We know a lot more than you think. Tell me the story in your own words."

A sigh this time. "Dude, Froggy Basquell and Belko Vaunt were hunting. Like they always do their shit, at night. This time they knocked down a big-ass buck with huge antlers, *huge*."

"Ten-point," Service told the caller.

"You know *that*?"

"I have the deer. Are you counting that among the seven?"

"No, dude, that makes eight," the voice said nervously.

"The chase?" Service said.

"Yah. They like looked for the deer, eh, but they couldn't find it. They went back to the car for a hit and a beer, and suddenly there were headlights behind them and Vaunt like split. Pete got left behind, so he run his ass up into the woods and kept goin'."

"Pete?"

"We call him Froggy."

"One of them dropped something."

"Man, the *saw*. They are so pissed about that. The next deer they shot they had to use an ax and they fucked it up. A car came along and they had to get the fuck out of Dodge and leave the horns behind."

"When was this?"

"Monday after dark."

"East county?"

Silence again. "If you know it all, man, you don't need me."

Kid's wavering, acting hinky. "Calm down. We know a lot, not everything. You're helping us. You're telling me there are eight deer and a *bear*?"

"Dude, only that I know of. There could be more. They are two crazy fuckers, sayin'."

"Did you actually see them shoot deer?"

"Yes, six of the deer, but not the bear, man. That was sketch; the dudes are like way off the hook."

The conversation had morphed inexplicably from near-English into Martian, which seemed to have the same words but diametrically opposite meanings from the English. "You saw them shoot deer, yes or no?"

"A'ight, I guess, dude."

"Is that yes or no?"

"Totes. You popo like don't speak good English?"

"Who did you see shoot deer?"

"Basquell. Vaunt, he just drives, and Pete shoots, like he's OD on guns man—guns and girly pussy."

"You've seen Basquell shoot?"

"Don't be so basic. Yah I seen. Fucker is *good*, could be a Marine sniper. You already got all dis, why you axing me shit?"

"We need a witness to corroborate."

"What's that mean, cardboardorate?"

"To verify."

"Like at court?"

"Not exactly. You just need to tell me what you've seen and when, and then we'll write it up."

"Like I don't want to be in this, dude."

"You're already in it, and we've traced your number and know exactly where you are." It was a lie, but he hoped it would freeze the caller, sap some of his will. "You know how much we know. How long do you think before we jump all of you and haul you in?"

"Dude, I like ain't gone lie to you. I . . . have . . . like . . . ain't . . . done . . . nothing . . . *wrong*."

"We need to talk face to face," Service told the caller.

"No way, dude."

"*Yes*, way. We know where you are. I can have a car on you in one minute. We've already got two squads in position."

"I just want do what's right, dude. That bear, sayin'."

"Let's meet."

"Marquette place with fucked-up roof?"

"No, we're at the DNR office in West Ish, right on US 41. You come in and we'll talk and get all this sorted out. You don't, you might risk going down for all of it. It's your call." Another sigh. "Take me half a six-oh, dude."

"Half hour?"

"Like dat, bra."

Service looked at his fellow COs. "Guy claims to be inside the crew, here in thirty."

"*If* he shows," Spear said.

"He'll show," Service said.

CHAPTER 5

West Ishpeming

FRIDAY, SEPTEMBER 18

Thirty minutes turned into two and a half hours. Spear and del Olmo both moved on to other tasks, but Grady Service waited and smoked and tried to shut off his imagination. *Damn no-smoking bugaboo. Friday's all over my ass over cigs, but geez, I've spent a life with them and it's deer season for cripes sake. Focus yourself, Service. Smoke and think. The kid will come. He wants out, not in. To get himself out of this, he has to come in, an algorithm even a fool can grab onto. Salvation lies here, not there.*

A red Toyota pickup pulled up and parked as it got dark. Nobody got out. Service's phone eventually rang. "Bra, I'm like out front now."

"Red Toyota?"

"Yah," said with reluctance.

"I'm coming out."

"Not in my truck, Bra. In the woods out back, eh. I'll go first."

Service made a mental note of the plate as he went by the truck, saw the kid—gaunt and skeletal as a longtime POW, pasty-skinned, evasive eyes that bulged slightly. "You packing?" Service asked and, seeing that the question meant nothing, added, "Are you carrying a firearm or any kind of weapon?"

"Unh, unh, Bra. Not my style, man."

"I need your name. I'm Officer Service."

"What's your *real* name, Bra?"

"Officer. Service. My first name is Officer and my last name is Service."

"You fucking with me, Bra?"

"*Your* name?"

"Clayton," the boy said after a long pause.

"Something Clayton, or Clayton something?"

"Clayton Tree, Clay Tree, Clay."

"Good, thanks for that. You got ID, Clay? This is standard, man. I'm not dissing you."

The boy handed him his driver's license. "This address current?" Service asked. It showed an address in Palmer, south of Negaunee.

"My 'rents, Bra."

"Rents?"

"Like parental units, dude?"

"You live with your parents?"

"I do, bra. I got a job, I go to school, tryin' to get my GED. I don't got time ta party twenny-four seven like those other douche bags."

"The others don't live with their parents?"

"No, dude. Got their own pad out off M-35 in Little Lake."

Clayton Tree's license put his age at nineteen. "How do you know these people?"

"Me and Shintner, we went to high school. I quit, he finish. Negaunee. Go Miners and all that shit, eh. Basquell and Vaunt from over Champion, I think. Cair's from Marquette."

"You know where they live?"

"Yah; they all crash at Cair's place. His grandfather buy him a truck and the 'parmen'. Truck in old man's name, 'parmen' too, but Cair got like deeds and like legalshit?"

"White Silverado, tricked-out?"

The boy nodded. "Okay, Clay, let's hear all about your role in the chase."

"Weren't no role, man."

"Don't bullshit me, Clay. I saw you and another individual headed south from that location that same morning. That's aiding and abetting flight, and it's a felony nowadays."

"Shit."

"Talk to me. Silence will screw you."

"Like I tole Vaunt, he panic; run and leave Basquell, but his ride crap out at Crossroads. Froggy he runned up inna woods and call me to fetch his ass. I get him, and then that asshole Vaunt call me for ride, so me and Froggy fetched him from Crossroads." The Crossroads was a bar south of Marquette, a local landmark for decades.

"Basquell in the woods, Vaunt in the sedan."

"Rye, how it went down, Bra."

"That was Froggy—Basquell—with you when I saw you."

"Rye."

"And you guys went and picked up Vaunt."

"Rye; I thought they gone fight on account Vaunt leave Froggy, see, but they just bump fists like it cool and no fight. Just light up joint and stare stoopid at each other all way out to crash, man."

"You took them to Cair's apartment, correct?"

"His crash, rye, dude."

"Was Cair there alone?"

"No, th' fo ho allas there; dudes don't never wear no clothes, man, like reg'lar nymph flecks. You know, like tote thirsties, dude, panting for Froggy's thang-bang; they all basic cray, sayin'."

"How old?"

"Don't be no numbers asked when ain't no clothes, man."

He has a point. "They over sixteen?"

Clayton Tree shrugged. "It matter, dey all got da good stuff, sayin'." *Probably under age.* "They drive?"

"No, bra. They be dropped."

"Where exactly is this apartment?"

"Can show you place, Bra. But I don't know no number. S'upstairs, dude. I don't know no more. Only been there few times."

"Where?"

"Tammy Ridge Parmens."

"Off M-35, close to Little Lake?"

"Atsit, Bra. Nice place when they move in. Man, you got keep me outten dis shit. I got job, skoo. I getting tired all their shit, and dat bear put me over top, sayin'."

"No promises, Clay. You play straight with me and I'll do my best for you. Lie to me and I'll cut off your fucking head."

"Hear dat, Bra. No lie, unh-unh. I wunt there for bear, but I seen, dude. They got vids, Bra. Got all da deer, da bear; got one of a coon dey make inna hamburger wit' fuckin' baseball bats! Girls like get it on to dat shit, all dat blood goin' ever'where. Sick shit, dude, sick. What up wit dat, wanna fuck when see blood and pain?"

"They have pictures?"

"Dude, they vid ever't'ing they do, even when dey scrompin' with da fo ho thirsties."

Good grief, *sex videos.* "Phone cams?"

"Phones, reg'lar cams, all those toys Cair got from his gran'pa, bra."

"How does Shintner fit in?"

"Like always, Bra. He shit for brains, follower; do what they tell him do is all. Loser, Bra."

"Are you on camera?"

"Not doing none a dat shit I ain't," the boy said. "Mebbe toking, could be, but not dat other shit. Dose fo hos allas want me hit dat baby fluff fo vid, but I tell 'em NFW, dude."

Underage sex is a separate issue in this. Stay focused. "You were with Vaunt and Basquell when deer were shot?"

"Six. Not dem las' two."

"What was your *job*?"

"No job, man, just dere, along, man, hangin'. They say, let's go party, but they, like, go shoot instead. I can't get out. All I can do is watch dat shit go down."

"You saw them take antlers?"

"Use cool saw till they lost it. Then they try an ax. I seen viduv dat one. Dat shit look so *nasty*."

"What's Cair's role?"

"His crash, his cash, his smokes, and his dope, Bra. Sugar daddy. Sometime he help cut horns."

"But not you."

"No, Bra. I smoke-toke some, eh. Dat's all."

"Dope comes from Cair?"

"Yah, always got stash, dude. Good shit. Get them girls naked and waxed and howling like beagles after rabbits."

"But you used dope and rode along."

"I *tole* you dat. I ain't gone lie, Bra."

"You did tell me. You know if we don't get them all, they'll just keep on."

"I know, bra. Why I caw you, sayin'."

"The red truck in your name?"

"My ma, she cosign, but yah, and I make payments, not her or my stepdad. What you do now?"

"I recorded what you've just told me. Now I'll get it transcribed and typed. You can read it and change it to make it absolutely accurate from your view; then you'll sign it and then I'll take it from there."

"My name stays out?"

"Right, you are Confidential Informant Number Nine." Service gave a false number to hide the fact that he had only two informants. The less exclusive they thought they were, the more informants tended to spill.

"Shit, you got eight dudes talk you? Shit, bra. I need me a lawyer?"

"That's your legal right and your call."

"Bra, there be stories, sayin'? Service, street dudes dey say, he tough but fair motherfucker, word good, don't never break 'is word. Keep me out, rye?"

He nodded at the young man. Two witnesses now, both confidential. The information was usable only if they could verify everything directly or through a third source. This kid seemed to be a fuckup with a good heart, and his own heart said to trust him.

"Rye."

• • •

It was well after dark when the other COs returned and he laid out what they had for a case.

Simon del Olmo said, "The search warrant is critical."

"First we nail down the exact location and address of the apartment."

Spear chuckled. "You start a deer season with a case like this, Grady, and you'll be shit out of luck the rest of the way. Eight bucks and a bear? No way you can top *that*. This is the case of a career. You might as well take off the rest of the season."

He knew that these were essentially baby violets. Full-grown ones, those with long years of experience in such matters, were doing as much or more damage and doing it with more planning and smarts. You couldn't hunt violets from your living room. More importantly, this case was not a slam dunk, not yet, and not by a long shot. Weird, unpredictable things sometimes happened in courthouses. Magistrates, prosecutors, judges, juries, defense attorneys—everyone could fuck things up.

CHAPTER 6

Little Lake, Marquette County

SUNDAY, SEPTEMBER 20

Weasel Linsenman was in civvies—black sweats and Nikes, light satin jacket with a faded Packer's emblem. He stared down at the beer can Service held out to him. "It's empty, a prop."

"Prop for what?" Linsenman asked.

"A morality play."

"Man, I get stage fright. Have you been drinking?"

"No but we'll both need to act like we have."

"Why?" Linsenman asked nervously. "Grady, I hate doing stuff with you. It always turns weird, man."

"Not always."

"More than it doesn't. What's this *about*?"

"Partly it's the case your two deputies blew."

"Mach and Cellini?"

Service said. "She has potential, but I think he just takes up space."

"He's young. Not everyone was born old and wise like you."

Service looked at his friend. He liked how he came to the fuckups' defense.

"You're right, the kid needs seasoning. Get him here in civvies. I'll take *him* instead of you." Service took back the empty beer can.

• • •

Tristan Mach looked sixteen in uniform and younger in civvies. "S'up, Sarge," the deputy greeted Linsenman.

The sergeant nodded at Service. "You're on loan to him."

"Chance to redeem yourself," Service told the young dep.

"I look like a frickin' coupon?" Mach shot back.

Perfect. "Hold the 'tude, dude. You'll need it."

"Did he just call me dude?" Mach asked his sergeant.

"Go with the flow," Linsenman told his man. "It'll be over before you know it."

Mach asked, "*What* will be over?"

Grady Service stuck the prop in the deputy's hand.

"This is the cheap shit," Mach said scornfully.

"Pretend it's full of chocolate milk or whatever shit you drink."

"My union does not call for me to work involuntarily for other agencies. I have a contract."

"You have *bupkes*," Linsenman said. "Do what you're told, and do it well."

"I'll file a grievance."

Grady Service pushed the man toward his personal truck. "Shut up. I don't need a snot-nosed cub cop. I need Brandname in all his fucking obnoxious glory."

The deputy lit up and grinned. "Say when, dude."

• • •

The parking lot at the apartment complex was surrounded by tamarack swamps, all the trees yellowing to the color of bananas. By December the needles would drop and the trees would look skeletal.

"We're looking for an apartment," Service explained en route.

"Do I get to ask why?"

"No."

Surprisingly, the kid said, "Okay," and remained silent the rest of the way.

They pulled into the lot and parked. Service lit a cigarette and handed it to Mach.

"I don't smoke."

"Today you do."

The deputy drew down a deep hit, held it, and exhaled a thin spout of smoke that curled like a snake.

Service expected a coughing fit, but none came.

Mach said, "I don't smoke now don't mean I di'n't used to, dude. I used to smoke all the time. This shit tastes good."

They were there ten minutes when Service saw a man in the lot. He went to a white Silverado, got something out, and started to walk away.

The two cops went after him. "Dude," Service yelled, "where the fuck is Sasha?"

The young man stopped and turned. He was frowning. Service immediately recognized Josh Cair from his operator's license. They had gotten photos of all involved from the secretary of state. It was Cair for sure—six-three, long blond hair, blue eyes, orange chook, faded jeans, fawn-colored Uggs. "Dude, like where that *bitch* Sasha?"

Cair squinted warily.

Service said, "Sasha say, 'Come over anytime, hang out, scromp, hit it hard, dude.' Whish apar'men she in, *dude*?"

Cair allowed the hint of a smile. "Sorry old-timer; ain't no Sasha here. Maybe you got played, dudes."

Old-timer? Service felt his temper spike, but his young partner stepped up in front of him. "I knew that be-otch be given us bullshit name. Sasha, who the fuck got name of some Russian cunt. We buy, bitch drinks, she lies; we'll kill 'at cunt we get our hands on it, eh, bra! You sure no Sasha 'ere? Mebbe you hittin' at shit 'n' try keep it to yoseff? She be like five two, big tits, hair color of a fire engine, bra."

Cair said, "There's nobody named Sasha here, dude, and nobody that looks like that. I been seein' 'at shit, I'd have to hit it myseff, sayin'?"

Mach turned to Service. "We fucked, partner. Gimme nuther stick; we got make us a thing on dis."

Service handed his cigarette pack to the young officer.

The suspect walked away. "Follow him," Service told the young officer. "We need the building and the apartment number. Verify it, but be careful, and don't blow our cover."

"Sasha's too?" Mach quipped, smart-assing.

"Do the job, rook."

Mach was back in seven minutes and held up his left hand. He had used a ballpoint to write on its heel, B-4, A-8. "Building Four, Apartment Eight, upstairs on the right."

"You certain?"

"Watched him into the door, went up, looked at number on door and plastic title on mail box for Apartment Eight. The tag says 'Cair.'"

"That was Cair you followed."

"Gimme 'nother butt, dude."

"Your mother's gonna curse me," Service said.

"Join the club. It has big numbers."

Service handed him the pack and told him to keep it. The kid had jumped right into the role and never wavered, a natural for undercover work. "Where you from, Mach?"

"East Grand Rapids, EGR."

"No cop work down that way?"

"Graduated Northern. I prefer the air up here; hunt, fish, you know. We do something good today?"

"We did, and you did. Now give me one of my smokes."

"This have anything to do with that night I fucked up the chase and prints?"

"Affirmative."

"You built a case?"

"Getting close."

"Cool," Mach said. "Is this what they call bonding?"

"A cigarette's just a cigarette."

"There a real Sasha?"

"Gotta be one somewhere."

"You were about to pound a head."

"Till you stepped in. Thanks."

"That like an attaboy?"

CHAPTER 7

Little Lake

WEDNESDAY, SEPTEMBER 23

They'd met at the old bare-boned DNR field office in Gwinn and gone over the plan to serve the search warrant, which had been obtained after an all-night session writing a detailed affidavit, which the judge used to make his warrant decision. Service would lead a soft entry. Knock on the door. But if there was no response in fifteen seconds, del Olmo would break it open and the entry would turn hard. They had a tactical plan for every eventuality, including one of them or the suspects being injured. COs John Spear, Sander Torvay, and Jop Volstaad, a newly minted CO, would follow the entry team and begin by guarding the back way out, meaning he would be below the balcony in case some fool tried to flee that way. They would interview suspects but arrest only Vaunt tonight on his warrants unless there was some sort of violent reaction from others. The mission was to serve the search warrant and look for the things the judge had approved. After the take was evaluated and analyzed, the business of bringing charges in a formal complaint would begin. The complaint would go to the prosecutor, who would decide which charges to pursue and seek arrest warrants based on that. All in all, Grady Service was sure they had planned for just about every eventuality.

And then came the naked underage girl greeting them at the door with the single word, "Dudes," and holding out the business end of a joint.

It was immediately clear that the apartment was trashed. This was a new complex, not three years old, but this particular unit looked like it had been lived in by camels and tramps. Dozens of old pizza boxes and petrified pizza slices looking like desiccated flesh. There was a large "lump" target against a wall and a dozen arrows in it. But there were also arrows in the wall, hanging down at peculiar angles, and all around them dozens of holes and slashes in the drywall, as if the wall had fallen victim to terminal woodpecker disease.

Decayed food scraps strewn everywhere. Sinks and counters over-flowed, dishes and pots stacked catawampus like cartoon piles, empty beer cans all over the place; several five-buck chuck empties were in the debris, and there was an overflowing cat pan, redolent of ammonia.

There was a small pile of used tampons in a corner and used condoms everywhere, including one inexplicably stuck to the fridge. Service saw the officers exchanging "looks" as they moved through the rooms.

Loose ammo and spent cartridges lay everywhere on the carpets. There were pockets of McDonald's bags smeared with ketchup aged brown, and petrified french fries. Pop cans overflowed a black plastic bag. There were cases of beer along the wall on the balcony outside, maybe ten cases, and in a bedroom, forty cartons of cigarettes bearing Missouri tax stickers—ciggies there selling for less than a fifth of the Michigan cost. What the hell was this?

A flat-screen TV took up an entire wall.

There were four young men, as expected. Only the owner, Josh Cair, protested, and that was mild and short-lived, nothing more than a show. Otherwise, Shintner, Basquell, and Vaunt were silent and distant. They had found Basquell in bed with a girl, with no indication that it was anything but by mutual agreement. Like the other three girls, she protested being inter-rupted and when asked her name tried to bargain, "Like I'll trade, man—."

Deal refused.

The boy, Shintner, eventually broke the wall of silence and gave them all the girls' names. Marquette Deputy Bettina Cellini called their parents to pick up their little treasures.

Service thought none of the parents seemed especially surprised to find their daughters in compromising circumstances. Was the world changing that much?

Only Vaunt was under arrest, but Service interviewed each of them, carefully separating his subjects. Deputy Mach sat with the others and showed a face that gave even Service a chill.

The harvest yielded a Marlin 895G Guide Gun in .45-70 caliber and a .30-06 Remington 700. There was ammo for each and for other weapons not on the premises, several compound bows, and two crossbows. Basquell claimed the two rifles and said proudly, "I'm the only shooter, dudes." They seized six sets of antlers and a bear skull from the fridge.

None of them claimed the other weapons.

The remainder of the haul included the illicit ciggies, sixteen cell phones, six digital cameras, two expensive video cameras, a dozen CDs, a box of forty thumb drives, and a box filled with photos on print paper—pictures mostly of dead animals but a few of the girls and boys engaged in sex, or posing. It was hard to tell.

There was a wooden box of old tools in a back bedroom, and Service had Mach take a look. The deputy said, "Antiques, worth a bundle." Several of the tools were saws, which they seized, along with a half-ax with deer hair and dried blood on the blade.

An older gentleman showed up after the girls and their parents were gone. Service figured one of the girls' parents had made the call.

"I am Parmenter Cair and this is my property," the man asserted.

Service said, "Do you live here, Mr. Cair?"

"My grandson lives here."

"Then you can't come in. Let's take a walk."

"I am the owner of record. I demand to know what's going on. I have a constitutional right to know."

"No, you don't," Service said and guided the man down the stairs and walked him toward a new Range Rover HSE. "Your grandson is in trouble."

The man had a stone face. "My lawyer will handle it."

"Your kid's being used, and so are you."

"You cannot talk to me that way."

"You mean straight, with no bullshit?"

"What is this about?" the man asked, obviously trying to soften his tone.

"Poaching, drugs, sex with minors. Contraband cigarettes. That's just for starters."

"Is Josh under arrest?"

"No, sir, not yet."

"I'll take him with me."

"After we're done."

"When will that be?"

"When we're done."

"You'd better make sure all your ducks are lined up and armored for a fight," he warned in a menacing voice.

"Thank you; we'll certainly keep that in mind."

When Service got back upstairs, the Basquell boy was mouthing off about needing a smoke and Mach was ignoring him.

It took some time to talk to each boy, getting their statements. It was obvious they had not practiced a group story. There were differing accounts and descriptions of nearly everything. They were on notice now, and lawyers would probably help them stitch something together, but this crowd was green and unlikely to be able to hold together. In a few years, if they kept on, lies would flow as smoothly as breath.

The search and seizure took six hours, with the careful logging of every item they took and the preliminary interviews. All the while, Service kept thinking he was missing something, but he put it down to his perfectionist streak and told himself they already had so much evidence they didn't need anything more. What they needed to do was focus on what they had, not on what they didn't know they didn't have.

The evidence all went into a locker in the regional office in Marquette, and Service drove to Friday's place and let himself in.

"It go down all right?" she asked from bed.

"So far."

"There's some stew in the fridge. You want me to warm it for you?"

"Not that hungry," he said.

He told her about the filth and the underage girls and the boys.

"Makes one wonder what lies ahead for younger kids," she said. As a state police homicide detective, she had seen a lot of death, as had he.

Friday said, "The good news is you scored a big case. Does this count for deer season?"

Service stared at her and moaned softly. Two long months remained until the statewide firearm deer season kicked in.

With luck, maybe everyone he checked in the weeks ahead would be acting lawfully. He didn't bother to share this with Friday. Even he didn't believe it.

CHAPTER 8

Marquette

TUESDAY, OCTOBER 20, 2009

The antlers taken from the apartment in Little Lake all matched the deer heads in the evidence freezer. All the videos had been reviewed. All the arrests had been made, all charges sorted out. All the boys had lawyered up, but the lawyer for Cair was the one who seemed to be directing an informal group show, the other three taking their lead from him. The forty cartons of Missouri cigarettes remained a mystery. None of the suspects or the girls who had been there claimed to know anything about them. The lawyer for the Cair boy was called Tegardle. He had offices in Traverse City and Rochester Hills and let everyone he met know that, but Service knew he was just a high-priced ambulance chaser who advertised legal defense of the American way while he vampired the system.

All the boys had pleaded not guilty through their attorneys, until the prosecutor brought Service into a meeting with Tegardle. The prosecutor laid out the charges again and said he would drop some of them in exchange for guilty pleas. A jury would no doubt find the boys all guilty of all charges.

Tegardle said, "We'll take our chances."

Grady Service said, "You want the jury to see your client on video screwing fourteen-year-olds?"

"This case isn't about sex," the lawyer said confidently.

"How about this then?" the prosecutor said and turned on a video monitor that showed the boys beating a screaming, squealing raccoon to death with a baseball bat. His client was among those wielding the clubs. "We put that up on YouTube," the prosecutor said. "Maybe you win in court, but that won't matter. This town will go berserk when it sees what your client has done. You might want to relay that to your client's grandfather."

"I don't need to," Tegardle said. "Let's talk."

The boys were already out on bail. Service had no idea when the judge might rule, but it didn't matter. His job was done. Time to move on. Only twenty-six days until the firearms deer season kicked off, and so far, following what he was calling the 8-1 case, it had been all quiet on the cedar swamp front. Maybe this would be an equally quiet gun season.

CHAPTER 9

Along the Escanaba River, Marquette County

THURSDAY, NOVEMBER 12, 2009

In the first blush of morning light, Service waded across the gray shallows of the Escanaba River, near where Sawmill Creek dumped in from the giant Cyr Swamp to the north. The CO's Danner boots were jammed into raggedy, patched rubber hippers, and it didn't escape him that only ten years ago he would have plunged across the river in his regular boots and said to hell with wet, cold feet all day. No longer. *My new reality: I'm looking at . . . God, I don't even know what, for sure. I've got the body of a beat-up forty-year-old but, thank God, the pain threshold of a reptile. I don't have anywhere near the flexibility I once had, and there's no way left for me to operate than to work smarter, not harder. Still,* he thought, *old ways die hard for an old boots-in-the-snow game warden.*

Conservation Officer Sander "Superman" Torvay was somewhere beyond the river, operating the drone, an RC Silent Screamer, their newest technological tool. It was rare in this era to have enough budget to put actual pilots and aircraft overhead for surveillance. But cheap-ass drones the state could afford, so it was drones overhead, not pilots in the sky. The idea of increasingly coming to depend on cheap toys like the noiseless Screamer rubbed him wrong. The drones were the result of some sort of deal with the military, arranged by Chief Eddie Waco. Had the chief arranged for the cost of maintenance too? Sometimes the department acquired new systems with what seemed to be an assumption they'd never break down, which meant the new stuff sometimes crashed and was little used thereafter.

"One, One Forty, you good for a TX?" Service radioed.

"That's affirm, Twenty-Five Fourteen."

Grady Service's life had been topsy-turvy for more than two years. He had been a detective (equivalent of corporal rank) before a sudden, unexpected, unwanted promotion to a newly created position—the state's senior noncommissioned officer for DNR law enforcement. He endured this for almost a year before turning his stripes back to Chief Eddie Waco. Top NCO had put him in endless meetings in district office buildings and kept him out of the field, which was where his heart lay. This far into a career, he wanted only to return to being the CO for the Mosquito Wilderness, where his old man had served before him. The chief had reluctantly accepted his resignation from the top NCO job and approved his request.

Then Detective Norm Kro developed some sort of ticker problem and was off duty for the next six to eight months. Chief Waco had called him last month and asked him to temporarily go back as a detective, with the stipulation he could work both as a detective and keep his boots in the Mosquito Wilderness and nearby terrain. Today he was in his dark green Class C uniform. If realities called for a detective, he'd switch to civvies. Maybe.

Service hit speed dial and called Torvay. "I'm across the river. You need my heading?"

"Negative, just don't take off your hat and Rosie will find you."

The CO's baseball cap had a small reflective patch Velcroed on top. The drone would use metallic fibers in the patch to find him and scan based on his position and directions. Service remembered how many times in his game warden career he had literally and painfully crawled miles through swamps and over nasty rock ridges hunting bad guys, found nothing, and limped back to his truck, bruised and bleeding.

Below the Bridge, especially in far southern Michigan counties, there were so many people that lawbreakers seemed to fly at COs in swarms; but up here Above the Bridge, officers often had to hunt their troublemakers, which required superb tracking skills and a lot of experience. The damn drone could make recon, surveillance, and following quarry a lot easier—*if* the weather cooperated, *if* there were no mechanical glitches, *if, if, if.* But when the drones worked as advertised, they were glorious tools and made the job so much easier. Still, he wasn't sold on the new toyology, not by a long shot. New did not automatically mean better.

Male COs were giving their drones female names and female operators were giving theirs male names, some sort of stupid psychological switchy-ditchy dance he chuckled at but had no interest in understanding. He had even been offered a one-week drone training class and guessed it was because of his age, that some up-tops in Lansing might be thinking he was no longer up to the physical demands of the job. Or someone down there was just trying to mess with him, which seemed more likely. He'd turned down the drone class with the explanation that flew through the ranks statewide: "I'm not worth a shit at naming stuff."

Deep down, he knew—jokes and skepticism aside—that the new toy could come in handy. Only three more days remained until the firearm deer season opened, and dirtbags from far and wide were already gathering in the camps that dotted the Upper Peninsula's cedar swamps and hardwood forests.

Torky Hamore had showed up at the house last week, standing in the front yard bellowing like a moose in heat for Service to "Show your bloody self." Service lived with Michigan state detective Tuesday Friday, and it pissed him off that Hamore dared invade their privacy. As a CO, he was used to it, but other cops didn't have to suffer such baloney from the public.

"How the hell did you find me, Torky?"

Hamore laughed. "Your woman. Wah, everybody know where youse two are, eh. So what's with the bloody deer herd?"

"Nothing."

"Bullshit. Wolves eatin' 'em all."

Not this crap again. "You know better 'n that, Torky." The man was a wealthy, successful logger in the central U.P., held a forestry degree from Michigan Tech, but like so many others, tended to dive off the flipping deep end every deer season, which in the U.P. was at least as important as monthly Social Security checks.

"Youse been out my camp, Grady, youse seen what's there."

Service had indeed. The camp was located in remote Delta County, an old log cabin filled with a collection of giant swamp buck heads dating back to the 1930s, when Hamore's great-grandfather bought the land and built the first camp building. Torky's father had passed the camp to him, as he would pass it to his sons. This was the U.P. way.

"At least one wall-hanger every year, some years two," the man said gruffly. "Until eight, ten years back, and since den, not a bloody one, eh. We didn't even see no damn does last season. I'm tell youse, she's got to be the bloody wolves."

Hamore, like many Yoopers, believed only bucks should be hunted, and that this approach to culling helped the reproductive health of the herd. In truth, buck laws had been instituted in 1913–14 solely as a safety measure, to require shooters to have a distinct target in their sights before pulling the trigger. Contrary to the baloney from old-timers, who bragged what great hunters they'd all been back in the day, historical records showed near mass incompetence then, with widespread disregard for safety and largely non-existent marksmanship. Most deer hunters in the earliest twentieth century had had no clue about their sport, or made up their own rules. Was it any different now?

"You know that deer populations fluctuate," Service said. "Cycles are nature's way."

Torky Hamore stuck out his jaw and shook a fist. "Since way back in thirties, one monster buck a year, now none for eight. That's bloody disaster, or a tragedy, and not no damn *cycle*. We got down to camp same natural feed, cover, genetics, but no damn deer. Explain *that*!" the man bellowed.

"I can't," Service admitted.

"Well, it don't make no damn sense, Grady. Tell you this: Me and the boys see a wolf this year, it won't never get seen again."

"Don't be stupid, Torky."

"Youse always been good guy—fair, talk, and shoot straight with people—and I thought youse should know. And we ain't onny ones think wolves are killing the deer. All camps out by us havin' the same damn experience."

Grady Service watched the man march stiff-legged back to his Chevy truck and roar down the street. Tuesday Friday came outside and looped her arm around his waist.

"Informant?" the state police homicide detective asked.

"Complainant," he said.

"Good one?"

"Same line we hear every year at this time," Service muttered. Yet he shared the man's concern and could understand his frustration. Cycles didn't happen at such rates, and department biologists, for all their impressive learning, did not always have answers to everything. Annual petty arguments simmering between various kin and camps somehow stayed tamped down between firearm deer seasons, but they were starting to fire up again, as invariably they broke out this time of year, every year, some of these tiffs dating back decades and generations. Talk about cycles. And all the damn fuss over . . . deer? What the hell is wrong with people? It was a strange phenomenon all around, and whenever he and Friday went somewhere and there was a mounted deer head, she would whisper, "Penis on a plaque." Like a lot of humor, it was based on truth.

Firearm season for deer. Complaints were starting, as they did every year, and almost every warden in the state was hearing whinging and carping complaints, and was on the alert for preseason oddities.

In that same vein, there was one particular situation that continued to nag at him. For going on two weeks he had seen a new red Chevy Silverado pickup truck parked in the same place every time he drove past a certain spot off one of the badly rutted Escanaba River Truck Trails. An all-day, everyday bow-and-arrow hunter? Bird hunter? Not *all* day. Both of those events were limited to certain times of day in specific habitats. Unh uh, this was something else here. Had to be. His gut churned each time he saw the truck, and this morning he finally stopped and ran the Illinois plate through the Michigan Law Enforcement Information Network (LEIN) a statewide computerized information system, which had been around since the late 1960s. The plate matched the truck and came back to a male named Kimball Gambol of Evanston, age sixty. A quick run through the Retail Sales Records database showed that Mr. Gambol had no Michigan hunting or fishing licenses for this year, or any other year, going back at least five years. Before that, who knew? So what the heck was Gambol doing out in the woods all day?

A look into the truck showed no ammo boxes; no signs of bait or blood; no rifle, bow, or crossbow case. So what the hell is this guy doing in the woods? Pats and woodcock are still legal, but morel mushroom season ended six months back. Fall shrooms? This was a remote possibility. Harvesting illegal dope grows? Nah, that's pretty much done by now. Photographer? Maybe. Or just a guy who likes to walk in the woods? The CO had called Station Twenty in Lansing, and Dispatcher Colleen Gonzalez had dug some more for him and found that Gambol's address came back to an empty lot in Evanston, owned by Northwestern University. Probably the identity was false too. The questions remained: Why, and who the heck is this wing nut?

Weird, troubling, and impossible to guess. Today Service was hoping to finally have an answer to the truck mystery. He had been back on duty only since late April, after he had been shot last winter and sidelined for a while. He called COs Torvay and Simon del Olmo. Del Olmo had driven up the River Road on the east side of the Escanaba and stashed his truck. The plan was for him to move up the east side of the feeder creek. Service slid on his go-pack and said into the mike near his chin, "One, One Twenty-Two, your position?"

"The creek we talked about earlier. You want me to move parallel to you?"

"Negative; the tracks I'm following, indicate *due* north, west of that creek. Come up your bank to where the next creek feeds in and then cross over toward me. Let me know when you're at the crossing."

Click-click, del Olmo replied, keying his mike twice.

It's the goddamn Federal Communications Commission's fault that we have to operate like this. FCC rulings had made it possible for manufacturers to create scanning devices that enable civilians to monitor all 800 MHz transmissions. What had once been an exclusive, private system for law enforcement and first responders was now totally public, which allowed violators and others to track cop operations. Typical cycle of the for-profit world buggering the country: First you give cops a tool to increase their safety and effectiveness and invest in all new equipment, and then you render it out of date and give it to the yahoo public. Typical bullshit from profit-chasers and by so-called public servants.

"Twenty-Five Fourteen, I think I remember an old tote road over by you. It runs due north and veers west to the river again," Torvay radioed.

"Affirm, but the sign is *between* there and the creek."

Click-click.

"Fourteen is moving out," Service radioed.

Who the hell is Mr. Kimball Gambol of Evanston, Illinois? Fake name? As it developed, tracking Mr. Gambol, if this was he, was not an easy task. His sign showed him doubling back, possibly to check his six for pursuit, and he made frequent sharp changes in direction before gradually returning to the original heading more or less toward the dense black spruce swamp to the north. Gambol's trail had led Service almost two miles, including crossing a two-track, which would have saved the man a good two miles of hard hiking. *Is this guy a masochist? Or doesn't he know the area that well? Latter seems more likely. You never know what sort of eight balls and ass-hats you'd encounter in the Upper Peninsula during deer season or just before the official opener.*

The trail eventually led into some aspens. Service took a knee to look, listen, and sniff. Sometimes you could smell a hunter's cigarette or cigar smoke. No smoke today, though, and no sound. He stood and moved cautiously on, his gut telling him the quarry was not far ahead. Thick swamp in front, river behind; there's no way for the man to go anywhere except where he was headed. Service touched his radio transmitter, "One, One Forty, Rosie up yet?"

"Affirmative," the CO answered. "I have a good picture of you on Channel Three." Service switched his handheld monitor to the channel and saw himself kneeling in the swamp. *Talk about an out-of-body experience.* All officers were issued small video monitors to carry when working under drones.

Del Olmo said, "Channel Three is clear and crisp."

Service said, "One, One Forty, send Rosie up that feeder creek for a mile, cut her west a half-mile and back south—then east to me to set a perimeter box."

There was a single gunshot not ten seconds later, roughly in the direction the tracks were pointing. It had sounded close, very low caliber and presumably subsonic, from neither a shotgun nor a deer rifle. A muffled crack, not even a .22. A .17, he guessed, the modern scumbag's precision tool of choice.

Did the others hear? "You guys hear that?" he asked his colleagues.

"Hear *what*?" del Olmo came back.

I heard it and Simon didn't. Means it's closer to me than to him.

"Rosie recorded what I think is a gunshot," Torvay reported. "Real low volume, but her audio sensors tagged it with a blip."

"That's a roger. Does she have a fix on it?"

"Negative GPS coordinates. The decibels weren't sufficient for a fix, but she's calculated a relative heading."

Service smiled. It was just like being with another CO when you heard a shot. Both of you would point and see how close you were. Maybe the drones aren't all that sophisticated after all.

"Okay, send her; I'll keep going north. One, One Twenty-Two, cross the creek northwest at first opportunity and start making your way toward me."

Click-click.

He watched the monitor for a moment, began walking, and didn't get twenty yards before stopping to squint at white objects hanging in a tree, swaying in the light breeze that had just arisen. The breeze was out of the east and suggesting possible snow, which the tree objects looked like at first glance. *Long white flakes of snow? Or ice? What the hell is this?* At first he saw one, then two, and shortly thereafter he had counted seven of the objects on one low balsam. He got out his digital camera, moved closer, and took photographs. He stared at the objects, mouth agape. *What the . . . ? Tampons. Tampons? What the . . . ?* Strings hung down like small white bombs. Service keyed his radio. "One, One Twenty-Two, you aren't going to believe what I have over here."

"Twenty-Two is sliding east."

Service looked at the drone monitor and radioed, "One Forty, circle Rosie over my position."

"Check your monitor."

Service looked and saw himself kneeling on a hummock in the swamp. "There's a bunch of stuff hung in a balsam right in front of me."

"What kind of stuff?"

"*Things* kind of stuff."

"Can you be a bit more specific, Twenty-Five Fourteen?"

On the radio? Jesus. "Uh, like uh . . . woman stuff, uh-you-know, like once-a-month-woman stuff?" Service radioed.

Del Olmo radioed. "If you're seeing tampons hung in a tree, I have two trees of the same thing so far."

"What brand?" Service asked, moving closer to his tree.

"Say again?" Torvay asked incredulously.

"Monthly feminine care items," Service said. "Uh, corks?" Which is what Friday called them.

"The ones over here appear to be used," Del Olmo said.

Service looked closely at his tree, made a face, and radioed, "Same here." *What idiot hangs used corks?* He watched the drone pick up del Olmo on the drone video monitor, and he knelt to await his longtime friend's arrival. He whispered into the radio, "Back when I was a kid, my old man usta tell me about old-timers who had their wives urinate on apples and corn when they were having their periods. They claimed it enhanced the value of bait, especially when the rut was on."

"Two comments. First, that's totally junk science," del Olmo said derisively. "Second comment: *Yah-uck!*"

"Deer hunters," Service said, as if that one phrase encompassed all the strange things they did, legally and illegally.

"Anything more on that shot heading?" Service asked Torvay as he looked at his monitor and thought he saw a human figure trotting between some trees. "Is that Sasquatch or a human?" Service asked the drone operator.

"Looks humanoid to me."

"Can Rosie stay on him?"

"We'll do our best."

"Got a heading from us?"

"Three five eight degrees, crow-fly."

As good as due north. Dead ahead of Service was a massive open expanse of sphagnum islands, clusters of spindly golden tamaracks that had started to lose some needles, and ragged rows and clusters of stunted, gnarled black spruces. In the near foreground he could see a looming line of tall white cedars with an interlaced canopy overhead blocking most light from reaching the ground, perfect protection for deer in winter. Service noted a browse line about seven feet high, confirming this area had been used as winter thermal cover and deer yards. He looked up to see if he could eyeball the drone, but it was butter-knife silent and he saw nothing. They could keep the heading and go under the cedars, but risk breaking an ankle on exposed roots in the dark. Better to skirt northwest and swing around to intercept.

"Moving," Service said, not looking over to confirm that his friend was with him. Del Olmo was the best kind of CO—one who charged toward the sound of the guns. With Simon, your six was always covered.

"Your mark's not moving," One One Forty announced.

"Keep Rosie circling him, we're moving up."

Click-click.

Fifteen minutes later the two conservation officers converged on a heavy foot trail into the thick, severely leaning white cedars. Both men knelt, opened their packs, and put on their night vision goggles to help them see when they moved into the blackness under the trees. "You see us, One Forty?"

"Roger, got a faint thermal sig on both of you. Your mark is about fifty yards north and stationary." Service was impressed with how easily the drone's thermal imaging camera penetrated the dense cedar grove.

The two game wardens entered the dark forest, spread out by twenty feet. "Report any change in position," Service whispered to the drone operator.

Click-click, Torvay answered. "I have a faint thermal signal twenty yards to the right of target," the operator reported.

"Another person?"

"Rosie shows four legs, and signature's heat is fading."

A deer, Service guessed, walking on. Ahead of him he saw a small log shack and a man squatting in the opening of the walled structure. He closed on the man, who popped up and quickly knelt again. There was a deer at the man's feet, a doe.

"Had some luck, eh?" Service said to announce himself.

The man turned, his face flushed and contorted in a rictus of surprise. "You! . . . Go! . . . Away!" the man said, struggling with every word, a rifle in his hand and leveled roughly at Service's midsection.

Grady Service said, "Department of Natural Resources, conservation officer. Point your weapon away and show me your hunting and driver's licenses."

The man stared at him. "*Going! Away!*"

Simon del Olmo swept in from the right and slammed the man down, separating him from the weapon and rolling him on his face as Service stepped in to pull back the man's arms and cuff him. "Sir, you are not under arrest. This is for everyone's safety, until we figure out what's going on here."

The man said nothing.

Del Olmo asked, "Sir, what's your name?"

"My name is none your business!"

"Show me your licenses," del Olmo said calmly.

"Go fucking yourself!" the man said with a hiss. He was not tall, but he was wide and strong and had reddish brown scars all over his face.

"Let's get him out into the light," Service said. "Torvay thinks there's another deer. See if you can find it." *Good god, the season's not even started!*

Grady Service snatched the man's rifle by the sling, hooked it over his shoulder, and roughly frog-hopped the man through the cedars out into the light and pushed him down onto a log. "*Sit.*"

"You treat me like dog!"

"What's your name?"

"*Neću razgovarati s fašističkim ološem.*"

"What the fuck is that, pig Latin?" Service asked. "We speak English here."

The man said, "*Jebite se ja više ništa reč*" and crossed his arms.

"Fourteen, this is Twenty-Two, I have a doe here, just been shot. You want me to field-dress it?"

"Yah, go ahead; it won't be staying out here."

Grady Service examined the man's rifle. It was a Remington Model Seven in .17 caliber, a poacher's gun, the barrel only twenty inches long and the rifle under seven pounds. But this weapon, made for close-in shooting, also had a lightweight Armasight digital night-vision scope mounted on it—the Armasight Drone Pro, a very current product and available only through the government. How the hell did this jerkwad get his hands on it?

Service pointed at the scope. "*Really?*"

The man stared past him. "You got a name?" the CO pressed.

"Fucking you."

"Listen to me, Mr. Gambol, if that's who you are. We could have done this the easy way but, because of your asshole attitude, we'll do it the hard way. You pointed that weapon at me, meaning you threatened a peace officer with a deadly weapon."

"No Gambol," the man muttered. "I no make no threat on you."

"So you do speak English."

"I make some spick."

"Licenses."

The man shrugged.

"I can't translate that. You don't have licenses, or you left them at camp?"

The man shrugged again as del Olmo came over, dragging the doe.

Service got on the radio. "One Four Zero, are we close to any roads?"

"There are two-tracks coming off County Road 444 across Mud Creek. That road dead-ends between Mud and Sawmill Creeks, about a mile north and east of where the two creeks intersect."

"Okay," Service said. "Our trucks aren't anywhere close. Call Marquette County and ask if they can do a prisoner transport from the 444 hookup point. How far for us to get there on foot?"

"I have you guys closer to Parker Spur. It crosses Sawmill right close to the area where you are now. You can follow that east to M-35. Five miles crow-fly, but the deps may be able to get down the spur road and shorten your hike."

"OK, change the link-up to the Parker Spur and let us know if you see anything else of interest. We want to deliver this guy for a jail run and then loop back here to look around more."

"You want me over there too?"

"Affirmative, and bring Rosie, but don't land her yet. Keep her flying in case this guy tries to make a run. Keep her flying until we pass the prisoner over to the deps."

"See you soon," Torvay said.

Minutes later, he called back. "Twenty Five Fourteen, I think I've got a vehicle parked just off the spur."

Service asked, "What kind, and where?"

"Not certain of the ID, but it's a good size, bigger than a pickup. You want particulars?"

The CO read out the coordinates and Service used a ballpoint pen to write them on the heel of his hand, a CO's forever, all-weather notebook. "It's just across the creek, just as you walk out of the swamp, pushed back in some trees on the south side of the two-track."

"See you soon, Twenty-Five Fourteen clear."

"You want me up with you or back here?" del Olmo asked.

"With me until we hand off this jamoke." If the prisoner ran, he'd let the younger legs run him down.

The two men helped their prisoner through the swamp and carried him across Sawmill Creek and quickly located the two-track. Just as Torvay said, they found the vehicle, which turned out to be a brown-and-green panel truck with no plate. But ten minutes after finding the vehicle, del Olmo found a nest of license plates in a plastic bag in the high grass not far from the driver's door: Michigan, Wisconsin, Minnesota, Illinois, Ohio, Indiana. "Pick your flavor," del Olmo said.

"Your truck?" Service asked his prisoner.

"I never see this."

Service looked at del Olmo. "No plates; could be stolen. Got your Sheena in your pack?"

The officer shrugged, put down his pack, and searched for the tool to jimmy open the door locks. His wife was CO Elza Grinda, nickname Sheena, and it did not make her happy to have a breaking-and-entering tool named for her by her colleagues, which of course was the whole point.

Del Olmo held up the tool.

Service said, "Hold off for now."

"Roger, *jefe*."

The Marquette County deputy who showed up was Sergeant Linsenman, who had been riding with a rookie. "Jesus, Grady. How do you find such *shit-hole* roads?"

"It's a gift."

Linsenman barked like an owl choking on a mouse.

Service and del Olmo looked around the van, finding blood and deer hair in several places, but the vehicle's rear doors were locked with three padlocks. After a thorough search of the prisoner's person, they found no keys, no wallet, no ID, no combinations to the locks, not even keys to the red truck. Had he stashed his stuff elsewhere?

Service leaned close to del Olmo. "Why don't you head back to where we grabbed this guy. Don't touch or force anything, but look around and see if there are keys or anything else. I'm going to request search warrants."

"Don't need one for the field stuff."

"I know there's plenty of probable cause, but I want to play this tight. My gut says this isn't our plain-brown-wrapper violet."

"Roger that," del Olmo said and loped away.

Was I ever that energetic? Two hours later he had his search warrants and four more conservation officers. Inside the suspect panel truck they found thirty skinned deer and boxes of dry ice. Del Olmo found more butchered carcasses in some balsam-covered pits packed with more dry ice—and six trophy-size buck heads, caped for shoulder mounts.

• • •

The additional COs included Sergeant James "Slick" Wooten, who, not yet thirty-five, technically was Service's newly minted boss. He was wise enough to let Service run the show and do whatever he was asked to help out, offering opinions only when asked—a good sign, Service thought. Three stripes on your arm didn't confer omniscience.

Service wanted to assist in the search but decided his time would be better spent with the prisoner. A deputy took him to his patrol truck and told him en route that the man the panel truck plates came back to wasn't named Gambol but someone else.

"Who?" Service asked; the dep only shrugged.

Grady Service headed for the jail, almost forty miles away. Goddamn distances were killers in this line of work, especially in some U.P. counties.

• • •

"Talk about poetic justice," Grady Service said when the U.P.'s leading attorney-to-assholes Sandy Tavolacci showed up with the prisoner, now identified not as Kimball Gambol but as Bojan Knezevich of Ridge Street, Chicago.

"What's that 'pose ta mean?" Tavolacci asked. The lawyer had a long rodentious proboscis that twitched and quivered like a hungry rat vacuuming a garbage bin.

"Asshole lawyer for an asshole violet," Service said.

"Let's try to civilize this situation right now," Tavolacci said sternly. "My client is a respectable member of the Greater Chicago Croatian community."

Service was unimpressed. "Good for him. Why's your client driving a truck registered to a bogus address in Evanston?"

Tavolacci furrowed his brow. "Did you personally *see* my client drive said vehicle?"

Goddamn lawyers. "I tracked him nearly four miles, and the boots on his feet match the pattern and size of tracks I followed in the snow from the truck."

"Four miles and no chance you crossed a second trail and got mixed up and followed the other trail erroneously?"

Service laughed. "No chance, Sandy. His tracks were the only ones out there."

"You're infallible, is that what you're saying, Officer?"

"Competent, not infallible."

"Did you ever consider that the boot he's wearing is probably one of the most popular among hunters, that such prints abound in the bush?"

Service saw how Tavolacci was going to play this game. It didn't concern him. "I want to talk to your client, Sandy. Alone."

"No can do, Grady. You'll have to wait for our translator."

"That's bullshit, Sandy. Your boy speaks and understands English. I've watched his eyes. He's following this whole deal."

The man immediately looked away.

"So he speaks a little of the lingo. You'll still have to wait. All citizens have their rights."

Service looked at the prisoner. "You don't have the balls to face this like a man?"

Bojan Knezevich's face reddened.

"Not a problem," Service said. "If you want to wait for your testicles to arrive from wherever, so be it."

Knezevich grasped the edge of the table so hard his knuckles turned white.

"How long?" Service asked Tavolacci.

"Tomorrow. The specialist, he has to like, you know, drive up from Chicago?"

Grady Service stood up. "Fine by me. Time?"

"Fifteen hundred."

"Cool," Service said, took one step and turned back to the prisoner. "It would be a lot more honorable to handle this man to man," he said.

The prisoner stared straight ahead.

"Your hands are shaking, Bub," Service said over his shoulder as he left the room.

CHAPTER 10

Marquette, Marquette County

THURSDAY, NOVEMBER 12

Grady Service was on his way to interview the suspect when a woman stopped him in the Marquette County courthouse. "You know my boy-friend, Harry Pattinson?"

Pattinson was a major property owner near Torky Hamore's camp in Delta County. The man owned several radio stations in the state and a res-taurant near Gladstone. "You are?" Service countered.

"Myra Steghouse. I work for Tom Neckers."

"How come we've never met?"

Neckers was the county's senior, longtime magistrate. Service had done business with the man for what sometimes seemed like forever. Tom "Ekey" Neckers had great rapport with conservation officers and knew fish and game law as keenly as the officers themselves. Service had less experience with the county's other magistrate, Kennard Dentso.

"I've just started," the woman said. She was fortyish, thin, wearing a sim-ple skirt and black boots with low heels. She struck him as a one-broccoli-floret-for-breakfast kind of person.

"Where's Lindsay?" Service asked. Lindsay Gillys was the magistrate's longtime clerk and assistant.

"She died a month ago, car wreck near Green Bay."

How did I miss that? He wondered but he had no time for sympathy or self-criticism. *You miss shit when you work all the time.* "Sorry, I have a meeting."

"I'm sorry," she said. "Harry is all worked up over deer and those dang wolves," the woman said. At second glance, she was a lot more attractive than his first impression, and her boyfriend was much older.

"He's not alone," Service told her.

"You don't understand," she said. "He's saying he's going to *do* something about it."

"What *kind* of something?"

"I don't know specifics, but it won't be good for the wolves. And that breaks my heart. They were here before us, weren't they?"

"They *were*," Service said. "If Harry's *something* starts to become real, call me, and not afterwards, *before*." He locked eyes with hers to make sure she got the message and waited until she nodded acknowledgement.

She mumbled, "I really care about Harry, and I don't want this to come between us." Relationships could be like minefields, every step important.

"Sounds like it already has."

"He's a good, moral man," she said.

"Good to know. Maybe his moral compass will keep him on the right path."

"Could he get into trouble if he like, *does* something?"

"Big, *expensive* trouble."

"There's no deer out to camp," the woman said. "Understand?"

Service nodded. "I've heard that same song before—from Torky Hamore."

"Judson Dornboek is saying the same thing," the woman said. "They had a meeting last night."

"Harry, Torky, *and* Jud?"

"Attilio Haire and Kermit Swetz were there too."

This smacked of big trouble, a landowner cabal. Pattinson, Hamore, Dornboek, Haire, and Swetz owned thousands of acres in the same remote part of Delta County, touching the Marquette County border. They were all self-made, had money and political clout, and weren't reticent about using it for their own ends. Swetz even had one of his U.P. hunting camps reserved only for judges and another for priests, covering all bets.

"Thanks, Myra. I'm sorry, but I have a prisoner waiting for me. Please call if you hear more." He gave her a business card.

"Will my telling you help keep Harry out of trouble?"

"It might," he told her as he moved on, knowing that for the next two weeks the sole subject of conversation in the U.P. would in some way involve deer. It was always a pain in the ass. And fun.

Twenty feet from the interview room, Marquette County Lt. Rusty Ranka tried to stop him. "Boy, do I have a story for you!"

Ranka was a good cop with diarrhea of the mouth and a tendency to exaggerate his fishing and hunting exploits. Service said, "No time for another deer story," and brushed past the man.

Ranka said thinly. "It was about some pats, eh?"

• • •

Service entered the room. "Sorry to keep you waiting, gentlemen."

Sandy Tavolacci said, "Officer Service meet Mr. Davorin Horvat, our distinguished translator."

"You don't need a translator, Sandy. I can understand your bullshit just fine."

Tavolacci flashed surprise but said nothing. The translator whispered something to his client, who showed no reaction.

"How much are you being paid?" Service asked the translator as he looked only at the prisoner.

"This is no concern of yours," the man said, clearly taken aback by the question.

"OK then," Service said. "Who actually *pays* you? Tavolacci or Mr. Knezevich? Or does the client pay through his attorney, who slaps a 20 percent handling fee on the transaction?"

Horvat said, sputtering. "I must object most vehemently. This is *most* unprofessional."

Service said, "I'm sure Mr. Knezevich doesn't want to waste his money on a translator when he obviously speaks English at least well enough to communicate what he wants with Mr. Tavolacci."

Knezevich eyed Service, who thought he detected a glint of something in the man's eyes. "Am I right, sir?"

"This is not acceptable," the translator said with a chirp.

"Go home to Chicago," Service said. "You're just a tit on a bull here."

"Sir?" the man demanded.

"Superfluous, useless, worthless—a hulking *Queen Mary* doing a rowboat's job."

Knezevich laughed out loud, looked at Tavolacci, and jerked his head at the door. "Out, da bot' a youse."

Tavolacci and Horvat exchanged glances. "I'm sorry?"

"Bot' a youse," Knezevich said again. "Beat it."

"But I'm your *attorney*," Tavolacci argued.

"Yes, my mout'piece on *my* dime. Me and da officer here can do dis t'ing alone."

"I strongly advise against this," the lawyer said, with desperation in his voice.

"Gedout," Knezevich said. "You can bring coffee for me an da officer," Knezevich looked at Service, "Whiteurblag?"

"Black."

Knezevich nodded. "Two blag."

Tavolacci and Horvat hurried out of the room.

"I seen you yesterday and I think dis big woods cop, he's got the *gravitas*. I think dis guy he don't think like udders. Dis guy is his own man. Then you walk in and bomb that pompous translator, and I know I'm right about you. *Gravitas*, you understand?"

Service said, "I'm not looking for your approval."

Knezevich smiled and nodded, "We all seek approval and acceptance."

Tavolacci brought the coffee and departed without a word.

Coffee in hand, the Croatian said, "You surprise me in the swamp. I never meant to threaten you."

"Motivation is irrelevant," Service said, "but the fact remains. Think of it as currency."

"I killed those deer," the man said. "I do it every year to pay back my most trusted employees and their families."

"In what business?"

"That ain't part of this parley," the man said.

"I was in that damn swamp late," Service said, gathering his thoughts.

Knezevich appeared to want to talk. "You were busy fella out dere."

The man sipped his coffee. "It ain't espresso. Oh for a splash of *rakija*."

Service didn't understand.

The man read him. "Fruit brandy, we drink it every morning, like Americans and your orange juice."

Service said nothing, wanted to see how the man would handle the lack of sound.

"*Kratka sprava je bolsi kakor dolga pravda*, understand? My people think a bad compromise is better than a good lawsuit."

"You're in the wrong songbook," Service said. "There's no lawsuit here.

We found thirty-five illegal butchered deer, three wolf skins, six buck heads. All evidence."

"No diff," Knezevich said with a shrug. "We negotiate. You want to *schtupp* your old lady, even then you must negotiate. That's life, am I right?"

This guy's got balls and he's used to getting his way, and he was a presence in a way Service couldn't quite peg. "Restitution for the deer here is a thousand a head. The wolves are fifteen hundred per; if the feds want the wolf case, then the court costs and fines can easily hit fifty grand."

"You want to play the hardball?" Knezevich asked in a flat, unintimidated voice.

"By the book is what I want, no more, no less. You tell me what you did, and we'll see where we can go from there."

"The why is not important?"

"It can be. But first I need the who, what, when, where, and how, all of that. The why comes later."

"Is difficult to be the king, yes?"

"I wouldn't know."

The man grinned. "We are, you and me, each king of something, or someplace. This is the beauty of life."

Service thought Knezevich had a long, sad face. His skin was abraded and leathery, maybe from too much sun and wind, the look of an outside guy. "I suppose there's some truth in that," Service admitted, thinking, *A violator spouting philosophy. This strains credulity.*

"You were a soldier," the Croat said. "Is in your eyes." The man touched his eyes with forked fingers. "I too," he added. "Our war against the Serbs, you know it?"

"Very little," Service admitted. The Balkans had been a shit stew, everything obscured, mostly hidden, odd, stinky, and mostly irrelevant.

"Our leaders they decide okay now we gonna make our own country, we will no longer be part of Tito's old Yugoslavia, but the Serbs in Belgrade they disagree, okay; I talk here JNA, Yugoslav People's Army. These peoples come to take our country, make it part of their territory. I am policeman at the time—in Vukovar. When invasion begins, we have no army and we policemen are told to fight. We have no idea what we are doing. I was in uniform four years and afterwards I come to Chicago to join my brother's business as partner. This was 1996. Five years later my brother dies, rest his soul, and I took over business."

The man stopped, and Service knew he was gauging his attentiveness.

"Every year, from the beginning, I bring to my top people a deer for their families to eat. In Croatia the poor hunt to eat, while the old nobility hunt for sport. My people do not need this meat. I pay them well, but this is a sign of my gratitude, a gesture, you understand?"

"Kings once owned all the fish and wildlife," Service said. "Maybe this is your way to remind them who is their king. How *many* top people are you talking about?"

"You have a policeman's mind. Thirty and six for gifts to others."

"The heads are gifts?"

"I give them, and what the gift-getter do I got no idea and don't care. A little profit, maybe. Who cares, my obligation is done."

"Profit how?"

"Don't be stupid. You know there are some guys want to buy such things down to Chicago. Okay?"

Service leaned forward. "Listen to me. If we push this over to the feds, I can do nothing for you. Nothing, you understand?"

"What must be done to keep this in your hands?"

"Your word," Service said. "Negotiate."

"My people say if you ask too much at once, you will come home with an empty bag."

"Americans say take it or leave it. To promise too much is to promise nothing."

"Where are your people from?" the man asked.

"Here."

"I mean before that?"

"Who cares?" Service countered.

"You have the power to make things happen?"

"I do," Grady Service said.

"There will be bail?"

"There can be," Service said.

"And charges?" Knezevich wanted to know.

"Taking with no licenses, taking with a firearm in a non-firearm season."

"Counts?"

"Thirty and the state takes the six heads and the three wolves."

"Ten and you keep the heads and pelts."

"Fifteen and," Service said.

Knezevich said, "Done. Okay, fifteen and . . ."

"You will give us the names of potential buyers of heads and pelts."

"I never said there was a market for the wolves. They would be too hot, and the Federals involved, yes?"

"You wouldn't keep them if they had no value."

"Some value is only personal, yes, as in mementos." Knezevich said.

"Not for you," Service said. "You're strictly a businessman. This deal will require a full written statement of what you did, and this is your opportunity to explain why to the court, to make your own case."

The Croat thought for a moment and smiled. "Let us call this thing what it is, a confession, yes? A turd may look like a black truffle, but remains a turd."

Service pushed a pen and printed form to the man, along with a tablet of yellow paper.

"You are expecting an opus?" Knezevich asked.

"I expect the truth," Service said, "However much that requires."

"In the war we called *Domovinski rat*, I led an independent brigade. I told my men I will ask you to do nothing I will not do. Do you think I was telling them the truth?"

"I wasn't there, and it doesn't matter. Your men had to judge for themselves, just as I will evaluate the truth of what you write."

"I think we must become friends," the man said.

"After you serve your time?"

"There will be jail?"

"That depends on what you write," Service said. He got up and stepped to the door, where he stopped. "The red Silverado?"

The man shrugged.

"I tracked you from it," Service said.

Another shrug.

"The red truck."

"I know no red truck. I think you are mistaking this for something it is not."

"I know differently," Service said. "And it had better be in your statement."

Service stepped outside to find Tavolacci pacing and looking conflicted.

"He's writing a statement, Sandy."

"You mean a *confession*?"

Service said, "You big-time lawyers always know the right word. No wonder you haul in the big bucks."

• • •

His parting words to Tuesday Friday this morning as they headed to work: "Econofoods, sixish. I'll start a basket." Then, a peremptory kiss before they went down their separate cop roads. Tonight he called out of service to central dispatch and to Station Twenty in Lansing, parked his truck in the Econofoods lot, and got out. It was beginning to snow.

He grabbed a basket in the slushy entryway, went inside, stopped, and sucked in a deep breath. His old man had been a drunk and largely inattentive father. Service had learned to cook out of desperation and self-preservation and eventually discovered he enjoyed both the process and the product. Nowadays there were foods and ingredients in stores seemingly from every remote part of the world, not just in big metro areas, but right here in Marquette. With combat in Afghanistan winding down, a lot of political cement-heads were making noises about America first, isolation, and other such malarkey. All they had to do was stand in a grocery store aisle to see how small and interconnected the world had become.

Friday sailed by him with her son, Shigun. Service hooked her waist and pulled her to him and placed Shigun in the cart. The little boy's face beamed and Service whispered, "How many widgets did you build today?"

The little boy giggled. "Midgets is people."

"Got me there," Service said. "Can't sneak anything past you anymore. Shigun's a smart boy."

Service turned to Friday. "Your day?"

"The usual crab-scuttle in the endless search for justice. You?"

"Deer hunters," he growled.

"I hate deer hunting season," she said.

"But you love venison," he reminded her.

She said, "Enough talking. Let's shop till we drop."

Service pulled out his list. "Cassava, parsnips, sweet potatoes, carrots, butternut squash, onions, jalapeños, frozen corn, fresh ginger, and lamb. You grab the veggies, and I'll meet you in meat."

Friday lowered her eyes and voice. "I hope that's prophetic. How long has it been?"

"Justinian or Gregorian calendars?" he asked.

"Glacial time."

"At least one full epoch," he quipped. "Go. The big boy will ride with me."

"*I'm* big boy?" Shigun asked.

"Damn straight, partner."

Grady Service had just selected a package of lamb chops when Shigun said, "Midget." And pointed enthusiastically.

Veraldyne Tice and her hubby, Hinch, were examining hamburger packages. Veraldyne painted her face white with thick cosmetics, and her stringy bootblack-and-gray hair drooped down all over her head. There was a large doll in a safety seat in her grocery cart. The woman wore an ankle-length fake leopard coat. Service said, "Looks like James has him a new snowsuit."

"Oh, yes," Veraldyne said. "We were just down to the Saint Vinny's. Thank you for noticing, Grady. You were always the most polite and helpful boy. I don't mean to brag, but my James is top of his class."

"Not surprised," Grady said, looking at the three-foot doll dressed in the snowsuit. "Chip off the old block. Your son's always been precocious."

"Midget," Shigun repeated in a more militant voice, pointing at the doll.

"Shush, honey," Service heard Friday whisper.

Veraldyne Tice crooked her forefinger and waggled it for Service to approach her. He had to lean way over to get close to her face. "Grady, I hate to tattle-rattle, but Klimik is up to dose ol' tricks again."

"Night shots?"

The woman nodded and whispered, "And donchuknow dere's a giant bait pile outten back and a light over it and a loaded .22 mag by 'iss window. Dey usual like shoot around four. Dat's when I'm up with James to check and make sure he ain't rolled onto his face and got hisseff smothered."

"Thanks, Mrs. Tice. We'll take care of it."

"Midget," Shigun said again as the odd pair whistled away with the doll in the bow of their grocery cart. Old man Tice had grinned the whole while and never said a word. It occurred to Service that he had never heard Hinch's voice.

Friday said, "What in the world?"

Service explained. "Tices. Their son, James, died in 1950. He was not quite two. They were twenty and just married. They never got over it."

"Died how?" she asked.

"Rolled over on his face in his crib and suffocated."

"My God," Friday said.

"I used to cut their grass and shovel their snow and make wood for them. Nice people, bent badly."

"No other kids?"

"Nope. Blame them?" Service saw Tuesday hug her son and shake her head.

"Those people have been crushed by life and still want to make a deer complaint?" Friday asked.

"Says something about skewed priorities," he said. "Life goes on, no matter what."

"Ya think?"

They were in the checkout line when Service saw a man come through the automatic in-door, spy him, and crash back through shoppers in flight.

"Handle the bill," he told Friday and took off, catching up to the man at the edge of the parking lot and pinning him to a metal light pole. "Willie Nelson Niemi. What rock did you crawl out from under? I haven't seen your ass in years. Why'd you do a one-eighty when you saw me?"

"Din't see you," the slightly built man said. "Forgot somepin' is all."

"Like what?"

"I don't know. I forget what I forgot. You scareded me."

"Did I? Where you been, Willie?"

"Vacation."

"Yah, where? Jackson?"

The man hung his head. "Newberry."

"For what?"

"Darn you, Grady, you know ain't polite ask such of a fella."

"You feeling guilty about something, Willie? We're just talking, a couple of old pals."

"My name ain't Willie. It's Virpi. Virpi Niemi."

"What did they get you for this time?" Service pressed.

"Meth manufacture. I got set up, I swear."

"Don't you hate it when that happens?"

"Ain't no joke. I didn't do not'in' wrong."

Nothing except to be born into a shallow family's narrow gene pool of law-breakers. "Guess you won't be hunting deer with a firearm," Service said.

"But I can still hunt with a bow, right?"

"When did Newberry release you?" Service asked.

"This mornin'."

Good god. "Virpi, I doubt you have the strength to draw back a bow, much less hold it back."

"Hey I pushed some iron while I was on vacation."

Service laughed out loud. "Please don't complicate your life with more stupidity," he told the man. "You need meat, call me, and I'll *bring* you a deer."

"No, sir, not me never. I don't take no handouts. . . . You'd do that, bring me a buck?"

It would beat chasing around a near-lunatic drunk on blood sport. "Sure. But just venison, not necessarily a buck."

"But a real man needs buck, show he's real man."

Service grunted. "You want the meat or not?"

"Okay, yah, t'anks."

"You got work?"

"Cuttin' pulps for my cousin Swinton."

Grady Service gave Niemi one of his business cards. "You need a deer, call me. Just use the number on the card and I'll hook you up. Okay? And if you hear of any of your asshole old buds screwing up, call me and I'll get you a buck. How big you want?" he asked.

"Ten-point?" Niemi ventured.

"Sure, ten is possible, maybe. I might could organize that—but only for the right information."

"How soon?" Niemi asked. "Man needs to get his buck on the opener, ya know."

Service knew then that Niemi was thinking about the various area big buck contests, which offered cash prizes. But most contests required a hunting tag on the dead animal, not a DNR donation ticket.

"I can probably do something on the opener." Sooner or later he'd end up confiscating a deer. Usually it was later in the season for the big ones, but you just couldn't predict.

"Cool," Niemi said, skulking away.

"*If* you call with the right information," Service yelled after the man, who raised an arm but did not look back.

"You ain't such a big prick," Niemi yelled from the shadows as Friday walked up and said, "I'd have to take issue with that contention."

"I think he meant it as a compliment," Service told her.

Friday squeezed his arm. "Me too. Did we have some flower business out here in the parking lot?"

"Violet fresh from the state greenhouse."

"Huh," she said. "Think it straightened him out?"

"Has it ever?" the conservation officer countered.

"There's Allerdyce," she reminded him.

"I'm not buying that program yet."

"The man very recently saved your life," she said. "And I am thankful."

"Nevertheless."

Allerdyce. His nemesis in so many ways. A poacher and a felon. And yet, the old reprobate had stepped up more than once to help Service, once to save his life, maybe even twice. *Claims he's reformed, but how does a lifelong violator actually reform? Is it even possible?*

CHAPTER 11

New Swanzy, Marquette County

THURSDAY, NOVEMBER 12

Just as he was driving down Friday's street, Service's work cell phone clicked into life.

"Grady, Chief Waco. Got a minute?"

"Yes, sir."

"This is about those kids in that case you fellas are calling the 8-1."

"Yes?"

"The Missouri cigarettes?"

"What about them?"

"There's an ATF agent from Springfield, and she's an old friend. The cigarette information got passed to the ATF here, and now it's out in Missouri with Special Agent Gelatine Neutre."

"Neutre?"

"She's an old colleague and a top agent, a lot like you. She never gives up."

Where was this going?

"She's coming to Michigan, Grady, and I want you to work with her. She thinks she's got a pretty substantial case lead."

"Eddie, it's deer season."

"You *are* an acting detective."

"I know, I know. When do I meet her?"

"That's her call. She'll be in touch. Be safe, and be gentle with her," the chief said and hung up.

Just what I need. Babysitting a damn Fed during deer season.

His work cell phone rang again just as he pulled into Friday's driveway. "Service."

"Grady, this is Krip."

John Krippendore owned Trophy Taxidermy. "I'm off duty, John."

"I'm thinking youse might want to make an unscheduled inspection."

"Tomorrow, John."

"Tonight, hey? The customer was showing max hinks when she came in."

"She, as in her?"

"Yah, she be a her, eh."

"Regular customer?"

"Never seen her before tonight."

"Give me an hour?"

"Yah, sure; just walk on in. I'll have 'er all unlocked for yas."

• • •

Friday rolled her eyes and sighed when Service told her about the phone calls. "Might as well pretend we don't exist for the next two weeks," she said sourly.

"Write a blues tune," he told her.

"Does this deer season feel different?" she asked.

"Each one is unique," he said, "its own weird thing. But the build does seem faster this year."

"Want me to push Thanksgiving back into December?" she asked.

"No, don't do that, but tell Karylanne we'll get over there soon, at least for an afternoon." Karylanne Pengally was sort of his daughter-in-law. That is, she was pregnant by his son Walter when his son and his girlfriend, Maridly, were murdered five years back. Karylanne had given birth to a little girl she had named Maridly in honor of Service's late love. Little Mar was developing into a pip and pill, truly precocious, and she owned him emotionally. She and her "brother" Shigun kept him entertained.

Tuesday Friday stared at him. "The real trouble is that you *love* dealing with scumbags and I hate it."

"There it is," he said, leaving her unhugged and unkissed. Realizing his mistake, he reversed course back into the house, put her into a bear hug, and laid an atomic smooch on her.

"Hold that thought," he said and marched away.

• • •

New Swanzy was a nondescript pile of pre-manufactured houses, garages, and pole-barn businesses stretched on both sides of M-35 a half mile east of Gwinn. *What the hell was pre-manufactured? It was or wasn't, right?* Visually, New Swanzy seemed a part of Gwinn, like a suburb. Back in mining days, Welsh miners had come to the area to work the iron mines and had created an ethnic enclave three miles from the old village. They had named (although misspelled) their new home Swansea, for the Welsh ocean resort. But there were no operational mines anymore, and no lake-shore or beach for twenty miles. Michigan law required a town to have a post office in order to post town signs; New Swanzy had no post office and posted the signs anyway. Typical of many U.P. places, what townspeople thought often did not mesh with what government and its regulatory agencies wanted.

Grady Service pushed open the door to John Krippendore's game-processing establishment and felt the temperature drop. The snow had stopped outside, but the temp out there was warmer than inside. Krippendore was a retired DNR wildlife biologist from downstate, a fact he kept carefully close. COs had gotten innumerable leads to good cases from Krippendore, who knew how to keep his eyes and ears open and his mouth shut. Known as a world-class taxidermist, he also was registered to process all kinds of game meat.

"Sorry about the timing," he said when he saw Service. "It's in the cooler."

Grady Service opened the cooler door and immediately saw the object of interest.

"Fourteen points?" he said, counting quickly.

Krip was right behind him, his white smock smeared with blood. "I rough-scored that thing at one eighty-eight."

"Holy moly!" *What do we have here? The Boone and Crockett typical whitetail buck record is something like 210, a total of inches taken from the thickness and length of various parts of the antlers tallied into an overall score. A near-190 was pretty much unheard of almost anywhere in the Yoop.* "She say where it come from?" Service asked. The license had been bought November 10 at 4:30 in the afternoon in Escanaba, twenty-five miles away. According to the tag, the deer was killed at five o'clock that same night. Not very likely—on the basis of geography alone—unless it was killed in downtown Escanaba, which would open another bucket of worms. This was typical thinking among some residents: First shoot a deer, *then* go get a license. Why waste money until you have a sure thing?

"You get a name?"

"Arletta Ingalls is the one who brought it in. Said her boyfriend shot it. Sort of."

"His name?"

"Penn Pymn." Krippendore spelled it out.

"Seriously?"

"You want to watch and hear the conversation?"

"You *taped* it?"

"Put the system in last winter. Button behind my counter. I'll put it through to the big screen for you."

Service watched a computer screen on a shelf behind the man's cash register counter. The woman he saw had bright green-and-orange hair and electric-red lipstick that made her look like a clown. Multiple earrings dangled from both ears, and she had multiple other piercings, in her lower lip, right nostril, and her tongue.

Krippendore said, "It was like talking to a cricket with a lisp, that damn metal post ticking against her damn teeth. It gets annoying fast."

The woman was on the other side of the counter from the camera. "I *click* shot *click* 'is *click* beauty, *click*."

"Shot?" Krippendore asked on the tape.

"*Click* croth *click* bow," she said. "Go *click* not shot *click*. You *click* want *click*, me to *click*, *click* to *click* say I *click* bolted *click* it?" she asked dismissively and laughed nervously.

"So this is *your* deer?" Krippendore asked her.

"*Click* yah *click* no *click*. Is *click* me *click* boy *click* frien's, his *click* bigges' *click* ever and I *click* wanted to *click* prise him *click* with a *click* shoulder *click* mount."

"So, you took it with a crossbow?"

"*Click* I just *click* said *click*, *click* eh?"

"You want to look at the range of shoulder mount forms?"

"Sure *click*, *click* good."

"Where'd your boyfriend bag this monster?"

"*Click* in' *click* a *click* field," she said.

"Private or public land?" Krippendore asked.

"I *click* got *click* mind to *click* take *click* my *click* business *click* elsewhere," she said.

"I'm licensed," Krippendore explained. "Which means I'm required to gather certain information, and you'll have to answer the same questions no matter where you take it."

"*Click* damn *click* governmenth," she said.

"State or private land?" he asked again.

"Uh *click* private, mostly *click*."

"Mostly?"

"Ran *click*, ya *click* know?"

"How far?"

"Didn't *click* measure the *click* distance. Some, ya *click* know? I wasn't *click* there. My *click* boy'riend, he *click* tole me."

Service watched them agree on a price and delivery date, which she sealed with a hundred dollar bill.

"She say where the meat is?" Service asked.

"Nope, probably in her freezer. It has to be a big-ass old swamp buck."

"Age?"

"Seven, pushing eight."

"Holy crap, an old guy for sure."

"Yah," the taxidermist said. "Like us, Grady."

Grady Service ignored the comment and said, "An animal that size with that rack and that old, there has to be a lot of locals who knew about him."

"I reckon," Krippendore said. "With all the wood ticks we've got up here, even big ass old swamp bucks get seen from time to time."

Service considered the rack size again. The Boone and Crockett record was not much larger, 210 or so. A mounted 188 Yoop buck would be worth serious cash from collectors and exhibitors at sporting goods and hunting equipment shows.

"Does she know you taped her?" Service asked.

"No, sir. You want the disk?"

"Please, I'll dump it into my truck laptop, and give the disk back to you."

Krippendore gave him the disk, and Service went outside to his truck and transferred the record. Back inside, he asked, "Got an address for her or the boyfriend?"

"Same place for both. La Branche."

Service said, "*Menominee* County?" This was pretty far away.

"Said she wanted an artist to render it."

"Did you feel the love?"

Krippendore laughed. "No, but I had the distinct impression she was seriously interested in trading certain favors for a price break. Flooze like that would kill me," he added.

"Did she mention where her boyfriend's bolt hit it?"

"I quote, 'Right where you're supposed to hit 'em.'"

"You buy that?" Service asked.

Krippendore said, "Feel under the left ear."

"Okay if I pull it out into better light?"

"Sure, I doubt it's gonna be staying here," the old biologist said. "Go for it."

Service pulled the head into the outer room, pulled on disposable blue latex gloves, and poked and probed. "I feel a hole. Your learned opinion?"

"Same as yours. Small caliber round."

"Bullet still inside?"

"Hard to predict. Probably fragments, but you never know until you look. Depends on the jacket, charge, all that stuff."

Service said, "I hope it's intact," knowing it was unlikely and that he couldn't match the round to a weapon.

"She's a real lulu," Krippendore said, shaking his head.

La Branche, Service thought. *Forty miles crow-fly from where they stood, twice that by road—a long damn way to drive for "art."* He copied the names and address into his notebook.

"She said they're north of M-69," Krippendore said.

"That's not known as big buck country," Service remarked.

"That might change," the taxidermist said. "Are you taking the head?"

"No choice, Krip. She give you a down payment?"

"She did."

"Keep it for your trouble; sorry you're losing the mount job."

The retired biologist shrugged. "Not my first dance."

Grady Service got into his truck and inserted the woman's address into his Garmin.

The sensible thing to do would be to go home and sleep, but he knew from experience that the best way to handle a situation like this was to take it head-on and as soon as possible, to get into the potential violator's face with as much surprise as you could bring to the moment. Middle of the night was perfect.

He headed south for Menominee County and called CO Herk Rice on his personal cell phone. Rice had transferred up from Grand Traverse County to be closer to his kids' grandparents in Stephenson. Rice lived near Spalding.

"Herk, Grady. I know it's late. You out or in?"

"Just now walked in. What have you got?"

Service explained and Rice said, "I kinda heard a big buck mighta been taken up that way, but never heard any details. Lots of talk with no specifics. You're heading this way now?"

"Yup."

"Want company?"

"You bet. And do me a favor; call our kid-sarge and let him know. My gut says we're going to have to seek search warrants on this. The sarge might want to be involved."

"See you about a mile south of the house," Rice said. "Take her easy. The rut's on down here, and the animals are out of their freaking minds."

"You know Ingalls and Pymn?"

"Not him. Her vaguely. No previous contacts, but I've seen her around. She sorta sticks in one's mind."

Service called Friday, woke her up, and told her where he was headed.

"Maniacs," she said. "I hope they don't shoot your ass over a stupid deer."

CHAPTER 12

La Branche, Menominee County

FRIDAY, NOVEMBER 13

Herk Rice brought a huge thermos of black coffee to Service's truck and got into the passenger seat. Service showed his colleague a digital photo of the fourteen-point buck.

"*No way,*" Rice said, shaking his head. "That came from *here*?"

"Allegedly. It's in back of my truck. You said you heard rumors of a big one?"

"There are always rumors in this county this time of year—you know, the old mystical swamp buck and all that crap—but nothing of this magnitude. This is something out of one of those expensive whitetail wet dream rags. It's off our charts of the possible."

"Nature still sometimes manages to surprise us," Service said. "But you heard a big one was bagged up here."

"Not details, just a murmur here and there. Like I said, we hear this crap every year, and it rarely pans out. I'm thinking you should confront the Ingalls woman alone," Rice said.

"Yah?"

"She's seen me, which makes me local and familiar. Better she is confronted by a total stranger. Then you call me in; when she sees me, she'll think I'll be her ally, but I'll jump her too."

"Bad cop, worse cop."

"Along that line."

"What do you know about the woman and her boyfriend?"

"Not much. Heard they're big into something called Keep Our Pets Alive. It's an advertising and fund-raising campaign. The money it collects goes to a snazzy pet rescue operation in Menominee."

"Legitimate?"

"Far as I know. A lot of prominent locals are involved, and I've never heard of any shady business."

"I like the irony," Service said. "Keep Our Pets Alive backed by deer violators."

"It *is* the U.P.," Rice said. "I called Sergeant Wooten. I think I might've interrupted him and his wife."

"Never have sex during deer season," Grady Service said. "You think a young buck would have learned that. I guess he's too green."

"That an official Department directive, or Grady Service Rule for the Road?"

"Sage advice, grasshopper. We need to keep our wits during deer season, not spill our wits out the south end."

"That's how you handle it, two weeks of celibacy?"

"It's a goal, but we are all imperfect," Service said. Rice laughed out loud and chugged his coffee.

Grady Service used his computer to pull up information on Penn Pymn and his girlfriend. She had been buying licenses for years, but his first ever was this year, and there was no record that he had ever taken hunter safety training, which was required for people of a certain age. She had a combo license and he had a combo ticket, with which the deer had been tagged, even though it was not yet firearm season. This wasn't technically illegal, but the purchase timing was highly suspicious.

Rice continued to stare at the deer head photo. "Unbelievable," he whispered.

Service wished he could talk to Allerdyce. For all his shady past, Limpy had near-supernatural knowledge of the U.P. and its people, geography, nature, history, everything. But he lived in a remote compound in southwest Marquette County with no landline or cellular phone and was basically unreachable by normal humans.

"Big into the pets op. What does that mean they're *into* it?" Service asked Rice.

"They raise money for the operation."

"How?"

"They make and sell pies."

"Good ones?"

"Like there's a pie that *isn't* good? They call their business Pies for Pets."

"They have an actual business selling pies?"

"That's how they bill it."

Service blinked, trying to hold back sleep, and took another long pull of coffee.

• • •

The house was a tri-level with attached two-car garage. There was a gigantic pole barn behind the garage, not attached. The nearest neighbor was about a half mile east down a gravel road that dead-ended in front of a farmhouse. The driveway here was paved. Service looked at his watch. Just past midnight, lights on in the house. Two trucks in the driveway. Sweeping, sculpted lawn, at least two acres. Considerable investment in landscaping. Clearly someone here had no apparent money problems.

Service turned on the tape recorder in his shirt pocket and knocked on the door. He expected a sleepy, surprised woman and instead found himself greeted by a smiling perky female, almost giddy, flashing a mouthful of horsey, shiny white choppers.

"Conservation officer."

"Been expectin' *click* youth," the woman said. "*Click* c'mon in, dude. Got *click* pithess in the *click* ovens, and we have *click* peths depending on our *click* sales. *Click* life and *click* death, ya *click* see what I'm *click* thayin'?"

Grady Service nodded, trying to make a quick assessment. She was all over the place, physically and verbally. "Did you hunt this year?" he asked.

"Yep."

"Any luck?"

"Nope."

"See any?"

"None I wanted."

Miss Communication had suddenly become Miss Minimal Syllables. "I guess I'm confused," he said. "I understand you got a giant fourteen-point buck."

She looked at him and frowned. "My boyfriend *click* got it, not *click* me."

"When did he get it?"

"*Click* ask him."

"Where is he?"

"Smoking in the *click* 'arage. You don't think I'd *click* allow toxic smoke to poison *click* our pies?"

"No, ma'am, I guess not."

"Well, I wouldn't. You *guess*; that's *click* all you've got?"

"Yes, ma'am. Where's the garage?"

She pointed at a door, walked ahead of him, and opened it.

The man was seated in a tall director's chair. A huge headless deer car-cass hung from a metal hanger and chain rigged from a ceiling rafter. There was a cigarette in the man's mouth and a Bud Lite in the chair's cup holder. The man had long blond locks that flipped up at the base of his neck. A tat-too of an apple and a skull showed on his neck.

"DNR," Service said. "Arletta said you were out here."

"Banished from Pieland by her majesty, dude," the man said, exhaling blue smoke.

"Your deer?" Service asked.

The man nodded disinterestedly.

"Buck or doe?" the CO asked.

Only then did the man take a serious look at him. "Are you blind or what?"

"There's no head, and it's been gutted."

"Dude, I forgot. It's a buck."

"Where's the head?"

"Taxidermist. Her majesty wants a shoulder mount."

"What do *you* want?"

"Dude, ya can't eat horns."

"Penn Pymn, right?"

"That would be me."

"Which taxidermist?"

"No idea," the man said. "She took it somewheres, said she wants it done right, and she's paying for it. Not my business, man."

"But you shot it?"

"Yessir, you betcha."

"Where'd you hit it?"

"Right where you're supposed to," Pymn said.

"Mind if I take a look?"

"Knock yourself out," the man said.

The massive deer had dark fur, almost black. Service turned it and saw no evidence of a wound. "Don't see anything," the CO said.

"Neck," Pymn said.

Service countered, "Risky shot."

Pymn: "Only if you miss, and I never do."

"You've shot a lot of deer?"

"Bunches."

Service keyed his microphone. "One, One Twenty-Nine, you want to run the RSS history on Mr. Penn Pymn?"

Pymn looked over at Service. "Who's that?"

"A colleague."

"Where's he at?"

"Around, you know?"

Service didn't wait for an answer because he had already run the search. "The license you bought this year is your first, and you've not had hunter safety training. Exactly how many are there in *bunches*?"

"Ten, twelve, like that. There must be some mistake. I been deer-huntin' all my life."

"How old are you?"

"Thirty and one."

"Maybe you had hunter safety when you were a kid and they lost your record?"

"Yah, that's probably it."

"Where'd you take this animal?"

"Took it right here," the man said. "Can't you see?"

"Sorry. Where did you shoot it?"

"Out in the cornfields, ya know?"

"You have some hunting property?"

"I don't. Her majesty does."

"Where is it?"

"Right here."

"How much property?"

"Ten acres? I ain't sure."

"Amazing to come across a monster buck on such a small parcel. What're the odds, eh?"

"I always been lucky," the man said, taking another hard draw on his cigarette.

Suddenly Arletta Ingalls was in the garage, standing between the carcass and Grady Service. "It wasn't shot on *this* property," she said.

Service guessed the garage was wired. "No?"

"Pie's ready in the house," she said. "C'mon back in the house, boys."

"I have to get some photos first," Service said, taking out his digital camera.

"There ain't no head," she said. "Why you want pitchers of a headless deer?" The clicking was gone from her voice. Had she removed the stud? Why?

Service said, "Penn said he shot it where you're supposed to shoot a deer, but I don't see any evidence of a wound on the body, lethal or otherwise."

"Was in the neck is why," the woman said, tapping a forefinger behind and below her ear. "Now come get *pie*," she ordered. "I got it out for you and everything, and all the good fixin's that go with it."

The woman stepped inside the door; the garage door raised and Penn Pymn ducked out of the garage while Service made photographs and keyed his mic. "Male subject is out of the house," he said. "Come on in, One Twenty-Nine."

"Rolling," Rice reported.

The woman said, "Did you say something?"

"I mumble sometimes," he said.

"God," she said. "Me too. What's *that* all about?"

The scent of fresh pie enveloped him as he stepped inside. "Wow," he said. "That smells good."

"Not good," she corrected him. "*Fantastico!*"

Service nodded as he heard the lock to the door into the garage pop closed. The whole place seemed to be wired.

"Describe the worst sex you ever had," Arletta Ingalls said, stepping close to him.

"Uh, I don't know."

"I do. The worst sex I ever had was fantastic, and I like to think my pies are better than the worst sex. I wanted to brand my pies Hot Pussy Pie, but my lawyer didn't like it, said it would offend some folks, that the word *pussy* puts people off; but half the people in the world have one, so what exactly puts them off? I don't get it."

Krip was right. A lulu indeed.

The woman stood by the island in her kitchen, her right hand between her legs, her fingers kneading the fabric of her apron. "What flavor pie you want, officer? I got Dutch apple, tart cherry, and Arletta's special hot pussy pie, which don't get served too often, even to Penn."

"Uh, no pie," Service said. "But thanks."

Her hand stayed where it was. "Ooh," she said with a little squeal. "Such a *fiery* pie!"

"I'm on a diet," Service said.

"Pussy ain't banned from no diets I know of," the woman said. "Specially my pussy."

"Is from mine."

Her hand finally moved. "Do we have a problem *here*?" Her voice had an edge.

"I don't know," he said. "*Do* we?"

Service heard a buzzer somewhere in the house and the woman said, "Another visitor at this hour! What the *hell* is going on here?"

Motion detectors on the driveway? If so, she had known when I drove up and she was ready for me. Curious: She acts the halfwit, but there's cunning here. A lot of it. The buzzer was reporting Rice's arrival. "You took a deer to a taxidermist in New Swanzy," he said. "This afternoon?"

"Where the heck is New . . . whatever you said?"

"Gwinn."

"Oh, yah, I did. So what?"

"You took in your boyfriend's deer?"

"Uh huh," she said.

"Some things are not adding up," he told her.

"Like *what* things?"

"Like there's no wound on the deer."

"Penn and I both told you it's in the neck."

Obviously the garage was wired for sound. "Well, that's the thing. I examined the deer and I found nothing."

"You . . . have . . . to . . . look . . . at . . . the . . . head and neck," she said, spacing out her words. "Not what's hanging in the garage. It was real high in the neck, see?"

She was pointing under her jaw again, below her ear, and she was obviously exasperated.

"I saw the head," Service said. "Tonight."

"Huh," she said. "Well I *know* it was there. A crossbow bolt, not an arrow. You musta had bad light or something."

"The light was fine."

"What is this *bullshit*?" she snapped, her voice sharpening.

"We're just trying to establish facts and clarify what happened," he explained.

"We, there's more than one of you?"

"Yes, ma'am, and if we don't' get some cooperation here, there will be even more of us."

"It's after midnight," she said. "What're you *really* here for?"

"We're following up on your deer."

"Did that asshole processor call you and tell you some story? You know, that asshole hit on me."

"I found your deer during a no-notice inspection."

"*Penn's* deer, not mine!" she yelped. "You gotta pay attention!"

"I am, but I'm confused," Service said. "You told the taxidermist it was *your* deer."

"He's a fucking liar!"

"I have a video."

"It's against the law to record someone without their permission," she said.

"Not in Michigan."

"You get that son of a bitch on the phone, and I'll straighten out his dick."

"I have a tape. We don't need to call him."

Penn Pymn came back into the house, with Herk Rice close behind. "There is a ton of bait around this place," Service's colleague reported.

"Storage," the woman said. "It ain't put out, so it ain't bait."

"You feed deer here?"

Ingalls looked past him, as if she was waiting for his words to compute. "All the neighbors around here feed deer. Every last one of them; look for yourselves. They even name them, treat them like they're pets."

"You two included?"

"We don't give no damn animals human names," she said.

"But you do feed them."

"I just *told* you everybody around here feeds them."

"But *we* don't feed them during gun season like them others do," Penn contributed.

"When's firearm season?" Grady Service asked.

The man looked confused. "Like now?"

"Not until Sunday," Grady Service said.

"I didn't miss by *that* much," the man said with a stupid grin.

"Why would you think it's gun season now?" Service pressed.

The man shrugged and turned away.

"Look," the woman offered. "We'll just go over to the taxidermist tomorrow and I'll show you fellas and we'll straighten all this out. It's just a mix-up. It's late, and we're all tired."

"That won't be necessary," Grady Service said.

"You'll take her word?" Penn Pymn asked.

Her word. Why does he put it that way? "Not exactly. Let's go outside."

"For what?" The woman asked. "It's cold tonight. The snow's been spitting, and I've got the thin blood."

"Put on a coat and boots," Grady Service said.

Ingalls grimaced. "I feel like I am being harassed."

"You do?" Herk Rice asked.

"I offered my personal pie to the big fella there and he turned it down. Can you imagine a man turning down my pie?" She reached toward Rice. "You want some of my pie?"

"Uh, ah, no ma'am," Rice said, stepping back.

"You need to come outside with us," Service said.

"Not until I take care of my pies," she said. "My ovens are filled. Can't this just wait until tomorrow?"

"No, ma'am, it can't. We'll wait outside. It's kinda warm in here," Service said.

The woman pinched his forearm hard, "You got no idea *how* hot it can get, dude."

• • •

It was more than thirty minutes before she ventured out, and despite her complaint about thin blood, she wore no boots or heavy outer clothing. Service led her to his truck. He had lowered the tailgate, and when he lit the deer with his flashlight, she let loose a piercing shriek that set waves of coyotes to howling and yapping in three directions. "You've ruined my beautiful buck, goddamn you, goddamn you you, you, you . . . fucker!"

"It's not ruined. You need to settle down," Service said sternly.

The woman shrieked again, and the coyotes went again.

Service touched her sleeve and she pulled away. "Don't touch me, you sonuvabitch. That train's done left the station. I'm gonna sue your asses!"

"You just told us you registered it as Mr. Pymn's deer, not yours."

She stopped. Hyperventilation to dead calm in an instant. "Okay," she said. "I ain't gonna lie to you boys." For an experienced police officer, this statement was tantamount to admitting all that came before had been prevarication. "Good," Service said. "We just want the truth, the facts."

The woman looked directly at Service. "Poachers shot that buck Monday night."

Service said, "But it's tagged Tuesday afternoon at five o'clock."

The woman looked away. "See, the poachers shot it night before and I seen the animal limping around, so me and Penn went and put it out of its misery because we love animals and we don't like seein' them suffer, even wolves, okay? It's in the Bible to take care of lesser creatures, am I right?"

"I don't know about the Bible," Service said. "Let's try to stick with here and now. You just changed your story from Tuesday night to poachers on Monday night. What time?"

The woman looked up at the sky. "I think it was after midnight."

"Did you see the shooters?"

"Yes and no," she said. "It was dark, 'member? As it is now? But I heard the shot."

"Just one?"

"I just said I heard a shot. You think I'm *lying*?"

"I'm only trying to determine how many shots you heard."

"I just told you that—it was one shot."

"You heard the shot Monday night, but if this was after midnight, it was actually early Tuesday morning. But you didn't see the wounded animal until the next day, which would be Tuesday?"

"Right."

"*Where* did you see it?"

"Out on the neighbor's one twenty," she said.

"Close to here?"

"No."

"But you heard the shot?"

"I guess the wind was just right and the good Lord intended for me to hear it so I could end that poor creature's suffering. God doesn't want any of His creations to hurt."

Obviously God excluded me from that dictum, because dealing with this woman is nothing but pain. "We'd like to see the place where you shot the animal to end its pain."

She said to Pymn, "Why don't you go show the boys."

"I ain't all that sure," the boyfriend said, "me being directionally challenged."

"Who shot the deer?" Rice asked in a harsh voice. "We're tired of all this word-dancing."

"Penn shot it," the woman said.

"But *you* just said *you* put it out of its misery," Service reminded her.

"Well, I was *with* Penn. Him and me are always one, you know like when I got my legs wrapped around him real tight and he's giving it to me, that's like being one, right, so technically I guess we both shot it."

"But Penn tagged it," Service said.

"I meant to," the woman said, "but everything got real confusing and we were afraid those poachers would come back and hurt us and grab the deer."

"So Pymn shot it and tagged it?" Rice asked.

The woman stared at the other officer. "Technically, I guess you could say I shot it," she said.

"With what?" Service asked.

"Crossbow."

"Show us the weapon and the bolt," Rice said.

She cocked an eyebrow and stared at him. "I've seen you around. You're local, and you're taking *his* side?"

"My patch says Michigan. Just show us the crossbow," Rice repeated.

"I have the bolt, not the crossbow," she said. "I sold that."

"To whom?" Service asked.

"I don't know, just a guy who come by and made me an offer I couldn't turn down," she said.

Grady Service took a deep breath. The two worst kinds of subjects were Sphinxes and Bouncing Betties. The Sphinx types said nothing, no matter what; the Bouncing Betties were all over the damn place and entirely unpredictable—like this woman. "That's pretty convenient," Service said. "When was this alleged sale?"

"I beg your pardon? Not alleged," the woman said. "It's real. I don't remember the exact day because I'm a very busy woman , but it's been since Tuesday, right Penn?"

Pymn didn't look at her, showed no reaction at all. "Check or cash?" Service asked.

"Cash," she said.

Herk Rice chuckled.

"How *dare* you impugn my honor!" the woman yelped.

"What's to impugn?" Service said. "Everybody here knows you're lying."

"That's libelous," the woman said.

"No," Grady Service said. "It's not libel unless it's in writing, and there has to be a witness who thinks the statement is wrong. Do you think it's wrong, Penn?"

Penn Pymn said, "Leave me out of all that shit."

The woman growled and moaned. "All you fucking peckers are ganging up on me! This is reputation rape; this is rape!"

Service said, "Save the theatrics. I've been recording everything since I stepped through the door. Every word."

"That's not fair," she muttered, quieting.

"We're after truth, not fairness," Service said. "Where's the crossbow bolt?"

"Prick," the woman mumbled and disappeared.

She returned with a bent, twisted partial aluminum shaft. It had no point.

"There's no blood," Service said.

"I washed it," she said, "as a keepsake."

"The keepsake's got rust on it," Service pointed out.

"You know how tough the weather is on things up here," she said.

"Aluminum doesn't rust, at least not in a couple of days."

She answered with a shrug . . . and an insipid look.

Going to be a long and tedious haul to break her. To get this kind, you had to pile her up in so many lies and inconsistencies that she couldn't bear the ultimate weight. He shook his head. "Show me where you shot the animal."

She pointed at a nearby field. "Out there."

"How far?" Service asked.

"All the way south to the property line."

"I thought the deer was on your neighbor's one twenty, and that's not close to here."

"You have to listen better," the woman said. "It's out there."

"Okay," Service said. "Let's go see."

"Where?" she asked.

"To the place where you shot the deer and to the place where you recovered the body. I'll shine my light ahead so you can look and show me."

Thirty minutes later they were stopped at the property line. "There," she said, pointing down a fencerow.

"Where?"

"Over there! Do I have to do *everything* for you?"

"Save your crap, and just show me, ma'am."

"Over there," Ingalls said, waving her hand.

Service looked in that direction and found nothing. "No joy, Arletta."

She scrunched her face. "What's that mean, no joy?"

"It means there's nothing there."

"It's dark. Wait until morning and then you'll see it."

"I have a good light."

Service saw another flashlight beam bobbing toward them through corn stubble. It was Wooten. "We squared away out here?" the young sergeant asked.

"This is Arletta Ingalls," Service said. "She says she put a deer out of its misery after poachers wounded it. We're trying to locate where she killed it."

"Forget that," Wooten said. "Where'd you gut it?" he asked her.

She sighed dramatically. "I supposed you're another one who don't like pussy."

Service said, "She's trying to shift attention. Where's the gut pile?"

"Did she call us when she put said creature out of its misery?" the sergeant asked.

"She did not. She took the head to a taxidermist."

Wooten turned to the woman. "You should have called us, ma'am. And it's against the law to possess an illegal deer."

"Ain't no point in wasting a creature, and I ain't no baggy-ass old ma'am. I'm Miz Arletta Ingalls, not Miss, not no damn ma'am. I ain't hitched, weighed down, nor nothing. I'm sorry we didn't call, but those poachers scared us and that is the truth."

"Where exactly did you shoot the animal?" the sergeant asked.

Service let Wooten take the lead for a while.

"Bolted, not shot. Crossbow, not rifle. Can't none of you people get nothing right?"

"Okay, bolted. Where?"

"Here . . . *somewheres*. We were just looking when you showed up, and now you've gone and got me all flummoxed. All this shit looks the same at night."

"Let's go look at the gut pile."

Service watched them stumble around, heard a voice in his earbud. "Pymn here is being very cooperative," Rice reported from the house. "The deer was shot close to the house with a rifle, not out there with a crossbow. There's a spotlight mounted on the back of the house. It's covered by a hood that's lifted by a switch inside. You can't see the light until the hood lifts. The deer was gutted back here too."

Service let the charade with Wooten continue for ten more minutes before he walked over to the searchers. "Is it possible you took the dead animal back to the house and gutted it there?" he asked.

The woman took the bait. "Yes, of course. I forgot. See what happens when you pressure people?"

Wooten said, "So you drove out here and loaded the deer after you killed it."

"Right," she said.

"Why a crossbow if you wanted to end the animal's suffering?" the young sergeant asked.

Pretty good question, Service thought. She answered, "Well, it's not gun season *is* it?"

"Penn helped you load the deer?" Service asked.

"No, I did it all alone."

"Really?" Service said.

"I can't lie. Pymn was sky high and of no use to anyone—for anything, if you know what I mean."

"This was in the afternoon?"

"No, the night before, right after the shot. I saw headlights, drove over here, and took care of the wounded animal."

"So you killed it Monday night, not Tuesday afternoon."

"What difference does it make? It was a mercy killing for God's sweet sake."

The deer in the garage, Service guessed, was well over 180 pounds with the guts out. Live weight would have been close to 250 pounds. Few men of any size could handle that much dead weight or an animal of this size alone. "You lifted this deer all by yourself?"

"I'm a lot stronger than I look," she said.

Ingalls was short and emaciated, bone-thin, a hundred pounds max, Service guessed. "Okay, you loaded the deer into your truck alone and drove it home."

"That's right."

"And gutted it at the house."

"Yes, I remember now. I was afraid the poachers would come back and grab me and the buck."

"Let's go," Service said. "And for the record, Miss Ingalls, I hate liars more than violators."

"Good, because I always tell the truth and play by all the rules, the way the Good Book says we should," Ingalls said. "It's Miz, not Miss."

Service laughed out loud and thought he could feel her glaring at him as they stomped back across the corn stubble.

• • •

It was one hour later. They were back at the house, there still was no gut pile, and the verbal dancing and sparring continued. They looked everywhere she directed, and eventually Service asked, "Could it have happened *behind* the house?"

"Let's try there," Sergeant Wooten said.

"There're no guts behind the house," the woman insisted.

"Humor us," the young sergeant told her.

"Do *you* like pie?" she asked.

"Sure, thanks," the sergeant said, "but first let's look behind the house."

"That is not allowed," the woman said firmly. "My backyard is a registered trademark and off-limits. You cannot look back there. I could lose some of my proprietary secrets."

"Come again?" Service said.

"I am a professional wildlife photographer, and that's my controlled and proprietary limited-access, top-secret restricted work area. Nobody is allowed back there, even Penn."

Sergeant Wooten said, "Go back inside, ma'am, and warm up. We'll get back to you in a while."

The woman left them and Wooten looked at his officers. "Are she and this thing for *real*?"

"Seems like," Service said. "I've got the head of a one-eighty eight buck in my truck."

"Holy shit."

The two men looked at the head and got into Service's truck. Herk Rice stood outside the driver's window while they all drank coffee and Service typed a search warrant affidavit. Forms done, he telephoned CO Nick Rolvig in Menominee.

Sleepy voice on the other end. "Grady Service here, Nick. I'm out at La Branche with Wooten and Rice. We need a search warrant. I'm sending the form electronically. Can you get it into the system, sworn and signed, and call me back?"

"What have you guys got out there?"

"Illegal fourteen-point buck."

"Are you *serious*?"

"I got it from a taxidermist check. We've been here since before midnight."

"What time is it now?" Rolvig asked.

"Oh three thirty."

"Okay, be there in one hour with paper in hand. This I have to see for myself."

"Thanks," Service said, but Rolvig had already hung up.

Service got out of the truck and showed the officers where he thought the lethal round had lodged. Both men felt around and agreed it was a .22 or a .17. The sergeant couldn't take his eyes off the antlers.

"That was shot *here*?" Wooten asked.

• • •

They served the search warrant at 0500, and by then a lawyer had been summoned by Ingalls from Iron Mountain. The lawyer was a former trooper named Alyse Merikanto, tall, sleepy-looking, yawning as she took her time going through the writ. "Four officers for one deer," she remarked. "Seems like overkill, a waste of public resources. There's nothing personal at play in this, one hopes."

"We're starting the search," Service said, "unless Miss Ingalls can produce the weapon she used to kill the animal."

"It's Miz, I told you, not Miss, and I already showed you the damn bolt," Ingalls said.

Grady Service said calmly, "We're looking for a small caliber rifle to match the hole in the animal's skin."

"Goddammit," Ingalls said. "How many times I got to tell you people it was a crossbow, not no bullet?!"

"Please get the bolt," the woman's lawyer said, "and we'll all take a look together."

They went out to the deer head in the truck, and Grady Service used a small pocket knife to open the skin to the hole in the neck. Ingalls placed the bolt on the small opening and pushed and grunted and struggled with all her might, to no avail. It would not fit the hole.

"There's no point on the bolt," the sergeant said.

"I think it mighta broken off inside," Ingalls said. "When we put the deer in the truck."

"*We* put the deer in the truck?" Service asked.

"I meant I, me," the woman said. "I guess when I put the deer in my truck. This is too broke up to fit."

Rice volunteered, "I have a good bolt with a point in my truck. I'll get that."

Despite a great deal more effort, and truly impressive grunts, Arletta Ingalls could not push the bolt with the point into the hole. Even so, she continued to stab at the wound until Service gently grasped her wrist. "That's enough. We know the truth," he said. "The head will be sent to Michigan State for X-rays, and a necropsy will determine what's inside. Let's get on with the search."

The woman loosed another shriek. This time there was no coyote refrain. The backyard showed hundreds of gallons of corn, sugar beets, browning apples, grains—all sorts of deer baits and feed—and animal tracks crisscrossed the yard. Not thirty yards from the house they found a pile of viscera. Service looked back and shone his flashlight up at a spotlight mounted on a roof peak. It had a hinged metal cover, but there was clearly a light under it.

"That device's strictly for my photographs," Arletta Ingalls said. "I sell my pictures and donate the proceeds to KOPA."

"Very commendable," Service said. "Where's the rifle?"

"What rifle?"

"The .22," he said.

The woman led him to a room with a dozen rifles of various calibers and makes, all of them loaded and uncased, standing in corners or against bureaus or bedposts. Empty and loose cartridge and cardboard ammo boxes littered the floor.

"Not these," Service said, listening to Herk Rice's voice in his earbud. "The boyfriend says there's a scoped .22 mag in the red bedroom."

"Red bedroom," Service told the woman.

"That's my sewing room," she said.

"Show us," he told her.

The woman went in first, reached into the closet, and threw an ancient single-shot .22 on the bed. "There, happy now?" Ingalls asked with an anxious snort. "You got me."

Grady Service sniffed the weapon. It did not smell like it had been fired recently. He tried to work the lever action, but it was rusted tight. "This hasn't been used for a long time," he announced.

The woman said. "Swear to God, that is the only .22 in this house."

Service walked to the end of the bed and saw a flat case between the bed-side and the wall. He picked up the case, lay it on the bed, and unsnapped the locks to reveal a small rifle with a scope. "What's this?" he asked, picking it up.

"Got no idea," Ingalls said. "It must be Penn's. Typical man; he never tells me nothing."

It was a Browning .22 magnum with a ten-round magazine and a Browning 5X scope. Service held the weapon out to the woman.

She looked away. "I have never seen that thing before," she said, folding her arms.

"What will fingerprints tell us?" Service asked.

She stared at the rifle. "*Game wardens* can do fingerprints?"

"Can and will," Grady Service said.

"That really sucks. Okay, I guess it could've been my rifle. You know, I got CRS, Can't Remember Shit disease."

"You shot the deer with this."

"I never said that."

"*I'm* saying it."

"Be still," the lawyer told her client. "Proceed with your search," she told Service.

The officers did a methodical sweep of the house, ending up in the basement, where a small cubicle had been built in front of a porthole out into the backyard and in line with the spotlight from above. There were a couple of .22 magnum cartridges on the floor, which the officers put into evidence bags and marked.

"What's this room for?" Service asked.

"My cameras," Ingalls told him.

Wooten said, "The opening is large enough only for a rifle barrel. No camera lens will fit."

"Well, I guess you haven't seen *my* camera lenses, have you?"

"You're right," the sarge said, "I haven't. Show them to us."

The woman brought a large hard-back camera case filled with cameras and lenses, all looking new and expensive, and a baggie with a half dozen disks and flash drives. None of the lenses fit the shooting port. "Tag everything," Service told Wooten and Rice.

"You can't take my cameras," the woman protested. "I make my living with them. I can't support the rescue fund without my gear."

"Where's your computer?" Sergeant Wooten asked, and this gave the woman pause.

"It's broke down and don't work."

"Show us," Service said, and when Ingalls looked at her lawyer, her counselor nodded. "They have a warrant," the lawyer said.

"Even for broken stuff?"

"Yes."

The broken computer was placed in Service's truck. It was not broken after all, and they took a smart phone as well as multiple photo albums. It was 10 a.m. by the time they cleared the premises. Charges would be recommended to the Menominee County prosecutor. What happened after that was up to the prosecutor. Service recommended that Pymn go uncharged for illegally tagging the deer, because he had cooperated and it had been her, apparently, who actually had the tag and affixed it to the animal.

Grady Service wanted to call Friday but had no cell service and was too tired to drive until he found it. He could hardly keep his eyes open. He turned north at Hardwood and got as far as a maze of two-tracks just north of the Sturgeon River. He nosed his truck into a copse of birches, piled his jacket behind his head, and closed his eyes. Sleep did not come quickly. Only two days until the firearms season began in earnest. How much more crap like this lay ahead? He didn't want to think about it. He wanted sleep, and then he wanted to get to the county jail to see Knezevich again.

CHAPTER 13

Deadhorse Creek, Northwest Delta County

FRIDAY, NOVEMBER 13

The first image when Grady Service awoke: snow coming down silently vertically in ugly, fat flakes, turning the landscape as white as a freshly bleached sheet. Looked first at his watch: 0814, and from his watch to the passenger-side window, where he saw a pair of beady eyes staring in that caused his heart to skip as he hurriedly sat up and heard someone fumbling with the door handle.

"Hey, Sonny boy," a muffled voice croaked. "Open bloody door; I goch-youse coffee."

Grady Service tried to rub the sleep out of his eyes and saw that his visitor was Limpy Allerdyce, who, like other supernatural beings, had a knack for materializing when and where you least expected him.

The old man tapped a thermos top on the passenger window. "Geez, oh, Pete."

Service tripped the door's auto-lock and the old man hopped spritely up into the passenger seat, his clothes dry, no evidence of snow despite the heavy downfall going on outside. "Snow doesn't stick to you?"

"Sure. I jes brusher off, eh. Heard youse pinched dat Crow-hat King."

"The who?"

"Not da Who, dat Cro-hat, Knezevich."

How the hell does he know the things he knows? "Who's that?"

"Geez, don't go clam on me, Sonny. Dis da guy I t'ought he never get pinched."

"Why's that?"

"Real smart Illinoider, sneaky, works alone, keeps 'is mout shut, don' live up 'ere, swoops in, makes da kills, swoops out, quiet as owl. You know what dey say."

"Actually, I don't. What *do* they say?"

"Keep your mout' shut is best armor."

"You know Knezevich?"

"Know 'is work is all, but youse pinch 'im. How youse dood dis, Sonny? Most dose udder COs coul'n't even find where he work, and nobody figure he all done by gun season. Like bloody ghost 'e is."

"You admire this . . . *king*?" The admiration was in the old poacher's tone.

Allerdyce snorted and chortled. "Youse know I know most evert'ing goes on in Yoop. Dis Knezevich, he's pret' good. Got give 'im 'is due, eh."

"Good as you?"

Allerdyce showed his noncommittal toothless grin. "Youse know I don't do dat stuff no more, but in my day? Nope not as good. Close dough, eh."

"You're surprised he got arrested?"

The old man grimaced as he uncapped the thermos, grabbed a cup from a holder, filled it with coffee and handed the mug to the conservation officer. "Al'ays knew he had one weak-knee-ass."

"What weakness?"

"Dat bloody red truck dose udder guys leave."

"Red truck?"

"Why you treat me like dis, Sonny? Me and your daddy was partners; now youse and me is. I'm frien', not foal."

Talking to the old man could be simultaneously illuminating, confusing, and disconcerting. Anything but stupid, his mangling of language was in a class by itself. "Foal?"

"Yah, like dat guy Ziggy Fraud tell, pipples is frien' or foal."

Service nearly spit out his coffee and, after recovering his composure, asked, "So what do you think the deal is with the red truck?"

"Like hammer judge got on desk in court, tell ever'body he da man."

"Like it's a symbol?"

"Not t'ing use wid drums," Allerdyce said. "Like judge's hammer."

"That's called a symbol."

"Yah, sure, youse sayso. See queen of the Englands how she carry dat fancy club sometimes, all gold, silver, jewels and shit?"

"Her scepter?"

"Yah, like short snowsnake, eh. You know why she gots carry dat t'ing?"

"Enlighten me."

"First, why youse sleepin' out here boonies middle of day? You have fight wit' your dickatective squeeze?"

"I ran out of gas."

"Truck gas?"

"Grady gas."

"Huh. So, dey make da queen, queen, dey give her all kinds fancy-schmancy food, booze, and den dey give her dat bitsy snowsnake ya know, ta fluff her dress to get rid of farts she let."

"Farts?"

"Ever'body got da gas, Sonny, even dat queen of dose Englands, and dey don't got no Beano over dere, so dey invent dat fancy stick for Queenie."

"Do you know everything?" Service asked the old poacher, suppressing a belly laugh.

"Not yet," Allerdyce said. "Mebbe someday."

"So the red truck is used by Knezevich against farts?"

"Holy Pete, don't youse listen, Sonny? Queen has fart stick so ever'body know she got gas *and* she da queen. Cro-hat, he got red truck so ever'body know he king."

"King of what?"

Allerdyce shrugged. "'is pipples."

"The truck is stolen," Service said.

"Dat's hull point. His boys steal new red truck, leave it for him, like pipples bring presents to dat queen of the Englands."

"Tribute."

"Yah," Allerdyce said. "Like t'ing youse jes said."

"He drives the truck?"

"Nah. Jest sits dere, like big red Bright Eye. 'is boys come get later, take to chop shop."

Bright Eyes were tacks used by outdoorsmen to mark roads and trails. They exploded with reflected light when a light beam struck them at night. "The truck marks his location?"

The old man shrugged. "Dose Cro-hats, who know what dose jamokes t'ink? Youse look back, youse gone find cops find red stoled truck ever' deer season, an' never find no owner. Mos time never get tow, 'cause gone."

"Going back how long?" Service had never heard this mentioned.

"Huh. Dis oh nine, I say back ninety-six, mebbe, ninety-seven. Been long while, eh."

"Don't bullshit me, old man," Service told the old poacher.

"Sayin' trut'. Cross my heart and hope for pie," Allerdyce said.

One of a kind; that aside, the old man was also an asset, a wellspring of precise knowledge and gossip. "Pattinson, Hamore, Haire, Swetz, what do you hear about the deer herd on their properties?"

"Ah," Allerdyce said. "So dat why youse is down dis way?"

The old man lacked formal education, but he did not lack smarts. "What've you heard?"

"Dey don't like no wolfies, dose lads."

"Your opinion on wolves?"

"We all got eat."

"Big wolf population on their lands?"

"Wolfies 'ere, but not t'ick like udder places in Yoop. Not 'nuff deer, eh. No deer, no wolfies."

Predator biology in four words: No deer, no wolves. The old man made sense. There were wolves only where there were enough deer to eat. So why no deer in that area? "You hear anything specific about that area?"

Allerdyce shook his head. "Jest know dose guys get' ole, mebbe, don't hunt so hard no more, den want blame somet'ing udder dan seffs."

This assessment might have some merit. "Where's your truck?"

"Got dropped. My grandkittle Johnny O, lives down Toledo."

"I don't know him." The old man seemed to have a lot of grandkids.

"Went school over Wisconsin, Insaned Somet'ing."

"And now?"

"Up to da codge now; teach maps, survey, gee pee ass, stadelites, shit like dat."

"Da codge" meant either Northern Michigan University or Michigan Tech. "Your grandson teaches geography?"

"Don't know da fancy name," Allerdyce said with a shrug.

"Why did Johnny O drop you *here*?"

"Seen youses' truck. Ain't seen youse for while. Miss me?"

"You came *looking* for me?"

The old man grinned. "Good, ain't I?"

Eerie was closer to the reality.

"Got suitcase in youse's truck bed," the allegedly reformed poacher announced.

"What?"

"Got have duds, gone stay while, eh?"

"Who said you could stay with us?"

"Wah! Not *youse* two, *us* two, youse an' me out to Slippy Crick camp. Dis is deers season, Sonny, game warden got stay camp, t'ink abut nuttin' but dose cheaters out in da swamps."

The old man had a key to Service's Slippery Creek house, which was not far from the Mosquito Wilderness. Allerdyce had copied the key without Service's permission and was forever letting himself in.

"Really?"

"Yah, sure, deer season, eh. Youse need me close to be advicer. So I t'ink best I stay right dere wid youse. Besides, youse gone be too busy make whoopee wid dat girlfriend."

Service gave the old man a long look. Why not? He picked up his microphone, called central dispatch and Station Twenty. "Twenty-Five Fourteen is in service with a ride-along. Make a note that said ride-along probably will be on board for the duration of the firearm season."

"She must be someone special," a familiar voice in Lansing said. Service recognized Candace McCants, his friend and colleague. She had just taken the job as lieutenant in charge of the state's Report All Poaching operation— the so-called RAP room, which had dispatchers on duty twenty-four hours a day, taking complaints from citizens and relaying them to officers in the field. Having McCants in the RAP room was a big plus for all officers. She had been a great CO, and sergeant.

"It's Allerdyce," Service announced.

The name was met with dead silence on the other end, then, "Station Twenty is clear . . . and yet . . . not clear at all."

"What dat about?" Allerdyce asked.

"Your fan club."

"I got fan club?"

"All across the state, even BTB."

"I'm like unfamous?"

"There you go," Service said, deadpan.

The old man crossed his arms and gummed his upper lip. "Dat mean I don't got no more piracy."

"You're probably okay for the moment."

"I like my piracy," Allerdyce grumbled.

Grady Service backed the truck out to the two-track. "A stolen red truck for the king every year, no bull?"

Allerdyce nodded, his head jerking like a bobblehead. "No bull, Sonny."

"You're saying the king never takes possession of the truck, just lets it sit there?"

"He never use it; don't know if he even know it dere."

"And the truck is intended to prove exactly what?"

"Geez, Sonny. It prove he da king."

"But he doesn't even know the truck is there."

"Sackly; kings don't pay no tension to stuff like trucks. Dey got important t'ings t'ink about."

Good god. If Allerdyce was right, Knezevich had not been lying about the truck.

CHAPTER 14

Northwest Delta County

FRIDAY, NOVEMBER 13

Torky Hamore looked hung over when he pulled open his camp door. His eyes were swollen, and alcohol fumes wafted off him, dragon breath so rich you could ignite it with a match.

"What time it is?" Hamore mumbled, looking past Service and stiffening. "What dat no-good old SOB doin' wid youse?"

Allerdyce said, "Nice see youse too, Torky."

Hamore said, "Youse can come in, Service, but dat piece shit stays outside in da bloody snow. I don't even want 'im on my proppity."

"You two got some history?" Service asked.

Hamore said, "Allerdyce, he got him some history wit ever'body. Shoulda been left down Jackson after he winged you."

"People change," Grady Service said, more an expression of hope than fact.

"Not dat one."

"Leave it alone. He's with me, Torky."

"Okay, but he don't touch nuttin' when he come inside," Hamore told Service, with another glare at the old poacher.

Allerdyce squinted at mounted fish and deer heads covering the log walls. "Ain't nuttin' but babies up dere, Hamore."

The cabin owner yelped. "You come inside and insult my *camp*!"

"Ain't no insult, eh. Jes' say trut'. You ain't got much up dere on dose walls."

"I suppose you *do* at your place?"

Allerdyce chuckled. "Can't eat no horns, Torky. Better to make moola an' sell dose t'ings to sports like youse."

Torky Hamore surged toward the poacher, but Service blocked the man by stepping in front of him. "What hell youse want 'ere dis time day?" Hamore shouted.

"Heard there was a little cabal here: Pattinson, you, Dornboek, Haire, Swetz. You guys aren't conspiring to take out wolves, I hope."

"What me and friends talk about ain't none youse's business. Last I knew, we still had bloody freedom of speech out to camp, eh."

"You certainly do," Service said. "But I thought I'd let you know I'll be keeping a special eye on all of you and your camps this deer season."

"What youse need keep eye on is wolf biologist, tell dat guy he need get rid some dose bloody deer eaters 'fore dey eat hull damn herd."

"We're working on it, Torky. First step is to get the Feds to downgrade the animals from endangered."

"Bloody bureaucraps," the landowner said. "All talk gobbledygook while dose wolves eatin' my deer now."

"They're not *your* deer, Torky. They belong to taxpayers."

"*Bullshit!* Dere on *my* land, dere *mine*."

"You fellas just need to hold your horses, let us solve this thing. Be patient."

"We all got grandkids we want kill deer outten our camps."

"They will—in time."

"We all gettin' old; don't know how much more time we got."

You're not alone, Service wanted to say, but all he said was "Okay." This was the standard cop acknowledgement that a statement had been made and heard, but implying neither agreement nor disagreement.

Allerdyce was quiet until they were back in the Silverado. "Torky dere din't drink so much, mebbe he shoot more deers. Dey can smell dat stuff long way off. Deers got long noses for reason. Mutter Nature she make dem so dey smell stuff good."

Grady Service took a deep breath and turned the truck toward Marquette. It was not quite noon, and he was tired and needing a good night's sleep. Maybe tonight, at camp.

With Limpy as housemate.

Good grief.

CHAPTER 15

Marquette

FRIDAY, NOVEMBER 13

Knezevich was freshly shaven, his eyes alert and twinkling. "Slept good," he announced to Service in the interview room.

"Jails aren't known for comfort."

"After you sleep on the ground as a soldier for years, any bed feels good."

Service wouldn't disagree. Over the years he had developed the ability to sleep almost anytime, anywhere, but seldom better than he slept in his own bed. He had called Friday before going in to see the Croatian man.

"Motel Patrol Truck last night?" she had greeted him.

"Worked all night, caught a nap this morning. I woke up to Allerdyce tapping on the truck window."

"Let me guess, you were somewhere east of Bumfuck, Egypt."

"Hell, I'm not even sure *where* I was."

Friday laughed, and Service suddenly wanted to be hugging her. "Allerdyce is gonna stay at Slippery Creek Camp."

"I assume this call is to inform me that you will be bunking there too."

"Do you mind?"

"No. It'll mean fewer middle-of-the-night whine-calls."

She always called citizen calls whine-calls. "Slippery Creek is for sleep," Service said. "But don't rule out road games for playtime."

Friday snorted derisively. "Playtime in deer season? That's *rich*."

"Okay," he said. "Gotta go. Hug our boy for me."

"Where are you?"

"At the jail."

"Ah, the Croatian," Friday said.

"Who told you about *that*?"

"The whole community is talking about how the great Grady Service pinched a legendary and uncatchable violator by following his nose-hair clippings, or something equally ludicrous, following them for miles through an impenetrable swamp."

"People exaggerate. It was his cologne. Jovan. A noseless dog could follow that stench."

"Yeah?"

"Eau de Violet."

Friday sniggered. "You *are* entertaining," she said. "Keep your powder dry, *kemo sabe*."

Service looked at Knezevich. "Did you give your statement to your lawyer?"

The man handed the CO some neatly folded papers. "I got no lawyer."

"What about Tavolacci?"

"He is a clown in bad suit. I don't need a fool. I will plead guilty, and you and me got an agreement."

"Understand, all I do is make a recommendation to the prosecutor," Service said. "*He* makes the decision."

Knezevich smiled knowingly. "I check around on you. You got the gravitas for sure. What you tell, others believe. So, this prosecutor makes the actual decision on charges and all? You make negotiation with this person, yes?"

Service nodded and read the man's statement. "Who dropped you on the other side of the river?"

"Mrs. Petrolli. She owns cabins called Escanaba Moons, near Gwinn."

"Giuseppi Petrolli's widow?" Service had suffered many contacts with the dead man, who couldn't or wouldn't follow rules and often wanted to fight him.

"That is her."

"How did you get up here from Chicago?"

"In panel truck."

"You park it, then go to the Moons. How?"

"First I drop gear at inn, then drive truck to where I will hunt, park truck, walk back."

"That's got to be fifteen miles."

"I like to walk," the man said. "You have sweet air here. Not like Chicago."

"And Mrs. Petrolli brings you back when you are ready to hunt?"

"Yes."

"You camp rough and kill deer."

"Yes. When I finish, I move all to truck, drive back Chicago."

"You don't stop to see Mrs. Petrolli?"

"Why? I have wife at home."

"And the red truck?"

"Knezevich grinned slyly. "*Ne crveni kamion. You* saw this truck?"

"I tracked you from it."

"Nothing do with me. Is nice one?"

"Tricked-out Ford 250, extended crew cab, big-ticket item."

Knezevich smirked.

Service said, "Tribute, I understand."

Knezevich said, "*Jeste li razum jeli*, you understand this?"

"Probably, the deer part of your deal I get. But why did you kill wolves?"

"*Vukovi su zli, da?* Wolves are evil, all of them. This country, Old Country, everywhere."

• • •

Service found the new Marquette County prosecutor in his office, his left leg in a cast. Kennard Dentso was forty, handsome, tall, and soft-spoken, a Chicago transplant. He had run as a Democrat and won in a landslide. Service knew he had a camp up near Big Bay.

"Figured you'd already be out to your camp," Service said.

Dentso tapped his cast. "Not this year."

"Ice?"

"My daughter's size 4 hockey skate on the stairs. Kids. Surprised you're not in the woods."

"Lodged a guy and doing follow-up."

"I heard the drums: You nabbed the uncatchable Croatian with thirty-six deer. Is that even possible?"

"Thirty butchered carcasses, six racks with capes, three wolf pelts."

"Commercial market operation?"

"If so, it's not like any I've seen before." Service then explained as best he could what was going on and ended by saying, "I've proposed a deal. We take everything, use the heads and pelts in our special ops, charge him with fifteen counts of deer out of season; he pays restitution, court costs, loses his equipment, hunting privileges, and gets no jail time."

"You're good with that?"

"It will slow him down and give us some tools to use. If we're lucky, he'll move to Wisconsin or Illinois for his next chapter."

"This is a real bad guy?"

"Not sure if bad's the right label. Strange bird for sure, yet he's honorable in some inexplicable way."

"Fifteen, and? That's the deal you're recommending?"

"Works for me."

"Bail or own recognizance?"

"Bail, in case I'm wrong on the guy."

"Okay by me. Done. You want to tell his lawyer?"

"He fired Sandy Tavolacci; thinks he can do this alone."

"Did you explain that justice is blind and dumb, and mostly the latter?"

"No."

"We'll make sure we get him a public defender. Tell Sally on the way out. She'll take care of it. I don't want this case bouncing back on us."

Service stopped at Sally Palovar's desk, handed her the paperwork, and explained about the public defender.

"Done," she said. "Newichyu?"

"Deer season," he said.

The woman smirked. "Give 'em hell, Grady. All of 'em. They're idiots, the whole bloody lot."

"Even your boss?"

"No exceptions, including my husband."

• • •

Town business done, radios quiet, Service decided they would head for Slippery Creek, get a good night's sleep, and see what tomorrow would bring.

A half mile from his house, he saw four-wheeler tracks cutting into the woods toward Slippery Creek. He parked the truck and they got out and started quick-walking along the illegal trail, which had been cut through virgin territory. A mile down, they struck the creek. A pair of four-wheelers were parked, and four men were spread out, wading the creek trying to dip spawning brook trout.

Service walked up behind one of the men. "That legal?"

"Who're you, the fucking game warden," the man muttered, not looking back.

"Conservation officer," Service said, and almost immediately the man had a cell phone in hand and was rabbiting through the woods, leaving his net and fish bag on the bank of the creek. "Get to the four-wheelers and disable them," Service told Allerdyce. "That will put them on foot."

The old man hurried downstream close to the bank, while Service climbed higher to more open territory and headed downstream until he saw two more machines. He slid down the slope and used his pocket knife to quickly put them out of commission.

Allerdyce soon joined him. He was grinning. "Da hunt an' da waiting game," the old poacher said. "Dis is fun."

"You see anybody on your way to me?"

"Nope."

"You want me go sniff 'em out?" Allerdyce asked.

"No, but work your way up to the other machines and collect all the fish and gear along the way. It's evidence. They'll try to get to the machines too. We'll start our work by checking ownership, find out who they belong to."

It turned out that all four machines were stolen—two of them just in the past week, two of them earlier in the fall from Baraga County. Dark came, and none of the men showed.

"Track 'em now?" Allerdyce asked.

"Not worth the energy. We recovered stolen property. That's good enough for tonight. We'll see these jerks again somewhere along the line." Service called the county and ordered a flatbed truck to haul the stolen goods.

"Dat firs' guy rabbit off t'rough woods?"

"The first guy? What about him?"

"Dat's Virpi Niemi's fodder-in-law, Dinty Peaveyhouse."

"You're sure?"

"Got short left leg, from g'enade, Fir't Guff War. Got full medical; don't work none nomore. In woods alla time, dat one."

"Good at it?"

"He look like he good?"

Service laughed. "Do you know where Peaveyhouse lives?"

"Yah, mebbe, I t'ink 'e got camp over old railroad grade and da pipeline down jest nor't an west a Alfred. Bear Creek, I t'ink."

The location was in Dickinson County. "They're a long way from home." "Got have truck hided roun' 'ere someplace."

Service ran Peaveyhouse through his computer and the state system and got a vehicle plate and description. White Toyota Tacoma, year-old eight-cylinder model. Service asked central dispatch to transmit the description and BOL for the central U.P.

"We'll wait for the flatbed; then let's go find that camp," Service told his partner. "That's where they'll head for, sooner or later."

Jesus, the official season hasn't even begun.

CHAPTER 16

Bear Creek, Dickinson County

FRIDAY, NOVEMBER 13

They had just crossed the pipeline on a two-track west of Alfred when Service saw a man in camo, maybe forty yards away. He was carrying a rifle and Service slowed, his mind ticking through what he had seen, small game? *No orange, the dumb ass.* He stopped the truck.

The man crashed into the cedar swamp.

"You see da scope?" Allerdyce asked.

"No."

"Wass one."

"Rabbits?"

"Got no dogs."

Shit.

"Look your computer gizzy dere," Allerdyce said, tapping the laptop between them.

Service shrunk the online map to one square mile so they could make out the contour lines.

The old poacher's yellowed finger moved across the screen. "Dis galoot 'eadin' dere; 'e gone turn east along swamp. Too much open coun'ry west, hardswoods an' stuff. He take dis dink ritch line, I t'ink; 'e run like hell, what I'd do wass me. Make us go on foot. No road, but look dere, Sonny, dere's two bitty-titty hills, eh. Dis second dink ritch got little overlook, mebbe right down on swamp. Runner gone go east on ritch, den down along da swamp. We get up top, 'e can't get by us."

Service's brain processed the information and map as Allerdyce jabbered about topography. The old man was right, and Service saw that the runner was making a tactical mistake. If he went the way Limpy said he would, he'd be trapped by Bear Creek on the north, the North Branch of the Ford River to the east; and if he bolted south through open country, he'd have to cross County Road 438, only to have to find some way across the main Ford River, which wasn't frozen and had some deep and dangerous hat-floating holes in this area. The man should have risked the open country to the west.

"I'm yore dawg," Allerdyce said happily. "Woof-woof. Sonny take truck over dere east end; youse get to dat ritch and come west. I push dis guy east and we get dis jamoke 'tween us. Youse come along edge of da swamp, bottom of titty hills." The old man pointed. "I follow track. We meet middle."

Do I give the old man a weapon? The runner is armed. Limpy's a felon and can't possess or handle a firearm. Not that this rule has been strictly adhered to or enforced. The way he saw it, there was law and then there was officer judgment, which was based on reality of circumstances, not words on paper. But Allerdyce was wily, and this was his kind of country and game. He didn't need a firearm. "Go," Service said, adding, "and be careful."

Allerdyce croaked, "Tree to tree like dat Nappy Buncoguy."

Service laughed as the old man slid on his battered pack, cackled, and went over the snowy field with the grace of a young animal.

Ten minutes later, Service had the truck moved and stashed and was hurrying westward for the rendezvous, trying to think like the runner. Fortunately, or unfortunately, most people who ran from cops and game wardens ran with no plan in mind, bolting on surges of fear and adrenaline, an instantaneous flight thing. Years ago the first instinct seemed to be to fight, but nowadays conservation officers were better trained and armed, and flee-and-eludes had become more prevalent than bone-crushing fistfights and wrestling matches.

The length of such chases was usually matched by the severity of the crime. Minor stuff, short chases. Serious stuff, drawn-out affairs; and the longer a chase lasted, the more dangerous it became, because all involved would be getting tired and frustrated and desperate. Service had been involved in such pursuits many times in his career and had experienced and known all the feelings and emotions involved. The problem with an unknown runner was that you couldn't know which kind of chase was facing you until the chase was joined. The only three facts certain here were first, the guy wasn't wearing orange; second, he was armed with a long gun with a scope; and third, he ran.

Weapons had to be factored into every pursuit, but something in his gut kept telling him Limpy would be all right, that the old man had probably been on the other end of such chases so many times that he could meld his mind to the runner's and know exactly what he would do next. In fact, over decades, Limpy had won almost all of his contests. Service and his late old man were among the few game wardens to ever get the best of the old poacher, much less pinch him.

Service followed the edge of the spruce and tamarack swamp, which connected two small hills covered with aspen and birch and maple. Tamaracks were now bright yellow and would soon dull to ochre, drop their needles, and spend the winter naked.

Reaching the west end of the tit hill, Service quickly scrambled up the western bump and found a place where he could see hundreds of yards out into the swamp. Naturally, his first thought was to light a cigarette, but he ignored the urge and told himself to tell Friday about his self-discipline, if and when he saw her again. In fact, nothing to do with discipline: Smoke carried out here in cold heavy air. One cigarette could tell your opponent where you were. No smoke. But he'd had enough presence of mind to stuff Limpy's thermos into his pack, which he set on a downed log.

He kept his Remington .308 slung barrel-down across his chest. The rifle was too long and heavy for most officers to carry, especially in an extended foot pursuit, but with his size he could manage it. Barely. The damn thing was heavy and unwieldy. Like most of his fellow officers, he preferred a shorter, lighter, carbine-type weapon, but state budgets precluded this. The one good thing now, in an open area like this, his .308 could reach out and touch someone with astonishing accuracy, even with its iron sights. Last summer, all officers had trained at Camp Grayling and had shot at 800 yards; he had socked five rounds into a tight pattern in the Coke bottle, all five kill shots. But this long-range possibility here was a fluke; most CO work took place within arm's length of the opposition, not at 800 yards.

He poured a half-cup of coffee, took a sip, listened. The fresh snow muffled sound, which would work into Allerdyce's advantage. Feeling alert and relaxed, he was content to let the little drama play itself out.

Until he realized how fast they were losing light. Dark would change everything. Or could. Was the runner capable of operating in the dark the way he and Limpy were? Or would the runner need a light to find his way? No way to know.

The only option: Sit back and watch for any light oddities.

The forest was silent, snow falling gracefully, dark settling quickly under a cloudy sky.

A flicker of light, close, not thirty yards, directly below me. How did this guy get that close without me seeing him? Geez. This is a disturbing damn thought. But no more flashes. Just one. Did I really see a light? This the standard doubt brought on by all crepuscular or dark operations? No CO, no matter their experience, was immune from imaginings spawned by darkness. Minds played tricks, and you had to be able to sort imaginings from reality. Easier said than done, and all but impossible for a few.

No, real, not imaginary. And it did not shine again. He slid on his pack and started downhill, angling to his right and anticipating the heading of whomever had been below. The snow was really coming down hard, the temperature holding around freezing.

"Hey, Sonny," a muffled voice said, and then there were other words he couldn't make out, but he moved toward the sounds. Allerdyce was the only person who consistently called him Sonny.

Service moved cautiously, one step, stop, listen, step again.

"Geez, oh, Pete; I hope you brung dat bloody t'ermos," Allerdyce said in the darkness. He cackled and hacked at the same time. "Youse got smokes?"

"I thought you quit," Service said.

"Dis young buck I got holt of make me want start 'gain, and he ain't got none."

Service found his partner sitting on a very still human figure. "Our guy?"

"Yah, you betcha. Kid's pret good. Dat li'l light 'e got screwed 'is pooch."

"Why is he so still?"

"T'ink mebbe he bumped his noggin, eh."

"Hit something while running?"

"More like turn to fight and run into branch." The old man chuckled.

Service had no doubt said branch had been in Allerdyce's hand. "Let's roll him over, cuff him, and get him to his feet."

"Gimme smoke first," the old man said, and Service gave him his pack. Then he cuffed the man and pulled him to his feet. He was awake, breathing heavily. Service lit the man's face with his Surefire.

"Hey, that makes me blind!"

Jesus. "Ah, Mister Willie Asshole Nelson Niemi."

"I told youse my name is Virpi, and dat old coot dere attack me and I want press charges."

"Did I or did I not tell you to not do anything stupid?"

"I ain't done nuffin stupid. Was comin' find youses."

"*Really*," Service said, his voice dripping sarcasm.

"Yah, I found some shit and was comin' tell youse."

"Where's his weapon?" Service asked Allerdyce.

"He hanged 'er in a tree 'bout hunert yards back. Seen dat, I knew he was losin' his balls, eh, gettin' ready get caught."

"He attacked me," Niemi repeated. "See my head? See it!"

It was bleeding but not profusely. "Okay, Willie, let's get you cleaned up. You didn't get attacked. You ran into a branch while trying to elude the law. That's God's way of saying 'bad boy.' It's also a felony."

"God don't do dat shit," Niemi said. "He too busy with sick kits and da poor and all dose goody-goodies."

Christian principle interpreted by a fool, Service thought.

Allerdyce coughed.

"What kind of rifle?"

"Just BB gun, eh."

Niemi yelped, "Air rifle, not BB gun. BB guns is for kids, eh. What people t'ink growed man hunt wit BB gun!" And then he was talking calmly and rationally. "Law say felons can't possess no firearm, but I got small game license and huntin' snowshoes wit' my *air* rifle. I ain't broke no damn law, and I come to find youse, not runned away."

"Couldn't you see the shield on the door of my truck?"

"In this snow, in a Silverado? Everybody up 'ere drivin' Chevy trucks dese days."

Allerdyce handed the boy a cup of coffee while Service cleaned the minor head wound. "Drink it down," the old man said. "You want smoke?"

"Be good," Niemi said. "T'anks." He coughed when he inhaled.

Service said, "OK, let's all relax and talk. You had no orange on."

"Look at my coat. It's reversible. I just forgot to put orange inside to outside."

"You ran."

"Onnaccount what I seen down in da swamp."

"Which was?"

"You got see it ta believe it."

"Your family's camp is around here, right?" Service asked.

"Not my family, my ex-wife's father's camp."

"Dinty Peaveyhouse?"

"Yah, dat's 'im."

"Does what you wanted us to see have anything to do with your father-in-law?"

"Yah, I t'ink so, but I don't know for sure."

"Well, why don't we just head for the camp and we can take care of several things at once," Service proposed.

"Can't do dat. Dinty shoot me, he see me. He make the wife divorce me when I go off jail. Her old man *make* her. Not what she want, eh. We love each udder."

"You still talk to her?"

"Divorce is just some paper, eh. She still love me, like scromp wit me."

"Womens," Allerdyce said with a cackle. "I know dis girlie?"

"Back off," Service growled at his partner, who despite his age and appearance was a much-heralded skirt-chaser . . . and catcher.

"Is your father-in-law at his camp now?"

"Him and his boys took four-wheelers out somewheres today."

"Fishing maybe?" Service asked.

"Dunno; I jes seen the trucks go by."

"Why are you here?"

"Great snowshoe hare huntin' oot innadese swamps."

"Where's the camp from here?"

The boy looked around. "She's 'bout mile nort' where I first seen youse twos."

"Up that two-track?"

"Yah, youse go left where she make da fork."

"Why'd you run?"

"Din't know what to do. What if youses was Dinty? Your truck, his, bot' look like dey dipped in mud. Las' I knew, game wardens drive green trucks. Now youses got black. All kinds shit changes when you go inside."

"Where is this 'thing' you want us to see, relative to your people's camp?"

"Tole you ain't my people no more, I don't t'ink."

"Okay, exactly in what direction and how far from where you ran into us is this place?" Service asked, talking slowly.

"Dat be to da nort'wes."

"How far?"

"'Bout halfway Dinty's camp."

"Tell us in words what it is we're going to see when we find it."

"Whacked deer."

"Whacked how?"

"Don't t'ink was arrows."

"Gun?"

"Could be, couldn't see. Somebody got dese deers hunged up in trees, gutted."

"How high?"

"Ten, twelve feet easy."

"One deer?" Service asked.

"I seen six, bucks and does."

"All in the same area?"

"Yessir."

"You see hunters?"

"No, but I can guess who easy 'nough."

"How?"

"Deers is wearin' coats and hats, strangest t'ing I ever see in woods."

"But you didn't see the hunters."

"No, but I guess I know dose clothes," Niemi said. "Was stuff da wifey and me give fodder-in-law and brudders-in-law 'fore I went off jail. My wife gone be pissed she hear dose duds get hanged on dead deers in woods. No respect, know what I mean?"

Grady Service tried to organize his thoughts. "What is it you wanted the DNR to see?"

"Dose deer ain't right is what."

"You find that offensive?"

"Yes, sir, I do. I did drugs, was wrong, I know, but I got respect for ann-mules, okay?"

Service tried to gauge if the man was lying, if this was some sort of revenge setup, which was possible but unlikely. Virpi was a simple soul.

"Could it be you broke into camp, whacked those deer, stole the clothes, and hung them on the deer to set up your father-in-law?"

"I ain't gone lie. No, sir, and I'll take trut'-checker machine, you want me."

Service sighed. "Okay, let's go look."

"In dark, in the snow?"

"We own the night," Service told the young man.

"Dude, I can't see nuttin' at night. How I gone find my way?"

"Just get us close and we'll take it from there. Can you do that?"

"Don't want my fodder-in-law see me."

"Was he born with night vision?"

Niemi giggled nervously. "Wears Coke-bottle-t'ick glasses; can't hardly see dick ta take piss."

"Then you're good to go," Service told him. "You'll be okay. I'm thinking he won't be back to camp too soon."

"Why dat?"

"Call it a hunch."

Dickinson County was in the same DNR law enforcement area with Iron and Gogebic Counties. Service called Sergeant Wooten on the cell phone and explained what was happening and where. He also explained how they found the Peaveyhouses trying to net spawning brook trout in Slippery Creek and how he had disabled their four-wheelers after they ran. "There's a BOL in the central U.P. for Peaveyhouse's pickup. Haven't heard anything on that, but radio reception down here is spotty at best."

The relatively new 800 MHz radios had been advertised as effective everywhere, but like all claims for most new electronics, this was less than accurate.

"You saw the dead deer?" Wooten asked.

"No, we're going to go find them now, but the camp needs to be covered so Peaveyhouse gets met when he and his merry fishermen finally get back."

"All right," the sergeant said. "On my way. Are these guys violent?"

Service leaned over to Niemi. "Are your in-law's scrappers?"

"Sometimes, if dey been drinking da hootch. Da old man sings da song and dose boys jes' follow, eh."

"Could be some resistance," Service relayed to his sergeant.

"I'll get backup."

There was currently only one officer in Dickinson County, and he lived way down in the southern part, in Kingsford. Service expected that the sergeant would also tap del Olmo and Sheena Grinda, who were in Iron County, and much closer than the Dickinson officer.

Service gave directions to his sergeant and hung up.

The cell phone immediately sounded. It was Simon del Olmo. "Mario Novello called and asked me to tell you that you should call him."

The season was heating up. He could feel it in his guts. "Has he got something specific?" Novello was in his mid-seventies, a long-retired CO from Iron County, but he had resented del Olmo and Grinda for never calling to pay homage to him and his knowledge of the area. When he had something, he called Service, which did not make either of the local officers happy.

"I'll listen to him and kick it over to you guys," Service told his friend.

"The guy's a fricking hardhead," del Olmo complained.

"Bump you later."

Grady Service called the number and Novello answered.

"Mario, it's Service."

"Thanks for calling. Here's the deal. There's this guy from Florence, name is Noble Chern. He comes up here to south Iron and drives along the grade. He only shoots big bucks."

"*Are* there big bucks down that way?"

"Sure was at one time, and maybe this guy is part of the problem nowadays."

Novello's camp was on the Michigan side of the Brule River, and the old railroad grade-turned recreation trail was a favorite route for road hunters, especially from nearby Wisconsin. Service put his notebook on the computer. "Give me that name again, Mario."

"Noble Chern is what I heard, which may or may not be right."

"From Florence?"

"That's the word."

Florence was just over the state border and not that far south of Iron County.

"What I'm hearing is this guy only shoots 140s and larger."

"Don't you think it would make more sense for Simon or Sheena to work this?"

"I want it to be you on this, not those two."

"How about I drive down tomorrow evening and we talk."

"I guess. You know why I don't like them two."

"I know, and you're wrong about them, Mario."

"Yah, yah, see you tomorrow night. Oh, Grady, almost forgot. This guy is 'pose to be big fella, six, six-two, clean-cut, military look, not the usual greasy-hair scumbag."

"Okay, see you tomorrow night."

"How's the overture going?"

"The what?"

"Overture, like the run-up to the show, this is the overture to the deer season, at least that's what some of us used to call it."

Service knew the retired officer was missing the job and the excitement of deer season and in the mood to talk and reminisce, but there was no time.

"Mario, I'm just getting ready to go look for some deer hung in trees in a swamp. They're wearing coats and hats."

"To keep the wolves offen 'em," the retired officer said. "Boy, does that sound like fun. Talk to you 'morrow night. You want some dinner?"

Why not. "Sounds good. Sixish GWT."

"Game warden time," Novello said, chuckling softly.

"Game warden time," Service confirmed, which meant "ish," or sort of, time being at best a plastic and approximate thing, especially during the firearm deer season.

Service reorganized and restacked the gear in his backseat, and Allerdyce crawled in back. Niemi rode up front and directed them to the approximate location of the dead deer. "You ever get scared, working out in dark alla time?" Niemi asked Service.

Allerdyce exploded in laughter in the backseat. "Why he get scared, kid. Sonny 'ere is *real* bogeyman!"

CHAPTER 17

Bear Creek

FRIDAY, NOVEMBER 13

It took almost four hours, but Service and Allerdyce found, photographed, and dragged six deer back to the patrol truck, a half mile away—three round-trips, each man dragging two deer through the snow, which made pulling somewhat easier and the walking a lot more strenuous. Niemi pitched in to help, but, true to his word, he was almost totally blind in the dark. What he did do was identify each piece of clothing draped on the animals—when they were bought, where, and for whom. And he agreed to write a statement providing the information for each garment.

"What about your wife?" Service asked. "Can she verify what you gave them?"

"T'ink she be too freaked, but store ought have receipts. We buy all dat stuff place called Da Legworks."

This was a not-so-old-line Marquette outdoor clothing and footwear shop owned by a family called Kallio. Service had met the grandparents who started the shop, but he didn't know the current operators.

"Me and Kallio's boy Deano usta fish a lot. Da Kallios know da wife and my folks and me real good. Youse'll see."

It was going to be interesting to hear what Dinty Peaveyhouse would have to say for himself. He'd bluster at first. He always had.

He got Sergeant Wooten on the radio when he met up with del Olmo and Grinda. They had apparently found the camp dark and empty and immediately withdrawn, up the two-track, and turned left up the other fork, where they found places to hide their trucks until it was time to move in. Service heard del Olmo on the radio and understood he had gone on foot back to the camp to call out Peaveyhouse's homecoming.

Service drove Virpi Niemi to his truck, west of where they had found the deer. Service told the ex-con to go home, and he and Allerdyce headed back toward the camp. Just as they got to the two-track where this had all begun, he heard del Olmo on the radio. "They're back."

"Four-wheelers?" Service asked over the radio.

"Negative," del Olmo reported. "But this is a really loud bunch."

"Drunk?"

"High probability."

"Where're your backups?" Service asked.

"Rolling," Grinda called on the 800 MHz.

"We're inbound," Service radioed.

"We?" Grinda asked.

"You'll see."

"Headlights nearing me," del Olmo radioed. "One, One Twenty-Two clear."

Grady Service said, "Twenty-Five Fourteen clear."

Service and Allerdyce pulled into the camp yard to find only one patrol truck, its lights and spots on. Service lit his to add shock to the scene, and Allerdyce growled, "What I 'pose ta do?" as they jumped out.

"Be useful," Service told him, running between two pickup trucks to the cabin. The first thing he saw was Sheena Grinda on top of someone in the snow, her forearm across the individual's throat and the night air filled with gagging and grunting and clouds of low-hanging pepper gas. Del Olmo was pinned to a camp wall by two men; one was punching him, the second man kicking. A fourth individual lay on the porch floor, face down, moaning.

Service unsheathed and extended his baton and chopped the legs out from under del Olmo's kicker, dropping him to the floor. With that pressure gone, Simon pivoted and drove the other man onto his heels and tackled him off the porch, where he landed with a loud hiss, all the air blowing out of his lungs.

Grinda and her dance partner were still struggling, and Service watched her strike the man in the face hard with the heel of her hand as he bucked her off. She immediately scrambled back at him from his side, attacking and finally getting back on top, pushed him facedown, and wrenched his arms behind him to cuff him.

The fourth man, the moaner, managed to get to his knees only to find Allerdyce's boot in his face, bouncing him off the camp wall, where he hit the floor hard and remained inert.

Grinda had her man on his feet, but he was unsteady and stumbling around like he was stunned. Both of them were snorting snot and coughing violently. "Get IDs," she managed between coughs. "Where . . . hell . . . Wooten? Right behind me . . . when . . . Georged."

"George" was game warden lingo for charging en masse. The word and concept came from a former officer in upper northern lower Michigan who never went into any situation quietly or stealthily. His preference was to charge in and then use the chaos he created to take control. Service looked around. Their sergeant was nowhere in sight.

"Did you see him, Grady?" Grinda asked, between coughing and hacking, frantically trying to wipe tears out of her eyes and snot from her nose.

"Nope."

"He didn't turn, he went straight. You guys should have passed head-on."

"We never saw him."

"Maybe he got another call," Grinda offered in a less-than-convinced tone.

"Yah, the radios suck back here," Service agreed. But he had heard no such radio traffic, and he had not seen the sergeant. Realization that Wooten had not Georged with del Olmo and Grinda made his stomach stir. Georging could be a risky way to do things, but sometimes it was the only choice, and when that was the case, game wardens had a single rule: One Georges, all George; no exceptions, no excuses.

Allerdyce nudged Service and pointed to the giant Grinda had cuffed. "Old Fart Peaveyhouse."

"Please settle down, sir," Grinda said firmly and politely to the man.

"Fucking Russian cunt, liberal commie DNR snatch, this is my private personal property and you are violating the constitution of this great country. This land is clearly marked No Trespassing. Youse can't bust in on a man's castle or his camp, goddammit, and what the fuck dat outlaw Allerdyce doin't here wichyouse?"

Service said, "Shut up, Peaveyhouse," and shoved the man over to his patrol truck, where he shone his Surefire onto the load of dead deer in back. "Care to explain what *that's* all about?"

"Why you ast me dat? I don't know nuttin 'bout dose deers dere."

"We'll get fingerprints off the clothes," Service said.

Peaveyhouse made a face. "Duds don't hold no fingerprints. Don't you try bullshit me. I watch da TV, I do."

Service pointed to buttons. "Plastic *does*."

Peaveyhouse stood silent, hacking and snorting. "I need doctor."

"What you *need* is a brain transplant," Service said.

"I'm taxpayer, your boss," the man said gruffly.

"There is absolutely nothing worse than a dumb-ass boss," Service retorted. "We've got you for four stolen ORVs, fishing out of season, flee-and-elude, resisting arrest, assault on a peace officer, obstruction of a police investigation, six illegal deer, and we haven't even counted the illegal fish yet, or looked to see what other goodies you've got here in your castle."

"I got nuttin' more say ta da likes of youse," Peaveyhouse said, turning away from the dead deer just as Sergeant Wooten emerged from the darkness.

"Where were you?" del Olmo asked him.

"Skin blew, had to fix it."

"Where?" Service asked him. "We came in the same road and never saw you."

The sergeant mumbled something about timing and walked away.

"We don't know nuttin' 'bout no damn stoled ORVs," Peaveyhouse said.

"They were in your possession. The rest is moot."

"Oh yeah?" Peaveyhouse said. "Where are dey now? Youse can't proof nuttin'."

"Got witnesses, Dinty. And we saw them on your trailers."

The man puffed up. "Won't stand up."

"Of course it will," Service said calmly. "This isn't the old days, when guys like you couldn't get convicted by scared juries. People these days *care* about the deer herd. When the jury sees photos of those animals in the back of my truck, that will be all she wrote. And when we throw in stolen goods, the fishing, well, they won't take an hour to nail your asses with guilty on all counts; the judge will take it from there and drop-kick your asses into Loserland with beaucoup fines *and* time inside."

"We ain't never done nothing before," Peaveyhouse said.

"Which means only that you've never been *caught* before," Service said. "This kind of knucklehead outlaw binge doesn't happen overnight." He let that sink in and switched tone and direction. "But this isn't the end of the world, so just settle down and talk to me. It's not like you murdered someone."

Service turned away from the man, took a step, and turned back. "You didn't murder anyone right?"

"Course not," Peaveyhouse the Elder said. "What the hull is wrong wichyouse?"

Service knew the confrontation was over. "Tell me about the deer, Dinty. I know they're yours, and we'll have ballistic tests that will match up to your rifles. Science will bring truth, so we might as well start with the truth."

"What're youse guys, like CSI?" the man asked.

"No, that's TV baloney; we're real and a lot better at what we can do. So what's with these deer?"

"The wolfs donchu know," Dinty Peaveyhouse said with a heavy voice.

"Wolves? What *about* wolves?"

"Dey killin' all da deers."

"But *you* killed the deer."

"First," Peaveyhouse argued; "'fore dose wolfs can eat dem."

"You killed the deer before the wolves could do it?"

"Right."

"Either way, the deer end up dead," Service pointed out.

"Our deers, not for wolfs. God put deers here for taxpayers. Deers is our right. We paid for 'em."

Service was almost at a loss for words, but he managed. "You paid God for the deer?"

Grinda interrupted. "I just ran the three of them through RSS. No licenses for anything this year," she said, adding, "or any other year."

"No licenses, Dinty. How'd you pay for those deer you were just lecturing me on?"

"I pay damn state an' poppety taxes. We meant get licenses, just forget. But we still got time. Season not open yet."

"The season's over and done for you and your boys."

"Dat ain't fair."

The man was a cretin. "Why the duds on the deer?"

"Keep wolfs and yotes offen dem."

"That's a myth. Putting human scent on dead prey won't keep predators away."

"Allas works good for us," Peaveyhouse bragged.

Service smiled. "So you've done this before, despite having no licenses."

"We allas got licenses."

"The state's computer says differently."

"What youse expect from craputers, eh?" the man said.

"I can understand how you feel," Service said, "but it's never been wrong for me."

"Course, your computer set up by state, so it say what you want it say."

"It doesn't work that way."

Peaveyhouse crossed his arms. "Me and my boys, we ain't got nuttin' more to say."

"Good," Service said, fetching his booze bag from the truck. All three men blew over the blood alcohol limit; the old man and the son driving the second truck were to be charged for operating while impaired.

Grinda radioed the Dickinson County sheriff's office for assistance with transporting prisoners. Service wrote tickets for fishing and deer violations and gave the Peavey clan's leader receipts for their trucks, eight rifles from the house, two more rifles that they had found loaded and uncased in the pickups, and the fishing nets they had recovered earlier at the stream.

"Why we got go jail?" Peaveyhouse demanded to know.

"How do we love thee, let me count the ways," Grinda said: "flee-and-elude, assaulting officers, resisting arrest, stolen ORVs, driving while impaired, hunting out of season, possessing illegally killed deer, loaded weapons in vehicles, the whole ball of wax."

The ORV thefts would be handled by complaint and warrant and passed into the prosecutor's hands.

Peaveyhouse snorted.

When the sheriff's deputies took the prisoners south to Iron Mountain, Service, Grinda, and del Olmo followed them. There Service wrote reports on the stolen goods and other events and left the reports and ticket copies in the magistrate's in-basket. The report would go to the county prosecutor, who would decide what complaint charges to bring, if any. Not all county prosecutors took fish and wildlife charges as seriously as statutes dictated. Service recommended court condemnation of all the equipment they had confiscated, and while he thought it likely the clan wouldn't get the rifles back, the state was unlikely to keep the trucks, preferring to give the guilty a means of transport to get to work to earn money to pay their fines. That was the twisted logic in such decisions.

"We're not starting real early tomorrow," Service told Allerdyce. "I really need sleep."

"I still got plenty pizzazz," the old poacher announced. "Feel twinny again."

Grady Service saw the twinkle in the old man's eyes, knew it was true, and shook his head. Allerdyce's constitution bordered on the supernatural.

It was past midnight and now the fourteenth. Tomorrow morning would be the fifteenth, and at first light the firearms season would officially commence. There would be some early birds trying to whack deer behind camps over lighted bait piles tonight, and he wanted to be out and about as this was going on. A light or shot at night was automatic probable cause during the deer season.

Sergeant Wooten did not make the trip to Iron Mountain, but Service called him on the cell phone and spoke directly and to the point. "Maybe you did blow a skin," he said, "and this time I'll assume you did. But next time your people are in George-mode you'd better be first in the goddamn charge, not the tail-end Charlie."

Wooten had no response, and hung up.

Grinda and del Olmo were married, and del Olmo asked, "You call Novello?"

"I did. Supposed to see him tonight, sixish at his camp. I think he wants company as much as anything, but he's given us some great cases over the years, so we can't just blow him off."

"Better you than us," Grinda said. "Every time I see him, he wants to tell me how to do my job and keeps calling me 'little girlie.'"

"Old school. Don't take it personally," Service said. "He was a great game warden."

"So are you," she reminded him, "but you're not like that."

"He's *real* old school."

"Right," Grinda said. "Jackwagon High, somewhere right of Attila the Hun."

"He gives us good cases."

"Gives *you*, not us," Grinda said, correcting him. "He gives *us* nothing."

"Are we or are we not one organization?"

"That's not sufficient justification to have to eat his shit sandwiches," she carped.

"I'll eat the sandwich, get the information, and pass it to you guys."

"Oh, joy," Grinda said. "If you're going to see him tonight, there's no sense driving home. Why don't you and Nature Boy come home, bunk with us tonight, and work over here today?"

Allerdyce perked up. "*Nature Boy*?"

"It's a term of endearment," del Olmo told the old poacher.

Tonight? Service thought and checked his watch. The season was still twelve-plus hours away, and time was already fragmenting and falling apart.

"Sound more like one dose whatdeycall sharkism t'ings me," Allerdyce complained.

As they followed the other trucks, Service asked his passenger, "Does your battery *ever* run down?"

"Nope, it's one them gymnetic t'ings. My famblee tell story my ancestor over in da Englands one day walk t'irty miles, hunt pats, eat big supper, walk t'irty miles home in 'leven hours, do work all day at house, walk sixteen miles to 'nother house for dance, scromp two womans dat night, walk sixteen miles home by seven morning, hunt pats all day at 'is place. T'ree days, two nights dis old boy walk niney-two an' t'irty mile, hunt pats, eat good, drink, fuck good. T'ink I got dat ol' gent's germs."

"You're making that up."

"Ain't not. I read in book, wrote by some guy name of White. You know best part today?"

"No, and I don't want to." Service glanced at the old man. "Nature Boy."

"Ain't too many pipples with sense of hummus no more," Limpy lamented.

CHAPTER 18

South Iron County

SATURDAY, NOVEMBER 14

Grinda and del Olmo were long gone when Allerdyce made breakfast at noon, and Service and his partner didn't get under way until 3 p.m. They refueled the truck in Crystal Falls and made their way south to the rec trail, an old east–west railroad bed turned road for hunters, fishermen, snowmobilers, trappers, and ORV riders. Mario wasn't expecting them until six. Service decided to set up along the rec trail and look for road-hunters.

The trick was to get up on a vehicle that was rolling slowly with open windows and hope for a porcupine (a vehicle with the tip of a gun barrel protruding from a window). Once you saw this, you had to rush them before they could unload. Unless you caught them with loaded weapons, the heaviest charge you could get on them would be uncased weapon and possession of a firearm inside a vehicle during the five days preceding opening day, referred to as the "quiet time." Some COs called it the Temptation Removal Rule, or TRR. Veteran road-hunters stayed alert for COs and were practiced in unloading weapons quickly while their trucks were still moving. It was a kind of cat-and-mouse game. The TRR was regularly ignored.

Service parked his truck so that he could see an intersection of the rec trail as well as another gravel road and a nearby two-track. With three good watch options, he hoped to up his chances for slow rollers.

Timing couldn't be better. Wisconsin's season was shorter than Michigan's by five days (nine days versus fourteen), started later, and ended earlier. Wisconsin's season opened on a different date every year, while the Michigan firearm season was always November 15–30. Michigan opened tomorrow, Wisconsin a week from yesterday, meaning for a few days it was predictable that some Wisconsin hunters would be operating both legally and illegally in Michigan, mostly in the four border counties: Gogebic, Iron, Dickinson, and Menominee.

Limpy said, pointing, "Sonny I t'ink dere's tan truck park back in dose popples. Be at youse's eight-clock."

"Got it," Service said. "Stay here and watch the roads." Service walked back into the aspens and saw the truck. He looked inside: no gun case, no ammo boxes, no bow or crossbow case, just an orange toque on the backseat. *What's this bird up to, scouting?* Only one set of tracks leading away from the truck and now beginning to fill with snow. One soul, and he'd been gone from his truck for a while. Service felt the hood; it was cold.

It would be difficult for him to explain why, but he felt a hunch taking root. There was no glaring reason for it, but the feeling was strong, and he had learned over the years to trust his hunches when they gnawed at him. He was still kicking himself over the little red truck in the 8-1 case. Had he made that stop, the case might have been solved a lot faster. All the most effective COs developed this extra sense of something being wrong without being able to identify how it worked, and the really top COs acquired it early on, or were born with it. He'd had it since boyhood, following his old man around. The old man could cruise past twenty or thirty parked vehicles and not even slow down; suddenly they'd come up on a truck and the old man would jam on his brakes and quietly say, "Oh, boy." Every single time the old man did this, he found some sort of violation. Grady had continually questioned him on it, but all his father would say was, "Do it long enough and youse'll get so youse just *know*."

The old man had been right. Service checked his watch. Almost four. He had read the light tables before they got in the patrol truck. Sunset today was 4:16, with shooting light to go for a few more minutes into the ensuing twilight. He decided to sit on this one, wait for the driver to come out. In the meantime, he decided to call Lansing. "Station Twenty, Twenty-Five Fourteen with a file. I'm in south Iron County on the rec trail and out of my vehicle."

"Ready to copy, Twenty."

"Wisconsin plate," Service said, and he ticked off the numbers.

Minutes later Station Twenty called back. "Your plate comes back to a 2005 tan Chevy pickup, registered to Noble Chern out of Florence, Wisconsin, no wants or warrants. Twenty clear."

Chern? *Isn't that the name Novello mentioned? What were the chances?* He couldn't stop grinning. This kind of coincidence almost never panned out, but now it was assuredly worth the wait.

No sign of the man by 4:30, and the light snow was getting heavier, making it more difficult to see in the failing light. Just as he was thinking this, he picked up some movement in the gloaming and hugged the far side of the truck, using it to hide him. The man was straight-backed. No long gun apparent, no orange either. The guy was decked out head to toe in camo and walked in cautious, mincing steps, using a cane.

Grady Service didn't announce himself until the man was reaching for the driver's door handle. "DNR, conservation officer, how's it going?"

"Great," the man said, his voice betraying no evidence of anything.

"Slow going in the snow with that game leg, eh?"

"Affirmative, but I'm used to it. My leg." He tapped the limb for effect.

"What's your name?" Service asked.

"Noble. Noble Chern, sir."

"Is this your truck, Mr. Chern?"

"Yes, sir."

"What's back up in the woods, Noble?"

"Not a darn thing. I was just doing some scouting."

"Good area?"

"Can be," the man said. "Got a thirteen-pointer near here last season."

"Very cool," Service said. "We don't see many like that down here on the grade. Why no orange?"

"I'm not hunting," the man said, his voice relaxed and calm. "I'm just scouting, want to see a picture of my deer?"

"Sure."

The man dug out his wallet, wedged a photo out of the plastic folder, and handed it to Service, who said. "Wow, *huge* rack. Score?" There was a Michigan deer tag wrapped around one of the long tines.

"One sixty-eight, but I never had it done officially. That's just the green score, which is enough for me, hear what I'm sayin'?"

"You get it mounted?"

"Sir, yes *sir.*"

Service kept counting the points and kept coming up with twelve, not thirteen. Were two deer involved with this guy? "Who does your work?"

"Always the same place. Jumbo Teller down to Spread Eagle."

"Don't know him. Has he got a shop?"

"He's good, and pricey. Cost me five bills."

Service whistled to make the man think he was awed. As he continued to look at the photo, he said, "I'll be right back." He walked away from the truck and said into his radio, "Station Twenty, Twenty-Five Fourteen, can you run RSS on the individual whose file I just ran, Noble Chern?"

"Affirmative. What are we looking for, sir?"

"Any deer licenses, oh five through this year."

"Stand by one, Twenty-Five Fourteen."

Service watched Chern, who stood like a statue, staring at him.

"Twenty-Five Fourteen. We show no licenses for Mr. Chern for any of those years."

"Can you check DNR priors?"

"Anticipated that, Twenty-Five Fourteen. Negative priors on Noble Chern. Twenty clear."

The registration date on the photo said 2007, which was two seasons back. But he had no license for that year, or any other. And he'd said he got the buck *last* year. Nothing tallied here, and the poofume of violation wafted up from the photo. No licenses and no DNR priors. Service guessed that the guy had never been stopped and had been operating under the radar for years with no regard for the rules or the law.

Service walked back to the man. "Whose license is on the deer?" he asked, holding up the photo.

"Mine, sir."

Wrong answer. "What were you doing in the woods just now?"

"I told you I was scouting, sir."

"How about we go take a look?"

"My leg," the young man said. "I'm not up to another walk so soon. Is there a problem, sir?"

The kid was clean-cut and shipshape in appearance. He had good posture, and he looked right into Service's eyes rather than down at his own boots. He was totally unlike the usual twenty-thirty-something, backward-hat, tattoo-drowned, mop-haired dirt-bird he normally encountered in the woods. "The deal, Noble, is that you told me you shot that thirteen-point last year, but your photo says it was 2007, which is two seasons back."

"I just made a mistake," the man said. "I shoot a lot of big bucks."

"In Michigan?"

"No sir, just that one in Michigan. I usually get mine down to Wisconsin. They have bigger ones over there, ya know, more farms, more food. Can I have my picture back, sir?" The man held out his hand.

"I think I'd better hang on to it for now." Service keyed his radio. "Twenty-Five Fourteen partner, you want to scoot over here to help me?"

Allerdyce was beside him in what seemed like an instant. "Let me have your truck keys, Mr. Chern."

"No, sir, I can't," the man said, his voice suddenly sharpening into a whine. "I have to go home now, sir. Please?"

"You will give me the keys now, son. You're not going anywhere until I say so, and that's not going to happen for a while, so relax." The man held out his keys.

Service looked at Allerdyce and handed the keys to him. "He doesn't leave until I say so."

"The old guy looks crazy," Chern complained, his eyes riveted on the old poacher.

Service said. "What you see is what you get."

Fifteen minutes later he found a loaded Remington .270 with a scope, a plastic chair behind a brush blind, and 40 to 50 gallons of bait in front of the rudimentary hide. He took photos of the setup and walked back to the truck, where he held up the rifle. "Look what I found."

"Not mine," Chern said. "I never saw it before, sir. Swear to God and on my honor."

Service showed him a photo of the bait and the blind.

"Not mine," the man insisted.

"I followed *your* footprints right to it. One set of tracks in, one set out. It's you, and all that out there is yours."

"Sir, no sir, not mine, sir."

"You were on private property."

"I have permission, sir."

"From whom?"

"The landowner."

"What's his name?"

"I don't remember his name. I've—."

The man seemed to snip off whatever it was he was about to say.

"You've what?"

"Actually, sir, *I* do not have permission on this particular property, but my friend does."

"What's his name?"

"Hill."

"Does Mr. Hill have a first name?"

"Henry, but everyone calls him Fat Henny."

"Where does Fat Henny live?"

"Someplace near Iron Mountain; I don't know exactly, sir. I never actually been there. His dad's sick, so they don't like visitors."

"What's Mr. Hill's phone number?"

"I don't know. I don't have no cell phone."

No phone in this age? Not buying that. "Landline then?"

"Not one of them neither. I don't call him and he don't call me. We just show up."

"Are you telling me you have no telephone?"

"That's affirmative, sir. No phone, sir. Money's tight, and I don't really need one."

"Are you telling me you guys communicate via ESP or something?"

"No, sir, I don't know what that is, that thing you just said."

Weird how he changes directions. "What about a phone for work?"

"I got no work, sir."

"Let me see your operator's license."

"I don't got it on me, sir," Chern said. "Forgot it. On accident."

"Yet you're driving."

"You can't hunt if you sit on the couch at home, sir." the man said.

"You said you were scouting."

"Hunt, scout, it's all part of the same thing."

"So, for clarification, that twelve-point you got, was it last year or the season before?"

"Well, I guess the photo is right. It was the year before last."

"You get a nice one last year too?"

"Yes, sir, a thirteen-pointer."

"But no photo of that one?"

"Didn't have no phone or camera with me, sir."

"Who took this photo, your friend Hill?"

"Not sure, sir. I guess I don't remember."

"Mr. Chern, the deer in this picture has twelve points, not thirteen."

The man stared up into the night sky. "My mind, sir. It goes soft sometimes. If this is the twelve, I ain't got no picture of the thirteen."

"To get this straight, you're now telling me that you shot a twelve two years ago and a thirteen last year?"

"Yes, sir, twelve, then the thirteen. Maybe I'll get a fourteen this year?"

"You shot a thirteen-point last year. Where was that shot, here?"

"No sir, that was in Wisconsin. The twelve was here, in that picture."

"Where's the twelve-point rack now?"

"I don't remember."

Service puffed up. "Do I look like I just fell off the rootabeggy truck? Why the hell are you lying? You just told me it was done for you by a taxidermist."

"*Honest*, sir. I'm not lying. My mom, she wouldn't abide lies. But my memory's funky and furry sometimes, from the war, ya know? It's at my house, *sir*."

"What's with your leg?" Service said.

"Eye-rack," Chern said quietly, in an almost sad tone.

"You got hurt in Iraq?"

"Sir, yes, sir, I did, wounded in oh three."

"What happened, if you don't mind me asking?"

"Nasariya happened, sir."

Like many Americans, Grady Service had not tracked the day-to-day details of battles in Iraq or Afghanistan. He had heard of Nasariya, but was not at all sure why. "Army?"

"No, sir. First Marine Expeditionary Force."

"Oorah," Service said. "Marines are squared away, so how does that explain you're not having your driver's license with you?"

"Truth, sir. I lost my license in South Carolina and moved up to North Dakota with my mom while my wounds healed and then I moved to Wisconsin, and I just never quite got around to it. Sir, I know it was wrong, but that's how it happened. I do have a military driver's license."

The man's voice dripped with sincerity and contrition. "With you?"

"No, sir. Back at the house."

"I'll tell you how this looks from my perspective, Chern. I don't like un-squared-away marines, wounded warriors or otherwise. I'm keeping your weapon, and I'm writing you tickets for no hunter orange, violating the quiet time, and using excess bait. I'm not going to hang you with hunting out of season or without a license, not yet."

"Oorah, sir. But that's not my rifle."

"True that," Service said. "It now belongs to the State of Michigan since it's not yours. You are going to take your tickets and drive yourself home and stay there until you get a valid operator's license. You can handle the tickets over a neighbor's phone. I'm going to wave bond on this," Service added. His gut was telling him there was so much wrong with this guy he couldn't even begin to scrape it all away, but the guy was a wounded vet, and that alone meant this would take some time, attention, and judgment.

"Thanks, sir. I don't' have no pot to piss in. Sir, what about my picture, sir?"

"Go home, Chern; get out of my sight."

"Sir, will I get my picture back?"

"That depends."

"On what, sir?"

"Too many factors to lay out tonight."

"Sir, yes sir."

Service and Allerdyce watched the truck drive east on the rec trail. "He say anything to you while you were alone with him?" Service asked.

"Boo-hoo, wah-wah, life tough, luck bad, ever'body pick on him, all he want do is hunt."

"It sucks to be him."

"Youse ain't done with that boy, are youse, Sonny?"

Service shook his head and made a loud sniffing sound.

Allerdyce nodded. "Wah! I smell dat too."

• • •

Mario Novello beamed like a child on Christmas morning when he saw Allerdyce.

"Thought you were dead," Novello told the legendary violator.

"Dose reports is flappergastered," Allerdyce said.

"You remember the time I got you up in Ericksen's potato fields?"

"Dat weren't me," Limpy said. "Youse never got me."

Novello kept talking. "I was right on your ass and you went into a sharp ninety right; I followed, but you were gone. Poof."

"Maybe da guy youse was after went ninety left."

"He couldn't have. There's only the river to the left."

"Could be dere's ford dere, I'm t'inkin."

Both men laughed.

"Do you want to hear about Chern?" Service asked his former colleague.

"Who?"

"The guy you called me about?"

"What about him?"

"We wrote him for no hunter orange and over-bait about an hour ago."

"No shit? That bird's been a ghost-killer up here for years."

"How long?"

"Oh four, oh five, at least."

Service showed Novello the photograph.

"Shit, I seen that big boy, wondered what happened to him. We've got a couple pockets of monster bucks over this way."

"Including a big thirteen-point last year?"

"Shit, did he take that one too? Every year we hear reports of monsters, only it's never the locals who get them. They just disappear."

"Says he's only hunted in Michigan the past two years."

"That's bullshit. You buy it?"

"No. You ever hear of Fat Henny Hill?"

"Elder or Junior?"

"There's *two* of them?"

"Major dirtbags out of Randville. They with Chern?"

"Possibly," Service said, sharing no more details. Randville was north of Iron Mountain.

CHAPTER 19

Florence, Wisconsin

SATURDAY, NOVEMBER 14

Wisconsin Conservation Warden Kelly "KTR" des Jardins de Richelieu answered his cell phone in a crisp professional voice. Some years back, Simon del Olmo had been pursuing a man south after the hunter sniped a buck off private property in broad daylight. The Iron County CO had the sense to call ahead to Richelieu, who answered the phone by saying he had the man in custody at that very moment. By sheer chance Richelieu had been by the Brule River on the border, and when he pulled out onto US 141, he had seen blood on the truck's tailgate, pulled over the driver, and found an untagged Michigan deer. Thereafter, Michigan COs called Richelieu Kelly the Rocket, KTR for short.

Richelieu had worked for many years somewhere near Madison and had transferred to Florence about ten years back. At one point he had a partner, who was killed in the line of duty on a case Service had been heavily involved in.

"Kelly, this is Grady Service."

"How's retirement?" Richelieu asked.

"The real thing, or retired on duty like you?"

"I ain't even close, and my two girls and their mother got private college aspirations. What can I do you for?"

"Noble Chern."

Richelieu made a sighing sound. "We call that jerk 'Chernobyl.' He's radioactive as hell."

"I met him tonight, stroked him for no orange and over-bait. I also found a loaded .270, but he insists it's not his, so it's now property of the state."

"It's his," Kelly the Rocket said.

"He showed me a photograph of a twelve-point buck shot up here in oh seven. He initially claimed it was last year but changed his story when I pointed out that the photo indicated it was 2007. There's a Michigan tag on one of the antlers, but our records show he never bought one of our licenses, not that year or any other. He told me he mostly hunts Wisconsin."

"Interesting. We've gotten him three or four times for failure to register deer kills, all does. No bucks." In Michigan, registration of deer was voluntary. In Wisconsin it was mandatory.

"Failure to register is all?"

"Well, we've heard rumors, mostly putting him across the border into your counties. What we hear is that he hunts continuously and takes only big bucks. Apparently he shoots our does solely for their food value."

"Probably taste like cheese," Service quipped. "Do me a favor; I want to go to his house and take the twelve-point mount."

"You mean tonight?"

"I have a feeling that if we don't act fast, Kell, that mount will go bye-bye to Nowhereland. He already told me he couldn't remember where it was. We may be too late already. Are you aware he doesn't have a valid Wisconsin operator's license?"

"Nope, I've never actually pinched him. Our guys down in Marinette County are the ones who've cited him. You want me with you?"

"If you can."

"When?"

"Sooner trumps later. We're ten minutes from the border."

"Okay; meet in thirty minutes at the Interp?"

"Works for us."

"We? Who's with you, Simon or Sheena?"

"Allerdyce."

There was a long, heavy phone silence, then a disbelieving, "Say again?"

"You heard me."

"This should be rich. I thought that asshole kicked it a long time back."

"I'd avoid that topic if I were you."

Service said, "Chern says he has no current operator's license for Wisconsin. So how does he buy licenses to shoot does?"

"My first guess is that he borrows tags from pals and uses those."

"Nice. So how does he get nabbed for failure to register?"

"Like I said, I'll have to check it all out. I've never made a case on the fool. And yah, he's a real work of art."

The Interp was the Florence Natural and Wild Rivers Interpretive Center, just outside town. It housed a number of state agency offices, including the local DNR. "Interp in thirty," Grady Service said.

• • •

They met in the parking lot, driver's window to driver's window. "You know where Chern lives?" Service asked.

"Indeed I do. Man, you are *really* going gray."

"And you don't have anything to go gray *with*, dude. What's with Chern and the military and his leg?"

"Not sure I know what you mean."

"There's an old Russian proverb used during the Cold War: Trust but Verify.'"

"That's way before my time, you being so ancient and wise."

"You never pursued his military record?"

"No reason to. Are you going to?"

"Probably."

"Isn't that an insult to all disabled vets?"

"Not to legitimate ones."

"You think he's a sham?"

"I'd like to know. How far away from us is he?"

"Under five miles. He's a mile south of the Brule Island Dam."

"Handy access to the border."

"Your words, not mine."

"Seriously, Kell, this guy feels like an iceberg," Grady Service said.

"Would not surprise any of us."

• • •

There was no ground snow south of the Brule River, which separated Michigan from Wisconsin. Chern lived in a neighborhood of ten prefab houses, a mini subdivision—small lawns, modest landscaping, snowmobiles and other toys, detached garages, middle class, working class, average. *Pick your own descriptor*, Service thought. The tan truck was parked on the grass driveway between the house and garage.

Service opened the rubber trash bin by the garage and peeked inside. Empty and pristine, like it had never been used. Not exactly normal.

Chern took forever to limp to the back door and arrived with his face flushed bright red. He glared at Service. "Don't you guys ever let up?" he lamented.

"We still have some unresolved issues, Chern. And until we get this all cleared up, I want that shoulder mount—the twelve-point."

Service saw the man break a sweat, like a switch had been thrown. "It's here, right?"

"Uh," the man said, and nodded dumbly.

"Remember," Grady Service said, "*You* said *you* shot it *last* year and *you* gave me the photo marked *2007*, and then *you* changed *your* story."

"But I told you that it was an honest mistake, you know, like on accident?"

Hate that phrase. "Which accident, killing that big buck or telling me the wrong year?"

Chern said nothing, and Service bored in tighter. "You've *never* bought a Michigan license, yet there's very clearly a Michigan tag on the antlers in your photo." Service could tell what year it was by color alone. "Is that license still on the mount?"

"No sir, I don't need none, right?"

"I don't know, do you?"

"*My* license," the man insisted, "*my* deer. *Fuck* your computer."

"If that's how this turns out, fine by me. I'll apologize. I know computers aren't perfect, but this will be first time for me that the license records would be wrong. Meanwhile, that mount is leaving with me."

"You make me sound guilty. What happened to presumed innocent?"

"You *are* guilty, and we both know it."

"Sir, I am a disabled veteran and a man of integrity and honor. I don't need to buy a Michigan license."

"What have you been smoking, Chern? Fermented sweat socks? Military personnel on active duty don't have to buy a Michigan license, but you're not *on* active duty. *Are* you?"

"You know I ain't, sir."

"Then you need to buy a license. Can we come in? It's starting to snow out here."

"Do I have to say yes?"

Kelly the Rocket spoke up. "Don't be a dick, Chern. We can have a warrant here in twenty minutes."

The man opened the door and stepped aside.

Service found himself in a small kitchen with a small round wooden table and two chairs. No dishes in the sink; the counters were clear. "Okay if we look around?" Service asked.

"Do I got a choice?" the man asked.

"Sure you do, but like Warden Richelieu just said, your choice to cooperate lasts only until we get a search warrant."

"But you're a Michigan guy, and this is Wisconsin."

"That's right, but we have an agreement with Wisconsin. Your wardens and ours can work both states. We go back and forth across the border."

"That sure don't seem right, sir."

"Take your beef to your legislators. Where's the mount?"

The man pointed disconsolately at another room.

Service nodded Allerdyce in and heard, "Whoa, then. Holy moly!"

Keeping his eyes on Chern, Service asked, "You got a copy of your DD 214?"

The man's eyes went wide. "Why would you want *that*?"

"Call it curiosity."

"Sir, this feels like, you know, an invasion of my privacy, and anyways, my lawyer's got my DD 214."

"Your lawyer?"

"From the suit against the sawbones who fucked up my leg."

"Thought you said you got wounded in Iraq."

"I did, but I didn't like how the government did my leg, so they discharged me. I found a civilian doc, and he *really* fucked it up and I had to sue him."

"I'm sorry to hear that. Is your case still active?"

"No, I won and got a settlement."

"Good one?"

"Could have been better, sir. My lawyer was for shit."

"When did you get this settlement?"

"Oh seven."

"And your lawyer still has the paperwork *and* your DD form?"

"Yes, sir. I never got around to fetching any of it. I didn't have no money for gas."

"But you'd just got a settlement?"

"I know," the man said, hanging his head. "I can't really explain it."

Allerdyce waggled a finger at Service, who joined him in the next room, where there was a four-foot flat-screen TV that took up most of one wall. There was a mounted pheasant, a pair of mounted largemouth bass and a muskie, two mounted turkey fans, a European mount of an antelope skull, the twelve-point, which was gigantic, and five other buck mounts, all large and impressive. A mink was mounted on a birch branch with a brook trout in its mouth. And there was a diamondback rattlesnake poised to strike; it was on an end table with an ashtray for its base. Most people didn't shoot one deer of this quality in a lifetime, much less six, but no sign of last year's thirteen-point. When he'd said he'd shot lots of big bucks, he hadn't lied. The issue now was *where* had he shot them, and when?

"Dandy bucks," Allerdyce said, "but dat minky and brookie is fine ark."

Service blinked and smiled. "Grab the big boy and put him out in the truck."

"Dude," Chern said, his eyes welling with tears.

"Where's last year's thirteen-point, the one you shot here in Wisconsin?"

"Only shoot does down here," Chern said.

"What about all those bucks on the wall?"

"I don't got talk 'bout them. I'm going to tell my attorney I'm being harassed, and I intend to let Fox News and CNN know too."

"We just asked where the deer are from." Service said. "You tend to change your stories a lot."

"That's not true, sir," Chern said.

Grady Service fished his tiny tape recorder out of a pocket and held it out. "Got the truth in your own words right in there. I'll be back," Service said. "While you're at it, get your DD 214 back from your lawyer."

"Yes, sir, I will, sir," Chern said with military crispness.

Outside, KTR said, "That place in there is bone-empty. I looked in cabinets, the fridge; nothing. The guy's got no food."

"Yet he's got money for ammo, mounts, and gas."

"The disease," Kelly the Rocket said. "Terminal hornophilia. Why are you hammering him for his DD 214?"

"The military doesn't release a man until his injuries are fixed to the government's satisfaction, not his satisfaction."

"You think he's lying?"

"I know he is," Service said.

CHAPTER 20

Slippery Creek Camp

SUNDAY, NOVEMBER 15

It was after midnight, and technically already opening day, when they pulled into Service's camp, which lay close to the Mosquito Wilderness. Sunrise would be in less than eight hours, and Service knew they needed sleep. Allerdyce had even nodded off on the drive from Florence.

The only chore now was to set the coffeemaker for morning. The one good thing about the firearm season opener was that you didn't have to race dawn. Unless you had known offenses or specific complaint situations that needed to be addressed immediately, it was preferable to let hunters enjoy their hunting experience without interruption. Tomorrow's weather forecast was for twenty-five and an inch of snow, not bad. Hunters would easily be able to sit in their blinds in some comfort all day, and some of the good ones would do just that, while bad ones, incompetents and cheats, would get impatient and start rambling and road-hunting.

Service heard a chirping sound, his phone announcing a text message, the latest in a seemingly unending technological irritant. His hands weren't made for pecking on pellet-size keys. The message he read blasted sleep right out of him. "Fire tonight in garage. Arson probably. We're okay. Three deer carcasses left out front. Again, repeat, we are okay. You're not picking up your phone. Repeat. We are okay, Shigun, me, the animals, all of us."

"Let's go," Service told Allerdyce, who chuffed for the truck without a word.

• • •

The garage was gone, reduced to a smoking black pile in the snow. Service looked at the three dead deer, killed today, backstraps removed. One was dumped by the garage, one on the sidewalk to the house, and one next to the back porch steps.

"We were asleep," Friday told him, holding him tight. "I heard some noise, you know like something that didn't quite fit, so I got up, looked outside; saw flames, grabbed Shigun, stuffed him into this snowsuit, and ran to the neighbors. I called 911 on the way. The fire guys were here in seven minutes, but it was too late."

"What time?"

"Tenish, I think."

"What about your car?"

"Left it out front, too lazy to put it in the garage. What's this about?" she asked.

"Me," he said. His anger had bled off during the fast drive north. "It's a message."

"Seriously?"

"Am I smiling?"

"What exactly are you being told?"

"I'm not sure yet," though he had a notion. *The deer are like conjunctions, joiners. If you kept up with something, your house was going to be next. What the firebug is referring to was anybody's guess.* "We need to move you and Shigun out to the camp."

"It's too far, Grady. We can stay with my sister."

Her sister was the boy's normal caregiver and lived near Skandia, south of Marquette, an easy shot to town.

The fire-moppers were still working. Service talked to the chief, who looked twenty and had the voice of an eleven-year-old. "Point of origin is the front door, east side. Some sort of flammable and an accelerant, nothing fancy. Set it quick, ignite it quick, and split. How many burnables were inside?"

"I cleaned out the chemicals and old paint cans last August."

"Good thing you did," the kid said. "Mighta gone off like a bomb, spit shrapnel and fire all over the neighborhood."

Service felt his legs start to turn to rubber. Friday had bugged him for a year to clean the garage, and he had finally gotten to it. The house was old, built just after World War II, the garage somewhat newer, but not by much. There had been multiple owners, most of whom left stuff behind when they moved on.

Allerdyce said, "Easy target, so close ta udder places, hey. Pipples don't notice somebody don't stop long. Out to camp dey got worry 'bout movement gizzies, trail cameras, some guys inside wit' rifles. You got all kinds open space your place too."

Not an accident, Service knew. He was a firm believer in clear fields of fire. Just in case. Provide as little cover as possible to wannabe intruders. Make it tough, not easy.

"This ever happened to you before?" Friday asked.

"Not to me."

"Did you fellas piss off someone today?"

"I'm always pissing people off," Grady Service said. "It's what COs do. Just leaving the house and driving down a two-track pisses off some idiots." He tried to play through the last few days and the players. His gut said Bojan Knezevich seemed unlikely. *Dinty Peaveyhouse? Possibly, but I don't know much about the man yet. He has the temper, that's for sure. Pie lady Arletta Ingalls? She seems the most unstable of all of them. Not Chernobyl. That's too recent, and he has an alibi. He was with us. This sick little deal required foreknowledge, and some nasty intent.*

The whole area reeked of smoke. "Limpy and I will follow you guys out to your sister's."

"You think we should plan to stay out there for a while?"

"At least for a few days. It's more private out there, lit better at night."

"I do *not* like this at all," Tuesday Friday declared in her steely cop voice.

"I know," he said. "But nobody's hurt, and that's all that's important at this point."

"When you find who did this, please don't kill him," Friday said.

"I'm a professional," Grady Service said.

"With a very large reservoir of testosterone," she whispered.

Two deps showed up, having canvassed the neighborhood, talking to all they could get to answer their doors. Nobody had seen anything.

Has to be evidence somewhere, Service told himself. *Somewhere. Has to be.*

"You see a signature in this?" Service asked Allerdyce.

"Mebbe. Got t'ink back. Dis make me t'ink old school."

"Explain."

"I'm 'memberin' east side over Hulbert, MickeyMillan, Seney. Back in da day youse hear game warden gone sniff around, youse send him message, leave me 'lone—or else."

"Preemptive warning—before the game warden gets involved in something, not after he's stirred the hornet's nest?"

"Yep, dat pimptive t'ing youse say. Way I 'member t'ings to back den."

"*You* ever do that?"

"Never had to," Allerdyce said.

"Seems way over the top to me," Grady Service said. "What's your take on the message?"

"Guy says what he gone do wit deer ain't none of youse's bus'ness. Youse keep gettin' in 'is way, he torch youse's house."

"But not somebody I've dealt with, is that what you're saying?"

"Only point dis deal is make youse stay away."

"How the hell am I supposed to predict the future?"

"Use youse's cripple ball."

Grady Service had no comeback for that.

• • •

They did not get back to Slippery Creek Camp until almost four in the morning, and both went to sleep in chairs. Grady Service awoke at 9 a.m. to the smell of coffee brewing.

Allerdyce mumbled, "Got 'er all ready. Youse want porshwid sinman?"

"What the hell is porsh?"

"S'like goatmeal and sinman; keep blood sugar down."

"That's your learned medical opinion?"

"What my mum always say back in da day. Sinman fight sweet bloods."

"Your mother was a doctor?"

"Wah. She was me mum. But she live ninety-five."

"And you loved her."

Allerdyce snickered. "Nasty old bitch. Hated 'er guts, but she know what she talk 'bout. What we gone do dis morn?"

"Stoke up on sinman-porsh and coffee, then go ruin the days of some bad guys."

Allerdyce cackled. "I usta be one dem pipples, eh."

"So you claim," Service said. *Who the hell is trying to warn me off? And of what, one of the camp owners I met with?*

"Youse got stubborn streak, Sonny, like youse's old man."

"That's a bad thing?"

"Nope; is all good."

ACT 2: UNDER WAY

Today you are you. That is truer than true. There is no one alive who is you-er than you.

—Dr. Seuss, *Happy Birthday to You*

CHAPTER 21

Near Watson, Marquette County

MONDAY, NOVEMBER 16

Opening day had been a zero. And it had been excruciating getting himself going this morning. Allerdyce made eggs and coffee and filled their two thermoses. No need to talk. Service wondered momentarily what lay ahead but quickly turned off his imagination. Yesterday had been a total bust. Maybe he'd had his shot before it all began. No sense pondering. It would be what it would be. No two deer seasons were ever the same, and this one was already in a class all alone, despite yesterday. The severity and incidence of law breaking varied from year to year, but stupidity and greed ran consistently high. This year both counts seemed severely elevated. Okay, some of it was stupidity and some was sheer ignorance, which you could forgive in a kid, but not in a twenty-something, and even less in a sixty-something.

They rolled slowly, got onto a two-track just over the Delta and Marquette County lines, southwest of Watson, the two-track west of County Road SC, an area Service called the Ford River Swamp. "Ever work this turf?" he asked Allerdyce, who shook his head.

Another inch of snow had fallen last night, and there was one set of tracks going down an old skid road. The tracks didn't penetrate far. He could see multiple stops, backups, pull-forwards, like those in the vehicle were looking at or for something. *For what?*

"You see any animal tracks out your side?"

"Not yet," Allerdyce said, and as quickly, "Over dere."

Service saw it too, a new model, gold Chevy pickup parked off the road. There was a camo popup blind, conspicuously set up on a four-foot rise, not thirty yards from the truck. The truck looked brand new. They got out, looked inside it, and saw a rifle case in the backseat. Even that looked new. Box of .308 ammo on the floor. Remington. The truck had Illinois plates.

"Might be good place bag some trucks," Allerdyce said. "You ever eat truck, Sonny?"

Service ignored his suddenly chatty partner. One set of boot tracks led directly from the truck to the pop-up blind. He checked his watch. A little after ten. He walked up to the back of the blind. "Hey, you inside the pop-up, conservation officer, DNR. Let's talk."

He heard a zipper, and a man in a full blaze orange insulated jumpsuit emerged. The color was so bright it hurt the eyes. Like an electric pumpkin.

"Any luck?" he asked the man.

"Not so far."

"You alone?"

"No, my brother-in-law is up the road."

"Your blind looks new."

"New everything," the man said. "The wives told us we needed to take up some manly hobbies. What's more manly than hunting deer?"

"You've hunted deer before?"

"I never hunted *anything* before, except the wife maybe."

"Your brother-in-law got experience?"

"Tommy? No, this is his first time too."

"Rifles sighted in?"

"Come again?"

"Have you and Tommy shot your rifles to make sure the sights line up on what you're aiming at?"

"I thought the manufacturer done that. They sure soak you enough."

Service explained, "Every firearm shoots a little differently. You have to shoot them in order to figure out if adjustments are needed in the weapon, and/or your technique."

"Ruskelt's Sports never mentioned none of that."

"Can I see your rifle?"

"Sure."

The man went back into his blind and came back out pointing the barrel at Service, who stepped aside, adroitly pushing the barrel away. He started to gently chastise the man when the silence was shattered by a shot that left his ears ringing. "Safety!" he screamed at the man, and quickly realized he had lost control of himself and was screaming at the fool.

The man looked crestfallen and afraid. "The w-w-what?"

Service took the rifle and activated the safety. "When this is 'on,' the rifle can't be fired. It's black, and means it's safe to handle. When it's 'off,' it will be red, and that tells you it's dangerous and ready to shoot. Always assume a gun is loaded, and check the safety frequently."

"Boy, that was *loud*," the man said. "Is it always *that* loud?"

The hunter was trying to act calm, but Service saw the man's skin had taken on the hue of ash.

Doofus. "Let me see your Michigan hunting license and your driver's license please."

The man unzipped his orange jumpsuit, which had at least a dozen visible zippers, and fished out a baggie containing several documents. He held the package out to Service.

"Please take them out of the bag and hand them to me."

"Okay."

Service's heart kept racing. Just like that, one damn millisecond of asleep-at-your-switch, and you might've taken a bullet in the guts, accidentally, the whole thing pure innocence. He held his elbow against his side to hide how badly his hand was shaking.

He read the Illinois operator's license. "Lewallyn Lewallyn Lewallyn, MD?"

The man said sheepishly. "I know, the name's peculiar. People call me Lew Lew-Lew."

"Date of birth?" Service asked.

"November 16, 1934."

"Today's your birthday." The guy was seventy-five and didn't look it. "What kind of doctor?"

"General surgeon."

"You almost shot me, Doctor. You have to keep the safety engaged until just before you're ready to shoot. Did you read the manual?"

"All that technical mumbo jumbo, who can read that gibberish?"

Service knew a congressman, a former surgeon, who claimed that all doctors were scientists and trained to evaluate complex technological and scientific issues. All but this septuagenarian, apparently. "I thought doctors were trained in mumbo jumbo."

"Our own, sure; other crap, no way," the man said.

"Have you ever killed anything, Doctor?"

"Only the occasional patient," the man said with a smirk. "On accident, my grandkids would say."

The rifle was a Blaser RB Jaeger in .308 caliber—a rare, expensive weapon, a serious hunter's tool, four or five grand a pop. "This is a beautiful rifle, but the trigger's set for 1.5 pounds per pull."

"Is that a little or a lot?"

"Ever hear the term 'hair trigger'?"

"Sure, everybody's heard it. From the movies."

"This has one."

"Geez, no wonder it went off so easy. My ears still hurt."

Damn fool. "Why is your blind set here?"

"To shoot a deer."

"This is a less-than-ideal location. You need to be farther from your truck and the road."

"Nobody told us."

It was common sense, but he held this back. Service leaned over and looked into the blind, saw a *DeLorme: Michigan Atlas & Gazetteer* on the floor. "Grab your map book, Doctor."

Even the book was new. The old edition had this spot on page 101. Now it was on page 43. Some bright nerd probably got promoted over the change. "This is a pretty good area, Doctor, but you need to move your blind deeper down to the edge of the swamp." He pointed. "Find a small ridge and set up there. Go a quarter mile or so in."

"Huh," the doctor said quietly. "I think I like it better right here. That damn rifle goes off again, I just may shit my pants."

"This was your wife's idea?"

"Mostly."

"How many days are you and your brother-in-law going to be here?"

"A week, which I realize may now feel like a month."

The guy's seventy-five. How old is his wife, and what's her motive? "Your truck's new too?"

"Everything is new, my first pickup truck ever. Makes my testosterone rise just looking at it. You think the effect will last a week?"

"You're the doctor."

"Not out here I'm not."

He felt sorry for the guy. Money out the wazoo and no clue. "Move your blind that way," he told the man. "For everyone's safety."

"Okay, I can do that. I'm really sorry."

"How far is your brother-in-law?"

"Half mile? I've never been good at measuring large distances. You can see his blind if you squint."

The man was pointing, and sure enough there was an identical blind not two hundred yards away. *God.* "Would you like us to help you to move your blind?"

"Thanks, but I have some self-respect left. I can do it myself. Sorry about the safety glitch."

"Unload your rifle, and reload it after you get the blind set up in the new location."

"I think I can manage that," the doctor said.

Service pulled the bolt to eject the spent round, popped the clip, emptied the weapon, and handed everything to the man.

"Don't mate any of that stuff until you're in your blind and ready to rock and roll."

"I guess. I never really experienced rock and roll," the man confessed. "Went to school most of my life."

Service returned to the Silverado, and Allerdyce was standing by the gold truck. "Got bullet hole in driver door. Nice deer, eh?" he said with his crooked grin. "It got horn in it. That make 'er a buck?"

The brother-in-law insisted he had read all the new product material, knew about the safety, and didn't balk when they told him to move his blind as well. He also never asked about the shot, which surely he had heard. Clueless, his life apparently having shut off some pathways still operating in other folks.

"What so funny?" Limpy asked.

"Life," Grady Service said.

"I hear dat loud and clear," the old violator said. "Dose two back dere goofy in heads."

Service thought, *Thus continues the 2009 deer season; poachers, poachers everywhere and damn fool green horns shoed in between them. Geez.*

They drove west, intending to loop south and east across northeastern Menominee County; but plans of game wardens, like plans of soldiers in war, tended to melt under the first shot fired with intent.

What asshole burned Friday's garage? It was one thing to have a hard-on for a game warden, but you knew to leave his family alone. That was the unwritten rule in the stupid game.

"Youse know Coppish?" Allerdyce asked.

"Knew him. He died, right?"

"Nah, he still suckin' air. Got camp south fum Arnold."

"Think we should give him a visit?"

"Wunt hurt."

Teddy Coppish had been a serial arsonist, targeting forests rather than people and their homes. He was the scourge of Delta and Menominee Counties for almost ten years. A nice enough guy, even normal, until the urge to make fire overcame him. "You can find his camp?"

"Wah," Allerdyce said.

Service took this to be a yes. *What the hell am I doing with Limpy Allerdyce?* The unanswerable Zen koans posed by philosophers and the like. "You can hear the sound of two hands when they clap together," the master said. "Now show me the sound of one hand. Or, what is the sound of one hand clapping?" He found himself grinning, looked over, and saw Limpy grinning. The mirror image gave him the chills.

CHAPTER 22

South of Arnold, Marquette County

MONDAY, NOVEMBER 16

The camp gate was wide open and a narrow lane cut through mature white cedars, the roadbed solid, the drive in to it almost a half mile long. Not cheap to install, even if you did most of the work yourself. The camp building was made of stripped logs and real chinking, not the plastic crap. There was bright green moss and a lot of it on ancient roof shingles. Service guessed this place had begun as a trapper's shack and had grown over time into something more substantial.

Teddy Coppish was outside and seemed to be waiting for them. Electronic motion detectors at the gate? Seems like trail cameras and other electronic devices were ubiquitous these days, and a lot of camp owners fortified their places like they were Fort Knox.

There was neither hand-shaking nor venom in the greeting from the arsonist. "Got coffee, boys. Want anything stronger, you'll have to go elsewhere." There was nothing personal in this invitation. It was merely an unwritten camp law to offer hospitality to visitors, even your enemies.

"No thanks. We had plenty this morning."

"Hear mebbe youse had fire dog recent-like," the man said, catching Service off-guard. *How did he find out so quickly?*

"Last night. Where'd you hear that?"

"Linsenman, he stop by, tell me story."

Weasel Linsenman?

Coppish added. "He don't live too far up road, stops by make sure I take my pills and meds."

"Dey got pills for fireomaniacs?" Allerdyce asked.

"Got pills for all kinds nutcases," Teddy Coppish said. "Prob'ly got pills help da likes of you too, old man."

"Me? I speck I don't need no pills."

"Service keeping you close like 'is pet Chihuahua, makin' sure you don't nip nobody's ankle?"

Allerdyce smiled.

It was like two old gunfighters working themselves toward a confrontation, or boxers trash-talking at the official weigh-in. "Linsenman told you about the fire?"

"Yah, just garage," he said. "Din't catch to house."

"Does that suggest anything to you, Teddy?"

The man ran a leathery hand through long white hair. "I ain't no coracle."

Allerdyce piped up. "Coracle is boat, you old firebug. You mean oracle, like da one out Phillydelp."

Oh, God. "Teddy, how do you read what happened?"

"Got nuttin' do wit' da likes of me, Service. It youse got da problem, I'd say."

"You think it's a warn-off?"

"Yah, prolly," Coppish said, nodding slightly.

"What else could it be?"

Coppish shrugged dramatically.

"How come youse not in youse's blind?" Allerdyce asked. "Season on, eh."

"Already got my buck."

"Mind if we take a look?" Service asked. This was standard operating procedure.

"Youse wunt be in here, gate not up."

"But it was and is up, and we just come in to say howdy, and here we are. Where's your buck?"

"I hung it. Got friend coming over, help me cut up."

"Lead the way."

The buck pole was fifty yards from the camp building, tucked back down a lane where it couldn't be seen unless you walked up to it. This was typical of old camps, whose owners were extremely secretive and many of them long-time violators. As they walked, Service saw what he knew was faded whitewash on trees back in the swamp, the whitewash up nearly six feet to provide a light background for a shooting silhouette at night. It was an old night violator's trick. It looked old, not of recent vintage.

Teddy Coppish stood mute.

Service checked the buck, a nice little seven-point rack, the tag on a string tied to an antler. There was a ladder against a nearby tree. Service looked at blood spots on the ground. There wasn't much. He put the ladder against the buck pole, climbed up, and looked at the tag. "When did you shoot it, Teddy?"

"First light, eh."

"Which day?"

"Opener."

"Tag's not validated, nothing's notched. You wouldn't be thinking of using the tag again."

"Tag's on the animal," the man came back.

"But it's not validated. That's a violation."

"I didn't break no law."

Service looked down. "Teddy, this animal's eyes are clear. You know the eyes film over in twenty-four hours and stay that way. This animal was killed today. Where's your blind?"

"Which one? I got ten out here."

"The one where this buck was shot."

Coppish waved his hand. "Back dere, eh, way da hull out by crick."

"Which crick?"

"Ellie."

"Let's go take us a look."

"She's long hike back dere."

"I like hiking. Humor me."

"I ain't got to. You hasslin' me."

"I'm just doing my job, and besides, what're you doing hunting? You're a felon and can't have firearms."

"I ain't hunting."

"There's no name on this tag."

"Did I say was my deer? Sorry dat. Mistake okay? Not mine, eh. Belongs friend. Shot it dis morning wit 'is crossbow."

"You told us *you* got a buck."

"I buy licenses, help state out is all. I don't actual hunt."

Service climbed down and activated his radio. "Twenty on RAP Two, Twenty-Five Fourteen. I'm at a camp south of Arnold. Run RSS for me?"

"Twenty ready to copy."

Service rattled off the numbers and watched the old arsonist nervously shifting his weight from boot to boot.

"Twenty-Five Fourteen, that number comes back to a male, Penfold Pymn. You want the spelling?"

"Negative; thanks Twenty. Twenty-Five Fourteen clear." *Pymn again? Geez.*

"What all dat jabber?" Coppish asked.

"It's not your license."

"But I got one."

"Not the one on the buck, you don't. You shot that animal for someone else."

"Nuh-uh; I jest go fetch for pal shot it."

"Penn Pymn."

"Don't know nobody by dat name."

"Who's the friend you dragged the deer for?"

"Jess somebody I let hunt proppity."

"Name of that somebody?"

"Never ast."

"You let somebody whose name you don't know hunt your land?"

"Not illegal do dat."

"Why didn't the hunter validate the tag when he shot the animal?"

"Was tagged. You *seen* antler."

This was going nowhere, the usual lies and dissimulation of hunters in the wrong. They'd wiggle like snakes with lie upon lie, hoping you'd miss something or get too tired to go on.

Service's radio activated with a burst of low sound. "Sonny, dis youse's partner on radio. Got gal in truck jes pull into camp."

"Does she see our truck?"

"Not yet."

"Good, don't let her leave; I'm on the way."

The CO sprinted back to camp, leaving Coppish far behind him. He turned the corner and came face to face with Arletta Ingalls.

"Hope you don't have that stud in your tongue, because we need to talk plain."

"You," she said. "*Again.* This is *harassment,* clear and simple."

Service held up the tag that had been on the deer. "This comes back to Pymn. It's hanging on an illegal buck."

"That so?"

"You want to see?"

"No sweat off my back what Pymn does. He's a grown man. Grown, yet not the brightest bulb."

Service held out the tag. "Pymn's, his second of the season, not validated."

"Men," she said, holding open her hands. "Can't never tell what a man will do in hunting season. Something in the genes and gender."

"That's how you're going to play this game?"

"It's Pymn's problem, not mine."

"Might've been you who was here."

"Not me. I ain't seen Pymn in days."

Interesting: Throwing her boyfriend under the wheels of the law truck. She is one nasty piece of work.

"When you see Pymn, tell him we'll be dropping by."

"Tell him yourself. I kicked his ass out. I need classy men in my life."

"Like Teddy?"

Service was pretty sure she had shot the deer, but not the how and why. And seeing her with Coppish told him she might well have been the one to set the fire at Friday's.

"Hey, girlie," Allerdyce cooed at her.

"Sick puppy," she said with a hiss.

"Reglar wildcat," Limpy said. "I like dis girlie."

"Fuck you, old man."

"Wah!" Allerdyce said. "I gone soap-out dat dirt-mout' youse betcha."

Service grasped the old man's shoulder to steady him. "Tell Pymn we're looking for him," Service told the woman as she walked to her truck, got in, and drove away. But she lifted both hands and flashed two birds as she raced back down the driveway.

"Dat one look like fun," Allerdyce said.

The arsonist reluctantly led them to the hunting blind, a ten-foot ladder onto a platform over some deer runs in the swamp. It took Service only five minutes to find boot prints matching Arletta Ingalls's size. No larger prints, just the small ones. They were at the base of the ladder.

"Where'd the deer go down?" he asked Coppish.

"Out dat way," the man said, pointing.

"Show me." There was a gut pile and hair. The prints fit Coppish's boots, not the woman's. He took more photos.

To Coppish, "She shot the buck, not Pymn. She killed it, and you fetched it. What did she give you so she could hunt here?"

"I got nothing to say."

"You like pie, Teddy?" Service asked with a straight face. "You might want to remember that sometimes the fucking you get ain't worth the fucking you get, savvy?"

Why did Allerdyce bring me here? He has to have a reason. The old man does nothing by chance.

Service looked at the firebug. "If I find out you're teachin' that woman how to torch, you're going back inside."

"I'm calling my lawyer."

"Do that."

Back in the truck and out on a county road, Service said, "What was that all about?"

"Heard on the drums Teddy datin' wild woman wit' mean streak. Jes wanted see her."

Service wondered if this was all of it, but there was no way Limpy could have known about the big buck and all of that. Was there?

CHAPTER 23

North of Helps, Menominee County

MONDAY, NOVEMBER 16

Harry Pattinson's camp was north of Helps, off an unnamed, unnumbered road. Allerdyce was clearly enjoying himself. Maybe too much. "Kinda blind luck we were with Teddy when we were."

"Guess so. Want coffee?"

"Sure. You and Coppish don't seem too fond of each other."

"All firebugs are shit bags, but not all shit bags are firebugs. Firebug shit bags, dey a mean lot dey are."

"Why'd you point me there?"

"Want catch one firefly, got talk 'nother firefly."

Solid logic. "We never really got to that point of discussion."

"Said he hear 'bout fire from da Weasel."

"Your point?"

"He heard from da Weasel, doubt he talk udder firebug."

"That's your carefully considered professional opinion?"

"Wah." Allerdyce said, grinned, and stared forward.

They were passing a house with a yard with no snow. Three blue jays were dancing on the grass fighting over some tiny morsel. "Dose guys, dey winter 'ere, dey dead," Allerdyce offered. "Nature, she a hard bitch. Stupid birds outten've gone south."

"Why Coppish?"

"I just tole youse, din't I?"

"I'm not buying your smoke."

"Really, Sonny. Dose firebugs all know each udder, watch each udder's work. Sick fucks."

Change directions. "The fire marshal didn't find anything special in the remains."

"Uh," Allerdyce said, and changed direction. "Youse know dat Arletta gal?"

"Took a big buck from her on the thirteenth. There all night. That's the same morning you found me. You know her?"

"Doggy queen, give a lot of money to one of them rescue outfits down Menominee."

"You know about *that*?" Typical Allerdyce, wired into everything. How and why were separate issues.

"I hear some t'ings mebbe."

"Some things, like *what*?"

"Mebbe selling racks, raise cash for dogs and stuff."

"She kills deer for dogs?" Service said.

"Smart girlie," Allerdyce said. "Looks pretty good too, eh."

"Don't even go there."

"Go where I want in my head. No guvmint in dere tell me what t'ink. Not yet."

Selling mounts for cash for an animal rescue joint? If true, this would be a first; and after so many years, firsts didn't come along all that often. "Know somebody I could talk to? Somebody reliable? I need more than hearsay."

"Might could fix dat. Where we go now?"

"Harry Pattinson's camp."

"We got complaint t'ing?"

Allerdyce's pronunciation came out more like cunt-plane. The old violator and simple king's English were sometimes on very separate tracks. "No, I just want to check in, see what sort of luck they're having, what they're seeing. We'll fly the flag for the DNR." This was bullshit; Allerdyce no doubt knew it.

"Dis hull country down dis way usta have some dandy bucks."

"Use to?"

"Not no more, I hear."

"Wolves?"

"Dunno."

"*You* ever work this area?"

"Way back, some. Youse's ol' man and me worked over dis way, time to time."

Allerdyce insisted he had ridden along with Service's father, but it was a hard thing to swallow. And while he did remember Limpy showing up with the old man once in a while, he couldn't remember any sort of what he'd call a relationship. *Mostly they got drunk together, but the old man got drunk with a lot of different people and was known to hit the sauce even while he was on duty. Even so, it never seemed to affect his performance. He had a sixth sense and maybe a seventh too. How good would he have been without alcohol? Stupid question. Runway behind you, not worth a thought. He was what he was. Now he's dead.*

"Pattinson's a straight shooter?" Service asked his passenger.

"Never heard he weren't. Got big yap sometimes."

• • •

The nine hunters at Pattinson's camp were unshaven, as morose a crowd as Service had ever encountered. "Any luck?" he asked when Harry showed them into the main cabin's great room.

"Ain't shot each other yet," one of the crew proclaimed.

"Ain't shot at nothing," this from another man.

"I seen me a gray jay," someone offered, "and a weasel. But no damn deer. Not even no tracks."

Harry Pattinson said, "It's the wolves, Grady."

Service asked, "Anybody see a wolf on or near their bait today or yesterday?"

Head shakes all around. "*Any* fresh wolf sign, scat, tracks, anything?"

Same reaction, which was either the truth or they had rehearsed for such questions. Wolf shooters usually tried to have a leak-proof story to tell.

"No sightings and no sign, how can it be wolves?" he asked them.

"What else *could* it be?" Pattinson asked.

"How about violators?"

"Bullshit, Grady. We take care of trespassers; don't usually need to call it inta you fellas, neither."

"Just a thought," Service said. "Take care of them *how*?"

"Let's just say we don't give 'em no tea and crumpets." The others all smiled and looked smug.

"Do you take names and ID?"

"Why do that?" Pattinson came back. "We give them a direct message, and they never come near here again."

"You mean you don't catch them when they come back."

Pattinson said quickly, "We know this ground like the insides of our houses."

Service looked at all the deer mounts on the walls, as good a collection as he'd ever seen in a U.P. camp. Even Limpy was gawking.

"Listen, Harry, you and your folks know you've gotta leave the wolves alone."

"We've got the right to defend ourselves," one of the hunters said.

"Yes, you do," Service said. "But this is not a war."

"Your opinion," someone said.

Service maintained eye contact with Pattinson. "True," he said, "but with all the talk around here about smoking wolves and such shit to bring back the deer herd, it's gonna take one hell of a story and supporting forensics to convince the law."

"You mean *you*," Pattinson said.

"That's right. I mean me."

"Who you been talking to?"

"Take a deep breath and think this thing through, Harry. You and your pals have what, seven, eight camps out this way? You've got people hunting just this one property. How many more in all the other locations? If all those guys get a hard-on for wolves, you think you can stop such momentum?"

"DNR's like KGB," someone said.

"The KGB doesn't exist anymore," Service said. "But *we're* still here. Leave the damn wolves be, boys."

Pattinson said, "They don't threaten us, they've got nothing to worry about from my boys."

Said Service, "Wolves never worry, Harry. We game wardens do that for them."

"I don't like how some of your people operate," Pattinson said, fumbling to light a pipe.

"That cuts two ways." Service looked around. "Nice camp, Harry. Thanks for inviting us in."

"Knew that scumbag was with you, I wunta," the businessman complained and scowled at Limpy.

"You've got a fan club," Service told his partner when they were back in the truck.

"Ain't 'at somepin," Limpy said.

It seemed the old man was pleased about something. "Big wolf numbers over this way?" he asked the violator.

"Not for few years. Ast youse's wuff man."

Service drove until he got a cell phone signal, pulled over, and called Zander Hecla at the Marquette regional DNR office. Hecla was the biologist now directing the wolf recovery program. He led a team that did annual surveys to estimate the number of animals and packs in the state. Everyone called him Lobo or Z-Man.

"Z-man, Service."

"So far so good," the wolf expert said. "No wolves yet reported shot."

"Menominee, Marquette, Dickinson border corner. What sort of wolf population there?"

Service heard papers rattling. "Steadily down over the past five counts, steep drop the past two."

"Particular reason?"

"The usual refrain: not enough deer. The wolves have been moving over to farm country in Northwest Delta, and numbers are up over that way, down where you're asking about."

"Thanks."

"Not a problem, Grady."

Service looked at his passenger. "Wolf numbers are down over five winter counts here, steep drop the past two."

Allerdyce said, "Somepin killin' deers. Got plenty food for deers here, so how's come no deers?"

The old man had a point, but how could they find the cause quickly and prevent a small war on wolves? "Any of your competitors working this turf these days?"

"Not no Allerdyces. My famblee outten da biz."

"Other violets?"

"Nah, dey all gettin' too long in toots or already in ground feedin' wormies."

"Could be some new talent," Service ventured.

"Yah, could be," the old man said. "More money in deers dese days den ever before. New talent wunt s'prise me none."

"How far back to when the deer population was still pretty good around here?"

"Ten years, mebbe, give or bake."

Service snickered.

"Wah," Allerdyce said. "What I say?"

"You'd think if a crew was seriously working this corner, word would be out."

"Would t'ink dat, but dere ain't nuttin I been hearin'."

Conclusion, a very preliminary one: Deer numbers way down, big buck numbers down, wolf numbers down, old poachers probably not in the picture. This might very well be the work of a new player, someone good enough to operate off all radars. Or was it something else entirely?

Service called Pattinson on his cell phone. "Sorry to bother you again, Harry. Which numbers are down, deer in general, all bucks, or real big bucks?"

"It's all deer—all sexes, ages, the whole lot of them, goddammit all."

Market hunters killed everything with meat, size totally irrelevant. Long time since he'd seen honest-to-god market shooters. This was the sort of problem he liked. Something not obvious, something only suggested, a ghost problem.

He asked Limpy, "Any good way to get a bead on a new operator around here?"

Allerdyce looked over at him. "Work alone, never talk nobody, process own meat, mount own racks, don't enter no stupid big buck contests, do t'ings dis way, nobody never know. Like dey say, silence is like night-guy's partner. Closed loop is way p'ofessionals do it. No way any outsider can get in on youse, 'ceptin' blind-ass luck."

Allerdyce was no doubt right about the best poachers' methods, but there was always a way in. He kept this thought to himself. Solo operators were virtually impossible to get to. Look at the Croatian, Knezevich. Pure luck, curiosity, and the red truck had busted his gig. Maybe Rosie could help in some way here, need to think more on this. There's no point in deploying a drone until there's a reasonable target and reasonable probable cause.

"Don't t'ink so much," Limpy said. "Hurts da headquarters." The old man looked at him and grinned.

CHAPTER 24

La Branche, Menominee County

MONDAY, NOVEMBER 16

Arletta Ingalls met them at the end of her driveway. She wore a dark apron spackled with flour or some kind of powder, and she was holding a shotgun. "Stay off my property!" she said with a menacing growl.

"We're here to see Pymn," Grady Service told the woman.

"He's gone, cleared out. I told you I threw his sorry ass out."

"Where'd he go, any idea?"

"To Hell for all I care. That man ain't no man at all, can't hold up his end of nothing."

"His end to what?"

"Anything," she repeated. "Are you thick? You people come back here again, you'd better have a warrant."

"If any more suspicious fires happen, we won't need a warrant," Service told her, staring her down. "All the proceeds from your pies go to Keep Our Pets Alive?"

"I don't have to talk without my lawyer present."

"It's a simple question, yes or no?"

"Less expenses, yes."

"Exactly what percentage actually makes its way to the rescue operation?"

"Get a subpoena, look at the records yourself. We do real good for everybody." There was pride in her voice and stance.

"On pies alone?" Service said, letting his words settle, and backed up.

The woman reacted with a strange muted grunt sound, like she swallowed a scream.

"Like lady moose callin' for 'er bull stick," Allerdyce said phlegmatically. "What we do next?"

"See Mario Novello."

Allerdyce said, "Good youse clear dat up for me. He hang up 'is stuff, what, seventeen years back?"

Probably that. The old violator noted every tiny change in and about his environment. Exactitude mattered for a poacher. A retired game warden meant new blood and an unknown for a violator, a potential sea change. Allerdyce had been top dog in the business so long because he paid attention to everything. It was astonishing to think how much he could learn from the old man, if Limpy was willing to share.

CHAPTER 25

Kingsford, Dickinson County

TUESDAY, NOVEMBER 17

The retired CO's first question: "How many did you stroke today?" *Stroke* was jargon for a ticket.

"None."

"Jaysus, it's the damn firearm season, son. Man don't get 'im dozen a day, he ain't earnin' his pay."

"It's not the same game these days, Mario. The job's changed."

"Glad I'm retired. People ain't changed."

"They have, and by a lot. Like everything," Service told the retired officer. "I came to talk about Noble Chern. I took a big rack from his place."

"You make 'im cry?"

"He wasn't happy about it. Tell me what you've heard about him, every little detail."

"Ex-Army, runs mostly alone. His truck been seen in border counties from Menominee up to Gogebic. Skinny says he cruises around in daylight, shoots anything he comes across."

"I found him sitting."

"Yah, they say he stakes out big bucks."

"When exactly did you first hear about him?"

"Five years back, maybe four; I don't really remember."

"Did you tell del Olmo and Grinda about the man?"

"This guy ain't no job for those pups."

"Mario, they're experienced officers, not pups."

"I don't like neither one."

"You're wrong about them."

"Been wrong before. Goes with bein' alive."

"How'd you first hear about Chern, Wisconsin wardens?"

"Landowners up here grousing. Damn guy likes to hunt open fields in broad daylight."

"He's got a bum leg," Service pointed out.

"That's why he only shoots trophies close to the road. Can't get to 'em if they're too far out. He whacked a big bear right off a road. Other hunters chased him, got the bear, and turned it in at the Crystal Falls office."

"How'd they know it was Chern?"

"They didn't. They saw a truck but didn't get a plate. The description matched the truck the landowners had been describing."

"When was this?"

"Two Septembers back. Big bear, skull green scored 20, which puts it way high on the Michigan list. Five thirty dressed weight."

"This bear was shot near Crystal?"

"No, was in a cornfield over near Iron River."

"What happened to the carcass?"

"Went to evidence storage, I guess."

"Who caught the case?"

"Don't remember. Prolly them snot-noses." He'd have to talk to del Olmo and Grinda about this, but it fit Chern's way of doing things.

"You talked about some people named Hill the other day, Fat Henny?"

"Randville, Smith Lane, double-wide house trailer on King's Creek; you can't miss the stench." Novello smiled, didn't elaborate.

"Elder or junior?"

"Scumbags da bot' a dem. Elder's late eighties, on oxygen, all sorts of health issues. Junior's in his fifties and not much better off than the old man, I heard."

"Violators?"

"Mostly fuckups, kind never gets away with nothing."

"You busted them?"

"Both, too many times to count. Too stupid for words, easily swayed and led astray. They mixed up with Chern?"

"Chern told me that a friend named Hill took the photo I showed you."

Service stepped outside and activated his radio. "Twenty, Twenty-Five Fourteen on RAP Two; run a file?"

"You're in line sir."

"I'll wait, Twenty-Five Fourteen."

He listened to the babble of officers around the state calling for information on citizens and situations; this was the time of year when the force of green and gray was in full gear. Eventually his turn came. "Looking for any and all DNR licenses, last five years, and DNR priors for two subjects." He passed the names to Lansing. "Elder is approximately eighty, junior in his fifties, both at an address of Smith Lane, Randville, Dickinson County."

Two minutes passed. "Twenty-Five Fourteen, Twenty. We have a Henry R. Hill, born 1922, and a Henry R. Hill Jr., same address, YOB 1943. Elder has no current licenses, and an arm's length of priors, both hunting and fishing violations. You want them all?"

"Negative on that. What about Junior?"

"He has three priors, two for no-orange and one for loaded firearm in vehicle."

"Twenty, can you cross-reference with RSS sales and see if there is a vehicle ID? This will probably be for the younger?"

"On it; Twenty clear."

Five more minutes ticked by. "Twenty-Five Fourteen, Michigan shows blank, but we have a 1999 Toyota truck for Mr. Hill Jr. with Wisconsin plates."

The dispatcher gave him the plate numbers, and he wrote them in his notebook. This dispatcher was top-notch and seemed to understand that a lot of Michigan people in the western U.P. cheated by registering their vehicles in Wisconsin to get lower rates. It was an old scam neither state had ever attempted to do anything about.

"Great job, Twenty. Fourteen clear."

He called Sheena Grinda. "You guys get a green score 20 bear a couple years back, one somebody tried to whack from a cornfield over by Iron River?"

"It's in the evidence freezer at the office. Typical story. Vague truck description, no plate, and it got brought in six hours after the events. Simon tried to run with it, but it led nowhere. Why?"

"I may have a lead on it."

"Novello your source?" she said, "and his phantom road shooter from Wisconsin?"

"Yah."

"It's bullshit, Grady. Simon thinks it was dumped by a sometime guide townies call 'Storebought,' actual name Rance Melk. Real piece of work. Drives an old puke-green Willys."

"That's what the complainants reported, green Willys?"

"That's right, but Mario has been running off his mouth about another color and make truck that fits stories he hears from landowners. They're not the same."

"Why would he do that?"

"Grady, that man goes out of his way to make us look bad every chance he gets."

He went back inside. "Junior is sixty-six."

Novello grinned. "Time flies."

"Does Junior work?"

"Didn't when I knew 'im. He and his old man were on full medical disabilities and sucking off the system."

"Fighters or resisters?"

Novello laughed. "Fight? Hell no. Coupla fat-ass *blobs*." He shook his head vigorously.

"The vehicle description on the bear shooter—Chern's truck, or an old green Willys?"

The old game warden grinned slyly. "Now youse mention it, mebbe was Willys."

"Chern doesn't drive a Willys. That rules him out."

"Speck, but worth a try to hammer him with everything you got open. That's the way it was done in the day."

"We aren't in the day, Mario. That time's gone. We do things by the book."

"Glad I ain't part of it no more," the retired CO said.

"One other thing, Mario. If I hear you bad-mouthing Simon and Sheena one more time, I'm going to drive over here and give you an attitude adjustment."

"I don't like 'em, and I don't like no women in our uniforms."

Service pushed his partner out the door, and they got into the truck. Novello might provide some good cases, but he was a jerk, and maybe it was time to ignore and avoid him.

"Too much time alone, dat one," Allerdyce said when they got back into the truck. "I'm hungry; could eat shit rolled in cracker crumbs."

"There are crackers in the food bag in back," Service said. "You're on your own for the other ingredient."

"Crackers ain't food. Pop Tarts is food."

"We've got one more stop."

Allerdyce made a point of checking his watch. "We been out twelve plus already, push fifteen, sixteen by time we get back camp. Youse's days allas dis long?"

"In the old days, when we had lots of overtime to cover us."

"You don't got no overtimes?"

"Nope, we're working for free."

"Dat don't seem right."

"Job's got to get done."

"Me, I'd go home, leave shit hang."

"Our people don't think that way." Actually some did, a very few. But most just donated time and finagled their records to make everything fit. "The job has to get done."

"Dat's legal, be cop and not get paid, arrest pipples when not on da clock?"

This topic was not going any further. "That's just how it is. Think of it as a fluid situation."

"Like da squirts from dying rear," Allerdyce chirped.

As apt a summary as any.

CHAPTER 26

Randville, Dickinson County

TUESDAY, NOVEMBER 17

"Twenty, Twenty-Five Fourteen on Rap Two, RSS check."

"Ready to copy, Fourteen."

"Noble Chern. Florence, Wisconsin, address. RSS on bear, past five years."

An almost immediate response. "Nothing, past five."

"All right. How about two Randville residents, Dickinson County. Henry R. Hill, YOB 1922, and Henry R. Hill Jr., YOB 1943?"

"The elder Hill had a tag in 2007, Menominee Unit. Junior had deer for same year, no bear."

"Great job, Twenty. When did Junior buy his deer license?"

"Third day of the season, Fourteen."

"What time?"

"1800 hours. Twenty clear."

"Kind of late go knock on doors in Yoop, Sonny."

"That's kinda the whole point."

"Just like darn game warden, pop up anywheres, even at front door. Wah, where hell *youse* come fumm?" Allerdyce was chuckling.

Surprise was the whole idea in some cases, to show up not just *where* you weren't expected but *when*. Some officers tried to carefully plan such events, but this case was more a matter of serendipity and fate, and he decided the timing ought to stay in that realm.

Mario Novello was right about the house trailer. It sat on an angle, sort of tipped up at one end, and every tree around it sported long chains of white LED lights. "Kinda like Heaven," Allerdyce said. "Or white Crisco-massed. I never seen so bloody many lights."

Who could interpret such nonsense? Outdoor decorations in the U.P. lay somewhere in the valley between eclectic and certifiably bizarre, with no obvious message inherent in most such displays. There was a small Toyota truck parked by the trailer. Light snow was falling in small round pellets.

"She gone get slickery tonight," Allerdyce said. "You want me stay truck while youse inside?"

"Come with me, but say nothing. Just look mean."

"Okay, Sonny."

Service banged on the door for almost five minutes. Curtains closed, the place smelling of ammonia, lights on inside, sound from a TV or something, no answer to the door. The sound had a thumping, heart-jarring bass.

"Smell dat?" Allerdyce whispered from beside him.

"Yut."

"T'ink dat's pussy cats?"

Cloying as that might be, it was better than a meth lab. He banged harder on the door and decided to keep hammering until someone answered.

When the door suddenly flew open, Service found himself staring at a massively wide male, obese, five-eight tall and wide; his red face a collection of circles and lumps; shirtless, rolls of fat piled on one another, some of them red, some white, some yellowish, scabs everywhere; and a shaved head, cleared not to a shiny dome but to a fuzzy nicked thing. The smell wafting from the interior made him gag and he willed his nose closed, an old trick he'd learned after a firefight in Vietnam, when heat began to accelerate the rot in the dead bodies sprawled around the camp. This guy was right off a sideshow freak stage.

"You the DNR?" the man asked, blinking, like the darkness behind Service was hurting his eyes.

"Conservation Officer Service. Who're you?"

"Henny Hill."

"Junior?"

"Ya-huh."

"Your dad here?"

"Inside, but he don't hear for shit."

"We'll talk first, and maybe we won't have to disturb your father."

The man stepped back, his heels pushing McDonald's bags and cups and wrappings, detritus spread on the floor to create a crinkling six-inch-deep carpet of decay. Service could see channels in the debris where the man's feet had waded through. The ammonia smell was sharp and overwhelming, but no cats were in sight. He heard Allerdyce cough behind him.

"You got cats?" he asked the younger Hill.

"Not as pets. Senior gets me litter of bitty kitties and we keep 'em couple months, then toss 'em out to feed yotes. Senior likes watch yotes eat cats. He don't like no cats. Me, I kinda like them kitties. You think this illegal or somepin'?"

Feeding kittens to coyotes? What the hell is wrong with people?! The interior was disgusting, stinking, cluttered, disorganized, countertops piled with dirty pans and food leavings. Baby toys and pacifiers lay on the floor beside petrified food remnants.

"You got kids in here?" Service asked.

"Girlfriend had three, but she moved out two years back."

No surprise in that news, though Hill's having a girlfriend was deeply disturbing on several levels.

"What's this about, sir?"

Hill was puffing like he'd just run up Heartbreak Hill in the Boston Marathon. "Your dad had a bear tag for oh seven?" Novello's half-ass allegation pissed him off, but RSS did show that Hill had a bear tag in the same time frame, and he decided to use this fact to open the discussion.

Blank stare, no answer, heavy, labored breathing. "He's on oxygen since oh five. You mind I sit down, sir?"

Some hunters still managed to get out with portable oxygen, but Service doubted either Hill fit this small group.

"Go ahead."

The man wedged behind a kind of kitchen nook table.

"How's your dad hunt if he's on oxygen?"

"Dey got portable units, hey."

Hill Jr. picked up a roll of paper towels, ripped off a foot of paper, and began blotting at his face and upper arms.

"Can your dad come in here and talk to us?"

"Invalid, can't move. Got him sittin' on toilet all time. I even got wipe his ass sometimes." This was said without intonation or consternation.

"How was he going to hunt?"

"Got around a bit better back then. We had him a permit, hunt from vehicle."

"Had?"

"It got losted." The man looked around and grinned sheepishly. "We're pretty sure it's here somewheres; we just don't know where. Happens a lot."

"'Magine 'at," Allerdyce muttered behind Service.

He sensed passive aggressive in the younger Hill—faint, but definitely there. "Let's get your dad in here so we can talk. All we need is information."

"That ain't happening," Hill Jr. said.

"Why's that?"

"I think youse know why. Been expectin' youse fellas, I guess."

"You were? Because your father drew a tag for a bear two years ago, or drew it for another person?"

"Look, sir. No bear got shot, so ain't no biggie, right?"

"Who was using the tag?"

"Me, I guess. I din't shoot nuttin', din't see nuttin', and bait cost too damn much, so I ain't done it since. I give up on damn bears."

"You were actually using the tag?"

"Yah, was me, jes me on dat. But not no more, hey."

"You know anybody drives a puke-green Willys?"

Hill stared at the ceiling. "Bear guide name of Milk, Malk, Falk, somepin' like dat."

Okay, he had admitted borrowing his dad's bear tag but had shot nothing, which put the bear clearly out of the picture for these birds. Now it was on to the main event. "And deer?"

"Never give up on hunt deers. Too good to eat and healthy too. Hey, no fat!"

"Our records show you had a deer license the same year as your dad's bear tag, but no deer tags before or since. Why's that if deer's so good for you?"

"Din't need one, I guess."

"But you use the meat?"

"Yah, sure. Love them venisons, but we got friends bring us meat. No need we got spend money on license, gas, ammo, all that junk."

"Did you get a deer in oh seven?"

"Zat last year?"

"Two deer seasons ago."

"I ain't sure, sir. Just minute, okay?" Hill Jr. picked up a roll of Life Savers, broke it like an egg on the corner of the table, poured several into his cavernous mouth, and took a long pull on a quart-size plastic bottle of Mountain Dew. "I got two kinds of the diabetes sweet blood; the one needs insulation, and the other one gets pills and sugar. One and two, man. God put His black-ass curse on me, and I don't know why. My blood sugar's a yo-yo. Goes so low I get dizzy and pass out, got take sugar, like right-quick-fuckin'-now, and then it goes way the fuck up and I am so screwed."

"Type I takes insulin," Service said.

"I run outten insulation last month; ain't been able get out, get more."

The guy was no doubt going to end up in a diabetic coma, soon to be followed by death. "You said you were expecting us, so you already know what this is all about, right?"

"Well, can't say I know nothin' for sure."

"Just tell us the truth, Mr. Hill, and we'll treat you fair."

"I ain't done nothin' wrong. You can call me Henny. Why that old fart stare me down like dat? Tell 'im don't be lookin' at me like dat."

Allerdyce's presence was having the desired effect. "Why were you expecting us, Henny?"

"Wait," the man said. He poured more candies into his mouth and commenced to crunch them loudly. "It's Noble, ain't it?"

"What's Noble?" Service asked.

"Noble Chern."

"Who is that?"

"Guy I know. Sometimes brings dad and me deer meat."

"Friend?"

"Nah, just know each other see what I'm saying?"

Hate that phrase. "Mr. Chern brings you venison?"

"He's a war hero, fought in Eye-Rack war. Army Ranger."

"Yeah, hero for doing what?"

"He ain't never sackly said, but he's got da limp, so must been war hero, hey?"

"You ever serve?"

Hill smiled sheepishly. "Where they find scale weigh the likes of me—at motor pool?" This set the man to giggling, then coughing, then clutching at his throat, followed by another long pull of Mountain Dew and a face wipe with a large swatch of paper towels.

"How'd you meet Chern?"

The man made a face. He was perspiring heavily. "Don't 'member."

"You guys hunt together?"

"I guess you could put it that way."

Junior's hoping I don't know the facts, trying to tiptoe around reality. "So you hunted together. Want to tell me about it?"

"Unh," the man said. "I just kinda helped him out, ya know?"

"You had a license to hunt, right?"

"Yes, sir," the man said with a decisive nod.

"Did Chern have a Michigan license too?"

Hill's head went from side to side, twice, emphatically.

Service said, "Yet he tagged a huge buck with a Michigan license. I've got the photo. Want to see it?"

The man nodded, said nothing.

Service showed him the photo. "See the color of the tag on the antler? That's a Michigan tag, not Wisconsin. Chern had no Michigan tag. We know you bought your license at 6 p.m. on the third day of the 2007 season, and here's what we know happened. You never hunted at all, but your friend showed up and asked you to go buy a license he could use on the buck he'd already shot and had no tag for."

"He drove me down to Red Owl," Hill Jr. said. "He paid the money, and I filled it all out."

"Your friend then tagged his buck with your license." Statement, not question.

No reaction other than labored breathing.

"Yes or no, Henny? It's late and we're all tired, and we already know the facts."

"Yah."

"You understand that you can't loan a license. It's issued to you only."

"But it was twelve-point buck," the man said.

As if rack size erased all rules. "You want to tell me in your own words what happened?"

"Do I got to?"

"Well, no, but I have to decide if I write a ticket for loaning a license or if you're conspiring to illegally take an animal that belongs to the people of Michigan."

"Like me and him was equal partners?" Hill Jr. asked.

"Yep, equal partners, equal guilt."

"Bullshit. I ain't got half that big rack. He got that *and* all the meat. He shoots deer, then comes, says he wants help, drives me over to store, gives me money. I go in and buy license, give tag to him, and never see 'im again. That seem equal?"

"You got no meat at all?"

"Said he was gonna, but never did."

"You bought the license *after* he killed the buck, right?"

"Yah. I buy tag, help war hero."

"He ever tell you how he hurt his leg?"

"Chopper hairsalt."

"Details?"

"No. You gone charge me wit' illegal deer?"

"No, just loaning your tag, but you have to tell me the whole truth of what happened. Your dad loaned his bear tag to Chern too, didn't he?"

"No, honest. The bear was just wounded and run off, so he never used it."

"Witnesses saw him shoot a large bear in a cornfield. They chased him away."

Hill made a face of disapproval. "At was dat bear guy Iron River. Word all over place. Not Chern." The man began chewing on his lower lip and eventually sighed and said, "That sonuvabitch. See, one night he come ast old man for his bear tag and he had bear claw on rawhide around his neck. I ast 'im where he got the claw, and he said it was from his girlfriend's father."

"A bear claw's not in and of itself illegal, Henny."

"He don't got no damn girlfriend, dat guy. When he got money, he spend all to hunt, buy heads for walls, fish an' horns 'n stuff, an' all shit an' like dat."

"Are you saying he didn't shoot the mounts in his house? You've *been* to his house?"

"Mebbe was dere just once long time back. He bought all 'at crap, stuff nobody picked up from taxidermists and they was gonna toss in trash."

"Which taxidermist?"

"Don't know, just heard name. Jumbo, somewhere over Spread Eagle."

"Wisconsin?"

"We got one Michigan?"

A hoarse voice yelled from another room. "I'm hungry now, fat ass. Where's my supper!"

Hill Jr. said, "Got go, take care my dad."

"In a minute." Service wrote a ticket, explained how to take care of it by phone. "I'm not writing your dad for loaning his bear tag. Not now. That's a break for him. I wrote something on the tag about the illegal deer. It's not a charge, but if Chern fights this and you have to testify and you change your story or fail to show up, I'll activate the charge. You understand what I'm saying?"

"I ain't no cheat. I'll pay fine and be dere, you need me." Junior flapped the ticket in the air. "My dad been real good dad."

Voice from the other room, "Hey fat fuck, get the lead out. I'm starving in here!"

Service said, "The bear tag. Chern asked to borrow it?"

"Not for him. Said he had bud over Iron River."

"The bear guide?"

"Never said da name, but wunt s'prise me none."

"One final thing here, Hill. Don't talk to Chern about any of this," Service warned.

"He ain't got no phone."

"Now or ever?"

"Now."

"How'd you know the DNR might come?"

"Noble stop by one night, say so; said don't say shit ta youse guys, just zip up and be quiet." Hill had lied about not seeing Chern, but it was not a major issue yet.

"You did the right thing."

"He din't give us no meat."

So much for the rationale for doing right. Service felt like rolling in snow to get the smells off him. Allerdyce was already in the truck, engine running.

"Some people too disgustin' for words," the old man mumbled. "We go camp now. This ain't fun no more."

Grady Service checked his watch. Five minutes past midnight. It would take an hour to get back to camp, and they'd just have to drive to Florence tomorrow. "We're getting a room in Iron Mountain," he told his partner.

"Okay, but make stop Golden Arches, get cheesyburks, fries, grease."

"I'd rather be shot. Did you not see the floor of that trailer? We have lots of food in the truck. We'll get a big breakfast in the morning."

The owner of the no-tell motel called Randy's Ranche watched Service fill out the registration card.

"Long day hassling people?" the man asked.

Service said, "We get the state rate, right?"

"Depends."

"On what?"

"If you want hot water."

"The state rate doesn't include hot water?"

"State rate comes outten *my* pocket. You people are 'pose to run lean."

"Whatever," Service said, too tired to fuss with trivial matters.

The man stared open-mouthed past Service, who heard Allerdyce cough behind him.

"Hey dere, Frankie-boy; youse got fire insurance, you cheap fuck?"

"*Allerdyce*," the man mumbled. "Okay, okay; the state rate it is. I'll be sure the hot water's on." The proprietor put a key on the counter and disappeared through a beaded curtain.

Service looked at his partner.

"What?" Allerdyce said.

CHAPTER 27

Spread Eagle, Wisconsin

WEDNESDAY, NOVEMBER 18

Wisconsin Warden Kelly de Jardins de Richelieu met them in the parking lot, still looking half asleep. "Jesus, don't you Michigan people sleep?"

Service said, "Not during deer season."

"Mine doesn't start for a week," the Wisconsin warden said.

Said Service, "No, yours has already started, Kell; you just don't know it yet."

The taxidermist was located on US 2/41, a huge, colorful sign announcing "Finning-Feather Memories Forever." The place was less than seven miles from the Michigan border. It was a standard commercial critter-stuffer's shop inside—black bear on a pedestal in one corner, several walls with whole fish, mostly walleyes and northerns. And there were birds and deer, half of them European mounts, bare skulls cleansed of flesh by insects. Nice heads, but neither significant nor eye-catching.

Allerdyce followed the two uniformed men into the shop.

"Teller here?" Service asked the man at the counter. He had blond hair, a bright red beard, and a crooked smile. He stood all of five-six, counting his unruly mop of hair.

"That's me and I'm here, so I guess I'm in. Yo, Kelly. You're out and about early."

"Tell me about it," the Wisconsin warden mumbled.

Red beard looked back to Service. "S'up?"

"You did a mount for a customer by the name of Noble Chern."

"We have privacy laws in Wisconsin."

Rocket growled. "Goddammit, just tell the man, Jumbo. It's too damn early for stupid-ass games."

"Yup, a twelve-point. Nice buck; scored 177, I think I recall."

"Chern's name on the tag?"

"Lemme look. My memory ain't that good no more." The man pulled a battered blue-gray ledger from under the counter, opened it, and leafed his way through. "No, he just brought it in. Tag goes back to an H. Hill Jr. over in Randville."

"That was oh seven?"

"Yes, but the work din't get done till last year on account Chern didn't have sufficient funds. I let him pay it off in installments. He's only had the mount a couple of months."

"You also do a thirteen-point for him last season?"

"No; he brought that one in, and I had the antlers out back in my shop until last night. He'd only paid me eighty bucks against seven fifty for a full shoulder mount, but he came by last night and took the antlers back, said he was going to make other arrangements."

"He mention where he shot the thirteen?"

"Not exactly, but I got the sense it was close to where he shot the twelve."

"A Wisconsin deer?" the Rocket asked.

"No, I think it was over in Michigan. Like I said."

"You see the tag on the thirteen?"

"Said he lost it dragging it out. You know, his bum leg and all."

The Wisconsin warden said, "Jesus, Jumbo, you *know* the rules."

"Course I know the rules, but this guy's a good customer, and a good guy. He's a war hero. I don't shit on our country's veterans."

Service took over. "He buy other stuff from you, stuff customers never picked up?"

"Has from time to time. That's not illegal. Was a time when he said he was flush with some sort of insurance payout and he spent like crazy back then. Bought a heap of stuff."

"Will your records show that?"

"Yep. You want a list?"

"Not now. Later we might."

"You say he grabbed the other rack last night?" Service asked.

"They're all his now, and I'm out of it. Those horns I green-scored at just under 200, bases big as my fists. So what do you guys want me to do?"

"Call me if he comes back," Kelly the Rocket said.

"Don't think the guy will be back. I offered him his eighty bucks back and seven hundred more to buy it for myself. I think I could make three grand selling it at a show. Chern told me money was no good. Can you believe that?"

They went outside. Richelieu said, "Chern's gonna dump the evidence."

Before Service could say anything, Allerdyce said. "Jamokes with horn sickness won't never dump no two hunnert rack."

The Rocket looked at his Michigan counterpart. "I think your partner may be right."

Allerdyce nodded his head emphatically. "No worry, boys; I know dis kind."

CHAPTER 28

Florence, Wisconsin

WEDNESDAY, NOVEMBER 18

Life right now was complicated. Technically, Sergeant Wooten was his immediate superior; Wooten, in turn, reported to the district lieutenant. But as acting detective, Service also reported to the new Wildlife Resource Protection Unit lieutenant downstate. Typically the downstate lieutenant knew to let his detectives do their jobs with as little interference as possible. But Wooten, as sometimes happened with ambitious new sergeants, had tried unsuccessfully to insert himself into a situation in which he no doubt smelled glory in the offing. Grady Service told the man to stay away, that he and the Wisconsin wardens had the case under control. He could tell that Wooten was not happy with him, and he didn't care. He'd be glad when deer season was over and his stint as a detective finished so he could settle back into protecting his Mosquito Wilderness.

Service found Allerdyce staring at him as he held the cell phone close.

"Why are you in Wisconsin?" Wooten demanded to know.

"I have a case here; it's not like this is some sort of exotic vacation choice."

Service knew that although the so-called buck sheet was no longer in official use, there were a lot of sergeants, including Wooten and even some higher officers, who used the tally to keep track of ticket numbers during deer seasons. Woe be to those who wrote few tickets during this time. There was no actual quota, but there was the mythical buck sheet, which was a score sheet for every officer and district in the state. Service hated the thing, which had been a big deal in his old man's day and early on in his own career as well.

Back in those days the paper kept track of every citation issued in the state. There were few women then, and all officers were assumed to be male. There had been women COs in the late nineteenth century, but in the wake of two world wars the job had become almost exclusively a male domain. Some district supervisors used the buck sheet to motivate their officers.

Captains, in turn, used it to motivate and evaluate their lieutenants, and the chiefs held the stats over everyone's head.

Like every bureaucracy and chain of command evolved by humankind, shit rolled downhill, and woe be to those officers whose deer season citation numbers were seen as lacking. Numbers were interpreted not just as a measure of performance but also as an indicator of officers' motivation and dedication to the collective mission. All of it was, in his opinion, pure bull.

The general public had forever seemed to believe that all cops were pushed forward by secret ticket quotas, and the DNR was included in this very wide assumption. Crap like the buck sheet only added fuel to the fires of citizen outrage.

The damn buck sheet caused some officers to write tickets when they might not have during another time of year, and this sometimes pissed off locals who they would have to deal with in the fifty weeks that weren't the regular firearm deer season. Even wildlife biologists sometimes clouded it all by using the buck sheet numbers to help them estimate deer populations: More tickets were assumed to translate to more deer in that area. This was the worst sort of nonsense, not to mention crappy biology.

Retired DNR Capt. Ware Grant had led the charge to obliterate any use, or mention, of a buck sheet in the department. And new chief Eddie Waco had in fact directly addressed this in meetings with officers last summer. He'd held up a sheet of paper. "This is the so-called buck sheet, and here's what I think of it." Waco had torn it into pieces and thrown it aloft like confetti. "That's the end. No more. Copy?"

Officers smiled, but their senior people simply took it back underground and said nothing to the chief.

"I'm just checking on your season," Wooten said, "to see if you need help."

"Sergeant, my season is going like every deer season, meaning I have an abundance of assholes and fuckups and not enough hours to take care of everything that needs doing. If we had overtime like in the old days, the overall challenge would be much less, but we don't, so we're left to deal with the shit as best we can. If we moved officers from low deer counties to high deer counties, as they did in the good old days, that also might help some officers. But we don't do that sort of thing anymore because we can't afford per diem and all that."

Service plowed on. "You know that we *all* know that it's unspoken policy to misrepresent our hours, especially in deer season, and you also know this puts us into liability limbo. Every officer is faced with not working and facing departmental wrath because of the phantom buck sheet or working the hours and making creative time cards to show less time worked than actual. So here I am in Wisconsin and, thank you, but we do not need any help."

There was dead silence on the other end of the phone. Then, almost meekly, Wooten said, "I take your point."

Service knew the matter should remain unremarked upon, like a fart in church, but he was tired and feeling less than generous. "I wrote one ticket yesterday and helped some Illinois droolers organize and locate themselves in such a way as to not shoot each other or some other unsuspecting hunter unlucky enough to get too close to them. One ticket; write *that* on your buck sheet."

Wooten said, "There is no buck sheet. You heard the chief last summer."

"I heard. Did you?"

"There's no such thing," Wooten said.

Service laughed into his cell phone. "I can hear you crumpling paper in your hand."

"You are not a team player, Officer Service."

Service fought to restrain his temper. "Listen to me, Wooten. The first thing any officer has to do, regardless of rank, is to decide which team he or she's on. I've got one ticket. There may be more to follow, but the numbers are irrelevant. I were you, Sarge, I would write the following word on a piece of paper and look at it and meditate on it every hour of every day. Ready to copy? Here's the word: G-E-O-R-G-E, George, common spelling. Want me to spell that again?"

Wooten said, "What. Is. *That*. Supposed. To. Mean?"

"It'll come to you," Service said, "Or it better. And soon."

The sergeant broke the connection.

"Youse ain't like your daddy, Sonny Boy. He always talk nice to bosses."

"He was a lush, continuously seeking grace and forgiveness."

"But he always top man on buck list," Allerdyce said.

"There's no such thing."

"You say so, Sonny, but we know jamokes down Lansing watch and keep count; and here we are, youse and me, still screwing around wit' dis Wisconsin jerk. Youse an' me is missing da deer season."

Service said, "Zip it, old man."

"Just sayin'."

He hated that phrase, the latest slang to grow out of "yada yada." "That's chicken-shit talking," he said with a growl.

This time Allerdyce let it go.

Kelly the Rocket's sergeant called him and wanted to be part of the crew to interview Noble Chern. The plan was to rendezvous at the man's house, go in, and hash it out, with the Rocket and his sergeant taking the lead this time. Service had already ticketed Henny Hill Jr. and got the man positioned against Chern. At this point, he could write Chern for borrowing a license, seize his weapons, keep the seized head, and let the Wisconsin guys do whatever they had in mind; but he didn't want to separate yet. Maybe Chern would spill more on his illegal Michigan activities. Service's gut said the Wisconsin man was a deep, widespread stain that desperately needed cleaning.

The sergeant's name was John Smith, an unremarkable name for an equally unremarkable person.

Most officers didn't kick over a single giant case in the course of a standard twenty-five-year career, but he'd had so many, especially lately, that he'd lost count and wouldn't be surprised if he sailed into retirement without any more icebergs—called such because some small things or events seen by an officer could lead him into a deep and complex case, far larger than first appeared. *How many big cases is one game warden entitled to? Nothing was written; instinct and decades of experience helped keep you motivated and on your toes. It was fine and dandy and necessary to deal with small-time fuckups, but the serial slime, they were the real quarry, real and damn hard to uncover—and to prosecute.*

Service went inside with his colleagues, leaving Allerdyce outside in the wet snow. The old man had the truck's backup fob, so he could get in and stay warm, and drink coffee and chow down on bakery with holes they'd picked up at breakfast this morning.

He fully intended for the Wisconsin guys to take the lead, but Kelly the Rocket started hemming and hawing. Before he could stop himself, Service said, "Listen, Chern, I talked to your pal Henny Hill last night. He says you were supposed to bring him and his dad some deer meat from the buck he tagged for you in oh seven. The meat never got there. He's not a happy camper."

Chern looked up at the ceiling, his eyes reddening and blinking wildly.

"There ain't no answers printed on that ceiling!" Service snarled at the man. "We have your photo, the mount, and Hill's confession. You shot the twelve-point and got Hill to buy a tag for you. That's hunting without a license, borrowing the tag of another, and taking game without a license, which means it's illegal. The mount stays with me. If there's meat, I'll take that too."

"I ate it, sir," Chern said meekly. The man's eyes were red and puffy. "You don't understand," the man said and began to whimper like a child, pouring out tears, sobs wracking his whole body. Service had never seen anything quite like it. In fact, it looked real and was convincing.

"Not our job to understand, Chern. The states pay us to enforce statutes. Period."

"But it was a twelve-point," Chern mumbled.

"Ya, a 177, Jumbo Teller told us."

"Damn cheat, that Teller is; ask anybody. Charges way too much."

"What's that make you?" Kelly asked the man, who opened his mouth and sighed.

"Have you got your operator's license straightened out?" Service asked.

"Like I ain't had time or gas money."

"Show us what you've got; the military driver's license will get us started."

"It ain't here," Chern said.

Kelly nudged Service. "We'll bird-dog all that crap. Go on and write your citation and we'll provide backstory as we get it. We'll see what our staff in Madison can harvest from databases. You keep the head mount."

"We're also going to keep your rifle, Chern, and we'll ask the court to condemn it."

"What does that mean, sirs?"

"Your rifle now belongs to the state."

"How I'm going to hunt bucks?" the man asked, his face glistening with tears. The man looked dumbfounded and broken, his face purple as a grape. "I hunt to live," Chern said.

"That's your problem, not ours," Service said.

"I got no money for food, how I hire lawyer?"

"There are public defenders. You'll have to figure it out."

"But you don't understand, that was my *grandfather's* gun. It means everything to me."

"Why?" Service answered. "Because he was a violator too?"

"He served in Europe, fought with Patton, got wounded and everything."

Kelly the Rocket asked, "What the hell does that have to do with your using his rifle to poach deer? Seems to me you're taking a crap on your dear old grandpop's memory."

Chern tried to stand up. "You can't take my gun!" his bad leg failed and he fell hard onto the linoleum floor and started moaning, "Oh God, oh God, I am so sorry, I am so sorry."

This brought another download of tears, which culminated in a wild tantrum of air-punching and kicking on the floor.

Kelly looked at Service and shook his head.

Service looked at a window and saw Allerdyce holding a massive rack above his head. A shit-eating grin covered his weather-beaten face.

Service looked back at Chern. "What happened to the thirteen-point you took in Wisconsin last year?"

Chern rolled on his back and crossed his arms. He was still sobbing, his nose runny.

"Get up," Kelly the Rocket told the man.

Chern remained on his back.

Grady Service went to the back door. Allerdyce was waiting. "Thirteen," the old violator said. "It's beaut. Was in trash t'ree houses down. I see dis woman, ast her when is garbage pickups? She says ain't till Friday. But dis one house got can out and wonder, why dat is for jes' dat one guy, eh? I go look. Wah! Here youse go. Like I tole youse, guys like dis can't t'row away t'ing like dis even if evidence gone screw 'im."

Service took the antlers inside and handed them to Kelly the Rocket, who held it in front of Chern's eyes.

The man's lips pooched out and quivered. "I've never seen that before."

Service said, "Neighbor was throwing it out. Can you imagine that, dumping a two hundred? That's a man with his life in the right proportion. You can't eat horns."

Chern began slapping the floor and wailing again. "I'm sorry, I'm sorry. I can't help myself, I'm *sorry*. You took my twelve you can't take that one *too*! I can't hunt, I'll die; I know I will."

"Listen, Chern, tell us one thing. How did you injure your leg."

Chern rolled to his side, away from the officers. "Fell outten a chopper."

"Fell?" Service said.

"They take us out to the trucks every day. I fall off, smash my leg bad."

"Thought this was an air assault?"

"I never said that, exactly."

A truck driver who fell out of his ride to work? Never mind that he was in a combat zone. Here lies a truly pathetic creature. Death might be a better place than he is mired in now.

The Rocket thanked Allerdyce, who said, "We done wit' dis jamoke?"

"Mostly. He took a dive off the deep end in there, complete breakdown. Says he'll die if he can't hunt. We took his trophies. We took his grandpa's gun. Wah-wah."

"Add old dogs and watermelon wine, and we might could get him on the Grand Ole Opry," Limpy said with a straight face and hopped up into the Silverado.

CHAPTER 29

Slippery Creek Camp

WEDNESDAY, NOVEMBER 18

Middle of the night and probably after midnight, but Service wasn't sure if it was today or tomorrow and it didn't really matter. They reached the camp just in time to see the camp's garage on fire. Grady Service didn't even attempt to get out of the truck. He didn't put a chokehold on the steering wheel and didn't pound anything in anger. He said nothing, just sat. And watched.

Allerdyce said in a barely audible tone, "Wah."

The two men watched the building burn.

"You want call basement savers?" Allerdyce asked, this a derisive Yooper term for volunteer firemen.

"No basement to save," Service said.

"Might she could spread to house."

"Built the garage far away just so that can't happen, especially this time of year."

"Can't just let burn. Youse got stuff in grudge we need get out?" Allerdyce asked.

"It's just stuff. God will let it burn out."

"Youse believe God? *Youse*?" Allerdyce asked, his eyes bugging out.

"Some days, sometimes."

"This one them days?"

"Not sure yet." Service reluctantly handed his partner his cell phone. "Knock yourself out."

Allerdyce made the call and Service got out and wandered over to the fire, *First the garage at Friday's, and now here? No coincidence. I've made more enemies than Nixon.* He broke his reverie to tell his partner, "Bump Pancho Frye down in Gladstone. Tell him I'd like for him to take a look at this mess. His number's in the directory."

"T'ought Frye and his woman move down some bluehairland," Allerdyce chirped.

"Only in January and February."

"He strange bird, Frye."

"But he knows his business." Pancho Frye had spent thirty years with the Michigan State Police, retiring as the MSP's chief arson investigator. Some said he was so good because he had the heart and mind of a firebug. Grady Service hoped so.

Allerdyce reported, "Basement gang here twenty minute, turdy; one dem say you live too bloody far out fum simplezation."

And yet not nearly so far that a torch couldn't find Friday's and now the camp. What would it take to be really too far out, to be unfindable by man or satellite?

"Hot dogs in the fridge in the house," he told Allerdyce. "Buns in the freezer."

"Grudge on fire and youse talking wieners?"

"The lads will need something to do when they get here. Only fire left by then will be barely enough to roast the dogs."

"T'ink we ought back truck up case some shit in grudge blows up?"

"Nah, God'll see to it."

"Dere youse go wid God again. Youse got youse's head on straight?"

"Ya, sure; everything's peachy."

A fire crew from Rock got to the place first, and Allerdyce greeted them. "Youse's ain't closest, 'owscomes youse get 'ere so quick?"

A fireman said, "This ain't the only burn tonight, old timer. We were already out this way."

Service leaned against the truck deer guard and lit a cigarette.

"Dose t'ings ain't no good for da healt," Allerdyce said.

"One data point is shit, two is better, three is a trend, four's a bonanza."

"Huh?" Limpy said.

"Ask the firemen exactly how many other burns."

"Now?"

Service said, "No hurry. Did I tell you how tired I am?"

Allerdyce went off to talk to the firemen and trotted back. "Dey got five fires tonight."

Grady Service grinned and nodded.

"Howscome youse ain't pissed. Youse got two fires youse's places?"

"You ever bet on instant replays?" Service asked his companion.

"Geez, oh Pete, no."

"Why not?"

"Already know how she come out, eh."

"Same here. Two fires on me, they're out. Why waste energy on what's done? All that matters is what comes next."

"Youse is more and more like youse's old man."

"He'd be serving beer to the fire crew."

"He wunt as bad wit' booze as youse make 'im out, eh."

"I lived with him."

"I partner with him. Him and me talk all time."

"Him and me didn't, partner," Service said. "He lectured. I listened."

"He had plenty ta tell."

"He was a drunk and a loser."

"He helped make youse youse."

"An entirely bullshit technicality."

"It trut', Sonny."

He felt oddly irritated, but the feeling was mixed with something else, an emotional non sequitur, elation. "Five fires *plus* here," he said out loud.

"Why youse keep sayin' dose numbers, Sonny?"

Go ahead and tell the man; share your happy with him. "You have one event, that's all you've got—one event, one thing; probably it stands alone, unconnectable to anything else. You have two, you've got to think they're probably connected. But you don't know how or why, and there is the possibility they could both be stand-alones and the connection totally coincidental. Following me?"

"Like follow da moose, but keep ways back so don't step in da doots, eh?"

"I'm trying to impart wisdom."

"Youse's partner is all ears."

"If we have two events, we might be able to draw a line between them, but it's not worth shit to do that. All you have is two points, and you can't say if they fit together or not. But then you get a third event, and *shazam!* You draw a line from one to two to three and you may begin to see a direction, you with me?"

"Wah, I t'ink mebbe youse got chunked on noggin' out to Peaveyhouse fight, got you dat pee-ess-tee-dee?"

"Are you with me?"

"Youse's partner, wichyouse alldaways."

"When the event horizon begins to grow to four, five, and six, that's when you can comfortably connect your line and see a more definite direction. This sinking in?"

"Yah, sure. Like when I was working in woods. I keep map on my table, mark down ever't'ing I hear bout big bucks. Summer, fall, win'er; I talk postmans, deliver-guys, anybody seein' anyt'ing anywhere, and I scribble it all down. Youse get enough dose over time, youse can start see picture."

"How do you decide when you have enough?"

"Youse'll jus' know."

"What amount of more is better?"

"More got to end somewhere."

"Infinite more is not as good as finite more, yes?"

"Got no idea what youse's talkin' 'bout, but whatever youse say, I'm wit' youse, partner."

Why am I blathering? Limpy's looking at me like I'm infested with psychic fleas gathering to swarm him. "We'll wait for Pancho, okay?"

"Youse da boss," Allerdyce said.

Service stood for the longest time looking around and eventually saw a flash of shiny out by the road, away from the house and garage. He walked out to it, leaned down, and picked it up. My brand of cigarettes. *You are a mindless pig*, he told himself, and went inside.

"Youse t'ink we get some slips tonight?" the old man asked.

"We're not going to roll tomorrow until we're ready. Our schedule is our oyster."

"Our *what*?

"Something a guy named Willie wrote a long time ago."

"Willie?"

"Some claim he was once a poacher."

"Don't know no Willie work up dis way."

"He didn't work in this state, not even this country. He reformed when he grew up."

"Geez, oh Pete; I'm not only one to turn da leaf."

"Actually, he never said anything about any of that stuff in his life. Others talked about him and what he did or might have done, but Willie kept his mouth shut. Nobody knows for certain he actually violated. All we can do is speculate and imagine."

"Dat's good; keep mout' shut youse gone do dat junk."

"Your record isn't rumor, it's fact."

"Cheap shot, Sonny."

"Like you said, I learned that from my old man."

"Sometimes youse creep me out, Sonny. Dis Willie got last name?"

"Shakespeare."

"T'ink dere was some Shakespeares over Painesdale back in da day of dose Cousin Jacks Welchingmans."

"Not related."

"Youse can't know dat for sure."

"Actually, I can."

• • •

Pancho Frye spent less than five minutes talking to the fire crew and fire marshal before joining Service and Allerdyce. Frye was an albino with a severe distaste for sunshine and daylight and a deep love of fires of all kinds and sources. He had pink eyes and white hair and was a small, compact man with feet meant for someone a foot or more taller and a hundred pounds heavier. It looked like he had been built from cast-off parts. The man's voice rarely got above a hoarse whisper.

"Big fire night," Service greeted him.

"Lots of dumbasses and booze in the old fire-tinder camps. Why am I here, Grady?"

"Had a fire in my girlfriend's garage just a few days back, and now this."

"Anyone hurt?"

"No. I think both were intended as messages. When a firebug wants a body count, he targets the house, right?"

"Could be, but bugs don't think with consistent lucidity. Most of them don't want to hurt anyone; they just want to make fire and get attention. They're impulsive and obsessive."

Frye looked over at Allerdyce. "When did they kick you loose?"

"Was years back," Limpy said.

"Had been up to me, I'd a kept you inside until you croaked," Frye said with a frown.

"Dat guy Jesus teach forgive people."

"*You* dare mention Jesus? You, the spawn of Satan?"

"That ain't nice."

"You catch this thing setting the fire?" Frye asked.

"Hey, Frye, I ain't no culvert," Allerdyce chirped.

Frye said, "It's pervert, you moron, and hah!"

"Wah, tell 'im back off, Sonny, or I wipe da floor wid 'im."

Service put a hand on both old men. "Knock it off you two."

Limpy said, "I go out wid his sis, long time back, but he don't never forget shit."

Frye bristled. "Go out? Hell, you ruined that girl."

"Pancho, I don't want hurt nobody, but youse's sis, Jen-Jan, weren't the Version Mary youse t'ink when me and her hook up."

Frye stepped toward the old poacher. "What're you calling my sister?"

"Jes say what youses don't want see. She was normal good gal, not no statue of saint."

"But she went off with *you*!"

"Youse ever bet on instant replays?"

Frye looked from the old violator to Service. "What in the dickens is he talking about?"

"Leave the past in its box," Service said. "Now that you know about my two fires, any thoughts?"

"That requires reports, point of origin, materials, accelerants, tactics, and all that other tiresome technical forensic stuff, but I'm thinking spates are usually one-bug campaigns."

"Meaning everything that happened tonight is connected?"

"Could be. Some bugs get their rocks off on chaos, so they set a series and watch the world scramble to react—to him, his creations."

"Could it be the other fires tonight were set to take attention off this one?"

Frye rubbed his chin. "Can't rule that out. You want to get all the reports down to me?"

"It's deer season," Grady Service told him.

Frye grimaced and popped his forehead with his hand. "Plumb forgot that, I guess."

"You didn't get out for the opener?"

"Went vegan."

Allerdyce blurted out, "Like 'at pointy ear, Vegan Smock guy on *Star Track*?"

Frye said, "I'll get the reports myself. What's your Marquette address?"

"Tuesday Friday in Harvey; sorry to get you all the way up here for this."

"Good to be wanted," the fire inspector said. "Gets the old ticker pumping thinking I can still help the cause, Grady. Don't never retire. You suddenly got more time than God and no damn purpose."

Service smiled. *Retirement? Not as long as I can still keep up.*

Grady walked the old fellow to his truck, and Frye said, "Everybody thinks this fire stuff is rocket science. It's not even close. The breaks almost always come from some simple piece of evidence. But don't tell nobody."

• • •

They slept in the main cabin, fully dressed, and in chairs again, like a couple of hobos.

It was full daylight when they woke up. They could still smell the stink of the fire. New snow was falling and some steam coming off the pile of black rubble. Service toyed with calling Tuesday, but this would just upset her. The first fire was enough on her shoulders.

Allerdyce was mining the pantry and fridge. Service said, "I froze some blueberry-peach pancakes in September. Pop 'em in the microwave."

"Got sirple?"

"I eat them dry, like Pop Tarts, out in the truck. I'll make the coffee." Both thermoses were on the counter.

"S'owers?" Allerdyce said.

"Why? We'll just get dirty again."

"Where we go taday?"

"Where're the biggest deer these days?"

"Mosquito, course."

"Not there. That's covered. I've got Duckboat on my beat while I'm working as acting detective." Duckboat was CO Dan Tooman, who years before had bought an expensive laydown duck boat and tried to hide it from his wife, Suzanne. But she had figured it out and made him sleep in it for a month, as penance. He had been Dan before that and Duckboat ever since.

"Kate's Grade, Bryan Creek. Soon as shootin' start, all big bucks head into da t'ick crap dere ta hide."

"Good a choice as any," Service said.

"T'ing 'bout dose big bucks. Mos fellas see one or two in life and can't do nothing 'bout dem. Takes killer mind be ready all time for dat one moment, eh."

Service looked at his watch. "Oh nine nineteen; our schedule is our oyster."

"Why youse keep saying oyster stuff?"

"Know what my pal Willie liked about oysters?"

"No offense, Sonny. I don't care."

"You can open them with your sword."

Allerdyce said, "Youse don't start talk normal, I'm gone smack youse's head, haul youse over to shrinkhead sawbones."

"I want to have another talk with Teddy Coppish."

"Kate's Grade ain't all dat far fum 'is camp."

"Very perceptive," Service said. *Why Coppish? He wasn't sure.* The old gut, mostly; something it had taken him a lifetime to learn to pay attention to when it started gnawing. As it was now.

It was zero nine thirty when he called into service with Lansing and central dispatch. A twelve-hour day lay ahead, but he'd be paid for only eight of them.

CHAPTER 30

Kate's Grade, Marquette County

THURSDAY, NOVEMBER 19

There were almost two inches of pure new snow and a light, snapping breeze out of the west, okay conditions for deer hunters. Too much wind made all animals wary and often made them stay put until the wind lay back down. They were cruising Kate's Grade in the south county, home to big bears, big deer, some moose, and more than a few big jerks. A truck came flying by them and raced north, fishtailing on the less-than-smooth dirt grade, a heavily traveled road with deep gouged ruts that never seemed to disappear, even in the deep of the driest summer.

"I know dat truck," Allerdyce said. "Belong dat chuck-knuck Jerzy Urbanik, Da Polack vickam."

Service glanced at his partner. "The *what*?"

"Long time back 'e got sloshed, smash truck into minivan, kill two preachers; was messytits, not 'is first drunked wreck, eh? Put 'im inside two year; he camed out, been vickam ever since. 'Look what state done me, boo-hoo.' Asshole."

Service remembered neither the man nor the events. "You know him?"

"Yah sure."

"Competitor or partner in your former line of work?"

"Holy Pete, no way. I wunt let no druggies or drunkies work my crew."

"There was your son, Jerry."

"Got no choice but put up wit blood."

"You worked with my old man."

"Geez, oh Pete, Sonny; crabapples and ground cherries, eh."

"Whatever," Service said, watching the van's brake lights suddenly come on and the vehicle slide until it came to a stop catawampus across the road. The driver bolted out of the door with a rifle case, unzipping it and dropping it as he ran, and crossed Kate's Grade with a sort of running, hopping gait. The man tugged on a blaze orange chook and took off into a massive cutover.

Service was beside the van when he saw ahead and to the side a huge deer in full flight between dozens of cedar trees and stumps. There was one shot and the animal went down, slid forward on its belly and was still.

The driver was running through the trees toward the downed animal and Service angled to meet him there. When he got close, he greeted the guy with uncut excitement. It was amazing what he had just witnessed, "Great shot. Running deer, with an iron sight? That really was one hell of a shot!"

"Jesus," the startled man said, "where *youse* come from? I'm in *trouble*?"

Service smiled. "No trouble; you did everything by the book except for the sudden sliding stop."

"I take my hunting real serious."

Grady Service looked down at the buck and gulped. The rack was *massive*.

The man knelt in the snow, took off his gloves, and notched his deer tag. He paused to count points and looked up at the officer. "That can't be right. You count too?"

Service had already counted and recounted. "Sixteen."

"You t'ink dis t'ing escape hunt ranch?"

"Don't know," Service said. A similar thing had flashed through his mind as he was counting antler points.

"Holy cow," the man muttered. "Holy cow, holy cow! Why me? Why now?"

Odd response, Service thought.

The animal was thick-bodied and dark, almost black. The man huffed and puffed, rolled the deer into a furrow on its back, took out a knife, and opened the body cavity like a surgeon. That done, viscera exposed and steaming, he used a coring tool to remove the bung and a small pull saw to split the breastbone. He reached inside, sliced the animal's windpipe, rolled the animal on its side, and tugged down the guts so that gravity took over and spilled them into the snow, turning it red.

"Got do dis fast," the man mumbled. "I'm in big hurry."

"I'll help you drag it," Service said. They each took an antler and took off through the cutover maze to the road and the van, where the man said breathlessly, "Up roof." The man reached inside, popped the hatch in back, got out some rope. The two of them hoisted the animal on top. He let the hunter take care of all the lashing.

There were three children in the van, all rug rats, all boys. Service hadn't noticed them before. His focus had been on the hunter and the buck. Now he looked and saw the passenger door open, a woman with her back to him on the driver's side, and Limpy Allerdyce on his knees in front of the woman, her dress thrown back up on her lap. Allerdyce looked up past the woman at Service and cackled, "Geez, oh Pete, she ain't got long, dis one!"

Grady Service said, "Long for what?"

"Wake up, Sonny! She's gone spit' out a kittle!"

A kid? "*Now*? Here? How long?"

"I look like bloody sawbones? Soon I t'ink. Dey got get goin' now! No kidding. Wah!"

The hunter driver said, "Hey, kids, want to see daddy's big buck?"

The kids piled out of the van and cheered and clapped and danced like little wild things.

Service said, "Sir, your wife's having a baby. You've got to get her to the hospital now!"

Allerdyce stood up. "Hey Urbanik, shit for brains. Youse leave dat damn deer, an' take care youse's wifey."

"Don't' get your skivvies in a big knot, old man."

Allerdyce came around the van and confronted the younger man, who was considerably taller and heavier. "What hell wichyouse, stop shoot deer when wifey ready spit out baby kittle?"

"None of your business, Allerdyce. I know who the hell you are. Everybody knows. We don't need advice from some dried up old jailbird. I pay dat woman's way over here fum Poland. Women dere know how drop kids anywheres, anytime."

Allerdyce moved toward the man, but Service grabbed his partner's sleeve. "Leave it."

The old man yelped, "Don't talk me like no damn mutt!"

"You need to get to the hospital," Service told the man, while he held Allerdyce back.

The man said, "Yah, yah," dismissively, and then, "C'mon kids, jump in; I guess we've got to get the rest of the way into Marquette."

"Chuck-knuck," Allerdyce said with a hiss.

This was the second time in a half hour that the old man had used this term, a new one in the ever growing and odd Allerdyce lexicon.

"Chuck-knuck, what is that word, a combination chucklehead and knucklehead?"

"Yah, like dumbass," Allerdyce said. "Onny worser."

The van resumed racing, and Service went around the van, turned on his blue lights, and led Urbanik toward town, calling ahead to alert police in front of them and in the city. The man had said not one word to his wife during the entire episode.

"Dose kittles grow up be shitbirds just like dat chuck-knuck Urbanik," Allerdyce muttered. "Poor kittles."

"Hey," Service told his partner. "Give the guy a break. He did some things right this morning."

"Youse t'ink?"

"Looked okay to me."

"Yah? When dey start let felons hunt wit' firearm?"

"That was a long time ago. He could have petitioned to get his rights back."

"Wit what? He don't have pot piss in. Take lots money do dat stuff wit lawyer. Question ain't could have, but did 'e?"

Service rubbed his head. *Blinded by the unexpected events and the animal. Lost your focus. Over a damn deer, just like the fools you're chasing. Doofus. Only Limpy kept his head on straight here. You could do a lot worse for a partner.*

"You gone check dat chuck-knuck's record?"

"Not this time. All those kids, a worn-out van falling apart, a record hanging over his head; he's got enough to handle. Everybody's entitled to at least one small triumph."

"Even if it break law?"

"Sometimes there are laws and there are laws," Service said. He thought about giving Urbanik a chewing out at the hospital, but why bother? The wife was in good medical hands now; Urbanik was what he was, and it was time to get back to real game warden work.

CHAPTER 31

South of Arnold

THURSDAY, NOVEMBER 19

This time they stashed the truck in the woods outside the camp gate and the two of them hiked into Coppish's place, going around the stakes that held the gate in place. The gate was closed, but they had business with the former firebug, and the gate was essentially meaningless in this situation.

Paroled firebug Teddy Coppish came to his door with an empty champagne flute in his left hand. "You two, *again*? I haven't done nothing illegal. You can't be on my private property. The gate is closed. You're trespassing."

"We found an illegal deer here yesterday, Teddy. That gives us the right to be here. You have some explaining to do."

"I already said all I have to say."

"I can write you for aiding and abetting the taking of an illegal deer. What do you think that would do to your parole status?"

"Wunt be good," Allerdyce said. "Dose POs don't like no monkeybiz."

"Why are you pounding on me like this?" Coppish whined. "Don't you got more important things to do in the woods this time of year?"

"Just work with me," Service said. "I'm not after you."

"It feels that way," the man said.

"It's the Ingalls woman we're interested in."

"Arletta ain't one to be foolt with," the firebug said. "She's a serious score-keeper, if you take my meaning—eye for an eye and all that stuff."

"What's your connection to her?"

"Whachu think?"

"I don't think anything, which is why I'm asking. Enlighten me."

"We . . . you know? Sometimes."

"But she has a live-in boyfriend."

"I guess he ain't enough for her. She a little thing with the big needs."

"Me, I had some womans like dat," Allerdyce inserted. "Anyt'ing got propellers, wheels, or titties gone venchly give a man trouble, wah."

Service had to force himself not to laugh. "You know, like how often?"

"I don't keep no count," Coppish said. "Ain't none your business, Service. You writin' a book? Ain't no law against help out a friend."

"This would be the friend whose name and ID you couldn't remember yesterday? Maybe you knew that helping her was not exactly legal?"

"Just helping friend is all I done," the man said.

"You think a judge will swallow that?" Service asked, making a show of flipping open his ticket book.

"What judge?"

"You'll have no choice, Teddy. I'll write you for aiding and abetting the taking of an illegal deer and other charges, and all that will jam up your parole status. You'll have to plead not guilty and take it to a jury, and how sympathetic you think a jury will be to a firebug?"

"You can't give me no ticket for nothing I ain't done."

"Chuck-knuck," Allerdyce said with a low growl.

Grady Service kept hammering. "I found an unvalidated tag wrapped around the antler, and you first told us it was your deer. The fact is that you were in possession of an untagged animal, and that makes it yours. In this business, possession trumps all words, Teddy. Give me your op's license."

"Oh shit," Coppish said.

"Eloquence is simplicity," Service said, holding out his hand. "What about your lady friend?"

Coppish stared at the ground. "She was here that morning. She shot the buck, told me to take Pymn's tag and attach it with a string, not to validate it, and keep it until she picked it up."

"For the record, she being Arletta Ingalls."

Teddy Coppish nodded. "Ya, Arletta."

"Taking the license from her makes you guilty of borrowing, you understand that?"

The man nodded.

"And it means Pymn loaned his, she borrowed it from him, and in turn loaned to you."

"Yah, but see, Pymn never bought no real license."

"No?" This was an entirely new and unexpected wrinkle.

"Arletta she screws young fella's a clerk at Stop-and-Rob up Gwinn. She gives him her stuff, and he gives her whatever licenses she wants. The system is set up so clerks ain't got verify no ID. I mean they do, but nobody holds 'em accountable, see; so this guy can give her what she want when she give him what he want, okay?"

"What's the clerk's name?"

"He's a Peaveyhouse is all I know. Junco, I t'ink."

"One of Dinty's sons?"

"Yah, I guess, probably."

Apples falling close to trees. Some stuff about human behavior was so true it could be summed up in five words.

"I getting ticket?"

"Not yet."

"You gone talk my PO?"

"No, not yet."

"What's all that not-yet shit?"

"First, you're gonna write this all down on paper in a statement—what happened, what you did, what she did, what you said, what she said, everything. Second, if this ends up in court, you will testify for the prosecution. If you renege on anything, I'll drop it all on you and let your parole officer take the next step."

"Nobody ever believes a firebug," Coppish said. "They'll never call me before a jury."

"Chuck-knucks of a fedder," Allerdyce said. "Jury see dat woman wit' likes of youse and folks vote guilty 'fore first bakery-coffee of day."

"I don't like any of this," Coppish says. "It makes me feel dirty."

"*Are* dirty," Allerdyce said.

"Driver's license," Service repeated.

Coppish went back inside.

"He says there are ten blinds on the property. The one I saw yesterday had minimal bait, and I'm thinking he cleaned it up after the kill. There's something more going on here. Why don't you make a sweep; see what's baited, and take a picture of anything you think is over five gallons." Service handed his digital camera to his partner.

"Law's only two gallon," Allerdyce pointed out.

"True, but we're not going to niggle here. Tonto effect," Service said. Allerdyce guffawed and took off in his predator gait.

Tonto effect was one of his old man's ditties. You do stuff close enough so that a drunk Indian on a running horse can't see the difference between close enough and right on. He had learned in his long life that this was as much truth as ditty.

Coppish came out and handed him the operator's license. Service made the man orally verify every item and fact, drawing out the time that Coppish was nervously looking around for Allerdyce. "Where go that old shithead?"

"He's my partner. Watch your mouth."

"Partner? He's a felon, same as me."

"He's not even a little like you, and he's learned his lessons. You might want to emulate him."

Just like that, Allerdyce was back, not breathing hard, not flushed. "Anything?"

"Twelve blind I count. One you seen is okay. Eleven got mebbe ten to fifty gallon."

Service put his hand up to get Coppish's attention. "Look at me, Teddy."

He activated his portable radio. "Station Twenty, Twenty-Five Fourteen with a file; op's license number follows. Cross-ref RSS and priors."

"Ready to copy, Fourteen."

Service read Teddy Coppish's driver's license number. Waiting for Twenty, he looked at the firebug. "You bought a license?"

"Yah."

"When?"

"July, August, like that?"

"Explain why you've got baited blinds if you're not hunting. And how come you lied to me about the number of blinds yesterday?"

"I get mixed up," the man said.

"And the baiting?"

The man shrugged, answered, "Habit?"

Lansing came back with a real surprise. Coppish not only had a combo license for himself but a crop damage block permit and ten individual doe permits.

"Crops?" Service said, staring down the arsonist.

"Food plots is crops."

"Food plots are deer bait, not human food."

"Word games, hey. Regs ain't so clear on that, an' if you think about it, they're same thing. You got something valuable and deer want eat it, you can shoot 'em."

"Deer eat lawns, shrubs, landscaping, flowers around houses, and gardens, and this doesn't entitle homeowners to whack them or to get block grants. Is this your deal or the woman's?" *How did he get the district wildlife supervisor's okay? The DWS has to personally inspect the properties and approve all such requests.* "Ten's the minimum you can ask for in this grant program."

"See, I ain't greedy; just want my share."

"Share of *what*?"

"You know," Coppish said, turning to Allerdyce. "Tell him."

Service looked at his partner, who looked at Coppish and said, "Gimme smoke."

Coppish handed a pack of Marlboro Reds to Limpy, who tapped out one and lit it with his own lighter. "See, farmers paid to grow crops, and not grow crops. If dey plant dey get paid for dere losteds after dey get bad wedders, get paid for everyt'ing, and most farms is big-ass company outfits, not little guys. So lotsa pipples t'ink dis not fair to little guy and dey ought get chance suck on govmen' tit too."

"Crop damage is real," Service said. "You're talking scam."

"Yah, sweet one too, if you get district guy buy into your claim."

The district biologist here was Maija Spong, stationed in Marquette. She had been around as long as Service, and as far as he knew, she wasn't one to claim a two-penny mistake on an expense report. No way it was Maija. His gut was yelling at him to go deeper.

"Who'd you work with at the district office?"

"Din't have to. Got contacts down Lansing."

"Bullshit; only districts can issue block permits. *Who* in Lansing?"

"Don't remember no names. Those Lansing types all look alike."

Change direction slightly. "Who came up with the license loan, you or Ingalls?"

"Who do you think?"

"Not you. I don't think you've got the smarts."

Coppish looked like a cat with a canary, a stupid grin on his face, sparkling eyes, like he couldn't wait to spit something out.

"Maybe you *are* smart enough," Service said, "but it doesn't matter. All that matters to me is the fact of possession. The grants and all that and how you got them, that will be your problem when your parole officer digs into this."

"Wunt my idea," Coppish said. "Arletta she set it up, the hull damn thing."

"And let me guess; Junco Peaveyhouse is part of the whole deal too."

"He got hold of some forms; I don't know how. He signs 'em, so how anybody gone know? Don't nobody give no shit about dis junk. There's no follow-up on nothing."

"What's Peaveyhouse get—beyond the obvious reward?"

"Don't know. Have to ask Arletta. She say something about three hundred, but all I heard was number, not no details."

"Okay, what besides the obvious do you reap from this deal?"

"She give me forty dollar per hunter. They buy state license, den I give damage doe permit, which 'pose to be only for da does, but we let da sports shoot bucks and pay by size. One eighty plus costs three K."

"You have one eighties on this land?"

"Nah, but most hunters dumb as bag of rocks, got roses in their eyeballs."

"Your cut is forty dollars on a thousand-dollar kill?"

"I get 10 percent on big ones."

"Which you've never actually collected, because there are no bucks in that class right around here."

Coppish grinned. "See, all you got to do is mention one eighty and dose guys get the tunnel vision, hunt on hope not facts."

Caveat emptor at its most elemental.

Allerdyce said, "Got look for crap when youse buy shit."

"Now you know everything," Coppish said. "We have a deal?"

"One more thing. Tell me about what you've taught Ingalls about how to start fires?"

Coppish looked dumbfounded. "Why I'd do dat?

Jesus, am I wrong on this? Is all this here just deer and money greed? Shit. Gut says more, but what and how?

Service patted his shirt for smokes. Pack must be in the truck. "Let me have one of my smokes, partner." He'd given the pack to Allerdyce to prevent indulging himself. This way he had to ask if he wanted to smoke.

Allerdyce grimaced and handed the cigarette to him; Service fished one out, lit up, and stared at the pack for a long time, not sure why. There was a blue state tax stamp on the bottom of the pack.

Coppish said, "Was all of it her idea. My land, her idea."

"Where's the money go?" Service asked.

"Some save-dogs t'ing. Were me, I'd give all damn dogs to Chinamen, tell 'em enjoy the meat."

"Chuck-nuck," Allerdyce said, but Service didn't quite hear the exchange. He was still focused on the Marlboro pack. *What the hell is it with these ciggies?*

"You'll work with me on this?" Coppish asked with hope in his voice.

"The woman pay you with cash or check?" Service asked, breaking his focus on the cigarette pack.

"Only cash."

"You get receipts?"

"For this? No way."

"You bank the cash?"

"Govmen' can watch bank. I got a safe."

"Show me?"

"Got warrant?"

Service flicked away the cigarette. "We can get one pretty damn fast and get the whole thing in the media too." He dialed the Dickinson County magistrate, explained who he was with, and was told he was being put through to Judge Cindra Csargo.

"Don't know her."

"Elected last year; good judge for your lot. She hunts and fishes."

"Grady Service," the judge greeted him. "Tell me what you told the magistrate."

He laid it out as succinctly as he could.

She asked, "You want all buildings on the grounds, all vehicles, and everything that could be related in any way? That work for you?"

"Might be a little wide, Your Honor."

"You do your job and I'll do mine. A deputy will bring the writ to you in thirty minutes."

"Thank you, Your Honor."

"No, thank *you*, officer. If you need more, call me directly. I hate cheats." She gave him phone numbers for home and the court. "Let me know how much cash is in that safe," she ended.

He stared at Coppish. "Verbal permission granted, but we're waiting for the dep to get here with the actual warrant. Unless you voluntarily want to crack open the safe for us and show us what's in there."

"Thousand in cash and ten permits. You gonna take everything?"

"No. I want you to keep working with Ingalls. Tell me the truth. How many deer have been shot on this property this fall?"

"Thirty-five mebbe."

"All bucks?"

"That would be stupid management. We make clients shoot one doe for a hundred dollars before they can even look at a buck. And they pay as soon as they pull the trigger."

The crop damage program dated back to 1992 or 1993, but Service couldn't remember exactly when, and it applied more to downstate than above the bridge. The deer herd had grown from a half million in 1971 to more than two million in 1989, spurred on by light winters. The result had been a disaster for some farms and orchards but a bonanza for hunters.

Coppish sighed loudly.

"Where exactly does the Peaveyhouse kid work?" Service asked.

"Cinche's Bait and Bottles in Gwinn."

"Don't call him or tell anyone we've been here."

"I tell Arletta, she'll cut off my balls."

"We wouldn't want that to happen," Service said.

"Got mouse in pocket?" Allerdyce asked with a cackle.

Limpy and Coppish reminded him of battle-scarred alley cats, survivors, the sort of men you might kill but couldn't break.

That his partner claimed to have changed lay somewhere between a miracle and a clever image. He still couldn't decide which.

"What now?" Allerdyce asked as they headed for the truck. "Deputy bringin' search warrant."

"We'll get him on the horn, tell him to hold it for later—if we need it. For now, let's cruise, find a camp to sit on."

"You believe what Teddy say about not teaching woman no fire stuff?"

Oddly enough, he did, and he couldn't yet say why.

• • •

They did not have to drive far. They moved up Kate's Grade again to a two-track he'd noticed earlier. He turned down it and drove a half mile along a ridge road that ended in a logged-over opening with an old sign: "Gleeson Creek Wild Man Camp: Invitation Only." There were three large army surplus wall tents, nine extended-cab pickups, three automobiles, five enclosed ORV trailers, and piles of empty beer cans gleaming in the sinking light. ORV trails spidered out of the camp center, all of them led onto property where ORVs were not allowed to operate.

"I t'ink dis gone be busy," Allerdyce said.

Goat rodeo, Service thought. He hoped the hunters would trickle back but knew they had to be ready for a jam. "How many loaded guns on ORVs?" he asked his partner.

"Camp like dis? Ever' damn one of 'em. D'amateurs never speck no wardens come."

"And professionals?"

"Dose jamokes all know just matter of time 'fore game warden pinches dem. Dey pay fine, don't make no fuss; know it just cost of do business, eh?"

CHAPTER 32

Gleeson Creek, Marquette County

THURSDAY, NOVEMBER 19

They walked the area separately and found nobody in the camp. Service weighed their options and decided to wait in the middle of the camp. When the hunters returned, he and Limpy would let them come all the way in before stepping out on them.

"Here's the routine," he told Allerdyce. "Shine your flashlight right in their eyes. Say, 'DNR. Is your weapon unloaded?' No matter what they answer, you tell them to unzip the case and show you. If you find an uncased gun, make sure it's unloaded right away and take it with their ID and tags. If you find a loaded gun in a case, same thing. Unload it, take the gun, and get their ID and tags. Keep it all together. Pick up ammo from unloading, and put it with the weapon. Send those who had loaded weapons to a particular area to wait." Service pointed. "Over there. I'll send mine to the same place."

He took Allerdyce through all the possibilities they might encounter: loaded guns on vehicles or in trucks, no orange, no helmets, no vehicle registrations, concealed weapons without carry permits, no hunting licenses—all the many permutations of waiting for a large number of hunters to return to camp after dark. Having briefed his partner, there was nothing left to do but listen, watch for lights, and wait. They were already well after legal shooting hours.

"Relax, Sonny. Youse t'ink I ain't been shaked down like 'is 'fore?"

"This isn't a shakedown."

"Feel like dat when youse on udder side. We check warrants on dese jamokes?"

"When we run their licenses and tags. All of this is gonna take time. When you first make the stop, give them a few seconds to declare if they're carrying concealed. If they have a concealed handgun and no permit, take it, unload it, and start a pile. If they have a permit and declare they're carrying and they aren't loaded, they're good to go. We need to get all loaded weapons out of the equation as quickly and safely as possible."

"What if dey piss-moan."

"Let 'em sing. They got a problem with the laws, we're the wrong people to talk to. They need to talk to lawmakers. All we do is enforce laws, even the ones we don't agree with. We don't like doing that we can resign."

"Might could be fiffy, sissy pipples wit' dis mob," Allerdyce pointed out.

Still no late shots, or ORV lights or sounds. *So far, so good.* Like his partner, he had also done the rough math and knew if this crowd was really large, they were going to be forced to call extra help. He decided to plan for the worst. He got on the radio and began checking on the whereabouts of other officers. If they weren't tied up, he asked them to move his way, just in case. This was standard operating procedure.

Service called Torvay. "One, One Forty, Twenty-Five Fourteen on D-One.

"You need something, Fourteen?"

"Where are you now?"

"Camp off the Floodwood Road."

"We're sitting on a gaggle at the Gleeson Creek turnaround. We might have a goat rodeo in the making. Your camp a hot one?"

"Nope; you want me to start heading that way?"

"Be good; Fourteen clear."

"Fourteen, this is One, One Forty-Seven. I copy, also starting your way. I'm not far, up on the Little West Road." One Forty-Seven was CO Angie Paul, one of the newest officers in the district and rock solid in all aspects of the work, especially dealing with the public. If needed, she'd be the one to keep the peace among the barbarians.

Service said, "This is Fourteen. Both of you stand off until we get our traffic stacked, and stopped. I'll let you know with the signal 'George.' Come in with lights and music."

"One, One Forty-Seven clear."

"One, One Forty clear."

"Dis is keen," Allerdyce said.

"*Keen*? Nobody uses that word anymore."

"Excitin'; dat better?"

"Thought you'd been through this stuff before," he whispered to his partner.

"Alone, not in no damn buffalo herd. I hate crowds, and dis bunch gone be grumpy."

"An assertion based on what?"

"Ain't no bucks hangin' on dere buck pole, and we in fiff day of season. Wah, dese boys got no clue how hunt, and dey be grumpy." Service weighed the information. They might already have moved animals to a processor, but it had been cold and there was no reason to hurry. Old-time woodsmen liked for their meat to hang for a while before butchering. He scuffed the snow under the buck pole, found nothing, no blood, no hair. *Nope, nothing shot here yet.*

As he heard the sounds of the first vehicle approaching, Service stopped and said into his radio, "George." He went about his business, knowing the cavalry was bearing down.

• • •

The ultimate body count, when all was said and done, was sixty-one people, at least ten of them from a nearby camp who decided to stop by to visit, commiserate, and share beers. Given sheer numbers, the rodeo's resolution had been pretty civilized and subdued, Service thought. There were some yappers, which was to be expected. Every group had them, but overall the hunters had chosen discretion over bombast; and when Torvay and Paul pulled in all lit up, the buzzing crowd went silent.

Service hoped all the flashing lights wouldn't trigger any epileptic seizures.

Sixty-one hunters total; fifty-nine loaded firearms on or in vehicles, including all the ORVs and three pickup trucks and all their passengers. There were forty concealed carry permits for the sixty-one hunters, almost all of them packing, and only two adhered to the law by immediately declaring they were carrying and had a permit. Three had concealed pistols but no permits. Magically, there were no outstanding warrants in the crowd, and no felons. Service had his colleagues split all the tickets to speed up the festivities. He confiscated the pistols from the three without carry permits.

There was not a single deer, and all the hunters were complaining about not seeing deer. A few claimed to have seen some wolves, which caused some of them to double up and triple up in blinds for safety. Fools.

All things considered, Grady Service felt at peace. The sheer number of tickets didn't sit well with him, and he knew his young sarge would be strutting like a rooster with his first hen. Sixty-eight tickets from one camp; fifty-nine loaded weapons and more. And they had given thirty-five formal warnings as well.

Business finally completed, the COs withdrew several miles and parked their trucks. This season was turning out to be remarkable: Knezevich, the Wisconsin big buck shooter; Chern; the damn Peaveyhouses; Arletta Ingalls and her deal at her place, plus her deer-for-bucks scam with firebug Teddy Coppish. It was beyond imagination, so much in the first full five days, and there were still eleven days remaining. This sort of mass encounter might boggle even the most fertile imaginations, but group things like this were not uncommon. The number of people here was high, but the percent of violations tonight was not even a little surprising.

Predictably, Wooten showed up, having seen the trucks gathered on his Automatic Vehicle Locator (AVL). The young sergeant was on him immediately to get his paperwork in. "Tomorrow, right? Tomorrow? It needs to be tomorrow, or all the paperwork will clog up the court."

Service said. "We'll turn in the paper work in chunks, not all at once, and this will keep the court docket from clogging up."

"What's going on with that Croatian you got? Do you have any idea how big an arrest that was? Huge, ginormous, a miracle."

"Del Olmo and Grinda told me that. I never heard of the guy."

"But *everyone* knows about the Croatian," Wooten said excitedly.

"Not me."

"Iron County officers have been after him for years and years."

"Yah, well."

Service yelled to the other COs and nudged his partner. "Been instructive, sports fans, but this old fella and me need to head for home. We need our beauty sleep."

"It okay break contact wit youse's guys?"

"We're good."

"Where're the smokes?" Service asked.

Allerdyce dug around and found a pack. "We need stop, get more."

"No problem," he said, looking at the pack as he lit a smoke.

"All sergeants is dicks," Allerdyce offered.

"Hey, I was a sergeant."

"Not long enough make youse a dick."

"I'll consider that a compliment."

"Din't know youse was needy kind."

"Shut up."

"Serious, needy make you look pa-tetic, and nothin' knock down man's dauber more den pa-tetic legend."

"Did you catch what Teddy said when I asked him about teaching Ingalls to make fire?"

"I heard. He sound s'prised."

"You buy it?"

"Don't matter what I t'ink. Youse da man."

"I think I believe him. You want to pick our route home?"

Allerdyce pointed. "That away, Mr. Sulu."

"Never knew you were a Trekkie."

"Lots youse don't know. Youse t'ink dat Sulu is girl, Sue and Lu? Or guy, or one dem cut-paste pipples?"

"Cut-paste?"

"Yah, transenders. God put here one way, does cut-paste make nudder way."

"You dwell on such things, do you?"

"Dawn to dusk."

"It's neither right now."

"An' I ain't t'inkin' on night-shooters and transenders."

"Focus, partner."

"Wah."

The deer season was going pretty well, especially for them. But there had been two burns on his property, and he was no closer to solving those. Until he did, he was worried about Friday. He'd thought it was Ingalls behind the fires, but now he wasn't sure that was the right road.

CHAPTER 33

Stalling Road, Dickinson County

FRIDAY, NOVEMBER 20

When you're on a roll, you're on a roll, and the camp roundup had given him a large burst of adrenaline. How could they go straight home when they were both still geeked up?

There was almost no snow on the roads as they moved eastward. It had either melted off, been worn off by vehicular traffic, or not that much had fallen here. People who didn't live in snow country never understood the randomness of it, or the vast number of microclimates that dotted the Upper Peninsula and could make weather drastically different only five miles from where you were.

Service pulled off Stalling Road onto a logging road through an area that had been selectively cut two or three years ago and was just beginning to provide a lot of new browse for animals. The magic formula: Browse in fields was bait for deer, and deer browsing in fields were bait for violators. They drove dark, and it felt as comfortable and familiar as day driving after so many decades of running without lights. All their windows were down. Allerdyce rode with his eyes shut, and Service knew his partner was focusing everything into his hearing. As they moved along, there was a snap where no snap should have been; he stopped the truck and looked over at Limpy.

"I hearded it," the old man said; he cracked open his door and slid outside. Service saw a dim red glow behind the truck, a small red penlight in his partner's hand. He was gone two minutes max, slid back into the truck, whispered. "Da get-guy out fetchin'. Two-stick set, one dis side make da noise, one udder side to mark spot. I put new stick where we broke old one."

"Footprints?"

"Yah."

"Think he heard us?"

"Nah; he'll be too catched up wit' findin' deer."

"Anything special about the tracks?"

The old man paused. "Look like itsy bitsy kittle tracks."

They both understood the scenario: A jacklighting crew had been slow-rolling, had seen a deer out in the cutover with their spotlight or headlights, and popped the animal. They had dropped off a man to find and maybe gut the animal and marked the place in a way only another violator would pick up on. The fetch would drag the deer back to the marker and await pickup. When the vehicle came back, the muscle would jump out and help the fetch throw the animal into the bed of the truck. Experienced three-man crews—driver, fetch, and muscle—could load and hide an animal in seconds and continue on almost as if they had never stopped, as quickly and efficiently as an Indy crew, and some of them practiced the skills to reduce exposure time to a minimum. While he couldn't admire it, he always wondered how such people of single purpose might fare if they turned their discipline and focus to legal pursuits.

"How much time, you think?" he asked Allerdyce.

"T'ink short to pig-up, mebbe half hour. Da get-guy in dere now, headin' back out."

Service found a place ahead, backed in, and shut off the engine.

"Youse don't know dey come out dis way. Might go back out same way come in."

Allerdyce was right, but this wasn't a sure-thing business. You had to make guesses and assumptions. "We'll play it this way and call your get-guy the fetch," Service said.

A cackle from the passenger seat. "We spick differ'net lingo," the old man offered. "I keep with get-guy, youse don't mind."

"Go. I'm going to hide the truck better and lock it. You take the get-guy side of the road, and I'll take the marker side."

"Not much time, speck," Allerdyce said; he opened his door, closed it without sound, and fell into the darkness like a frogman into the sea.

Service moved the truck, locked it, got out, and found his partner between a couple of humps of debris, just up from the marker stick, which was like a black snake protruding into the two-track. It would stand out on lighter colored sand, or snow. He knelt by a stump, suspecting their wait would be a short one.

Three minutes later a pickup truck came silently and darkly up the road in the same direction they had come. The whole thing was predictable, such patterns developed by violators over generations and eventually discovered by game wardens. Jacklighting crews always made a right-side pickup. If this was the same crew, they would stop. But if this was a different crew, they would move on past; they didn't. Service heard the new marker stick snap and the truck stopped.

He charged directly to the driver's door. Drivers in this situation were supposed to be watching the road ahead, but most of them rarely did. Human nature being what it was, most drivers turned to see what kind of deer had been killed. Predictably, all the pickup's windows were down.

Service got to the driver's window, paused, heard mumbles and a strange, off-key thump in back; he thrust his hands through the window, turned off the engine, pulled the keys out of the ignition, and threw them up the road. Only then did it occur to him that the sound in back was not exactly the right sound, but done was done. In these situations you had to act fast and without hesitation.

"Hey!" a voice yelped from the truck cab, the voice followed quickly by three inhuman shrieks that rent the night air and his eardrums. He unlocked the driver's door, grabbed a puny shoulder, and jerked the surprisingly small driver down to the road, where he pinned the driver in place and growled, "Conservation officer, DNR! Do! Not! Move!"

He could hear Allerdyce on the other side of the truck and then, "Got da fetch. Geez, oh Pete, Sonny; dis 'ere's little kittle girlie!"

Service dragged the driver around the front of the truck to the passenger side and grabbed at a figure scrambling to get into the truck. "Who's the crew leader?" he thundered.

"We ain't no crew, we're sisters," a high-pitched youthful voice shot back, this from the muscle, who he had snagged at the passenger door. They moved all three prisoners to the front of the truck and lit them with their Surefires. Three young girls, none of them more than a hundred pounds. Talk about firsts.

"You scared us," the driver complained.

"You're killing deer at night. You don't get to be scared."

The driver said indignantly, "We did not kill anything from the truck. We stopped, got the rifle from the bed of the truck, and shot."

"You used a light."

"Did not; that would be cheating."

"And breaking the law."

"We don't care about stupid law. We got our own standards, and we don't ever cheat or play dirty."

"Shooting at night is playing dirty."

"We beg to differ," one of the girls said.

He took a deep breath of cold night air. Encounters like this were inherently dangerous for all involved. *Kids? Girls? What the hell?* He shone his light into the fetch's face, but she looked away. Allerdyce gave her a little push and she snarled, "Keep your hands off me, you old asshole!"

The girls were runts in jeans with flapped mad bomber hats nearly obscuring their tiny faces. They wore boots and layers of oversize sweatshirts with hoods.

"I suppose you guys are checking your trap lines?"

"What?" the driver yelped.

"Your hats, *trapper* hats? It's a joke."

The driver said, "That is not funny, and this is not a joke. We're working here. Besides, they're mad bomber hats, not mad trappers," she added.

"That certainly polishes your image."

"Don't look at me," the fetch yelled at Allerdyce.

"Got us three bad-ass little bunny rabbits," the old violator said.

"We need names," Service said. "All of you calm down. I need driver's licenses, but obviously none of you is old enough to drive legally."

"We have our hunter safety cards," the muscle said. She was the smallest of the three.

"Okay, hunter safety cards and your deer licenses."

"Dude, no can do. You two must be the worst game wardens in like . . . the universe."

Was this real? "*What?* Let me see some ID."

"Dude, we don't got ID. We're like, not hunting. We're making a documentary on poaching and cop abuse for YouTube."

He blinked. *Are they naïve or accomplished liars?*

Allerdyce rooted around in the truck's glove compartment, came to the front to Service's side. "Ain't got no registration inside, nor no plates."

"Whose truck is this?" Service asked the girls.

The driver said, "None of your business, dude."

From the great roundup tonight they had descended into this . . . whatever it was, which was anything but clear. The girls looked very, very young. "What're your names?" he asked politely.

"Up yours," the driver said.

"NOW!" he roared like a drill instructor intent on delivering dire bodily harm.

The driver froze and looked down. "J-June," she whispered in a reluctant voice.

"YOU!" he roared at the muscle.

"I'm July?" the girl said.

"July question mark, why the question mark? Are you July or are you not, YES OR NO?"

"Yes, sir. I'm July."

"I'm January," the fetch contributed in a whisper. "Please don't yell at us. Everybody yells at us."

"June. July. January. Last name, RIGHT NOW!"

The girls joined hands. Driver June said, "Can we go now, or does your savage male ego require that you verbally abuse children in order to make you feel like real cops?"

He almost swore, but suddenly realized he was being baited.

"Addams," the fetch blurted. "We're the Addams family."

"The entire family unit or just the sisters part?"

He saw the girls exchanging glances. They said nothing.

"Dese guys got da lockjaws," Limpy said.

"What year is this truck?"

Allerdyce said, "Ninety-nine, I t'ink."

Service hit transmit on his radio and spoke into his chest mic. "Central, we're out on a logging track off Stalling Road. We've got a ninety-nine Chevy stopped, color dark blue, no plate and no registration. The people claim their name is Addams."

The dispatcher came back, "Is that two dogs for d, or one?"

"They say two, but run both." He was losing patience.

"Easy, Sonny," Allerdyce whispered. "Just kittles."

Central dispatch came back, "Nothing on the truck, Twenty-Five Fourteen. Can you get the VIN? Is this for real, or is it that movie thingy?"

Real or that movie thingy? What the hell is going on?

"Movie thingy?" Service hissed into his microphone.

"Sorry," Central said. "Wasn't supposed to say that over the radio. You get that VIN?"

He had no desire to crawl around looking for the manufacturer's vehicle identification number. "Stand by," he said.

The dispatcher said, "Don't know if this helps, but we have a BOL out of Marquette for three runaways, sisters, Adams with one dog for d."

"June, July, January?" Service said.

"Affirmative, Fourteen."

"Ages on the BOL?"

"Fourteen, thirteen, and ten."

"Thanks, Central. Fourteen clear."

He turned to the girls.

"See," the fetch said. "We didn't lie."

"Whose truck is this?"

"We have permission," the driver said.

"None of you is old enough to drive legally, so permission is irrelevant."

"We have not stolen anything," the driver said. "Deer belong to the citizens, which means us."

"You don't even pay taxes yet, which doesn't qualify you as persons, and you're too damn young to be driving, much less blacked out at night."

"Mere technicalities," the driver said dismissively.

What is it with kids these day that so little intimidates them? Okay, stay calm, let them take out some line. "Okay, documentary sisters, where's your camera?"

The group was suddenly illuminated by bright lights, and Service had to squint to see. "We're here," a male voice said from the dark beyond the lights in front of the truck. "Still rolling."

Service saw Allerdyce grinning. *The old fart is enjoying himself? Good grief.*

"Conservation officer, Department of Natural Resources. Kill those lights now, step forward, and identify yourselves."

A tall man came in from the driver's side of the road. "I'm Doctor Jay Jay Emerson Adams, assistant professor of film at Northern. These three desperadoes are my daughters. My lovely wife, Doonoona, is up the road with the camera. Our sons Augie and March are handling the sound."

Service could hardly contain his rage. "You think this is a game?"

"No, Officer, we take this to be a very serious film effort."

"Do you have any idea how easily your girls could have gotten hurt? Driving dark at night and taking deer is not just illegal, it's all dangerous as *hell*."

"You're arguing theoretically. No one got hurt here. This has all been expertly rehearsed, and it went down like clockwork, thanks to you two fellas. Actually we thought you were our actors, but apparently they got lost—and what happens? Real game wardens show up. How cool is *that*?"

Seething, trying to hold it in. Service walked back to the truck bed, flipped up the corner of a plastic tarp, and found a heavy Styrofoam deer target. No wonder the sound had seemed off. It had squeaked, not thumped when it landed in back of the truck. He looked out at the field. "Bring the camera to me."

A woman came forward. "We're sorry if we've upset you, but this has been a wonderful and delightful learning experience for our children."

"You could make the same claim for funerals," Service grumbled. "Somebody could've died here tonight."

The woman didn't acknowledge him. "They're gifted, you know, and living up here in Nowhereland. I'm certain you can't imagine how difficult it is to find the necessary educational opportunities."

"You're right," he said. "I can't imagine. Give me your camera."

She handed it to him. "How many disks are there?" he asked.

"Three."

"Put them in my hand."

The woman hesitated. "This is private property. Tell the man, Jay Jay."

"Give the man the disks, Doo."

Service felt two disks in the palm of his hand. The woman said, "Two plus one in the camera, which you already have. Do be careful. That is a valuable, professional-grade piece of equipment. You can't just abuse private property."

"I can't?" Her tone grated him. "You just participated in a conspiracy to mislead law enforcement in the process of doing their jobs. That's a crime."

"Oh pish," the woman said. "We just hurt your feelings because the girls had you guys fooled. Men are always so damn sensitive, and you are blowing all of this way out of proportion. Tell him Jay Jay."

The professor kept quiet.

Service said, "Bring your boys forward. I want the whole family right here in front of me."

When they gathered around, he asked the age of the boys.

"Eighteen and sixteen," dad said.

"How did you all get out here?"

The professor said, "We have a van parked near here."

"The real thing or movie thing?" Was the county somehow in on this bullshit, and if so, why? What's up with this *crap*? Now he was really steamed.

"This was not supposed to go down like this," the man said.

"Adams, it's deer season and night in the ass-end of nowhere. This time of year, nothing goes down the way it's supposed to. There's a BOL out on your daughters. They're runaways."

"That's part of the script, and I suppose we should apologize."

Script? "Fool!" Grady Service said sharply.

"I'm sure that attitude is unprofessional even by backwoods standards, and it is uncalled for rudeness," the wife interjected icily.

Service just shook his head, grabbed Allerdyce and said, "We're out of here."

"Sir, Officer," Professor Jay Jay said. "The keys to our truck?"

Service said, "What keys?"

The professor said, "Seriously, we need the keys."

"Look around. They gotta be here somewhere. My arm strength isn't what it used to be."

"This is behavior *unbecoming*," the wife said to their backs.

They didn't talk until they got into the patrol truck and started the engine. Service called dispatch, "Twenty-Five Fourteen is clear of the last, but you'll hear from *me* again about this movie *thingy*."

The dispatcher did not reply.

"Just great," he said to his partner. "When this gets around, we'll never live it down."

"Youse not gone arrest dat gaggle gooferballs?"

"I'll talk to a judge. At this time, I don't know what to do. I've never seen anything like this before."

"Me neither either," Allerdyce said. "T'ink dey let us watch da flick dey made?"

"Shut up."

CHAPTER 34

Slippery Creek Camp

SATURDAY, NOVEMBER 21

They slept in real beds, and when Service got up just after sunrise, he looked out front and saw a second black patrol truck parked next to his, its engine running. His truck was frosted over. The other one looked like it was just out of its new-truck wrapping, sparkling clean, no dents, no U.P. pinstriping, and no character. Had to be Duckboat, who was anal about caring for his equipment, state and personal. He opened the front door and waved the man in.

Allerdyce came padding past and went into a bathroom, cutting off the other officer.

"Jerk," Duckboat complained.

"Age has privylatches," Allerdyce called out. "Why you t'ink dat word got maked up?"

Service moaned. His partner was exhausting to be with 24/7. Duckboat walked stiff-legged into the kitchen.

"How long have you been parked out there?"

Yawn. "Dunno, but I had this great dream going."

"You want coffee?"

"Please."

"Gotta make it first."

"No hurry. How's your season going? Mine is *SO SLOW*."

"Have you not talked to anyone?"

"Texts, e-mails, cell phones, gossip; I hate *all* that shit. Just let me do my job and go home whole. What I want to know is what the hell you did to deer hunters in the Mosquito. There are some big bucks back in there and no hunters."

"Wasn't me; McCants was in there before you. She was pretty hard on people."

"Point is, ain't nobody coming in no more, which is a shame. I got two loaded guns on the perimeter road opening night, and since then, not a damn thing. I think you and McCants put a curse on the place."

"Work smarter."

"I didn't come here for slogans or advice. What the hell is *Allerdyce* doing here?"

"He's my partner."

The poacher picked up the coffeepot, saw that it was empty, and made a face. "I got do ever't'ing dis joint?"

Duckboat said, "Are you crazy? Is it even legal to have the likes of him in your truck?"

"I forgot to ask."

The other officer shook his head. "Seriously, Grady, what's the deal with the Mosquito? There are big bucks in there, and nobody's after them."

"No ORVs or snowmobiles allowed. It's like a sanctuary, and nobody wants to make the physical effort anymore. The Mosquito makes you walk and rewards only those who do."

"That's not fair. Not all hunters are lazy."

"Not all, but a lot. Got a whole generation now that knows nothing but elevated stands, food plots, and bait. Put them on the ground with no bait, and they're clueless. They couldn't track a wounded elephant from the shower to the toilet."

"My pipple don't use no blinds," Allerdyce said, joining in.

Duckboat bristled. "What exactly constitutes *your people*?"

Allerdyce smiled. "Youse know."

"No, I don't," the young CO said.

"Youse's job ta know such stuff," Allerdyce said, turning to his partner. "Ain't it?"

"Who the hell are you to tell me how to do *my* job?" Duckboat challenged.

"Sonny boy's partner is who." Allerdyce handed a cup to the man. "Pour youse's own; ain't no wait-on-your-asses in dis camp."

The junior CO poured coffee and grinned. "You sure are feisty."

"Learn it fum best," Allerdyce said.

Duckboat turned back to Service. "Seriously, I'm going to start sleeping out there to look for hunters. Is everybody seeing the same thing? It's slow."

"Haven't talked to everybody."

"What about you?"

"This and that, you know; the normal dull roar."

"Geez, everybody calls you the Main Shitmagnet, and if it's slow for you. . . ."

"Every season is different; each one has its own pulse and speed."

"But there are trophy animals in the Mosquito and nobody seems to care. How can that *be*?"

"Lotsa pipples scared by da wolfies," Allerdyce said.

"They may carp about wolves, but they still hunt."

"Talkin' two-leg wolfies wit' da long memories," Allerdyce said.

Duckboat downed the rest of his coffee. "Thanks, guys; I gotta roll. Boredom and dream time are calling my name."

Service put a finger in the young officer's face. "You slack for one minute and it can kill you. Keep your head in the game, copy?"

"Yes, sir, I copy."

"Use your head. If you wanted to go deep into where the animals are, and not walk, how would you do it?"

The officer stared at him and went out to his truck.

Service guessed that the heavy hand he and McCants had laid on the Mosquito was still being felt. Few outsiders had the nerve to even find the place, much less hike into it.

"Normal dull routine," Allerdyce said. "Why you don't tell 'at boy trut'?"

"Don't want to demoralize him." Service looked at his partner. "Two-legged wolfies?"

Allerdyce raised his cup in salute.

He called Friday on her cell phone. "Everything all right back there?"

She said, "I don't know. Is it? Sixty-eight tickets in one stop and I don't hear a peep out of you? Seriously, what the hell is going on, Grady Service?"

No easy answer for her. "Not sure. You don't sound happy."

"Happy? What exactly *is* happy? We've just learned that a deer hunter beat his wife to death in Palmer, our garage got burned down, my insurance agent says my coverage does not cover arson, and I'm so horny I'm making goo-goo eyes at green bananas in the grocery store, bananas named for a goddamn woman, and you have the gall to ask if I'm happy?"

"Don't worry about the garage," he said. "It may be time you and I had a talk."

She countered, "A talk or *the* talk?"

"There's a difference?"

"You don't know, *seriously*? You are such a guy, Service."

"We can talk about talks when we talk," he said.

She laughed out loud.

"I mean it; don't sweat money or the garage. I've got this," he said.

"I wish you had *this*," she said in her wily feminine voice. "What's ahead for you guys?"

"More patrols and trying to solve the big mystery."

"Which is?"

"Why Harry Pattinson and those camps are not seeing deer. I talked to Wildlife. The answer is not wolves." This had been scratching at the back of his mind since his first talk to Torky Hamore. "I love you," he told Friday.

"Talk is cheap, bub. Be safe, please?"

He closed the phone and looked over at Allerdyce. "Do you like puzzles?"

"Not lessen dey harder'n Finnlanders' square heads."

They got into the truck and were about to pull out when he saw something red. The damn cigarette pack he'd seen before. He got out, walked over, picked it up, threw it into the bed of the truck, and pulled out.

"Should leave dere, Sonny," the old poacher said. "Snow make go 'way till da birdies comes home."

CHAPTER 35

Harvey, Marquette County

MONDAY, NOVEMBER 23

Yesterday had been uneventful and unproductive, but not a total loss, because they'd managed to get two consecutive nights of normal sleep. Friday had texted him that she was moving home tonight and had dropped off the pets this morning on her way to work.

First stop this morning was the Marquette courthouse, where he handed in tickets and the cash he'd collected as bond money, mostly from the outlaw gun camp. He saw Sally Palovar in the magistrate's office. She smiled at him and asked, "Any excitement yet?"

Had she not heard about the crap they were colliding with? Everybody else seemed to know, and the backslappers were out and full of attaboys as he moved through the building. Lt. Rusty Ranka tried to tell him about a case he'd once made and how it had propelled him to sergeant. He excused himself from the bigmouth, stepped away, and saw Sally Palovar again, this time outside her office in the hallway, staring at him. He sensed she wanted something. She had said something odd a few days back, but so much had happened in the intervening days that he no longer remembered details or contexts. "You okay?" he asked her.

"Which part of me are you asking about," she came back.

Peculiar response. "Not sure, I just thought . . ."

"What exactly *did* you think?"

Her voice had a grating quality. He shrugged because he had no idea what else he could or should say.

"Do not interrogate me. I've been trained to resist."

She said this with a slight smile, and it seemed to him she was straining, like a truck trying to pull an overloaded trailer. He gave her one of his cards. "If you ever need to talk . . ."

She rolled her eyes. Was she vamping or blowing him off? "Call *you?* You, the *game warden?*"

He knew he was missing something, but he had no idea what, or how to connect to her. He said, "You've got my number," and started to leave.

She tugged on his sleeve and turned him. "Do you have *my* number?"

He looked at her and found her glaring at him, almost angrily. *What the hell?* This wasn't a come-on. That he could have and would have read. *This is something else, something subtle and troubling, something beyond my grasp, a reminder that you don't know this woman at all.*

The encounter left him uncomfortable as they headed for Friday's house. He'd made a call to an Ishpeming company that specialized in demolishing and hauling contaminated debris, especially rubble from burned buildings. They promised to take care of the garage within forty-eight hours. He didn't ask for a price estimate. The black pile looked ugly. *Do we rebuild or not? She's gotta have a garage for winter, something to keep her vehicle out of the snow and ice. Forget that stuff now. Get it out of your mind. You can solve that later. Keep your mind on real business. It's deer season.*

Allerdyce was at the truck with two cups of coffee. "We workin' outten truck t'day?"

"If we go out in the snow and dirt, people will just irritate us."

"Dere problem, eh. Youse want shake trees, dat's what I want, Sonny."

"Knowing that affords me great peace of mind."

"Dat piece like womans give, or da kind like dove birdies bring?"

"At some point we were sort of talking about how you tracked big buck locations."

"Weren't no pocket science. Jes wrote down ever't'ing heard, see?"

Pocket science? "You wrote it all down on a piece of paper?"

"No; I got dose typogrammical maps from guv-mint."

"Topographicals from USGS?"

"I don't know all dat letter soup, Sonny, t'ink youse need youse's ears-check."

"You mean a hearing check."

"Dere youse go again. Why you do dat me? I say what mean. What dey check when want know youse can, hear? Ears, it an ear check."

Hopeless, unwinnable battle to debate or correct the old man. "Okay, so you made notes on the maps?"

"Jus' tole youse dat."

"Over how long a period?"

"Dunno, one second, two mebbe."

Good God. "No, I mean over how long a time did you keep your notes?"

"Keep t'ree set. Dis year, last two years, last t'ree years, diff-ren' color ink each year."

"Do you still have those maps?"

"Guess, dunno. Why?"

"I'd like to take a look."

"Youse want bust my chops for ole stuff?"

"Not that. Can I see them, yes or no? The statute of limitations is long gone on your stuff."

"Got drive all way out my place. What if youse see some'pin dere not gone by statue of imitations?"

"I'll ignore them. We'll make a quick stop at the Harvey house, and head out your way."

• • •

Newf, Service's Presa Canario, was 160 pounds of bulging canine muscle. She went ballistic when she saw Allerdyce behind him. Soon thereafter, Cat, the nameless feline misanthrope he had saved years before, took umbrage at the old man's singular attention to the dog, hissed like a cobra, sprung up, and viciously chomped one of the dog's ears. The dog batted the cat away like an annoying fluff ball and kept by Allerdyce's side, leaning into him, whining, and begging for him to pet her. Service had been deathly afraid of dogs most of his life, until an old girlfriend gave Newf to him. Living with the giant dog all the time began to lessen his fear. Not entirely, but enough not to be immediately horrified and petrified.

Why the animals adored Allerdyce escaped him. You'd think they'd sense what a multispecies murderer he was and run for cover. Instead they battled each other for his attention.

Allerdyce rubbed Newf's large head and cackled and grinned and coughed; Service could stand no more of the display and headed into another room where he didn't have to watch.

He called Tuesday on her personal cell phone. "We're at the house."

"Is Allerdyce included in that we?"

"*Oui*, we" he said. "The animals like him."

"They also like to drink fetid swamp water and smell each others' butts," she reminded him. "There's no accounting for taste, and they have IQs of what, like 14 tops?"

"Still," he said.

She said, "My day's great, how's yours?"

"You know," he said.

"No, in fact I *don't* know, which is why I asked. The killing I told you about? The father copped to it out of the gate, but I'm not buying his story. I have two sources telling me that the son hated his mom and batted her around on more than one occasion. I smell dad taking one for junior. What the hell is wrong with people?"

This was not a question she expected an answer to, and he knew to keep his yap shut. She was venting. It had taken most of his life to figure out that when a woman was in vent-mode, the last thing she wanted from her partner was problem-solving. His job during a vent rant was to shut up and listen, period. No exceptions.

She continued, "I mean, if the father wants to do time, why should I care? It's his life, right? Never mind that junior will be free to strike again. It's not my place to interfere, right?"

There was a question here, not quite rhetorical, but neither was it sincere. It was more in the line of a feint designed to find out if he was listening. "OK," he said in neutered cop talk, which translated to "I just heard the words you said," which is to say, the sounds that came out of your mouth, "but I neither agree nor disagree, and, yes, I am listening to your every word."

She plowed on. "Maybe I should shoot the punk and do everyone a favor before he strikes again. What do you think, hon? Should I?"

Now it was time to answer.

"If you do that, use a shotgun with birdshot, number sixes. Birdshot's a lot harder to trace in the lab." He heard her voice catch, followed by a girlish giggle.

She asked, "Whatever do I see in you? Seriously."

He answered, "Seriously? I've got no clue."

"Yet I love you."

"It's as mysterious as pocket science."

"*What*?"

"An Allerdycism."

"I have to tell you that it makes me shudder to think that creepy old man is inside our house."

"We won't be here long. We're headed out to his place."

"Out in the jungle?"

"You want help from the beast, you have to go to its lair."

"You have a peculiar way with words."

"Yah?"

"No," she said. "Be safe." She hung up.

"Do we need to grab groceries on the way to your place?" Service asked his partner.

Allerdyce cackled with obvious pleasure. "Sonny, my place is da grocery store."

This was not exactly what he hoped to hear from his "reformed" partner. He got his bag of plat books from his basement corner office and grabbed a bottle of 2007 Coppola Claret from the wine rack in the living room. "I bet we'll have venison," Service said to the old poacher.

Allerdyce smiled and said, "Wunt s'prise me none."

"Long frozen and not fresh, I hope."

"Why youse say dat, Sonny?"

"Because you've been with me the entire firearm season and you've not had time to hunt."

"Dere's bow and arrow before, eh? An' road kill keep-papers. Youse want, check craputer stuff on what license I buy."

Service laughed.

"Dare youse," Allerdyce said. "Youse and me need get dis shit straight."

Service called Station Twenty, checked the retail sales database, and found that his partner indeed had bought an archery tag.

"How many you got so far?"

"Two," the old poacher said.

"You arrowed deer with your bow?"

Allerdyce went into a laughing fit, and when he finally got himself back under control, he blew his nose and said, "Arrow a deer sound stupid—like wrench a nut, knife a steak, bullet da bear." The laughing jag began anew.

Grady Service drove on, suspecting he was going to need a serious vacation when this deer season was over. Buckular dystrophy, deer-killing disease, it seemed, was everywhere, in various forms—an unseen epidemic yet to be identified by public health experts.

ACT 3: A SOUP CALLED SERENDIPITY

Unless someone like you cares a whole awful lot, nothing is going to get better, it's not.

—Dr. Seuss, *The Lorax*

CHAPTER 36

Southwest Marquette County

MONDAY, NOVEMBER 23

They made the drive quickly and uneventfully, stopping only to wait at a parked truck and check licenses of three NMU students coming out of the woods to get some coffee before they went back in for the end-of-day sit in their blinds. Everything checked out—unloaded guns, no concealed weapons, proper amount of orange, tags matched driving licenses, all had hunter safety training. This was, Service thought, the equivalent of the doctor checking your virgin teenage daughter and reporting back, "Everything is A-OK."

"Great work, fellas," he told the students. It was nice to see not just young hunters out in the woods but the young ones actually following the rules in letter and spirit, something a lot of older hunters increasingly seemed unable or unwilling to do.

"Think the deer will be moving tonight?" Service asked his partner after they left the trio.

Allerdyce answered with a disinterested shrug. "Will or won't. What we do t'day?"

"Visit camps, schmooze, listen, keep our eyes and ears open, check whoever we run into, handle complaints as they come to us."

Sadly this described the routine activity during a lot of deer seasons. It was also a fact that in many counties in the state, complaints would not roll in until days and weeks after the season ended, when nothing could be done about them. Trespassers, over-baiting, shots before and after hours, hunter harassment, no orange in the field, all sorts of things COs might have been able to take care of when they were occurring would go unaddressed if the complaints came too late.

He was of the opinion that late calls were largely nothing more than hunters and camp owners trying to set themselves up for the next season by putting DNR pressure on certain competing camps, individuals, and situations. Got a problem this year, don't call yet. Grin and bear it. Wait until the season is over so you can make sure your own house is clean. Then you lodge the complaint to get your local CO looking in the direction you pointed when the next season rolled around. He knew this view was jaundiced, but he had seen evidence that it was often true and part and parcel of the trivial unsubstantive, neighbor-versus-neighbor, relative-against-relative conflicts that marked most seasons. Conflict, justified or not, was the air most cops breathed.

And it was a pattern every DNR officer quickly came to recognize and loathe, especially in those counties composed mainly of private property. Many such complaints were disinformation and smear campaigns, not genuine calls for righting serious legal wrongs, a sort of low-intensity gossip-information war aimed at only one outcome, improving the complainant's imagined competitive position. Many of these calls, maybe most of them, were a waste of time because they were so late and therefore impractical and most often unactionable.

Although some complaints *were* serious, many were trivial at best.

Their route was a zigzag across the southern reaches where a chunk of Marquette County thrust south and lay between segments of Delta to the east, Dickinson to the west, and Menominee County on the bottom perimeter—an area some of the old-time officers referred to informally as the Quad of Mutes, a wild and woolly area where camp owners rarely called the DNR and tended to deal with their own problems and perceived slights.

Those not in the know were under the opinion that the Quad was some sort of gathering place for an amazing array of outlaws and lowlife characters. It was far from that. This area's camps tended to be large, their owners serious hunters, and most landowners had the resources and power to get their way on just about anything that money could affect, which meant just about anything. With one exception: A hunter on public land got no less fair treatment from conservation officers than landowners with four sections and obese bank accounts. To a game warden, equality meant something real and tangible about your actions in the woods, not your credentials in some other venue.

His having unexpectedly come into substantial wealth had not altered his personal and fundamental belief that money was either a weapon or a tool, depending on who wielded it, how, and to what end. His own money rarely scratched his thoughts. But he knew others used money as the sole gauge of quality of life, and this belief sometimes took certain individuals into some strange territory.

They were in their seventh camp of the day, checking deer on buck poles, hearing nimrod hero tales the tellers were certain were unique in the annals of hunting but which Service had heard so many times he could have given the new tellers their own blow-by-blow. It was to the point now that he'd rather hear the story of someone's hemorrhoid surgery than some blowhard's William Tell shot "swear to God" made on a doe from 290 yards. "I paced it off myself, through a small tunnel of branches moving in the breeze, and I had just one shot, and I . . ." It was so damn predictable and boring. *Ho-fucking-hum.* And this baloney not from knuckle-dragging wood ticks so much as some CEO from Chicago with a vacation villa in Martinique and a winter place in Tucson, and all he could talk about was a pitiful doe he shot in such a way he now imagined he could have had a career as a military sniper. As if that one shot through a black spruce tangle put him on the list of hunting's top ten accomplishments. *Disgusting.*

Today they had seen some questionable things, but nothing that overwhelmed or called out for the steely cold hand of justice. It was just another morning in hunting season in the U.P., a stretch of time where they made contact with fifty-six people (which he kept count of with hatch marks on a notepad). The current politically appointed leader of the DNR had decided that all of his employees needed to count the number of people they interacted with daily in order to create a sort of public scorecard for the agency. Most COs simply shook their heads at such foolishness and kept the count as they were instructed.

Service remembered the days when COs were expected to count and report on wildlife movement. This was how things like the state deer herd size were calculated back then, and the public was assured it was science at its best. Bull.

The number of contacts got noted on electronic dailies and in weekly summaries to supervision. It was a standing joke in some counties with sparse human populations that officers counted dogs, cats, sheep, horses, and even Amish buggies to inflate their numbers.

He hated all such artificial nonsense but dutifully kept his count (no dogs or canaries), and because of this he knew they had been in contact with fifty-six citizens so far, and never mind that conversations in most cases were brief pro forma rubber stamps of previous conversations. The conversations tended to follow the same outline and order:

"Seeing many big bucks?"

Define big. "A few."

"Wolves a problem?"

"Don't seem to be so far."

"What's the biggest buck you've seen so far?"

"Sixteen points." This answer invariably broke down the script.

"No shit, *where*?"

And once that aside got exhausted, it was back to standard bullshit.

"We sure are glad to see you guys. We all follow the rules, but not every camp is like us."

Right. On and on, a continuous conveyor belt of pabulum. Later, if he found one of these same self-proclaimed law abiders outside the boundaries, they would flip out over being picked on. The tone and fabric were in some ways all predictable, day after day, season after season. *People.*

They were back in the truck and headed for their eighth camp. "Youse got same gift of gab youse's old man had."

"I'm hearing the same bullshit stories too."

"Ya sure, but he knows how get good dope frum camps; use ta make some real good cases, Sonny."

"Dope to smoke?"

Allerdyce frowned. "Youse's daddy din't do no damn drug crap. Dope mean inflammation."

"Information," he said, correcting his partner.

"Wanted said dat word, woulda said, hey. Inflammation mean more dope youse can put toget'er, more dope you want make youse's brain get smarter and smarter."

Service rolled his eyes. His alcoholic old man had eventually killed himself with booze as surely as, although more slowly than, with a bullet. But Allerdyce was loyal and unshakeable in his support and faith in those things he believed in, and you had to admire that in a man, even a specimen such as Limpy.

Ironically the eighth camp was called Camp Eight, and there was an open camp gate. They drove into the camp on a road along a finger of land above a deep gorge, got to the end where the camp itself was, and saw no sign of human life other than seven trucks, all newer models—GMCs, a Lincoln Blackwood, couple of Fords—most of them punked and tricked-out, and all with non-Michigan plates.

The buck pole was empty. He could see a floodplain below the camp and a ribbon of stream cutting through a kind of swamp meadow. There was no blood on the backs of the vehicles or under the buck pole. He wondered how unhappy this crowd would be.

He didn't need to speak to Allerdyce. They had evolved a routine: Service went to the camp door to knock while Limpy made a hurried circle around the camp to see what he could see. No answer at the door; he saw Allerdyce pointing downward, over at the edge of the drop-off to the floodplain.

He joined his partner, who held up six fingers, pointed downward, and made his crooked grin as he cupped a hand behind an ear.

They moved closer to the lip. Allerdyce used split fingers on his eyes, pointed, and made his fingers walk. He made a sign like he was choking, put his hand on his head and moved it like he was feeling nothing, and held up six fingers and pointed off into the dense black spruces near camp. They had not worked out a code, but Service understood Limpy had found six does hidden somewhere in the trees, not on the buck pole. Service heard free-flowing water music and no human voices below. Allerdyce made a gesture like he was casting to fish and raised an eyebrow.

Service tried to orient himself and closed his eyes to create and visualize a map in his head. This was probably Skimpy Creek or an unnamed branch of it. Skimpy was said to be fair brook trout water, which got little pressure because it looked so unimpressive, was so far off the beaten path, and the bulk of it ran through private camp properties. Most anglers didn't want both an exhausting walk and a potential argument with landowners, who wrongly assumed fish in the creeks on their property belonged to them.

Service pointed at the camp and gave Allerdyce a small push to head him that way, which he did immediately. Service looked around and found a worn trail leading below through heavy cover and descended the steep hill. He was hidden at the bottom by heavy brush and tag alders; he stepped into them and looked out and saw four men in waders in the stream and three other men coming out of a draw on the far side of the marsh. The three were dragging a deer, and the anglers stopped fishing and gathered to greet the deer-slayers. When the seven were together, he stepped out of hiding, strode quickly to them, and greeted them, "Looks like we've had some luck."

A large man with flat gray eyes bent slowly down to pick up a branch about three feet long and as thick as a baseball bat, the only sounds that of heavy breathing blending with moving cold water. "I hope that's for the campfire, Ace," Service said, locking his gaze on Gray Eyes. The man showed no emotion but let the branch drop to the ground by his feet. He was a big man with a menacing, hollow look. Relieved there was no escalation, Service turned his attention to the deer, a doe.

"Hmm, no tag, why might that be?"

One of the seven stepped in front of Gray Eyes, whose look had gone from impassive to fiery. "The truth is that we just found it," the man explained, pointing north. Service noted that the man with the explanation had not been with the hunting group. They all had rifles slung. The self-appointed ambassador had been in the fishing party but obviously knew what had taken place.

"Shot it, tracked it, and found it?"

"No, sir; we never shot anything. We just found it out in the woods."

Service studied the seven, trying to assess the threat level, if any; and though all was quiet at the moment, he figured he was about to be engulfed in a verbal shit storm. The man to watch most carefully was Gray Eyes, clearly the alpha threat, now glowering and not trying to hide it.

A scream such as he had never heard from human lips shattered the moment. All seven men were startled and turned clumsily to see Limpy Allerdyce, shirt off, face and torso covered with blood, shotgun in hand. He plowed right at Gray Eyes until the bigger man stepped back, tripped over the doe, and landed on his back in the snow and mud. The man lay there with his hands outstretched to ward off the attack, as if flesh could deflect slugs.

Allerdyce was frothing at the mouth. "Eatem now boss? Eatem now *please*, boss!"

Jesus, God. Has the old man lost his mind?

Limpy was thrusting the shotgun forward and jumping back, like it was a spear or something, and mumbling, "Shootem, eatem up, shootem, eatem up, okay boss; big ones got lotsa good eatem up!" Allerdyce was making slurping sounds as he blathered, standing over Gray Eyes with the shotgun pointed just over the man's head.

"Leave it!" Service commanded.

Allerdyce squealed pathetically, "fugingfuginfrickinfug," stepped back sharply, and came crisply to attention, the shotgun held diagonally across his chest in the position of port arms.

"Good boy," Service said. "At ease."

"Please boss, eatem now," Limpy said. "I reeel hoongry!"

"No."

Service knew the shit storm had passed; Limpy's outrageous behavior had ripped the guts out of whatever the group might have had in mind. Service kept his eyes on Gray Eyes and pointed for the others. "You four, get your fish and lift them so I can see them." He locked onto Gray Eyes and pointed. "You are going to drag that doe up the hill to camp." No one moved.

"*Now*." Service yelled. The anglers lifted their brook trout; Gray Eyes bolted for the hill, with Limpy hopping along and waving his arms and making strange guttural sounds.

"Fish!" Service shouted, and the men danced over to the stream.

Service asked, "Okay *who* found the deer?"

One of the three hunters waggled a finger. "That would be me, sir."

"But you didn't shoot it, right?"

"Absolutely correct. We do not believe in shooting does in this camp. It's against sporting principles."

Service allowed, "Shooting does can be good for the herd."

"We are aware of that theoretical position, sir, and we certainly respect that view, but it's just not for us and, in any event, the point is moot, yes? There are no doe permits for around here, so even if we wanted to shoot does, which we don't and didn't, the rules would preclude it and, as already noted, we do not knowingly break rules. You now know the truth of the matter."

"Nice speech," Service said. "How does your bullshit square with the six does you've got hanging in spruces over that way?" he pointed.

The group's spokesman gulped. "Can we talk, man to man, no bullshit?"

"It would warm my heart," Service said. This group was not of this planet.

The man said, "Mistakes have been made, see what I am saying?"

"Mistakes made by whom?"

"Let us just leave it at mistakes were made. Why needlessly and injuriously point fingers when we know where all this ends up? This is about money to the state. Why put everyone through the inconvenience of paperwork and a rubber-stamp kangaroo court? We're all responsible adults here." The man made a show of getting a wad of bills from his pocket. "Cite us a number, Officer, and let us return to the business that brought us here. Are we on the same wavelength here?"

"How about we start with the fish," Service said. "Empty your creels on the ground at your feet, turn the creel inside out, and spread out the fish so I can count them."

"Sort by size?" one of the men asked.

"That's not an issue in this case. The season's been closed since the end of September, and a six-inch trout is the same as a sixteen today. They're all illegal, and size isn't an issue."

The count came to sixty brook trout among the four anglers, all of them barely legal fish had the season been on. "Hand me driver's licenses and fishing licenses."

Not one of them moved. They were all studying the ground. "Don't have one with you, or don't have one, period?"

Still no change in posture or any response. "Driver's licenses, then, and deer tags." These they produced.

The self-appointed ambassador asserted himself once again "Our land, our fish, fourth-generation camp; we set the rules here, and we enforce them."

"What do you do for a living, sir?"

"I am a certified professional planner."

"What exactly is it that you plan?"

"You name it."

"Well," Service said, "this camp is one mega fuckup. Did you plan this?"

The man turned red and stepped back.

Service whispered to Allerdyce. "Stay with them and schmooze them to keep their attention, and make sure they can see the shotgun." He glanced up at the group and added loudly, "If any of them gets out of line, go ahead shoot them. You can eat the meat later."

Allerdyce cackled, yelped, "Wah, wah, yah, yah, eatem up boss, eatem up!" and slapped the slide on the shotgun like he was thumping a guitar.

Service checked Gray Eyes again. The man had sunk to his knees and had blood coming out of his nose and a mark on his cheekbone. *What the heck?*

It took a long time to run all the licenses, interview all the idiots separately, get all the charges sorted out, write tickets, and collect the right amount of bond money. He and Allerdyce took seven deer from the camp—none of them tagged, the first six hidden in the trees—and he took all their deer tags. None of the men would admit to shooting any of the deer. Gray Eyes, it turned out, owned the camp. Service nailed him with all seven illegals but took all their rifles and fishing gear.

The contact left Service's pockets overflowing with bond money, most of which the man with the money roll supplied.

They were on the road out of camp with another fistful of tickets. "What the hell county are we in?" He lifted the top of his laptop on the pedestal between them, checked the AVL, and saw they were barely in Marquette County. "We're gonna jump back to town and turn the cash and the tickets in to the court. By the way, partner, what happened to Gray Eyes back there?"

"I t'ink mebbe he piss off God or somepin."

Service took a container of sanitary wipes from his door, handed it to his partner. "God still has bloody knuckles."

Allerdyce grinned and started cleaning himself.

"Weren't you cold with your shirt off like that, and where'd all that blood come from?"

"Can't get cold when do what God say do."

He had no idea if the old man was pulling his leg. What he did know was that his partner's unexpected appearance had seized the initiative and badly shaken up the hunters; had he not done what he'd done, the contact might have ended a lot differently.

Once again, he owed the old man.

"Those jerks claim this is a fourth-generation camp. Can you imagine what's gone on back there, undetected?"

"Been dicktected now."

"Do you know what *laconic* means?"

"Lake over Schoolcraft County?"

Allerdyce. "We'll grab chow at home after we drop the stuff at the court. I still want to talk about how you usta track big bucks back in the day."

Allerdyce said. "Usta. I like the sound of dat. Sonny, weren't no ammo in scattergun back dere camp. I know bettern's play with the loaded gun, eh."

Grady Service nodded and added eight marks to his contact list.

"Was onny seven," Allerdyce corrected him. The old man was leaning over to peek.

"I'm including the wild thing in red war paint. I have no idea who he was, do you?"

CHAPTER 37

Tri-County Swamp Camp Country

TUESDAY, NOVEMBER 24

Getting rid of the confiscated firearms wasn't easy. The gun locker in Lieu-tenant Livorno's office in the Roof was full and locked, and he was off duty. But Carrie Ericksen told him Captain McKower had just gotten a gun locker for her office and Ericksen had the key. She opened it and they dumped the tagged weapons; he left a note on the captain's desk.

They dropped the tickets and cash at the court, had dinner with Tuesday and Shigun (who, like the animals, thought Allerdyce some sort of gift from the heavens), drove all the way out to Limpy's compound, talked briefly about tracking big bucks, and crashed for the night. Service knew that phys-ically he was pushing his limit, but he couldn't really assess his partner's energy level, which seemed to be limitless, despite their age difference.

Morning came, coffee got made, breakfasts were consumed to refuel bodies, and the two men wearily trudged out to the truck in silence. Service was in a reflective mood, a sure sign of sleep deprivation. To get into the patrol truck was like a cowboy being reunited with his horse—that single-minded creature that lets you cover far more ground than you could alone and, like the horse, needs fuel. Service popped down to Channing to top off their fuel tank.

They began to make their way from the gas station east to where the wolf-hater properties lay at the intersections of Delta, Marquette, and Menominee Counties.

Service had just called into central dispatch and to Station Twenty when he got a cell phone call. He took the phone from its visor case and flipped it open. "Grady, Linsenman. Are you in service yet?"

"Just."

"Where you at?"

Service gave his friend an approximate location. "Why?"

"We've got something we think you ought to have a look at. I'll explain when you get here." Linsenman gave him an address in extreme southern Marquette County, coincidentally in the same area they were heading toward, though he didn't know the actual place. He wrote the address in his notebook and figured he would recognize it when he saw it. There were not many places in U.P. counties he didn't know, at least by sight or reputation.

"There a name there?"

"Buckshow, first name of Jesper."

"No mood for deer season jokes," Service said, sniggering.

"It's not a joke, Grady. The name really is Buckshow, and I don't think you'll be grinning when you get here."

"Guess where we're going?" he asked his partner.

"Ain't no mood for puzzles, Sonny. Youse drivin', I jes lookin' outten window, eh. Ain't had nuff coffee yet. What dat call 'bout?"

"Linsenman has something he thinks we ought to see."

"Din't hear youse tell 'im I'm witchyouse."

"I'd rather he get the full effect when you step out of the truck."

"Why dat boy so grumpy roun' me?"

"He thinks you're the devil incarnate. You have that effect on a lot of lawmen."

"Not youse."

"Once somebody shoots you, the relationship changes."

"Was sort of accident," Allerdyce said wearily.

"You know and I know, but most cops are not so sure."

"Dat 'urts my feelin's," Allerdyce said, and added in the next breath, "Sure could use us some fresh bakery wit' dis coffee."

All U.P. sweet rolls and doughnuts were lumped under the phrase "fresh bakery" and separated into two classes, holes and no holes. Grady Service loved this small wrinkle in local life. "No stop-and-robs down in this neighborhood. A good host would have made some fresh doughnuts."

Allerdyce grimaced. "I don't do no woman's works."

Service said, "Maybe Weasel will have bakery."

"Don't t'ink he given me da sweat offen his nutsack, dat one."

"One can always hope." The old man's way of relating to the world escaped all known classifications.

"I ain't inna hope business. Dat way t'inkin' got no teeths. Me, I like pick where I go and steer my own way."

"You're not steering today."

"Youse is partner and youse steering, same t'ing iffin I do, ch."

Service wondered what Linsenman had for them. He and his partner had talked no more than fifteen minutes last night before sacking out. The old man had shown him on a map how he charted large animals and, by writing down dates, how over time he was able to roughly approximate travel patterns and timing. This had predictive value, which let him pop big bucks others only saw. "Never let me down, dis way din't," the old violator had concluded.

. . .

Linsenman had a smug look on his face, but it changed quickly to near-panic when he saw Allerdyce.

"What the . . . ?" was all he could manage.

"My partner for the season."

Linsenman scrunched his face. "Part of some wacky new parole program?"

"I invited him."

"Doesn't your department require an annual mental health check?"

"Not that I've heard."

"It should," Linsenman said.

"Why the heck are we here?"

"We got a complaint from Harry Pattinson. One of his nephews had his new pop-up blind stolen. Pattinson says this has happened before, but this time the nephew tracked a four-wheeler back to this house and there sits the stolen blind in the side yard.

"Jesper Buckshow, yes? Never heard of him. Is he here?"

"No, we just transported him to jail. We went to Pattinson's last night, looked at the scene, and followed the tracks to here, just as the nephew did. We came here first thing this morning, and when Buckshow eventually opened his front door, a wave of dope smoke rolled out so thick it will have hunters high for a two-mile radius. Geez, Grady, that shit gave me and my boys a buzz, which reminds me, you guys bring bakery?"

Service said, "We were banking on you having some."

"We did, but we got so damn hungry here we ate all the bakery *and* our lunches. Why am I *so* hungry?"

"One of life's small mysteries. You don't have a drug test scheduled for today or tomorrow, do you?"

"No, why?"

"It's gonna take your body several days to shed the secondhand dope."

"We should charge this asshole with tainting officers."

"I don't remember a criminal code for that."

"Should be one."

"Your mind is drifting off course."

"Tell me about it," Linsenman said. "I thought the family dog here was a wolf!"

"*What* family dog?"

"Biggest, loudest goddamn German shepherd I've ever seen, and it's trained to put up a big-time defense."

"This is all fine and dandy, and entertaining and interesting and all that junk, but why are *we* here?"

Linsenman grinned sheepishly. "Oh, yah, almos' forgot."

"So Buckshow opens the door, got a cane in each hand. The smoke rolls out and we say, 'Are you smoking dope in there, sir?'"

"He goes, 'Nope, and if I was, it ain't none of your fucking business.'"

"We ask him if we can we come in. He says, 'You may not. This is my castle.'"

"I tell him, 'We don't care about your castle; we're here to talk about your neighbor's hunting blind.'"

"What's he say to that? 'I don't hunt. I'm disabled. Go the fuck away.'"

"Sir, we followed four-wheeler tracks from the complainant's property. There's no doubt."

"'That don't prove shit,' Buckshow says."

"Sir, the blind is sitting in your side yard."

"'Can't be,' he says."

"But it is. Step outside and look."

"He tells us he can't *do* that because of his medical problems. 'Why you think I've got these canes?'"

"I tell him we're sorry for his condition, but we have to deal with the stolen blind. And he says, 'You should be sorry. This goddamn country makes no accommodations for special needs.'"

Service listened, let his friend talk, knowing he was still a little bit jacked on dope smoke. It was kind of fun, the non-talker suddenly turned garrulous storyteller.

Linsenman continued. "I said, 'Mr. Buckshow, we can smell dope, we have a complaint, we have evidence, *and* we have enough probable cause to load a small trailer. Please let us in now.'"

"Then he wants to know if we have a *warrant*. I tell him, no, but we can have one in half an hour, so stop acting the asshole, let us in, and let's be civilized and talk about all this."

"Naturally, he insists on his rights and demands that we call his lawyer. 'For what?' I asked him."

"'I have a severe, chronic medical condition that requires marijuana for palliative relief. I am under a doctor's orders and prescription.'"

"I thought you weren't smoking."

"Says the man, 'I ain't.'"

"What's your doctor's name?"

"'He's not local,'" Buckshow says."

"How not local?"

"'Pakistan.'"

"I told him, 'We'll talk about the dope in a minute, but first we need to talk about the stolen property.' The dog was behind him and going apeshit the whole time, so I told him to secure the damn animal so neither it nor any of us got hurt. Bozo said, 'Deano? He wouldn't hurt a soul.' That's when we pushed him out of the way and grabbed the mutt. Understand, dear old Deano has a head the size of a donkey and teeth like a tiger, and he's snarling and growling and drooling yellow goop all over the damn floor! Long story short, we finally got the dog secured in a bathroom and nobody got bit, and Buckshow called his lawyer. But before the lawyer got here, we found six hidden dope grows and almost two hundred plants."

"And strictly for personal use?" Service said. "Just a wild guess."

"There it is," Linsenman said, "quote, unquote."

"What about the blind?"

"Swears he's never seen it before, and it's in part of the yard he can't really see unless he goes outside, which he can't easily do because of his alleged but unspecified disability."

"Why are *we* here? You don't need us for stolen goods."

Linsenman's eyes narrowed. "Oh, yeah, come take a look."

Every room in the house, including the garage, was filled with deer antlers in various mount styles. Some of the antlers had tags with names that were not Buckshow's. Six of the tags belonged to Sally Palovar, which stopped Service in his tracks. "Who's this?" he asked the county sergeant.

"Exactly who you think she is: Magistrate Kennard Dentso's assistant is Buckshow's wife. They don't share a married name."

Service made a note of this then went around and very quickly counted more than eighty deer skulls and antlers, four full turkey fans, and two wolf pelts; with that he stopped. "When's Buckshow getting kicked?" he asked Linsenman.

"Not tonight. He's going to be in jail at least until tomorrow morning; with dope charges, maybe longer."

"Where's his wife?"

"She'd already left for work when we got here."

"Has anybody informed her that hubby's headed to the can?"

"Not unless Buckshow or his lawyer called her."

Service knew that the way information traveled informally up here, she'd know pretty quickly.

He left Limpy at the truck and made one quick circuit around the house and then one through the house, room to room, touching nothing. The place was a massive mess of evidence, and he was determined not to blow the case with hurried, sloppy work. The round count was now more than a hundred antler mounts. This deal was going to require the cavalry and the methodical, deliberate, fully thought-out evidence-collecting process the department's detectives used more than field officers.

His first call was to Sergeant Wooten, asking him to meet ASAP at the Roof in Marquette.

Call two was to Lieutenant Livorno, to give him a quick head's up. A third call went to a judge, deliberately avoiding the magistrate and his assistant for obvious reasons. The final call went to Dave Dejinois, the Wildlife Protection Unit's newly promoted lieutenant.

The case would be complicated somewhat by the marijuana. The legislature had last year passed a law that "sort of" legalized dope for qualified patients, but the law did not address how the stuff would be legally distributed or sold. The whole arena around legalized medical use was unsettled and in legal limbo, which put cops at a bit of a disadvantage in enforcing the law. Predictably, almost all cops were hearing the defense of legal medical marijuana in nearly all their stops with toking suspects. He wished lawmakers in Lansing would legalize the whole damn thing, soak the sellers with big taxes, and be done with filling jail cells with minor dope players and idiots. Meanwhile, he was determined to handle this case by the book: Create a team, map out what needed to be done, and write a seamless, thorough, airtight affidavit for a search warrant. His time as a detective was welcome now and would pay off. The Wildlife Resources Protection Unit had made sure he was thoroughly trained, and all the detectives were prickly about getting warrants exactly right. Buckshow would not get back here before late tomorrow afternoon. He checked his watch. They had just over twenty-four hours to prep, obtain warrants, search, and seize evidence. It was going to be a long night.

He talked to his partner. "We're going to have to come back here. You won't be able to go in with us, but I want you to scour the property and see what you can see. If you find something you think we need to know about, you tell one of the outside officers and they'll come and tell me."

"What's dis jamoke done?" Allerdyce asked.

"I found three inside shooting rooms with ports, connected to outside lights and visible bait piles, and more skulls, antlers, and full neck mounts than I can count alone. I stopped counting at over a hundred."

"Big deer?"

"No; it's weird. They're all sizes, and a lot of them have the tags of other people. He's even got some doe skulls mounted. There's not one item with his name."

"What dis guy's name is?"

"Jesper Buckshow; you know him?"

Allerdyce shook his head. "Stupid name like dat, I'd 'member."

Service made a point to look at the blind. According to Linsenman, the name on it belonged to Harry Pattinson's nephew. He decided to call the camp owner and confirm this.

"Harry, Grady Service. Do you know Jesper Buckshow?"

"Don't know him real well, but I've met him, and that's for damn sure where my nephew's stolen blind ended up. I heard the Buckshow's got ALS, Lou Gehrig's disease, something like that, which limits his mobility. You think the thieves dropped the blind in his yard to point the finger at him?"

Interesting notion. Why would someone do that? "I haven't really thought about it yet. You should ask the deps that question."

"Why're you calling me?"

"To find out if you know Buckshow."

"Well, it ain't politically correct, and maybe it's his damn wheelchair. I don't really know the man, but excuse me if I say he comes off as one very creepy fuck, and I'm sorry to say that about a guy with a terrible disease like he has."

Service hung up and called Linsenman. "Did you see Buckshow in a wheelchair?"

"Negative, just with canes, which I thought he didn't use all that much, now that you mention it. There's a wheelchair downstairs somewhere, under the cellar stairs, I think. It don't look much used."

Why was Pattinson talking about the wheelchair? What was it Sally Palovar had asked him? He shook his head. *Too damn cobwebby. How does she fit into this crap? Did the thief abandon the pop-up blind, or had it been put deliberately in the yard, and, if so, why? And how exactly did it end up in the only blind spot Buckshow had from inside the house? You could see it from the road but not from inside. Coincidence?* He did not believe in such things.

"We grab bakery on way Marquette?" Allerdyce asked meekly.

"Your need ranks right up there with starving kids in Africa."

"Youse's bein' what da codge boys call iron tonic, eh?"

"You nailed me."

Service's mind was occupied with other things. Goddamn dope and dopers. He'd once found a man in his tree stand by smelling dope curling to him a hundred yards away.

He had announced himself to the hunter, who whined, "Dude, don't go bustin' my happy. I'm up here talkin' to God."

"God, *really*?"

"Yah, dude; the old Hebrooms, those motherfuckers called it *kaneh bosm*, the tree of life."

"I thought that meant roots in hell. Where's your stash, *dude*?"

"You can talk *Hebroom*?"

"No, I made it up, foghead. You can't hunt and handle a firearm when you're high."

"But *dude*, I am so mellow, and mellow's like safe, sayin'?"

"Look at that buck," Service yelled.

The hunter neither moved nor reacted. "Wha?"

"Get out of the damn tree, and do it carefully."

"Got ask God 'cause I ain't making 'is one happen all by my lonesome, sayin'?"

"I'll help you."

"Only God can lift men up."

"You're only half right, dude; give me your hand."

Dope and deer hunters: disgusting.

CHAPTER 38

Marquette

TUESDAY, NOVEMBER 24

The sight of the Roof tended to affect new officers and first-time visitors the same way. The architect had slapped a Chinese pagoda roof over the heads of DNR personnel. The public was puzzled, those under the roof embarrassed, and all officers pissed off every time they had to assemble in the peculiar building. Despite facing Lake Superior and the wind, the place was a total loser by feng shui standards.

Slick Wooten was first to arrive. "What did you get?" he asked as he walked in.

Service laid out the details quickly, seamlessly, efficiently.

"What do you want me to do?" the young sergeant asked.

"Help assemble a team to plan this deal: Superman, Simon, Sheena, Angie Paul, Volstaad."

"Volstaad and Paul are green."

"We were all green when we started. They've got good minds and good eyes." Service had partnered several times with the young officers and found them good company, serious about their work, and consistent. Three or four different times, Volstaad had read angles on situations Service had missed on the first sweep. The young officer had unique insights and new ways of looking at things.

"What about Duckboat?" the sergeant asked.

"No, the Mosquito needs him where he is."

Wooten smirked. "Since you got back, the Mosquito's been the most boring spot in the district."

Wasn't the whole point of police work to pacify places? "We're not here to debate trivia, Sarge. We have a case but not a lot of time. We need to stay focused. Get our team together."

"Right," the sergeant said.

Service continued. "Simon, Sheena, Superman, and let's call Magic in from Dickinson and Rice up from Menominee. Here's my thinking: Sheena as recorder. She's thorough, never misses anything. Simon as touch-man on evidence. I'll do the actual evidence logging. Superman on camera. We'll want to record the whole deal, start to finish, stills and video. Magic and Rice, Volstaad and Paul handle outside security. Wait, move Volstaad to the inside crew. I want him to fill out evidence tags."

"That old man out in your truck can't be part of this," Wooten said. "I'm not even sure he can be *in* your truck legally."

Wooten knew that the officer who broke a case was in charge, and this pushing in now showed his immaturity in leadership. Service said gently, "That's my concern, not yours. He won't be part of this. I'm going to have him scout the property, report findings to the external team."

"I don't like it," Wooten said.

"Drop it, Sarge. Allerdyce has forgotten more than we'll ever know. You need to get on the horn and get the team moving this way. We don't have a lot of time. Have I missed anything?"

"My job in this?" Wooten asked.

"Overall site security, no visitors, liaison with other agencies."

"You said something about a dog?"

Shit, forgot about the dog. "Right. I heard it when I was there but never saw it." The thought made him shudder.

"Let's take Animal Control with us, let them handle the dog," Wooten said.

"Good idea."

"What time do I tell Animal Control to meet us? And where?"

"You're jumping too far ahead of us. Get a name and phone, and after we get our plan and timing down, you can let that person know."

"No idea of timing?"

"Rough. I'd like to make entry at 1700 today and be clear of the place by midnight, but I don't know if that's realistic."

"In seven hours we could clean out a museum," Wooten said.

The sergeant had no idea what lay ahead of them. "That's pretty much what we'll be doing," Service said.

Captain McKower wandered in. She and Service had been friends for a long time, more than that for a short period of shared wildness. She had moved from CO to sergeant to lieutenant, and Chief Eddie Waco had promoted her to captain when he arrived, putting her back in Marquette, where there had been no captain for some years. Lisette McKower was a veteran and one hell of an officer and still so good looking she was what Allerdyce called a turn-head.

"I talked to the county," McKower said. "How do you find so much crap?"

"I was called on this, didn't do anything but answer my phone." He could tell she was pleased and proud of him, had always been, and would always be candid and direct with people, especially him. "Serendipity," he said.

She smiled her amused smile. "Lot's of syllables for the likes of you. I heard Allerdyce has been riding around with you?"

Wooten, no doubt. "Yes, Ma'am."

"Interesting choice. Is he actually helping?"

"Heaps."

"That's high praise from you."

"Seriously, Lis, riding with him is like having a living encyclopedia next to you. He knows shit about almost everything in the U.P."

"Did your Limpopedia know about Buckshow?"

"Nope. This one caught him short."

"Then he doesn't know everything, does he?"

"C'mon Lis."

"Don't go first name on me when we start hauling around a felon like he's a legit VCO—an agency program, I should remind you, that our lawyers deep-sixed years ago."

"That was a stupid mistake on their part," he argued back. VCOs were partial game wardens with minimal law training. Some of them had helped make some major cases over the years.

"Never mind that. I only said that Allerdyce is an interesting choice. I didn't say I endorse it."

"Chief Waco will back me on this. Back in Missouri he had a guy he called a shadow wolf, his words for what we called a VCO, and his guy was far from an angel."

She gave him her steely eye. "Don't you dare name-drop on me. I will back you too, but that doesn't mean we don't talk about it, you big lummox. Was his shadow wolf a felon?"

"I think so." But he wasn't that certain and couldn't remember all the details of what turned out to be a deadly and bloody case. "You want me to call the chief and get details?"

She smiled. "I know you and how you think. You're not telling me everything. You're trying to fake your way though this shit, right?"

"Yep."

The smile turned to a smirk. "I always hated playing poker with you."

"The way I remember it, we never cared who won the game."

She blushed and said, "Yaah," drawing out the word. "I remember that too. Okay on Allerdyce, but for the record, I don't like it. He once shot you, and now you're treating him like he's one of us."

"The shooting was 'on accident.' He's also saved my life, more than once."

The captain sighed dramatically, rolled her eyes, wheeled sharply, and was gone.

The team would be arriving over the next hour or so, and he planned to use the time to think out the organization of the group and outline what lay ahead. First thing he needed to do was list everything that could conceivably, even remotely, impinge on the case and serving the search warrant. He pulled out a notepad and began to write: all buildings, all rooms in all buildings, houses, sheds, outbuildings, any structure anywhere on the property. All storage areas, bins, compartments, closets. All vehicles and their contents, visible and not visible.

He stopped making notes and called Linsenman. "Did you get prints off the blind?"

"Yah, our techs got some stuff, but none of it comes back to Buckshow."

No prints came back to Buckshow?

Linsenman said, "With two hundred plants we don't give a shit about the blind. You can throw that into your overall case of other stuff if you want. That's why I left the blind there for you."

Service told his friend, "Do me a favor, and have your people keep looking at possible print matches."

"Is there something you're not telling me, Grady?"

"No; I'm just trying to cover all of my bases."

"Cool. I'll give you a bump if we get a match."

Back to his notes and planning. If nobody's home—i.e., Sally Palovar, the wife—they would have to force entry. *Animal Control will come directly behind the team with me leading. First task, get dog under control and safely secured. Step two, move all equipment inside.* He quickly sketched a rough floor plan. *We'll work in the upper level first, and work room by room and floor by floor, basement next to last and the garage the last place. Simon will touch items and give verbal description. Sheena will write down that information, and I will give the item an evidence number and declare either take or leave. Volstaad will be beside me and make actual evidence tags and affix them, reading data to Sheena to make sure A equals A and so forth. We'll have to keep moving steadily, no goofing off. Five-minute breaks in place between rooms. We'll order some sandwiches made up and some drinks and collect them as we head south.*

He called Allerdyce, who was out in the truck. "Come inside, partner."

"T'ink I like 'er better out here."

"I need help, partner."

"Youse better if youse make me go inside. Youse know I hate dat place."

Allerdyce came inside and walked like he was barefoot on snakes. Service met him in the lobby and took him back to the conference room. He explained about the sandwiches and pointed at a phone with an outside line.

"What flavors youses want?"

"Don't care. It's just fuel. Just don't get fancy."

"I like cudighi."

"I don't."

"Youse ain't ever'body."

"*No cudighi.* It tastes like spiced spoiled roadkill and makes big gas." Cudighi was a kind of Italian sausage, an obscure local delicacy of widely varying quality and flavors, all homemade. Service loathed the stuff, which left him farty and lay in him for days like lingering poison gas in the trenches of Flanders.

He stared at his partner. "*No goddamned cudighi.* The stuff came here from Italy, and now you can't find it over there because it's so damn nasty."

"Youse don't trust youse's partner?"

"In some things, no."

Food handled, back to the plan. He had seen three shooting rooms for sure and suddenly felt the need for nicotine. "Want a smoke?" he asked his partner.

"Youse betcha."

Service got his cigarettes out of the truck, and they stood near the tailgate. He was staring off when the color blue got his attention again. All the trash in the truck needed dumping. He picked up the cigarette pack and turned it over in his hand. There was a Missouri tax stamp on the bottom. He'd been pushing after Ingalls for the fires, but they had found contraband Missouri smokes in the kids' apartment in the 8-1 case. The kids all denied any knowledge, as had the apartment owner's pushy grandfather. Jesus!

"You ever feel stupid?" he asked Allerdyce.

"Nope," the old man said. "Leave dat to udders."

The two men finished smoking. Service felt like a leper, hiding from public view, waiting for food to be thrown over the wall.

"Been t'inkin," Allerdyce said. "I look some of youse's plat books in truck. All dose bucks, all dose years, Torky and dose guys. I call guy handles da deets for county, he tell me dis Buckshow jamoke buy dat house ten years back, eh. Was 'pose to become subdecision, but enveloper guy onny sold da one place. Buckshow bought all da enveloper proppity later, now got seven, eight acres dere."

"Does that show in the plat book?"

"No 'cause was zone small parcel, eh. Jus not big nuff make da plat, deet guy tole me."

Service smelled a rat and called Linsenman again, this time finding him at home and off-duty. "Now what?"

"Country registrar of deeds, what's the skinny on him?"

"Balfour? Nice old gent, kinda slow, there but not there? Got a gal, Shelley Jaaskelainin. She runs the show, and word is she's partial to favors."

"What kind of favors?"

"Kind that fits in your wallet and can't be traced."

"Cash."

"Give that game warden his Kewpie doll. That's even the name people call her behind her back, Cash Jaaskelainin. She knows they refer to her that way and thinks it's cute."

"If this is true, why doesn't the county clean house?"

"Because in these times it's not that important in the big picture. She runs the outfit pretty damn well, and she keeps them on budget. That's the Holy Grail at all levels of government these days."

Governments, Service thought. *Why did idiots get elected and then choose more idiots? Like damn zombies comfortable only with their own kind.*

Somewhere down the line he'd visit Ms. Cash, have a heart-to-heart and find out if Buckshow paid her to misrepresent his property in the plat book. *At this point, Buckshow's property doesn't even exist in the plat book. He was invisible, and what if he had paid Jaaskelainin to keep him that way? And, more to the point, why?*

The answers and reasons might very well be on Buckshow's walls. All he owned was a house the wolf haters were unlikely to even notice, not when they collectively owned more than three full sections between them. Buckshow was a speck and less. He looked at Allerdyce. "Show me."

The old man got the book, turned to the page, and pointed. The property of all the others turned into an hourglass, with Buckshow right in the middle, meaning almost all animal traffic had to cross through his land. How the hell had this guy stayed invisible all this time?

Service's radio crackled. "Twenty-Five Fourteen, Station Twenty on D-One. We have a message asking you to call Sally Palovar at her office. She said this number's not on the county register." The Lansing RAP room dispatcher read the telephone number to him, and he wrote it in his notebook. It was the same number she'd given him when he'd seen her recently.

He punched in the numbers and she answered immediately. "You never called," she said. "I heard you were at that house."

Not my house or our house, but *that* house. Strange. "True."

"You know my husband has been arrested and won't be home tonight?"

What's she trying to tell me? "Okay?"

"I thought you ought to know the house will be empty—if for some reason you need to go back."

"Thanks, but I guess I don't understand."

"Think hard. Maybe it will come to you."

Why this strange little dance? "Can I ask you something personal?"

"No law against it, just as there's no law that compels me to answer."

Fair enough. "What's your relationship with your husband?"

"Conjugally or biblically speaking?"

"Er, overall?"

"Dead in all ways. For a very long time."

"But you're still there."

"Obviously spoken by someone who's never been on the receiving end."

What was she driving at? "That's a bit vague for me."

"Listen carefully. The last thing I want to be is specific with law enforcement and then have my husband come back."

Now it was pretty clear. She was afraid. "There was a neighbor's hunting blind found in your yard. Four-wheeler tracks led right to it."

"Imagine that," she said.

"It seems to have been placed so it can't be easily detected from inside the house."

"And yet," she said, "easily seen from the road?"

"It was and is," he said. "Makes one wonder."

"No doubt you have to solve a lot of small mysteries in your work."

"The county is running prints."

This brought a delay in answering. "You'd think someone devious enough to leave that thing where passing cars can see it but residents of the house can't, you'd think that sort of person would be smart enough to wear gloves, wouldn't you?"

"One might think that," he said. He knew it was her; this was a deliberate setup of hubby.

"I don't think you should trouble yourself with trifles and theoreticals," she said. "He'll probably be out on bail late tomorrow."

"Theoretically?"

"I see no great divide between real and theoretical in this instance."

"Will you be home tomorrow?"

"I *have* no home," she said.

"Whoever gets there tomorrow will no doubt find the furnishings and decorations somewhat reduced."

"Gut the whole thing," she said with a sharp voice.

"All those mementos?"

"They're not mine."

"Your name is on some of the tags."

"Not mine," she repeated. "My licenses and my tags, yes. My bullets, bolts, arrows, and my hands, no way. Not once, not ever."

"You loaned your tags."

"There are no loans with that man. You do as you're told, or else. With him, other people are just so much fodder."

"You know I'll have to pursue this."

"*Mea culpa, mea maxima culpa.* Done is done. I don't fear truth."

"Unless you're physically close to him."

"You have drilled into the heartwood of my conundrum."

"You could have told someone in law enforcement, Sally."

"I *tried* to tell *you*, but you are apparently too dense when it comes to understanding women."

He thought he was good at reading people, men and women. How had he missed this? Troubling in so many ways. Decision time. "Your spouse will not be home tomorrow or the next day."

"No."

"You have time to get what you need and want out of there."

"It's mostly clothes, but I don't want to spoil your investigation."

"You can assume if something's still in the house after we're gone, it's not of interest to us."

"I wish I could believe you."

"You can call the court or the jail tomorrow; they'll tell you Jesper's release timing. Two days, all yours."

"I'll do that. Thank you for calling me back," she said, "and don't feel you have to break down the door. There's a geranium plant on the porch and a key underneath the pot," she said and hung up.

He immediately called Linsenman. "Buckshow's a wife-beater."

"Says who?"

"The beatee."

"Will she press charges?"

"I don't know. She's just coming to grips with bailing out."

"Are you telling me she needs more time to get it together?"

"Couple of days, at least."

"The sheriff will talk to the prosecutor. We'll keep the crime scene in place until we're done, and this being deer season, everything gets bumped back at least a week. What about your investigation?"

"We're shooting for being done tonight."

"You people move fast."

"This is our fast season."

Linsenman laughed and hung up.

Service found Allerdyce staring at him. "What?"

"Youse know how good youse are at all dis crap?"

"There better not be cudighi," he told his partner.

The search warrant was all that mattered right now. But when this was over, he was going to pay a little visit to Mr. Parmenter Cair and talk about cigarettes and fires and whatever else might pop up. Maybe Cair didn't set the fires himself, but he might well know who did, and Service had a hunch that it would turn out that he gave the order. He wasn't quite clear on a motive yet, but his gut was now fixed on the older gent.

CHAPTER 39

South Marquette County

TUESDAY, NOVEMBER 24

It was not quite 1700 hours when they were assembled one mile from the house, down an old tote road, out of their vehicles, and gathered around Service. Most of them were giving Allerdyce something between light razzing and the cold shoulder or some form of the evil eye, depending on each person's confidence in dealing with the legendary violator. Allerdyce stood back to back with Service and showed no emotions of any kind.

Wooten had made a drive-by on the house and found Animal Control parked out on a nearby gravel road. She was now melded into the entry team.

Sally Palovar said there was a key, but they couldn't confirm this until they got to the house. The key would be a big help; lacking that, they had a ram to knock open the door if that became necessary.

Service got the animal control technician close to him. She was fortyish, with bouncy eyes and a serious squint. "We'll open the door for you, but Officer del Olmo and I will go in first and clear the space. When we say the word 'dog,' come right in and do your thing. If you need help, del Olmo will do that. Just tell him what you need. Your heart rate will be jacked up. This is normal. Try not to hurt the animal."

"Let me do my job," the ACT said. Her face was leathery, her tone resolute.

"You've done this kind of thing much?"

"What is this, a fucking audition? You don't get to pick people; you get whoever's on duty. We don't hire fuckups."

Service grinned. His kind of woman, direct as a punch. He looked at his watch. "Do we have enough evidence tags?" he asked for the hundredth time.

"Six hundred and fifty," Volstaad said. "We should be covered."

"Don't be such a worrywart," Sheena Grinda said. "We need Patton out front, not Jimmy Carter."

This made everyone laugh. "Okay, one more time. Enter, neutralize and secure animal, then Simon and I will do a fast walkthrough. We will then clear you into the house with your gear. The plan is to start upstairs and work our way down. Five-minute breaks between rooms. Limpy has sammies and pop and lots of coffee, but that's for after we finish."

"Did you bring a taste-tester too?" Superman asked.

Allerdyce spoke for the first time in his characteristic cackle. "Sonny say dat *your* chob, bucko."

Service was taking it all in. His partner had been good natured, but he wasn't going to take shots just to take them. He liked his partner's flint. Service looked at his watch. "Okay, trucks, we George in three."

He and Limpy in the truck. "Ready?"

"Youse bet, Sonny. Dis is hoot!"

"Once we go through that door, it's gonna be go go go go."

Said Allerdyce, "Like chug from spiddoon—can't stop once start, all in one string."

"Disgusting," Service said.

"But true."

"George," he said over the 800 and pulled out, running the truck hard for the property.

The key was located where advertised. The dog was flipping out inside as he disengaged the lock and cracked the door. He went through with Simon right on his back. The dog was wolf size with an immense head and fangs and throwing yellow drool all over the floor, its claws scrambling for purchase on a smooth tile. Service said over his shoulder, "Dog," and the ACT was inside and had the animal by its neck with a catch-stick; she dragged it into the bathroom and closed the door. It immediately stopped making a ruckus.

"Clear," the ACT said, "mostly."

Service saw fresh and runny dog feces from the front door to the bathroom. They had literally scared shit out of the watchdog. Only then did the stench register. "Good God, Simon," Grinda said from the door behind him.

"Not me," del Olmo said. "It's the dog."

"Typical man," Grinda said. "Blame the poor dog."

"Knock it off," Service said. "Equipment in, go to the start room."

Wooten came in and said, "I'll clean up the dog's mess. You guys move on." Service couldn't believe the sarge had volunteered, but was glad he had.

As they piled upstairs, passing walls filled with antlers, Service heard a half dozen whispered "holy shits."

Everybody was assembled in the start room. The plan was to work north to south and west to east in every room, no exceptions. Simon took an eight-point mount off a wall. It was on a plaque marked 1999. Simon said, "Yay or nay?"

Service said, "Yay?," the others said "yay," and del Olmo said, "Echo item number one, one eight-point mount, dated 1999." He handed this to Volstaad, who filled out the tag and said "Echo One, eight-point mount, dated 1999." *Echo* was for evidence.

Sheena then said, "Check." Del Olmo reached for a small skull cap on the wall, also marked 1999, and they repeated the process. This done, Volstaad started a pile by putting the first two pieces of evidence by the door. They moved on, taking skulls and horns and feathers and skins, as well as four computers, four digital cameras, a bag of flash drives and boxes of disks, some old floppies, and two smart phones, every item carefully noted in their records. It took them almost no time to establish a smooth working rhythm as they tagged and bagged evidence, and before they had finished the rooms on the top floor, Service began to wonder if they had enough storage in their trucks to get the stuff back to Marquette. His truck, Wooten's, Simon's, Sheena's, Volstaad's, Superman's, Magic's, and Herk Rice's were all there. No worries, he decided; but the rest of the night, he kept silently trying to judge the sheer volume of the take against space available. The stuff Buckshow had accumulated defied logic. How much money had he spent on all this junk? What happened to all the meat? *Save the questions,* he cautioned himself.

Wooten popped up every now and then to make sure they had what they needed and to ask if they needed help with anything. It was a new side of the young sergeant Service had never seen before. "Tell Allerdyce to keep sweeping the property and reporting his finds back to Herk. Nobody is to go anywhere on the grounds except Allerdyce until we're all done here."

"Dark outside," someone mumbled. "Should have rolled sooner, when light was better."

Service said, "Knock it off. Stay focused. We didn't get the search warrant until 1650 hours. Besides, the old man sees like an owl in the night."

Securing the search warrant had not been a problem. Judge Callie Doster had not altered a single word or request from the affidavit; had, in fact driven to the Roof with Magistrate Ken Dentso. The judge's color had gone from tan to red to pale by the time Service laid out what he had seen with a brief walkthrough. The judge said, "You get there and find more, call me directly; we'll handle it by phone." She gave him her card with multiple phone numbers. The judge and magistrate had nearly lost their composure when Service told them that the house was owned by Sally Palovar and her husband, who had a different name. It was his opinion that she was probably involved to some extent by being forced to loan her tags as an unwilling participant.

At the first five-minute break, there was not much small talk. Service could see that the COs were staggered by the sheer magnitude of what they were witnessing. He went to the front door, and Herk Rice came up to him. "Allerdyce says there are poured concrete spider holes, four feet deep, each with a seat, a heater, and one window port that pushes up. Lift the roof, get down into position, close it up, and you're ready to shoot. Wait until you see."

"Lights too?"

"Limpy's not seen any yet, but he's looking. There's a four-wheeler trail from each spider hole, which makes them easier to find once you see the pattern. Your partner is scary out there in the dark. You don't hear shit, and suddenly he's damn near breathing down your neck. He's like us—only better."

"That's him," Service said. "But he doesn't bite." He hoped this whole deal didn't come back to bite them all on the ass because he had deployed Allerdyce in the team. More than that, he was worried about Sally Palovar's safety, if and when her old man got out. The more he thought about it, the clearer it became. Sally had stolen the blind and put it in a place where her husband couldn't see it, hoping that someone from Pattinson's camp would drive by, see it, and call the cops. Which is exactly what had happened. Damn clever move on her part, almost too subtle, but he guessed her thinking was that any cop would quickly see the situation for what it was and that the law enforcement cascade would bring in the DNR. Working for the magistrate, Palovar knew how the county and state worked, or didn't. Without the stolen blind, none of this would be happening.

When they came to what Service had named the Main Shooting Room in the middle basement level, the group was struck silent. There was a window with a special automated curtain around it. You stepped to the window, hit a button, and the curtain closed to engulf you at a shooting port. The port also had a movable plastic port; the same switch controlled both the curtain and the port. There was an elevated bed twenty feet from the window. The mattress was built up so that whoever laid there was looking directly out the window. Just to the left of the bed there was a TV on a pedestal and a bookcase filled with porn disks. Next to the bed on a nightstand there was a small red plastic wastebasket overflowing with tissues that contained suspect dry substances.

Grinda said, "I'm guessing that's not a sinus condition."

"Disgusting," Volstaad said.

"People are disgusting," del Olmo said. "Only cops see the reality, and somehow we still don't want to believe what our eyes and noses are telling us. This Buckshow has some serious issues."

"Sally Palovar is married to . . . this . . . *thing*?" Grinda said.

"Unfortunately." Service told himself, *Okay, knock this off and back to work.* He told his friend, "I think the marriage status is in the process of changing, as we speak."

They went to work on the room, and Service didn't try to stop all of the nasty cop jokes and black humor that flowed.

He telephoned Linsenman at their next five-minute break.

"This better be good," the sergeant said.

"It's Grady."

"Are you still working?"

"You bet."

"Crazy fucker. How do they find people like you?"

Service said, "There's a whole roomful of us here. Who the hell *is* this Buckshow?'

"Retired from Corrections ten years ago on a full medical."

"Medical as in what?"

"Not clear. I know he was a sergeant at the prison."

"Marquette?"

"Yup, for eighteen years, and by all accounts he was a hard-nosed, no-nonsense motherfucker feared by residents and other officers alike."

"Power tripper?"

"I don't know the medical term. What we heard unofficially is that he got crossways with an inmate from Detroit, black dude name of Tyrene Talent, hitter for some dope mob down to the Twat. Inmates call him T-Rex. We heard Buckshow made this guy lose face, and the man jumped Buckshow and did some serious damage before Buckshow's people intervened."

"That's what put him on the medical?"

"No. He lost some teeth is all and took some stitching and staples and such, but his people say Tyrene took Buckshow's cojones that day; he never came back to the job full-time, not even on light duty."

"Medical injuries and problems real or imagined?"

"You'd have to consult with a pill pusher."

"I'm hearing talk of ALS."

"That's news to me," Linsenman said. "The judge is holding him through the weekend."

"Good. We ought to see if we can arrange to talk this Talent into making a conjugal visit with Buckshow."

"Cops are not allowed to say such things out loud, Sergeant. You can think 'em, but you can't say 'em."

"You must have ESP. I never said nothing out loud."

Service closed his cell phone, decided he wanted to see Tyrene Talent and talk to him eyeball to eyeball.

The team left nothing unexamined, and at 2330 Service summoned a wrecker with a flatbed to take Buckshow's pickup truck, side-by-side ATV, and his golf cart. They took thirty-four rifles, five shotguns, two crossbows, two compound bows, arrows and bolts, and four handguns out of the house, all of the firearms loaded and laying around in the open. They also took boxes and boxes of ammo, a Russian-made night-vision scope, an infrared scope, three top-end Zeiss binoculars, and a spotting scope.

Their photo sticks contained close to 1,000 photos and a couple dozen videos. There were six freezers in the garage and various rooms in the house, all of them empty. One hundred ninety antler sets went into the trucks, 174 of which would eventually make it into the indictment, along with turkey fans and wolf pelts. Service guessed as they loaded evidence that the court might very well take the man's house. Too bad for Palovar, but she had put up with it. He had some compassion for her, and a lot of admiration over how cleverly she had engineered this thing, but there was real help for people in her situation, and she had not come forward.

They transported the haul to the Roof, unloaded and sorted it, and stood around talking. Service knew they were unlikely to ever see another take of this magnitude. The team estimated that Buckshow had killed an average of twenty deer a year, some on borrowed tags, but most with no tags at all. He had not bought tags himself since retiring. These were just the deer they knew about. They had no idea how many more there might be, or how many he had wounded and left to crawl off and die. Wolves killed for food. Buckshow? For the sheer pleasure of killing, it seemed. Sicko.

Captain McKower showed up with bottles of nonalcoholic champagne and led them in a toast to the team's success. They ended the night by securing the take in evidence lockers and in one whole room of the Roof that McKower gave them for the case.

It was 4 a.m. when they finished. They drove to Friday's. Allerdyce fell onto the couch, Cat materialized and hopped on the old man, and Newf almost knocked Service down as she raced down the stairs while he was headed up. He undressed and got into bed, wondering if his dog had even wagged her tail at him on her way to Allerdyce.

"Am I dreaming again?" Friday mumbled.

"Probably."

"What time is it?"

"You don't want to know."

"Maniac."

"No argument."

She moved her hand to his shoulder. "Pew," she said.

"I'll jump in the shower."

"Like hell," she said, clutching him tightly. "I'm not letting go."

"Limpy's on the couch," he whispered.

"You sure know how to charm a girl."

"Really?"

"No, fool. Go to sleep."

"Not . . . you know?"

She started giggling and punched his arm playfully.

CHAPTER 40

North of Helps

WEDNESDAY, NOVEMBER 25

Grady Service called Harry Pattinson's camp late morning and reached a machine instead of a human. "This is Grady Service; I need to talk to you and your landowner compadres, Harry. You have my number."

Three minutes later his cell phone rang and Harry Pattinson asked, "When?"

"Let's say one this afternoon. That will give your guys plenty of time to get back out for the afternoon hunt after we're done."

"We'll try."

"Do better than try, Harry. Make it happen. You and your guys swagger around shooting off your mouths, and now you need to sit and listen to what I have to tell you."

"Which is?"

"I'm not doing this five or six times, Harry. Just get the gang there; I'll explain to all of you then. They don't show, tell them I won't be doing individual encores."

"Why the hard-ass?"

"Just do as I say, Harry, and make sure Torky Hamore shows up."

"You must've heard something that brings you this way."

"Should I have?" Service countered, letting the question hang and closing his phone.

• • •

It was like old home week with all the camp owners and their hunters all gathered in one place, most of them irritated to be called away from the woods. The place stank of BO, flatulence, smoke, and garlic, something less than a chichi sachet.

The whole crowd was crushed into the great room, all of them talking, trying to talk over and outdo one another, the typical all-out competition of male lions basking in the sun on a hill.

"Seeing any deer?" Service began.

"Some does is all," Torky Hamore said. "But no bucks. Damn wolves."

Service said. "Torky, do you think wolves eat only bucks?"

"Din't say that."

"You said, and I quote, 'No bucks. Damn wolves.'"

"The DNR got roving English teachers oot in da woods now, eh?"

This drew snickers from the gathering.

"Why're we here?" Kermit Swetz asked. He owned a small grocery store chain that stretched from Sutton's Bay to Alpena.

Service ignored the man's question. "Answer me this: If you've seen a wolf during this hunting season, raise your hand."

No hands went up, but Hamore said, "But we seen no bucks either, eh."

"If you're not seeing wolves, where have they gone?"

"To where there's food," Attilio Haire said. He was a prosthodontist in Marquette.

"Exactly. They've gone to where there's food because it's not *here*."

"Onaccount wolves killed and ate it all," Hamore said.

Grady Service said. "No deer and no four-legged wolves."

This last phrase stopped the buzz. "What the hell is this about?" Pattinson demanded. "All wolves got four legs."

"Do they?" Service said.

Now he had their attention.

"Do you guys know Jesper Buckshow?"

Hamore said, "Cripped prison guard from up Marquette. What about him?"

"The county busted him for a dope grow, took a huge number of plants out of his house."

"Good God," Pattinson said.

"Your call on the stolen blind took the deps to the house. When the man opened up, they smelled the dope, and that gave them probable cause to enter and do a limited search."

"What about my nephew's blind?" Pattinson asked.

"I have it in Marquette as evidence. I brought you another one as a loaner. I tagged it with my name."

"What about the nephew's blind?"

"Got to hang on to it for a while longer."

"So, Buckshow stole it?"

"That's not entirely clear yet," Service told them, "and as it turns out, it's probably not important. How much land does Buckshow own?"

No immediate response. It was Torky Hamore who eventually ventured a guess. "Got house, mebbe an acre 'round it, eh. Spit out what you tryin' ta say, Service."

"The state is going to indict Mr. Buckshow on scores of game violations. I can't give you the exact number yet, but when it goes public, I think you'll understand that the wolf killing your deer is named Buckshow."

"Bull," Dornboek said. "Don't seem possible one man could have that much effect. None of us see no deer no more."

Service had drawn a rough map for just this moment. He unrolled it, spread it out, and waited for the men to gather around. "Buckshow owns these seven acres, which just happen to connect the two chunks of property you people own. Any animal moving east or west has to pass through Buckshow's parcel. A lot of them never got through."

"He's a crip," somebody said and quickly corrected himself, "disabled or whatever the politically correct bullshit term is right now."

"One man can do that?" Pattinson asked.

Service went to the front door and admitted Allerdyce. He could feel the crowd compress into one another as the old man walked into the great room.

"You all know or know of Mr. Allerdyce," Service said. "We might characterize him as an expert on taking deer by means other than legal."

Limpy grinned at the description and nodded.

"I asked Mr. Allerdyce to look over the property in question. Mr. Allerdyce?"

"Bes' bloody spot ever see—an' I seen plenty, youse guys."

"I'll kill that motherfucking Buckshow," Torky Hamore said, jumping up, but Service stepped over to him and pushed him back into a chair.

"You are not killing anybody over some damn deer. And if you ever show up at my house again to whine like a baby, I will beat on you until you shit out your brains."

Hamore glowered and tried to stand, but Service kept him pinned in place.

"But this Buckshow's like a total cripple," Pattinson observed.

"Are you certain about that, Harry? Do you even *know* the man? Maybe he wants people to *think* that's his condition."

"You sayin' he running a scam?" Haire asked.

"I'm not saying anything other than he's been arrested, and the investigation is under way. I just wanted you fellas to have a head's up on this deal. Your problem isn't wolves."

Torky Hamore said, "What state gone do fix dis t'ing?"

Grady Service said, "Nothing. Time will take care of it, that and all the food plots you guys have on your properties."

"They're not illegal," Pattinson said.

"Nor are they natural, Harry. You plant, then everybody plants, because if they don't, the first plot pulls the deer to it. It's a damn stupid game and artificial. If Buckshow has been the problem, and I think he has, removing him won't automatically fix the situation here. That will take time, and you guys ought to talk about what's best for all the deer, not just the few big ones you want to shoot. You, me, the deer, the wolves, we're all in this thing together."

Dornboek was scratching at his face and eventually said, "Our buck kills started falling off after the guy moved in."

"Your overall deer count and sightings are down too," Service said.

All the men nodded.

"Put a lot of that on consecutive hard winters, not wolves or violators."

"Wolves kill some," a voice said.

"True," Service said, "but they don't kill every deer they see."

"Buckshow's been killing everything?" Pattinson asked.

"Wouldn't be surprised," Service said.

Pattinson's eldest son Henry had out a plat book. "How come the plat doesn't show all the land he owns?"

Torky Hamore said, "Cash."

"What's that about cash?" Service asked, pretending ignorance.

"Nickname for Shelley Jaaskelainin. She works for Balfour in the deed office, calls all da shots," Hamore said.

"What's that got to do with Buckshow?"

Pattinson said, "I am not making a charge here, but it is common community knowledge that the woman is amenable to certain pecuniary incentives."

"Spell it out, Harry."

"It seems that one might be able to pay her to have something depicted or not depicted accurately in the plat book."

"Are you talking about bribes, Harry?"

"I never used that word."

"Of course you didn't," Service said disgustedly. "What do you care if she's taking a little *mordida*?"

Torky Hamore asked, "A what?"

"*Mordida*, Torky. It's Spanish for a 'little bite,' which translates to a bribe."

Hamore smirked and Pattinson said, "Are you guys certain about Buckshow?"

"We are."

"Why weren't we informed earlier?" Dornboek complained.

"You just own some land, Jud. You aren't a bunch of European nobles. Here each of you counts no more or less than my partner or me."

Allerdyce smiled at this.

Torky Hamore stood up and announced, "I think I'm gonna puke," and pushed his way through the crowd.

There were no more questions.

"Dose guys din't look too happy," Allerdyce said in the truck.

"Those guys like to be right. They think owning shit automatically makes them right, and makes them smarter than people who are less fortunate and don't own as much. They just learned they were wrong about a bunch of things."

"Youse t'ink dose fellas been shootin's some wolfies?"

"What have you heard?"

"Ain't hear nuffin'."

"Then we'll assume they haven't."

Service's work cell clicked anxiously as they rolled along. It showed Sandy Tavolacci's name.

"Counselor."

"Thought you ought to know, Jesper Buckshow's now my client, Grady."

"He can't afford a *real* lawyer?"

"That isn't funny, and we'll see who's laughing when we get to court."

"It's not funny to you, Sandy. Is to the rest of us."

"I'm tired of you interfering with my clients and my practice."

"I'm glad you said that, Sandy. Why would anyone hire a lawyer who is just practicing? Me, I'd want one who is actually performing. Game time beats the hell out of bench time."

"I'm bringing charges," the attorney said.

"It's a free, free world—in principle," Service said.

Tavolacci hung up. Service thought, *He and I need to have a heart to heart.*

"Who dat?"

"Sandy T."

Allerdyce said, "Asswipe."

"Your eloquence sometimes leaves me speechless."

ACT 4: "TELL ME AGAIN WHY I DO THIS JOB?"

Step with care and great tact. And remember that life's a great balancing act.

—Dr. Seuss, *Oh, the Places You'll Go*

CHAPTER 41

Harvey

THURSDAY, NOVEMBER 26

It was Thanksgiving Day, and granddaughter Maridly launched herself from six feet away, landing against his chest, squealing, "BampyBampyBampy," which was what she insisted on calling him and he insisted she not. But she continued to do as she pleased, and deep down her little streak of stubbornness and defiance made him happier than the stupid term made him unhappy. She was almost five and jumped like a monkey, six feet horizontal, four or five feet vertical. *Does Guinness have categories and records for tots?* he wondered.

The little girl's mother, Karylanne Pengally, had been his son's girlfriend when he died. The baby was his son's, which made Maridly his granddaughter, even if that didn't quite plot on legal paper. Karylanne Pengally was a beautiful and sweet young woman and a terrific mother. She was now working on a PhD in some arcane field at Michigan Tech in Houghton.

He was not quite certain what it was she was chasing so hard in the classroom, and it didn't matter to him, though in the back of his mind he was afraid that when she finished, she might have to move elsewhere to find a job. If that happened, what would he do? He honestly had no idea, and thinking about it made his stomach knot up.

Karylanne had brought a guest—a slump-shouldered, skinny, long-haired boy who looked like he was mourning his lost skateboard.

Allerdyce pushed his way past Newf, marched straight to the guest, and stood in front of him, staring into his face, his own face not six inches away. "Who youse, Bucko?"

"His name is Charles," Karylanne said. "But he likes to be called Bebop."

"I'm talkin' dis boy," Allerdyce growled menacingly. "You got own voice dere, Bucko, or we got use sign linkage?"

Service wanted to smile, but didn't dare. Limpy was a better guard dog than Newf, but the kid needed the break. "Hey, we've got grocks in the truck," Service said and pulled the man back from the visitor.

"What the hell is wrong with you?" he asked when they got outside.

"Dunno, Sonny. I seen dat twerp and start see some mind pitchers in head don't like."

"He's a guest. Be nice. If Karylanne likes him, we'll like him."

"Wah," Allerdyce said. "We see 'bout dat."

Their second entry was quieter. Shigun came over, and Service picked him up, hugged him and gave him a loud smooch, and set him down; he and Maridly each grabbed Bampy's trousers and followed along like goslings. Newf was crawling all over Allerdyce, and Service didn't even try to tell her to get down. Where the old man was concerned, she did her own thing and called her own shots. Allerdyce was snuggled with the giant dog, making sounds of affection that had no known connection to English, much less any other language Service had ever heard.

Friday wore slacks and a sweater and looked happy as he patted her butt and began removing groceries from paper bags, which he chose over plastic because both youngsters liked to draw and paint; paper bags were great painting surfaces, and already paid for.

He and Friday had put the turkey in the oven this morning, before he and Allerdyce had gone to the store. Karylanne, Maridly, and Bebop had arrived while they had been strip-mining Econofoods.

Allerdyce set down his groceries, pulled a chair over to the guest, and sat right in front of him. "How old youse?"

"Twenty-four."

"Look twelve."

"Sorry."

"You hunt?"

"No."

"You fish?"

"No."

"You like boys?"

The visitor made a face. "As a matter of fact, I do. Are you trolling?" The man looked at Karylanne, who was laughing. "Who *is* this person?" the guest asked.

"Family," she said, then paused and amended this to "ah, er . . . *like* family?"

She looked at Service, who said, "He's family. I guess. Sort of. Right."

Allerdyce looked at Karylanne. "Dis guy no hunt, no fish, an' he fairy boy. What you see in dis guy?"

Karylanne smiled and said, "He's my boss, and my friend."

"What you boss her of?" Allerdyce asked, turning back to the man.

"We teach and do research."

"What kind church?"

"Not church, *r*esearch."

"Teach what, dancing for longhair fairies?"

"Are you asking me to dance?" the guest asked.

Allerdyce pulled back. "Wah! No way! I don't dance wit no mens."

Karylanne intervened. "This is Professor Rosslind Fynes Pechta."

"What kind name dat for boy?" Allerdyce challenged.

"Earthling," Pechta said, and all but Allerdyce laughed out loud.

"Porfessor? How come you not better one dey give you name like goodfessor?"

Allerdyce. "We've got to make cornbread dressing," Service called from the kitchen, from where he had been watching.

Allerdyce was immediately in the kitchen. "Like cornbread stuffing, eh."

"Dressing; it's only stuffing if it goes into the turkey."

"Dis gone go inta us, so what difference dis makes? Why youse knick-pick words all time?"

"It's not nitpicking."

"Okay; dis feel me like youse stick pins in old doll look like me."

"You're being overly sensitive."

"Man can't have too much sense," Allerdyce said.

Service could see what he took for relief on the professor's face.

It was the kind of day he both coveted and loathed. The house was warm, the smell grand. Aaron Rodgers and the Packers were kicking the stuffing out of the Detroit Lions, the animals had glommed onto Limpy like he was pure pet dope. Karylanne, her boss, and Tuesday were deep in conversation, and the kids were playing nicely with some sort of goofy electronic game. But he knew that this was a false security blanket, a mirage, that outside the confines of the house there were bad guys doing bad things, with nobody out there to stop them.

While the others enjoyed the moment, he began thinking about Parmenter Cair, who owned the apartment "hideout" in the 8-1 case.

He was in the kitchen, hovering over the turkey and fixings, when Lions rookie quarterback Matthew Stafford threw his fourth pick of the game and put another nail in Detroit's game coffin. The sad sack Lions were the perfect symbol for the long-dying city, most of the roster consisting of guys making big salaries and living outside the city in GP—a term his friend Luticious Treebone had made up to represent greener pastures. Most people took it to mean Grosse Pointe.

His best friend would get in the face of white guys who called themselves Detroiters. "You live inside 8 Mile?" he'd challenge.

"No, I live in Royal Oak."

"That ain't Detroit, motherfucker. That be GP."

"Not Grosse Pointe, Royal Oak."

"Shit for brains, GP mean white-boy-green-pasture-land, and donchu be tellin' peeps y'all Detroit boy when yo ain't."

Allerdyce disturbed his reverie. "Ain't nuffin' cooking faster jes' cause youse puttin' eyeballs on it," the old man said. "I need smoke."

They stepped outside together. What was the name of the ATF agent from Springfield, Neutre? The chief said she'd call soon, but what did soon mean to a Fed? It also dawned on him that he couldn't recall how many days had gone by since that conversation. The answer was in his notebook, in a coat or shirt pocket, or in a bag, or somewhere in the disarray of the truck, this being the time of year for most officers when in-truck organization went from random clutter to all-encompassing chaos.

"We hit road aft'noon?" Allerdyce asked.

"Nope. This is a holiday for us."

"Where dat word come fum, holiday?"

"Originally meant holy day, I think."

"Wah. Santy Claus day, dat holy day when Jesus guy borned. Easter, dat holy day when Jesus guy buy big farm in sky. Turkey day ain't no holy day."

"I'm passing information, not defending the history of words."

"Youse is all antsinpanties bein' 'ere. Look scared as two-head buck."

Service smiled and took a pull on his smoke. "You know, we might just take us a little drive after dinner."

"Do what?"

"Same reason the bear went over the mountain."

Allerdyce grinned. "Wah! I know dat one. Ta pee in da Saltine Sea."
Grady Service laughed out loud. *Allerdyce.*

CHAPTER 42

Marquette Über Dem See, Marquette County

THURSDAY, NOVEMBER 26

Fighting through the paralysis of postprandial food coma, the partners took Service's personal truck to find the house and property of Parmenter Cair. The address was in his notebook, which Service fished out of his work truck. He knew Marquette fairly well, as did his partner, but neither of them had heard of something called Marquette über Dem See. He used his cell phone to call central dispatch and get directions. The place was in a new development of estates slightly north and west of the Marquette Mountain ski complex, and it was set onto a hump of rock that was higher than most other local elevations south of town.

Service had no idea developers had penetrated this area so deeply, but he wasn't surprised. Developers were calling Marquette the next Traverse City—like this would be a wonderful thing. He knew some developers would, for the right return on investment, bury the entire Upper Peninsula in concrete.

They eventually found the street, which appeared to be newly paved. It was unplowed, and there were no vehicle tracks; the road meandered like a river around the bottom of a series of steep ridges and deep, narrow valleys. Cair's house was one of only three in the development, the farthest east and the one with the best view, catching the end of Intimidation Lake to the north and Lake Superior to the east.

"Geez, oh Pete," Allerdyce said. "Dis jamoke must be loaded, have place and view like dis."

Service wondered what the price was for lots. He was aware of one developer over by Munising who tried to lure Japanese and Californian investors with unique lots starting at $250K. The development remained nearly empty, much to the happiness of most locals.

There was a dead end turnaround not a hundred yards past Cair's driveway, and Service stopped there, turned off the engine, and put down windows.

Snow was falling, adding to the rolling white vista, grayed-out in the darkness. It was almost idyllic.

The engine was off, the windows were down, and there was total silence except for small snow pellets pecking at the truck. A spotlight from the house clicked on and flashed down into one of the narrow defiles close to the house, momentarily illuminating a half dozen shadowy deer; just as suddenly it went dark again. Off.

"You see any horns?" he asked his partner.

"Too quick, but I seen 'em paw da snow. Want bet dere some bait under dere?"

"No bet, but that light wouldn't be out of place in Hollywood." It had been large and intense.

"Go see da man now?"

Too dark and too little to go on at this point. "No; we'll wait for daylight so we can be thorough."

The light came on only the one time, and only for that instant. They sat for another thirty minutes as the snow pellets began to show some fast accumulation. Service was about to start the engine when something touched his shoulder. Utterly surprised, he lurched and recoiled violently and hit his head on the truck roof, the response totally out of proportion to the stimulus. This sort of reaction was normal when you were trailing night-hunters. Even when you knew a shot was imminent, the suddenness of it would cause you to pop upward and hit your head on the roof. To prevent this, you held the bottom of the steering wheel or something else when you expected a shot to be coming soon. This he was totally unprepared for.

"*Service*," a husky voice whispered from his open window.

He looked left, found himself face to face with a Cyclops, a single eye, which his brain quickly sorted out and registered as night-vision goggles, military issue. His voice was gone, and he had no choice but to wait until it came back.

"Sorry about that, guys," the voice said. "I'm Special Agent Neutre, ATF. I believe your chief told you I'd be in touch?"

Service chuckled. "He didn't say literally, or with such a dramatic entrance."

"Like I said, sorry. You mind if I jump in back and catch a ride out of here? This snow's looking serious. My truck is over in a lower ski hill parking lot."

"You walked from there to here?"

"It's not that far," she said.

It had to be three or four miles and almost all of it vertical. A hike from where she was parked to here was a major deal, even without snow and ice and wind.

The woman started for the back of the truck and Service said, "Jump in up front. My partner will fit fine in the backseat."

"You're sure?"

Allerdyce already had the back door open, had squeezed behind the passenger seat, and was stacking their gear and supplies into a single mound behind the driver's seat.

The ATF agent slid into the passenger seat after she chucked something heavy in the truck bed. "My trash and surveillance gear," she explained as she groped under the front of the seat for the mechanism to adjust the space. She removed her goggles. She had a military haircut Service knew only as high and tight. She found the seat handle and pushed back with a solid thump. She was dressed all in white, some sort of coverall made of silent material.

Service drove out of the area, maintaining dark until they got out on the Intimidation Lake Trail and almost to County Road HJ. The woman said, "Stop here please."

He did as she asked. The woman in all white was out of the truck in less than two minutes. She came back wearing faded blue jeans and a heavily cabled white sweater, her feet in fashionable Italian Chamonix fur boots the color of new honey. He'd proposed such boots to Friday once and she had scoffed at him. "At four hundred bucks? I've bought used cars for less."

Friday had no way of knowing that money meant very little to him, that fate and inheritance from his lover Maridly Nantz had left him way beyond well off. The ATF agent's boots were a reminder that he needed to have a serious talk with his . . . what? Girlfriend?

How lame is that, Service? Girlfriend's so high school.

Allerdyce passed a thermos cup of coffee to the agent from behind.

"Ah," Neutre said. "Warm again."

Service guessed she was six-four, perhaps taller, solidly built, blond hair, ruddy face. "I suppose you fellas have questions."

"Just the usual stuff," Service said, "no brain-busters. Let's start with what the hell were you doing out there, and how the hell did you identify me?"

"I've been on a stakeout for seventy-two hours, and Eddie Waco sent me your photo. This new snow gives me a great opportunity to bail and leave no traces behind."

"Seventy-two hours in *this* crap?"

"No problem. I have a thermal pop-up shelter and a state-of-the-art, lighter-than-a-fart solar heater. The one good thing about working for the Feds is they give us great toys."

"What exactly are you staking out?"

"The domicile of one Parmenter Cair and Kerny Pascal-Veyron."

"Cair I've met."

"Kerny's his main squeeze of the moment, his almost-significant other. He has a wife, of course, but she is of the stay-at-home bling-less flavor, living frugally in a 900-square-foot Monkey Ward bungalow in Brentwood, a burb of St. Louis. Parmenter is a true entrepreneurial phenom, self-made, wealthy as Midas, ruthless as Machiavelli. He started as a small plumbing contractor and parleyed himself into the third or fourth largest privately held construction company in the world. Name a place and you can bet he's built something there. His outfit's made billions off DOD contracts in Iraq, Afghanistan, and related locations.

"He still runs his company?"

"He's now chairman emeritus, still on the board but not involved in any day-to-day stuff."

"What's ATF's interest in him?"

"The thing about Parm is that he can't sit still. Asperger's probably. All he can think about is making money. His middle name should be Busy."

"Your name popped up from Eddie when we found contraband ciggies at Cair's grandson's apartment."

"Right. To Parmenter, ciggies and other stuff are like a hobby. He has one minivan a week run from Rolla, Missouri, to Detroit, and he nets a quarter million from sweet, low risk, no-deep-thought cash."

"The smokes we found at the apartment."

"Our guess is that grandpap gave the boy those to use as a little cash cow for his pals and gals, and himself of course. Parm always takes good care of Parm. But we're also of a mind that grandpa may be teaching the kid the biz and young Cair is making some actual runs to Missouri and back. We don't know this for sure yet, but we've got some pretty good camera

systems in place in St. Louis, with some amazing state-of-the-art facial rec-
ognition software. We've ID'd the kid three times, always in the same van,
which belongs to grandpa and is, as we talk, parked in his garage back there
on the hill.

"The chief thought you could help us with our case."

"Yes. We have been running a little sting at the behest of the Iowa and
Illinois DNRs, and young Cair has gotten snared in our net. He's taken a
contract to shoot deer with large racks for three grand per, no questions
asked."

"When was this?"

"Early fall. He's not been back to talk to our guy, so we figured he hasn't
scored yet. Our UC has upped the ante by promising five grand per, for any
racks of 140-plus. You fellas know what that means, other than big?"

"Total inches based on a certain measuring scheme. What do you have
on grandpa?"

"Smoke-wise, nothing yet. But I heard shots from the house and down
in those nearby draws."

"How many shots?"

"Between two and four a day, all emanating from near the house. But
there were also some other shots coming from the apple orchard downhill
and east of him and two more from uphill to the west. If you drop me at my
vehicle, I'll get out of your hair."

*She must have made a major recon of the man's property and everything
around it. Impressive.* "How long are you here?"

"Until I nail Cair or decide I can't."

"Can you tell us exactly what you're looking for?"

"The van he owns, full of Show Me State smokes, with the grandson
driving the internal combustion mule."

"Got a plan?"

"The venerable stakeout: Sit till you shit."

Service said, "The weather in these parts is about to turn real owly, and
you can assume it will stay that way until early May. You'd do better to pull
out and wait for spring breakup."

She sucked in a deep breath. "I truly loathe the phrase 'pull out' and all
that it might imply."

"Is Cair some kind of special case, something personal in this for you?"

"Eddie Waco said you've got a sixth sense about people. The English author Henry More once wrote of 'men of shallow minds, and lickersome bodies, cleaving to the pleasures of the flesh.' The stay-at-home flavor of wife living frugally in Brentwood? She's my mom. Parmenter left her high and dry, and I intend to nail him to the wall of shame."

"You're Cair's daughter?"

"Indeed, the product of a single one-night stand many years after he left dear old mom. He stopped back one time for another dip in the pool, and here I am."

"What's that make Josh to you?" Service asked.

"Half-something, I suppose; but tell truth, we're not sure whose loins dropped Josh."

This was not someone to be toyed with. "We'll eventually be going back to Cair's. Maybe we can join forces and piggyback. You have my number?"

"That's affirmative."

"Let's check in once a day."

"Goody," she said. "We can sext and talk dirty. Stakeouts always put me in the mood."

He did not have to ask what mood. They dropped her at her vehicle, and Allerdyce hopped out and helped her brush off snow.

"Geez, oh Pete," the old man said when it was just them in the truck again. "Dat one's da real Hammerzon, wah!"

CHAPTER 43

South of Greenwood, Marquette County

FRIDAY, NOVEMBER 27

Linsenman called to let him know that Marquette County's Lt. Jack Tax was taking the Buckshow case. This reminded him that he needed to talk to Sally Palovar before he interviewed husband Jesper and before Buckshow got sprung from jail. The whole line of befores made him think of the Bible and begats.

Jack Tax was a bit of a mystery—a grossly obese man who could hardly breathe, was almost pathologically introverted, and virtually impossible to converse with on any subject. But he had made countless good cases for the county and was respected by drug cops across the U.P.

The lifelong bachelor lived with his mother, Tavi, who was a pathological extrovert, never shutting up. It was put forward by cop-house wags that her continuous yap had squeezed Jack into silence. The only point of this knowledge was for colleagues: If you wanted to talk to Jack Tax, do it by telephone. He got tongue-tied in face-to-face meetings. Further, if you wanted to talk to him on the phone, make sure to do it when he was not within Mama Tavi's earshot. The detective's mother tried to wear his badge every chance she got.

Service had reached him this morning. "Uh huh," Tax said when he answered the phone. "Grady Service; you caught the Buckshow case, eh?"

"Yep."

Tax said, "I've got it from our side of things."

"Heard that."

Tax wanted to know, "Is Buckshow's wife involved, other than being married to the guy?"

Hard one to answer. "Not so far," Service said. "I assume you're looking at her for possible involvement in the drugs case."

"We are."

Service said, "I need to talk to her about our case, but I don't want to step on anything you're going at. We know she loaned a license on several occasions, but I'm thinking this is a technicality, that she was coerced. I want to use her to strengthen our case, but not at the expense of yours."

"Okay."

Service thought, Okay *what*? Jesus.

"Wife's not on the radar," Jack Tax said eventually. "Do whachu gotta do. One thing. You talk to her, let me know whachu get, eh."

"Glad to. I think we should work as close together as our supervision will allow us."

"Sounds good."

"Be back at you."

"Okay."

What a pain in the ass to talk to.

Talking to Sally Palovar, it turned out, was problematic. Service called her boss, Kennard Dentso. "Grady Service here, Ken. I'm looking to talk to Sally. I know she's not at home. Have you got a personal cell for her?"

The magistrate gave him two numbers, Palovar's personal cell and the cell of her sister, Pokey Brownmill, who taught some sort of freshman ecology class at Northern called Sticks and Stones. It was a hugely popular course at the school, and Brownmill was well known across the U.P. as a mentoring teacher and hyperactive activist in numerous environmental causes. Service knew about her because Lisette McKower had mentioned her from time to time.

"Do you know anything about Sally's home situation?" Service asked the magistrate.

"Obviously not. Met the husband of course. Creeped me out, my wife even more, but Sally's no complainer or whiner. She's damn smart."

"You think one of those numbers will reach her?"

"Should. She called me last night, and she's taking some time off. I told her that might be a good idea, but not to make it too long. I need her here."

"She talk about what's going on?"

"Only that Tavolacci's taking the case for Jesper."

"Did you advise her to get a lawyer for herself?"

"I did. Why?"

Service said, "Because she was loaning her tags to hubby."

"I didn't know that."

"I doubt she'll be charged in the case, but I'd sure appreciate her help in sorting out some details."

"She doesn't have to do that, you know."

"I'm hoping she'll want to, and I suspect she will. Has she lawyered up yet?"

"Not that I know of, but she did mention something to Mary Helen about Kenya Maki, and I also advised her to get representation."

"She and Mary Helen are tight?" Mary Helen Huaanpaa was the sheriff's secretary.

"Pals at work, but after hours I got no idea."

He toyed momentarily with telling Palovar's boss his theory that Sally had ruthlessly and efficiently set up the scenario by stealing a hunting blind and relocating it where police couldn't ignore it. But a theory was only a theory, and he might be wrong. Better not to talk about it.

No answer on her personal cell, but he left a message and texted her.

Her sister, Pokey Brownmill, had not talked to Sally in a week and had heard nothing about her brother-in-law; Service decided to let it stay that way. So far the media knew nothing about the case, but it being deer season, they were always on the hunt for relevant stories. He hoped the bust would stay unreported for a while longer. Deep down, he knew it probably wouldn't. Why it wasn't already moving around like wildfire was beyond him.

He then called Mary Helen Huaanpaa. She didn't know where her friend was and made it clear they did not socialize outside work because neither her boss nor her husband could tolerate Palovar's husband, even at holiday parties and such. Yes, she had talked to Sally about defense attorney Kenya Maki, a hard-nosed Finn who hailed from Champion, had practiced in Lansing for ten years, and moved back to Marquette County.

The fact that Maki answered her own phone impressed him. He explained who he was and his reason for calling.

The lawyer said, "She's my client as of last night, and I'm advising her not to talk to anyone but me for the time being."

"How about if I talked to both of you and you can run interference?"

"Are we talking with some sort of notion of leniency in play?"

"The truth is," Service said, "I think she set up this whole deal."

Maki said nothing for several seconds. "Do you know where Four Moose Bend is?"

He did. "South of Greenwood off 452 near the old Greenwood Mine."

Maki gave him a fire number, which he wrote down. Fire numbers were posted at every remote camp to guide EMS and fire personnel in the event of emergencies. "There's a driveway just before Larson Creek. There's a small log cabin at the end, right at the pond, about one mile back. The road is *terrible*. We'll meet you out there. Noon work?"

"It does."

She said, "I don't like weekend work, especially during deer season, but this time I'll make an exception if you're coming in peace."

"Definitely." He didn't bother to point out that today was only Friday and not quite the weekend.

She said, "You know Tavolacci's representing her husband?"

"I heard. He called me and tried to game me."

"Idiot," Maki said. "You two have a history?"

"Sort of," he said and broke the connection.

• • •

He wanted to know what was waiting for them, so he dropped Allerdyce out on the county road and waited. They then met near the entrance to the driveway.

"Two womans outside cabins takin' pitchers of big old bull moose and 'is cowgirl."

"Just the two of them?"

"Two womans, an' two moosies is all I seen."

"How close to the cabin did you get?"

"Close enough see panty lines in dere pants."

Service shook his head. "They see you?"

"I don't want get seed, I don't get seed, Sonny. Like youse."

No doubt. The man was a magician in some ways.

"Dere somepin' else did see, Sonny," the old man said with uncustomary reluctance. Usually he spit out what he was thinking, had no filters to pass things through. "Dese two, dey like hold hands?"

Hold hands, what the hell does that mean? "And?"

"Jest dat dey hold hands and grin a lot."

The old man demonstrated, and the effect was startling and scary. "Let's stick to words," Service said.

"Wah," Allerdyce chirped softly.

As soon as got to the cabin, Maki came out to the patrol truck and introduced herself, looking past him. "Is that Limpy Allerdyce?"

"You know him?"

"*Everybody* up here at least knows *of* him, and lots of people Below the Bridge do too."

"Most of what you've heard is probably bullshit," he told the lawyer.

"I take what most people say *cum grano salis*," she said. "That's Latin for 'with a grain of salt.'"

"Me too," he said. "That's English for 'also.'"

Maki smiled. "You're not the macho beast some people make you out to be."

He shrugged

"What's Allerdyce's part in this?" she asked.

"Consultant."

"Wow," she said. "That defies too much to even generalize."

"You just did," he said.

Her left eyebrow shot up. "Not macho. Smart and quick too, a cop who's almost human."

"Like some lawyers—not many."

Sally Palovar said, "Hi," when Maki showed him into the cabin. The women offered coffee, which he accepted, not wanting to hurry anything. The presence of an attorney during an interview almost always complicated questioning of any kind.

"I'm not recording anything," he told Maki. "Today is entirely preliminary and off the record. I'm just trying to wrap my arms around this case."

"Acceptable for the moment," Maki said.

He decided to dive deep and fast, get everything out on the table and see their reaction. He started with the stolen blind and pulled no punches. "You took the pop-up and placed it on your property so it could be seen from the road but not from the house."

Palovar looked at Maki. The attorney took her hand. Palovar said, "Placement was insurance to my way of thinking."

"You guessed the theft would be reported, and you made sure the trail could be easily followed from Pattinson's to your yard so Pattinson and his people would follow it, find the stolen blind, and call the sheriff, or us."

Palovar said, "Yes, I did."

"What if Pattinson had instead confronted your husband directly?"

"He didn't," Maki said. "Stay with reality."

"You knew the blind would get the cops to the door, where they'd smell the dope, and that they'd call us in."

"I didn't know the exact protocol or cascade, but that's what I hoped for."

"You know your husband will try to implicate you."

"I don't care. This is all on him, not me. When he was still working, it was somehow manageable. He worked variable shifts and wasn't in my space too often. I could cope and deal. Then he got the medical, was there all the time, and everything got worse—the dope, the hunting , the . . ." She stopped herself. "What he does is not hunting. It's killing. He's a pig who can't stop eating."

"Are you telling me your relationship—your marriage—was off the rails for a long time? Why didn't you leave?"

"Catholic, for better or worse, until death do us part. Honestly I thought about killing him too many times to count, but the Church has rules against that too."

"How many people bought licenses for him?"

"Me, our three kids, his mother, some old pals from the prison. I don't know exactly how many, and he lies so much I don't know what's real and what's bullshit."

"Nobody objected to giving their tags to him?"

"I think some of us felt sorry for him, thought it would be good for him to have something to do, even if it was on the shady side."

"There's a wheelchair at the house. Does he use it?"

"It's only a prop for his play. He gets around with a limp, but he does get around. Obviously. Sometimes he uses canes, but again mostly for show."

"You're telling us he's mobile."

"Have you searched the grounds?"

"We have found some interesting things."

"Then you know the answer to your question. All those pits? He calls them deer digs. Our property? He calls that Ambush Alley. He's been off the deep end on killing wildlife for a long, long time, ever since he shot a wolf and went on a three-day jerk-off fest with his sex vids."

"You know about that?"

"Better those vids than me," Palovar said. "I'd been down that road and didn't care for it one bit."

Service watched the women's hands, saw nothing other than an attorney trying to steady a client's jangled nerves. Even if there was something personal, why would he care, except that it might point at some motives for making this thing public now. *Not your job to sort that out. Stay focused.* "Can you tell me when your husband's *spree* started?"

"Please don't call him my husband. It began soon as we bought the house in ninety-eight."

"Was he in kill mode before his medical retirement?"

"To some extent, it's been as long as we've been married, but back then he didn't push it in my face all the time."

"He abuse you?"

She tightened her lips. "The thing is that prison guards always seem to know how to get what they want without leaving visible evidence. My husband is an artist when it comes to that. Maybe it's occupational?"

"It's not," Service said.

"I hate all this," Palovar said. "I feel filthy, and if he makes bail . . ."

Maki said, "We'll have a protective order in place. And with his dope troubles, he'll have to keep playing the innocent cripple desperate for pain relief or get his ass kicked in court." The lawyer paused and added, "The drugs are off the table for my client?"

"You know the prosecutor will make the final call on that. I don't think she's going to be in this drug thing as long as she cooperates, but this deal overall is going to be a big-ticket item. The wildlife poaching alone is going to push two hundred grand."

Palovar's eyes went wide and blinking wildly. "Two . . ." she couldn't finish. "They'll take the house!"

"They could," Service said. "They'll definitely put a lien on it to hedge the state's bet."

"But he's going to do time in jail, right?"

"Honestly, I don't know. A jury could be sympathetic to a wheelchair."

"Jesus, Joseph, and Mary, this is a nightmare," Sally Palovar said. "I work for a magistrate, a man of honor, and here I am up to my neck in . . . *shit!*"

He tried to refocus and calm her. "What I need is for you to help me understand how your husband operated, every incident and kill you can remember, every detail no matter how inconsequential it may seem."

Maki said, "And in return for this, she gets what?"

"I will recommend no fish and game charges of any kind. Her licenses were bought under duress. The theft of the blind was a desperation move made to attract help."

Maki said, "She's filing for divorce. If Sally testifies, a jury may see her testimony as sour grapes and vengeance."

"Understood," Service said. "What I want is to have her husband cold on facts and data. Between our stuff and the drug felonies, the prosecutor will hammer him until he spits it all out, admits guilt, and throws himself on the mercy of the court, of which there will be none."

"You don't know Jesper Buckshow," Palovar said.

"He doesn't know me," Service came back.

"You're going to try to break him?" Maki asked.

"My goal is to win the war before the battle even starts."

"Tavolacci's a fool, but he's not incompetent. He has gotten a whole lot of assholes off," Maki said.

"Sandy and I have gone head to head many, many times over the years."

"How many has he won?"

"None when I'm the principal officer."

"That's a little too *mano a mano* for my taste," Maki said.

"The record is the record."

Maki said, "You just nailed the legendary Croatian. Word's everywhere. And sixty-eight citations in one camp in one night. You're on a roll. Nobody nails this many big cases in such a short period. Not nobody, not no how. Pride goeth before the fall."

"In or out?" he asked Sally Palovar. "I need a lot of details before I interview your husband."

Palovar looked at her lawyer but pointed a finger at Service like it was a pistol. "In, but you *can't* lose this one."

He took out his tape recorder. Maki nodded. He said, "Start remembering."

Which she did, well into the evening, for the record, on tape. At one point Maki fetched Allerdyce into the house and made soup for them while Sally Palovar talked and talked. And cried and cried, and lamented, and cursed her husband.

Service listened and thought, *This is how a priest must feel.* After awhile he found himself relying on the recorder. The oceans of detail were too much to write down. Transcripts would allow him to sort the information and data and organize it all into a logical, orderly case.

Sally talked, Maki and he listened, and Allerdyce seemed especially absorbed by her story. It was pushing ten when they drove out of the camp.

They traveled in silence. "Got an opinion on what you heard?" he asked his partner.

"Better prolly shoot some pipples den put t'ru court."

Service couldn't disagree. "Do you know where Tavolacci's camp is located?"

"Wah, I know da place. It belong to da clown's daddy, Berard."

"Still alive?"

"P'etends 'e is, eh."

Allerdyce despised Tavolacci, who had been his lawyer when he had accidentally shot Service during a scuffle as Service was trying to arrest him. He blamed the lawyer for not getting him a lighter sentence and less time in prison.

CHAPTER 44

Marquette

SATURDAY, NOVEMBER 28

Snowbound Books was a magnet for reading addicts, the curious, the bored, wannabe intellectuals, social misfits, aspiring authors, and people just looking for a quiet place to meet in a space that was public, private, and homey, all rolled into one small store.

It took twenty-six telephone calls to find Hamnet Eyquem, who had been Jesper Buckshow's supervisor at the time Buckshow was granted full medical disability and retirement by the state. Eyquem was less than enthusiastic about a meeting but eventually acquiesced to Service's insistence and his understated professional-to-professional appeal for cooperation.

The man was in his mid-fifties, tall, broad shouldered, and looked more fit and alert than many corrections people still on the job.

"Service," he greeted the man. "Eyquem?"

The man nodded, did not proffer a hand. He seemed uptight, even more in person than on the phone. *Professional tight wrapping, an emotional shield.* "I want to ask you about Jesper Buckshow."

Service noticed they were in front of a line of books by Henry Kisor. The author's main character was a U.P. lawman named Martinez, an Indian raised by whites and forever seeing the world from different and sometimes conflicting perspectives. Service admired the character, envied his ability to see sides so clearly. Not so different from talking to a corrections guy who spent his professional life warehousing the people cops and COs arrested and helped put there. Both jobs were under the umbrella of law enforcement, but there was little similarity other than perhaps a sense of right and wrong, and process of law. At least he hoped so.

"What *about* him?"

"You were his supervisor when he retired."

"Only on a technicality. He was off the job eight months before the paperwork was final, and I was newly promoted and inherited him. There wasn't much face time."

"But there was some."

"More than I would have liked."

Squeezed tone in the voice, almost exploratory. Sometimes you had to wait out something like this and other times you had to George it. "Why do I get the feeling you're skating around something?"

"Are you impugning my integrity?"

"We've got some heavy stuff going with your former employee, and I don't have time to foxtrot on eggs. Buckshow is in deep trouble, and we need all the leverage we can get."

"We live in an ever-litigious society. Blame that for my reticence. You bust your balls for thirty years, and then you have to watch your back. Lawsuits can come both from sleazy cons and worthless officers."

The voice sounded like one who had been burned by such suits. "Buckshow fit into one of those pigeonholes?"

"Both, if I had to be candid."

"He wore stripes."

"Unearned, in my view. My chickenshit predecessors were afraid of him and promoted him, when they should have sent him out on his keester. Buckshow was one of those anal types who filed grievances against anyone about anything and everything. You never knew what the man would do next or how he would react, other than in his own self-interest, which is the alpha and the omega with that one."

"I heard he had some sort of punch-up with an inmate."

Eyquem sighed. "He had dustups with everyone, but mostly verbal. He had the power and used it as a weapon."

"The name I heard was Tyrene."

"You live in the jungle, bullshit and artificial power will take you only so far. If you insist on keeping to the Hardass Highway, you tend to get back what you put in."

"Can you tell me what happened?"

"Only God and those two men know. You'd have to ask them."

"Talent's still around?"

"Gang-banger, lifer, a reptile in human flesh. Thing is that the man that came here, whatever he once was, seems someone else now."

"Found Jesus?"

"Muhammad, Buddha, the Wicked Witch of the West, the Easter Bunny, who knows? He arrived angry and snarling, me-against-the-whole-world; he stayed that way for a long, long time, and one day out came someone entirely different. Angry and warlike one day, mellow and at peace the next. I've seen this happen before, but never expected it from T-Rex, which is what others call him. I guess aging reduces testosterone, and one day the resident looks around and thinks, *Hey, life here ain't all that bad, it could be a lot worse.* Buckshow saw this as a weakness in the man and as a chance to use what he seemed to think of as leverage to show other inmates his ruthlessness and power as the king of the cellblock."

"You don't know what went down between them?"

"Don't *want* to know. I'm retired, and I no longer have to swim among the turds in the cesspool. I like my life; all that other business is behind me and locked in a box that I'm never going to open again. Not for anyone, not for any reason."

Service gave the retired Corrections Department lieutenant the litany of Buckshow's transgressions. Eyquem listened and shook his head.

Service asked, "You think his wheelchair's a scam?"

"Based on all the other stuff you've caught him doing, I'd say it has to be. But I'm not a doctor. It certainly wouldn't surprise me that he would game the system. Word on him was he was always a stickler for making others follow the rules, so much so that it made me wonder, you know, protesting too much and all that? Listen, if you really want to know what happened, you'd have to talk to T-Rex. He's the only one who knows for sure."

"You think this Talent will talk to me?"

"You can ask through channels, but after this, please leave me the hell alone. Buckshow is not worth another second of my time."

"I take it you won't be showing up in court as one of his character witnesses?"

This drew a slight smile. "I'd be first in line to give the man a lethal injection," Eyquem said, "and God forgive me for that."

"We don't do that in Michigan."

"Damn pity," Eyquem said.

"He's not killed any human beings," Service reminded the retired corrections officer.

"You don't have to stop a man's heart and brain to kill him," Eyquem shot back. "You can hound a man until all he wants is death, and when you reach that point, you've killed him."

They finished their conversation while standing in front of a used four-volume edition of the *Oxford English Dictionary*. Service was fascinated by the sheer size and touched the collection. A clerk whispered, "That's a facsimile of the 1936 edition. An original of that edition is priceless. Took from 1857 to 1928 for the first edition to come out, and that was in ten volumes. By 1936 they reduced the type size and got it down to four volumes. Fifteen and a half thousand pages, 178 miles of type, fifty million words, and pushing two million illustrative quotations." Talk about a commitment. The editors would have made first-rate corrections officers.

Service walked away thinking, *must've been nice to work in a time when commitment could be gracefully stretched over decades.* Cops had no such freedom or leisure. This case with Buckshow was pressing, and he was still thinking in the back of his mind about Cair and the bizarre night experience at the man's house, two garage fires, and so damn many active major cases he was finding it increasingly difficult to concentrate and sort them all out.

• • •

Late afternoon, and after a dozen more phone calls, Service found himself with a deputy warden at Northern Michigan Prison. The man had veins in his nose and tousled hair and listened politely until he got his spiel all out. His name was Hass Remington.

"Buckshow, eh? I'll ask T-Rex myself. Me and him been knowing each other a long, long time."

Two hours later, Grady Service was in a small beige-and-maroon room with a very large black man with dead eyes the color of brown chalk and movements so slow and deliberate he wondered if the man was on prescription meds.

"Appreciate this," Service began.

"Ain't no big thang," the man said. "I got me the time."

Service thought there was the slightest hint of a smile. "You remember Buckshow?"

"I 'member, yah."

"There are legends here about you and him."

T-Rex nodded solemnly. "Bullshit like money inside this place, sayin'. Get along in here, man got learn to be like tha' blond bitch wit' the long-ass hair tell stories till her tongue get sore."

"Rapunzel?"

"'At's 'er."

"So, there's a lot of bullshit in here?"

"There be fiffy-eh story 'bout me an Buckshow, none of 'em rye, sayin'."

He told T-Rex about Buckshow's problems.

"What id it 'bout white man got kill 'em cute li'l Bambi deers?"

"Can't explain it. Is what it is."

"I hear dat, but why you t'ink I gone spin you true?"

"Buckshow's defense is going to lean hard on sympathy, 'Boo hoo, poor me.' The prosecution needs to be ready to show the man as he really is, not as his lawyer paints his portrait."

"Trufe is, I ain't much on vengeance no mo'."

"What about justice?"

"Ain't same t'ings."

"Something obviously went down between you and Buckshow."

"Inside game, you know?"

"Not like *you* know it."

"Trut' dere. You gone try make me come tessifye?"

"Might could get you some time reduction."

"Don' wan' 'at. Wan' stay, do tye, ride dat sof' row."

"Would you testify?"

"I try not t'ink down no roads of 'morrow, sayin'. I try keep here-now, and like dat."

He couldn't blame the man and opted for silence to see what the man might offer next.

T-Rex scratched his forehead. "Oh why not put Massa Trut' on the flow? Buckshow was up in mah shit all tye, but me, I be duck wid oil in fedders, let his shit frow right offen me. Coul'n't get no rise fum me, that man coul'n't; and one day ah'm in room, cuffed up tye, and that man do

Willie Horton on me wid baton, fuck up mah back, rips, kidneys; I piss da blood fo two week when he be done. One day, monce later, I see him doin' his mad-dog bark on man; go over, tell the con, beat it bro. Look Buckshow inna eye. I tell 'im, 'I got contrack on your sick sorry ass. You ain' gone know where it come fum or whin, but it gone be fo sho Judgment Day for yo, motherfucker.'" T-Rex paused. "See, I see in dat motherfucker's eyes, all way deep down, an' I see I got myseff in real good. Ain't no need beat man's body if you can get inside 'is haid. I ain't no eddicated man, but if I can get in dere, speck you can too."

It was perhaps the strangest interview in his long career. And yet there was something reassuring. Of what, he was not all that certain. T-Rex, Eyquem, none of this was essential for the case, but Buckshow was a wiggler. You need to be ready to hold tight, like putting a sharp hook through a wiggling leech.

He called Jack Tax at home. "Service here. You going to talk to Buckshow soon?"

"Monday; no reason to hurry."

"You can't hold him indefinitely without charges."

"Drugs in the picture change everything, and his lawyer hasn't piped up yet."

"You want me to take him first? We're about to push him into the Grand Canyon on our stuff. He might look to you as an easier road."

Pause. "OK."

"You want to sit in with me?"

"No."

Special Agent Neutre called as Service and Friday were making a fresh harvest pork stew with roasted squash, carrots, and apples. "Neutre here. I'm back at the stakeout. Cair had a male visitor this afternoon. I got a photo with my long lens, uploaded it to my phone, and shot it off to you."

"Stand by one." Service found his phone, took a quick look at the e-mails, and saw the photo.

Penfold Pymn? What the hell?

He returned her call and said, "I know this guy. He's involved in another couple of cases of mine. Do you know him?"

"Not yet, but I will. What's his name again?"

"Penfold Pymn. Any sign of the grandson yet?"

"Negative down that path."

"You could be sitting out in the snow a long time."

"Or the opposite of that. You know, shit happens."

"Well, I'm thinking we should make our visit on Cair tomorrow. You want in?"

"Be good. You got a time?"

"Not yet."

"Let me know. I'll slide down the hill by the driveway and jump in back. I'm all in white."

"You'll leave a snowsnake trail."

She said seriously. "I don't even know what that *means*."

"I'll explain when we get time."

"Tomorrow then. Stay near your phone, in case."

CHAPTER 45

North Iron County

SUNDAY, NOVEMBER 29

The camp was near Shank Lake, less than a mile south of the Iron-Baraga county line. It was a throwback—tarpaper-covered, thick, gray moss on a warped shingle roof; no doubt there were asbestos strips under the tarpaper, because back in the day this was how most camps had been constructed. This was considered top-of-the-line construction in the 1940s and 1950s.

Service cringed whenever he came upon such primitive set-ups, and it always made him wonder if anyone had ever studied the life expectancy of the owners of such dumps. He knew dozens of places where the old toxic buildings were left to rot in place and fall back to nature, while new camps were built nearby from safer modern materials. Few camp owners wanted to spend the dollars needed to have toxic materials hauled away and legally disposed of. They'd spend initially on the camp, and not a penny on the old crap.

Luke's Road was as rocky as an old streambed and tended to put major hurt on vehicles that ran it regularly. Some camp owners had a special parking lot out near US 141 and drove sturdy beaters from there into the actual camps. Even with the Silverado's heavy suspension, road vibrations and oscillations made it difficult to move quickly or carry on a normal conversation.

An old sign proclaimed, "QUARANTA LADRONI, QUARANTA ANNI."

"What's it mean?" Service asked his partner as the truck continued to be bashed and bruised by the road.

Allerdyce was bracing himself. He shrugged and said, "Wops, dey have like hunnert year 'ere 'Merica, still wan' spicka da spaghetti, eh."

White smoke was curling up from the camp chimney. "I guess dey god a new Poop," Allerdyce said.

"Pope."

"Whatever. Why hell we got come dis place, Sonny? Dese guys like dog shit on boot bottom."

An old man was standing at the camp door on a crude porch, smoking a pipe.

"Da camp clown Poop," Allerdyce said.

Service left him in the truck and announced himself. "Conservation Officer Service, DNR."

The old man took the pipe out of his mouth and pointed with it. "Why're you on my private proppity?"

"Is Sandy Tavolacci here?"

"Get offa my proppity 'fore I *make* you get off."

Sandy Tavolacci appeared in the door with a huge cigar in hand. His eyes bugged out when he saw Service. "Pop," the lawyer said firmly but respectfully. "It's okay, I've got this." Another man stepped out, pulled the older man into the cabin, and closed the door.

Tavolacci wore old-timey red plaid wool pants and knee-high blaze orange wool socks. He had a black mug in one hand, and Service guessed it contained something other than tea or coffee. "You got some nerve barging into my dad's camp," the defense attorney said.

"We need to talk, Sandy."

Tavolacci craned at the truck and squinted. "Allerdyce? You've got *Allerdyce* in your state truck? What's he done now? You can tell that piece of shit I ain't available to represent his ass."

"Never mind Allerdyce, Sandy; and as for him needing your services, he thinks you're a fool."

"That's the thanks I get?" the lawyer said.

"He went inside seven years."

"Would've been worse if not for me."

"He doesn't see it that way."

"You come all the way out here to bust my balls—over ancient fuckin' history? How about Knezevich? What you done there does not sit well with me. I lost a client because of your unethical crap."

"Sandy, we both know Knezevich didn't need you. You were nothing more than a cheap prop until he could recon the field."

"I don't like being dumped. Word gets around."

"Clients who don't need you aren't going to swallow your big fees. Knezevich wanted to come clean. He's an honorable man, not one of the scumbags you tend to attract and run with."

"Are you calling my family scum?"

"If that was the family apple tree who greeted me, I'd say the apples don't
fall all that far from it."

Tavolacci said, "One of these days . . . you and me."

"Find another fantasy, Sandy. That turd won't flush."

"Say your say and get that asshole Allerdyce off our property."

"Jesper Buckshow."

"You people went t'rough 'is place like Nazis t'rough a Jew house."

"Yah?"

"Dep tole me."

"That dep, if there *is* such a person, is full of shit. No deps were there
when we went in."

Sandy quickly moved to another proposition. "My client has special
medical needs, and the things you did have harmed his health."

"He wasn't there when we were there, Sandy. He was already in the can."

"My client served the state honorably."

"Your client's a fraud, Sandy. If he's been confined to a wheelchair all
these years, how does he haul in all the animals he's whacked? Or build
cement bunkers?"

"He don't kill nothing. His wife does. You see his name on anything?"

*How does Tavolacci know what the evidence looks like? Has he been
Buckshow's lawyer for a while? Curious.*

"Bag the attitude, Sandy. I'm actually trying to protect you on this one."

The lawyer grinned with incredulity. "Really."

"Your client has personally and singlehandedly vacuumed most of the
major game off more than a couple thousand acres."

"Bullshit. Everybody knows it's the wolves, and you people just don't
want to admit it."

"Wolves don't bother with places that have few or no deer. They need to
eat, just like ambulance chasers."

"You come all the way out here to my dad's camp to lay this *shit* on me?"

"Listen to me, Sandy. You need to think this through. You've earned
a certain reputation and notoriety for representing your darkside clients.

Everyone knows that. Everyone knows that under our law, every citizen has a right to legal representation. But most of your practice is plain old law-abiding clients who hunt and fish. There aren't enough high-profile cases up here for you to make a living off them."

Tavolacci stared, puffing on his cigar.

"If you represent Buckshow, I'm pretty sure that Harry Pattinson, Torky Hamore, Kermit Swetz, Jud Dornboek, and Attilio Haire will paint a target on your chest. One of them has already threatened to kill your client."

"This is nothing but intimidation," Tavolacci said, "tampering with legal counsel. *Who* said they'd kill Buckshow?"

"Irrelevant. My point is that these fellas have deep pockets, long memories, and you know how long such memories tend to persist and grow into get-evens. They're like chicken salad at a picnic. If you represent Buckshow, they're going to pull strings to cut off your professional nuts to teach you not to interfere in their affairs."

"*Their* affairs? You their messenger boy?"

Service said, "You know better than that, Sandy."

"Buckshow's being railroaded."

"Your client's a loser. Not only will you lose this case, just representing him is likely to face-plant your reputation."

"I ain't afraid of nobody," Tavolacci said.

Clearly there was other than coffee in the man's mug.

The old man pushed back out the front door, waving a shotgun. Sandy blocked the barrel upward with his forearm, and four other men poured out to grab the old gent. They looked like cookie-cutter Tavolaccis.

The old man was shouting with a hoarse voice. "Dis game warden, he tells trut?'"

Sandy said, "He's bluffing, Pop. Take it easy."

The old fellow said, "Pattinson, Torky, Swetz, Jud, Haire, I know dese guys. Dese are men wit da clout. You pissin' off men like dat make no sense. Da client, da client, who da fuck is 'e? Shit from a rat's ass is all."

"Pop, go back inside. This is not your business."

"Got do wit my sons, is all my bidnit, *capisci*?"

"Not *this*."

"Dese five dis game warden talks, dey make war on Tavolaccis? We don't need dat shit. Old days is gone." The family elder spit. "Ciao to d'old days.

That stuff no fuckin' good for nobody, tough guys runnin' round with guns, waving em like *cazzi giganti*. Casa nostra, *casa di baciarmi il culo*."

"*Dad*!"

"Listen you me. You make dat bunch mad, dey take it out on you and me, and your brothers and your sisters, and all the families, *capisci*? We all doin' pret' good, don't need this *merda* on case you know you gone lose anyway."

"You don't understand what's at stake here."

"I unnerstan. *You* one don't see! Pattinson and dose guys make you into garbage, an' me and hull family too."

"My client's innocent," Sandy Tavolacci argued, his voice reedy.

The elder Tavolacci shrugged theatrically. "Innosin, guilty, who gives the shit which. Family all dat matters."

The father and brothers were all glaring so intensely at Sandy that Service felt compelled to do something to shift their focus. The first thing he thought of was out of his mouth before he had a chance to run it through his filter. "Listen, fellas. Since I'm already here, I guess I ought to check licenses and your camp buck pole. You guys had any luck?"

The men on the porch froze.

Tavolacci said, "You're not here legally. You're trespassing."

"Your gate was open."

Tavolacci glared at one of the other men. "Joey."

"I was like, late. There wasn't time to lock the chain, Sandy."

The elder Tavolacci declared, "You'da stay like I tole you and your brudders, we got none dis crap we got now. Goin' home for pussy!" He spat again.

The man called Joey defended himself. "I'm still a young man, Pop. My bride's young, not like you old farts."

"Young ain't 'nother word for *stupido* in *Italiano*."

"That's not fair, Pop!"

"What'sa fair, *questo grande stronzo con il distintivo d'oro*? Dis is my family, and all you *I* maka decides for." The old man turned back to Sandy. "You tell you client go find somebody else wipa 'is ass."

"You don't know what this is about, Dad."

"You deaf, boy? I don't care none what. Pattinson and others, dese're serious men with serious money. You don't get rich with pussy feet."

"There are ethical concerns, Dad. Even in your day, there were. You know that."

The man glared. "Only et'ical concern 'ere is how dis hurt my family, all of you. All da rest is rain dat never toucha da groun.'"

Sandy Tavolacci looked over at Service. "Is this what you wanted?"

Service fought back a smile. "Nope; this is pure bonus, Sandy. You might want to think hard on what your father's advising you to do."

"Buckshow's promising big bones for this."

"On what? He's on a medical pension from the state, and his wife works for the county. You think they've got magic trust funds stashed in the Caymans?"

Tavolacci said, "The big payday was *his* offer, not my demand."

"Big bones from *what*? The man's a liar, a cheat, a thief, a wife-beater, a doper, a killer, maybe a pervert. You have absolutely no idea what the hell you are biting off, but I can tell you it's gonna bite back."

"We should not be talking about this," the lawyer said. "This is not according to Doyle."

"It's Hoyle, not Doyle, and those are rules for games. We're talking hard reality, Sandy. Now show me your buck pole."

The group moved en masse. Service glanced at the truck. Limpy was no longer in the passenger seat, and as they got to the corner of the main camp building, the familiar voice said, "Dey gots some dandy horns back dere, Sonny. I coun' eight on buck pole, t'ree more spikes hangin' in black spruces farder back. Fee, five, fo, flum; I smell the real big stink all over dis one."

Allerdyce had somehow gotten out of the truck during the verbal fireworks and reconnoitered behind and beyond the camp.

"Six hunters in camp," Sandy Tavolacci said. "That number eleven is not an automatic wrong."

"Ain't no tags on nuttin,'" Allerdyce whispered.

"Ah," Service said. "Life gets more interesting by the moment. Okay, counselor, let's go see what you've got back there, and what kind of story you've got for me."

"We got tags, just ain't put on da deers yet," the patriarch announced from behind.

Service looked back. "This isn't a new requirement, sir. You have to tag it when you bag it. And if not, well, it's either a tagging violation or an illegal deer."

"Who maka da decision, tag or illegal?" Tavolacci Senior asked.

"That would be me, sir."

"Unfair," one of the brothers said.

"I hear that a lot, but only from those who never expected to see me." Service looked over at Limpy. "Let's see what all is here."

"Like spotlight over da camp window, blood on bait pile, dat kind stuff?"

"Yessir, partner. Exactly like that."

"Got bait pile mebbe hundred yards; got shooter lanes, bait pile mebbe t'ree feets high, ten foot long. Seen t'ee blinds too; dey all got way over two gallon, eh."

Tavolacci washed his face with the heels of his hands and keened, "Jesus Christ. This won't go away, will it? You know this is nothing but harassment."

"There's always a backstory and a bigger picture, Sandy. Sometimes it's hard for us to see it when we're inside it."

Three hours later, the patrol truck left camp with all eleven deer, including a thick-necked ten-point. There were no tags, except for Sandy and his father, and both of them claimed they hadn't shot anything. The other brothers hadn't yet bothered to make purchases and planned to process the meat right in camp, so there was, to their way of thinking, no need to buy licenses. A quick RSS search showed the brothers had not bought licenses in five years. Yet there were skull mounts in the camp with the brother's names and dates on them, all within the past five years. Service pointed out he could take all the mounts as well, but wouldn't. Yet.

He also issued a ticket for the camp bait pile and ordered the men to clean up the over-baits at their blinds.

"Din't speck all dat," Limpy said as they headed for Harvey.

"Me either," Service said. "I just wanted to talk to him."

"You t'ink dat bastid see big pitcher now?"

"One can only hope."

"Dis camp bin dirty long, long time."

"You never said anything."

"Youse din't never say where we go, eh. When I see dat camp sign, I t'ink, 'Geez, oh Pete; dis might be fun.'"

"You know what the Italian on the sign means?"

"Est. 1949. Fortyeth year. I like check buck poles part dis job, but not all dat jaw-jaw youse got do. Youse's old man was bullshit jaw-jaw; youse all bidness jaw-jaw. He couldn't done what youse do."

"Times change, jobs change," Service said.

His final words to Sandy Tavolacci had been, "I plan to talk to your client in the morning at nine. See you there, Sandy."

The lawyer looked at him with a stone face, a rare moment for such a volatile personality.

To Allerdyce, "One thing we know about that family."

"Eh?"

"They can't count for shit. The number of years since the camp was established is sixty, not forty."

"Wah," Allerdyce said, cackling.

CHAPTER 46

Marquette Über Dem See

SUNDAY, NOVEMBER 29

The plan was to have a quiet night to think about the impending Buckshow interview, but a call from Special Agent Neutre killed that and sent them in another direction.

"Pymn was at the house this morning," Neutre said. "I thought he was still here, but a silver minivan drove in just a few minutes ago and Pymn got out. I don't know how he got out of here or when the car got moved. I don't believe in magic. I am thinking that this van is full of cigarettes and they'll soon unload. We need to get in there now and catch them with the contraband."

Service told her it would take forty minutes to an hour to get to her from their present position. The woman grumbled and reluctantly acceded. "I'm moving my blind to the bottom of the hill directly across from the driveway opening. They'll never see me."

He called CO Angie Paul on his cell phone. With 800 MHz scanners now available to the public, COs were reduced to old methods of keeping operations secure. Paul answered and he gave her a quick rundown on the situation. "There's an ATF agent sitting on the place. She's got a hidey-hole across from the driveway, about eighty yards south of the house. There are two more houses up the hill from there, both unoccupied, with good drive-ways. Duck into the one up the hill on the southeastern side of the road. You'll have a garage to block anyone seeing you from Cair's place. When we come in dark, I'll give you a radio bump and you can jump in behind me. I'll stop to pick up the agent, and we'll turn up the driveway and make contact."

"Shall I call Volstaad to help? He's in this part of the county today, working a processor follow-up."

Young legs. "Good call; have him jump in with you."

"How far out are you?" she asked.

Typical of the U.P. to ask for a distance but really wanting to know the time involved. "Three zero mikes if I keep pushing it."

"Is this on some kind of urgent timetable?"

"For the ATF, not for us."

"Be careful," the young officer said.

Service heard her call Volstaad on the district frequency and ask if he was available for a TX, to which he replied, "Affirmative."

Neither of the young officers had radio diarrhea. They didn't waste words. He liked that.

• • •

Given the sudden intersection of circumstances, there was little time for careful thinking or chitchat. *What the hell is Pymn doing at Cair's, and what does Neutre know that she's not giving up?* It was still pretty much standard for Feds to withhold information, never mind declarations of transparency between law enforcement agencies in the wake of 9/11. That was lip service and little more. Nothing much had changed if you weren't considered part of the varsity.

Service pulled up to the end of the driveway dark. Allerdyce bailed out, and the special agent took his place. Paul and Volstaad were black and directly behind him.

"Where's he going?" Neutre wanted to know. She was visibly nervous.

"Recon, and don't worry; he's invisible."

"A physical impossibility," she said.

"Granted, but it is what it is. I want him in there first."

Ten minutes later, Allerdyce was beside the truck and the special agent was muttering, "Where the fuck?" Allerdyce leaned in and whispered, "Got the bloods all over sout'wes' side dere grudges, blood'n hairs on four-wheeler backside, more blood'n hair all over two plastic barrel."

"You look in the cans?"

"No need see. Can smell, Sonny. Deer parts in cans; smell head up on firewood pile. Got tarp froze down over top, 'nother buncha parts furder nort' along grudge wall. Lights on inside, pipples talkin', 'lectric saw buzzin', chains rattle. T'ink dey cuttin' one up."

Service turned to Neutre, "They're probably not even thinking about cigarettes."

"Where did that *man* come from?" the agent asked incredulously, pointing at Limpy.

"He's got superpowers."

"Bullshit."

"You just told me his being invisible was a physical impossibility."

"You can trust his words, take them for gospel?"

"If my partner says that's how it is, that's how it is."

She looked and sounded a little flustered. All that time alone and cold, and now all this action all around her. He knew how she felt, had felt it himself many, many times. You never got used to going from solo to team in a finger snap.

"Can we *go* now?" she asked impatiently, her voice clipped.

Service whispered to Allerdyce, "Tell Angie and Jop to park behind us but go around to the front door and knock. Tell Angie to ask if they can come inside to talk, and after they're inside, find a reason to continue talking in the garage." He could see the door was up on one of the garage bays.

"Me?" Allerdyce said.

"You push past the stuff you found, post out on the front of the house to the north. Don't let anyone get past you."

Allerdyce was gone in a blink.

"We're wasting time here," the ATF agent complained.

"Do you have a warrant?"

"You know I don't."

"Then chill. We have to finesse our way into this place, and our stuff will be the ticket to opening doors for you. Let's go about this thing deliberately. No rushing. Step by step."

From the driveway they could see one bay in the four-car garage open, and Service could see part of a silver van in the easternmost bay. The westernmost bay was closed up, but lit inside.

"We need to get inside," Neutre said.

"Angie will get us in. People always want to please her."

"She looks twelve."

"Maybe that's the key."

Allerdyce came back by, whispered "Okay," and raced up the driveway ahead of the trucks.

"I can't believe how fast that old man moves."

"This is nothing," Service said. "You should see him when he's trying to get away from the law."

Service stepped aside as COs Paul and Volstaad went by to the front door, which was to the east of the bank of garages.

He couldn't hear the conversation as it happened but would later hear it played back on CO Paul's digital recorder.

AP: Address, time, about to seek entry. Knocking could be heard, then a woman's voice.

Voice (later identified at Kerny Pascal-Veyron): "Yes?"

AP: "I'm sorry to bother you, ma'am. I'm Conservation Officer Angelina Paul, Department of Natural Resources, and we are here to investigate shots that have been reported up here in the hills. Have you heard anything?"

Voice: "You mean like tonight?"

AP: "Yes, ma'am. Tonight, any night recently."

Voice: "I'll have to think about that."

AP: "Is your husband here? Maybe he's heard something."

Voice: "He comes and goes. There's no clock to punch here."

AP: "Does he hunt?"

Voice: "I don't really know. You'd have to ask him."

AP: "Do you hunt?"

Voice: "No."

AP: "Has your husband gotten any deer this year?"

Voice: "I think, maybe. You'll have to ask him."

AP: "Is he here?"

Voice: "I already said I don't know."

AP: "Can we come inside and talk? We're letting cold air into your house."

Voice: "Oh, thanks. Please do come in. Would you like some coffee? It's already made."

AP: "No, thank you. Where does your husband process his deer?"

Voice: "I stay out of all that business."

AP: "That's a sweet pup you have there."

Voice: "She'll jump all over you. She's just five months, a Rhodesian ridgeback."

AP: "Lion-hunting dogs. My uncle had one. I'm a dog person. Can I pet her?"

Voice: "Sure. Rhodie, be nice to the lady."

AP: "She's so soft. Do you think we could talk in the garage. My partner and I are kind of overdressed to be inside."

Voice: "I suppose."

AP: "Is this the door into the garage area?"

Voice: "Uh, yes."

AP: "What space. I *dream* of such space! You have a gorgeous home. It looks new."

Voice: "Thank you. We built it a year ago, but Parm's already making noises about building a newer, bigger place, ya know, with more privacy?"

AP: "This looks quite private to me."

Voice: "It's a mirage. When all these lots get sold and other plat houses built, this will be just like other neighborhoods. We need real space and privacy."

AP: "You have plenty of both right now."

Voice: "Who are those people outside our garage?"

AP: "Don't be concerned. They're our colleagues."

Voice: "But why are they here?"

AP: "A gorgeous house like this, you don't mind if we look around, do you? When you're on the state payroll, you can't even *think* about places like this."

Voice: (tentative answer) "I guess . . . it would be all right."

AP: "There's some kind of blood and hair all over the garage floor."

Voice: "It's always a mess this time of year."

AP: "You mean during deer season?"

Voice: "I guess, yes."

AP: "Other times of the year too?"

Voice: "Parm can be more specific. He's got a steel-trap memory for everything he does."

AP: "That's a real gift."

Voice: "I told him that."

AP: "Do you ever hunt with him?"

Voice: "With who?"

AP: "Your husband."

Voice: "I never hunt with my husband."

AP: "Never?"

Voice: "Well, we used to, you know, as something we could do together? But I get too cold too fast."

AP: "Me too."

Voice: "You poor thing, and you must be out in the cold all the time."

AP: "More than I'd like."

Voice: "God, I know. I have the hot flashes and all that."

AP: "My mom went through the change. She said cold was good for hot flashes." Service heard Angie call the woman on the cold thing, then change directions. Great technique to keep the subject off balance. "There sure is a lot of blood and hair in here. It looks fresh."

Voice: "I wouldn't know anything about that."

AP: "What does your husband do for a living?"

Voice: "Imports and exports."

AP: "That sounds cool. Like what kind of stuff?"

Voice: "I don't pay attention to man-business. How do gals do your job?"

AP: "We just copy what the men do."

Voice: "You're a clever girl."

AP: "Do you have children?"

Voice: "No, and it's just as well, given Parm's emotional struggles."

AP: "He has some health issues?"

Voice: "Vietnam, you know? It turned him into a risk taker."

AP: "Really?"

Voice: "Oh, yes. He's a regular for counseling at the VA in Iron Mountain."

AP: "What's through the door over there in the corner of the garage?"

Voice: "That's Parm's man cave."

AP: "The lights are on. Is he in there?"

Voice: "I would not know that, would I?"

AP: "Have you had any visitors today?"

Voice: "No, none. In fact, I've got cabin fever."

AP: "It sounds like somebody's in the man cave."

Voice: "I don't hear anything."

AP: "Mind if we look?"

Voice (resignation): "I guess."

In real time, this is when CO Paul went through the side door into a garage bay littered with dozens of used latex gloves in several colors, all thrown around the floor; boxes and plastic bags with bloody cloth and paper towels; severed deer legs here and there; blood and hair; a legless carcass hung from a chain over a recessed drain in the floor, most of its meat gone and piled haphazardly on the floor. Service was behind her, heard her yell "Stop!" and saw her slide in blood on the floor as she scrambled toward an open side door to the outside. Special Agent Neutre was behind him, ordered Parmenter Cair to not move.

Service went through the side door and found Paul and Volstaad, who said, "He came out the door, sprinted for the hill to the north and jumped. Your partner was posted north, saw him, and jumped after him."

There were two paths in the snow down the steep hill—two people who had slid down on their butts. Service hopped down and followed, hurtling pell-mell after them, not thinking before he committed himself. The rough descent lasted seconds and stretched close to a hundred feet at a steep angle that bounced him at the bottom, but he quickly got back on his feet and followed two sets of boot prints in the eight or nine inches of snow. He followed them downhill through a series of ravine bottoms until he heard something directly ahead; he turned on his Surefire and saw an Arctic Cat side-by-side ORV. Allerdyce was on his knees with a stick or something across Penfold Pymn's throat; Pymn's right leg was deep under the ATV and the left leg sort of half up the side of it.

"What's up?" he asked Allerdyce.

The old man released his hold on the younger man's neck, and Service saw not a stick but a crowbar, which Allerdyce dropped in the snow. "He mighta coulda bumped inta somepin' kinda hard."

Service got down and looked at the leg. Compound fracture, some blood, swelling fast. It was ugly. Pymn wasn't moving. "Is he alive?"

"Wah, I t'ink he jus' bump noggin'."

Service got on his radio, told Angie Paul to yell for EMS. Bump on noggin' hell. *How will I explain this one?* His first task now was to splint and secure the leg so the injury wouldn't be worsened when they moved Pymn.

• • •

They were all in the workshop; Parmenter Cair was studiously examining the floor, or his boot tops. Special Agent Neutre said, "We can clearly see cigarettes in the minivan."

"There's no law against smoking."

"The cigarettes have Missouri tax stamps."

No response came from the man for a few seconds. "You can't possibly see that from outside."

Neutre said, "You just told us."

Cair: "I did no such thing."

Neutre: "Not intentionally. Where are the keys?"

Cair: "It's not my van."

Service whispered to the agent, "Pymn probably threw them when he ran."

"We have more than adequate probable cause," she told Cair.

"Again, that is not my vehicle."

"No? Whose is it?"

"How should I know?"

"It's parked in your garage."

"One of life's little puzzles," the man said.

"It was observed arriving here today."

"Not seen or driven by me. I don't know anything about that vehicle."

Neutre said to Service, "He's all yours for the moment," and left the workshop.

Grady Service said, "We've got Pymn, but he's hurt."

Cair only shrugged and showed a quizzical look: "Pimp? I know no such person."

Service said, "He says he knows you."

The man looked at the ceiling before answering, "Ah, *that* Pymn? He's shirttail kin to my wife."

"He says he's done some work for you. He's willing to talk, and he wants to clear his conscience," Service said.

Cair countered, "Prevaricator."

"He seems convincing to me," the CO said.

Cair grinned crookedly. "Donchu know that's the first test of a liar?"

"Are you telling me that if someone's convincing, they're telling a lie?"

The man nodded. "Absolutely. You see it in the private sector all the time. *Caveat emptor*, right?"

"So, if I find what *you're* telling me seems convincing, that will be my way of knowing that you're lying?" Service asked, playing the man's own words back to him.

"Not *me*! Others. I'll be telling the truth. It's others you have to concern yourself with. I'm a man of honor."

Grady Service said, "Well, that's a relief. So, now we need to talk about all the deer and cigarettes you've got here."

"Those cigarettes are not mine."

"We found cartons of the same brand at your grandson's apartment."

"You'd best talk to him then, not me. I know nothing about that."

Allerdyce summoned Service to the outside door. "Two gut piles down where we was, and girlie says fresh blood up above on road in. Gone take ORV up dose hills and see where it lead, okay?"

"Go."

He stepped back into the garage. "I don't care about the smokes. I want to know about the deer. We've got four outside your workshop, two in the garage, and my partner has found evidence of two more, which makes at least eight. This is your chance to come clean and prove you're a man of honor."

"I don't have to prove anything," Cair said.

"You say that with great conviction. Are you lying? Tell us about the deer, Parm. C'mon, this isn't a capital crime, it's just some deer. No biggie. Get it off your chest."

"There aren't any deer."

"Look around you."

"I don't have to look. I know my house and my workshop. There are no deer here."

"Where's the venison?"

"Ain't no venison," Cair said. "We do not consume such unspeakables."

"We interrupted you butchering a deer. There are parts and meat all around on the floor."

"I see nothing, and none of it is mine."

"None of what?"

"None of what you see," Cair said.

"How do you know what I see?"

"You just told me."

"You've been hunting."

"Absolutely not."

"I checked our computers. You have a license, as do your wife and your seventeen-year-old son. By the way, where is *he*?"

"I have no son."

"Our retail sales system says differently."

"Computers can be wrong."

"Not this one. You bought licenses. I can even tell which day and time."

"I don't remember."

"You've been hunting."

"I don't remember."

"Somebody killed the animals here."

"Not me."

"You didn't do it, or you can't remember if you did it?"

"Can't remember."

"No?"

"The war."

"Which one?"

"Vietnam."

"You were there?"

"I'm still there."

Neutre never mentioned any military service for the man. "Where was there?"

"Long An Province, I Corps, Ninth Infantry Division, Operation Enterprise."

"When was this?"

"I remember it like it was yesterday; 1965."

"Ninth Infantry Division?"

"Oorah."

"Bullshitter," Service said without hiding his disgust. "Op Enterprise ran from early '67 into early '68; Long An was in III Corps in the Delta Region, not in I Corps by the DMZ; and soldiers say 'hooah,' not 'oorah.' That's reserved for Marines. Like me."

Cair was studying the floor again when the special agent returned. "Your wife knows nothing about cigarettes."

"She's a pathological liar."

Neutre said, "I don't think so. I talked to her in St. Louis."

Cair looked startled. "You've made a mistake. My wife's in the house here."

"No, that woman in the house is your girlfriend, or however you guys put it. Her name is Kerny Pascal-Veyron, and she was once a titty bar stripper in Las Vegas."

"Exotic dancer," Cair said. "And she was the headliner."

"She was a fifty dollar whore," the special agent said. "She admits it, why can't you?"

"Pathological liar."

Neutre looked at a rifle case in the workshop. "Yours?"

"Yes."

"For hunting?"

"No, for shooting."

Service asked, "Can we see it?"

"Yes, of course."

Cair opened the case, broke the rifle, and set it in Neutre's hand. She hefted it and made a sound of admiration. "Beautiful work. Fieldstar Smackdown, single shot .45-70." She looked closer. "Says '3 of 30.'"

"Custom-made. The wife gave it to me last Christmas. Still makes me kinda weepy."

Service had shut out the man's voice. There were two crossbows hanging in the garage outside the workshop; two rifles cases in the garage, three more rifle cases in the workshop, deer parts all over the damn place. No telling how many firearms in the house.

"You use the .45-70 to shoot all these?"

"No," Cair said. "That's the job of the .30-06." He pointed at another gun case in the workshop.

CO Paul picked it up, unzipped it, checked the breech. "Loaded," she said, popping the clip. "Two rounds gone."

"I do not hunt," the man said. "I collect."

Carcasses. "You just told us the .30-06 was used to kill the deer around here."

"Not by me."

Allerdyce materialized in the side door. "Got two bait piles in field quarter mile up road, two gut piles, drag marks out to road, I t'ink to haul on snowmobile under tarp by woodpile."

Couldn't count all the animals right now. Too confusing. "Where's all the meat?"

Cair shrugged. "There isn't any."

"I can see deer parts. We can all see them. And meat. Some of it's right there on the floor."

"That's not mine."

Service was looking at his partner. Angie Paul had gone back into the garage. He heard the following:

Paul: "That's a fine rifle, a .45-70, right?"

Cair: "I got a sweet deal on that. Paid a man twenty-nine hundred. New she would go for four grand, easy."

Service had had enough and stepped back inside. "You just told us your wife gave that to you as a Christmas gift."

"That's the story she tells. She don't like to say what she had to do to get it off the guy."

"You just told Officer Paul you *bought* it."

Cair paused. "Well, if my wife bought it, then I bought it, right? Do you follow my logic?"

"You said *you*."

"You're being a strict constructionist. My wife bought it, but not with money, if you get my meaning. I don't want her humiliated in public when all she wanted to do is surprise me and make me happy."

"Your wife is in St. Louis," Neutre said again. "Not here. Your happiness isn't on her radar and hasn't been since you abandoned her."

"I beg to differ, and you have to bear in mind that I have some difficulty remembering things. Nothing is my fault."

Neutre took Service outside. "I talked to Pymn. He drives for Cair, takes a nice cut, which he passes to his pet rescue operation partner."

Service: "Keep Our Pets Alive, KOPA. His partner is Arletta Ingalls."

"You know her?"

"I do. She claims to finance the group with pie sales."

"You believe that?"

"No, but I honestly haven't had time to look deeper into the case. I've been jammed since before the season began, and it hasn't let up."

"Have you gotten everything you need from here?" Neutre asked.

"Not yet."

There followed a strange conversation with the fake wife, woman whose first name was Kerny.

Service: "There are three chest freezers in the garage, and two more in the workshop. How many are in the house?"

Woman: "Uh huh."

Service: "That question calls for a number."

Woman: "The usual, I guess."

Service: "How many?"

Woman: "Two chests and the freezer side of the fridge in the kitchen. That makes what, seven and a half?"

Service: "How much venison do you have?"

Woman: "I have no idea. I don't cook, do I? Parm cooks on account of his dietary needs. You know, he got gassed in the war."

Service: "Did he? Which war?"

Woman: "Persian Gulf, the first one, when that nice George Bush was our president, not when his fool son was in office."

Angie Paul intervened. "Ma'am, you told me your husband was in Vietnam."

The woman sighed. "He lies all the time, and how am I supposed to keep it all straight? I mean one stupid war's pretty much the same as another, right?"

Service was fed up. "Do you mind if we look in all the freezers?"

"Of course not. Take everything you find. I don't want that filthy stuff in my home."

"Filthy stuff?"

"You'll see."

The freezers were filled with venison, all packaged and neatly labeled. They stacked packages, used a scale, had right around a thousand pounds. Service calculated that at an average of eighty pounds of processed meat per animal, the meat in hand accounted for right around a dozen animals. It was close enough.

Neutre said, "You'll probably never get him in a state court."

"Wah," Service said and looked at his watch. It was pushing midnight, November 29. Only one more day remaining in the 2009 traditional firearm season. What more could happen?

CHAPTER 47

Marquette

MONDAY, NOVEMBER 30

How did you interview a snake like Jesper Buckshow? This had been simmering in the back of his mind for some time, knowing the moment was
coming, but only late last night had it struck him that the task might be a lot
easier if he used all the tools at his disposal.

Marquette State Prison Deputy Warden Hass Remington answered as if
he had been awake for hours. "Service here. Got a wild proposal for you," he
told the man, who listened quietly.

"You think this would help your case?"

"It sure can't hurt it."

"Okay then. I'll see to it myself, but only if I can watch."

"By all means," Service told the man.

• • •

Jesper Buckshow was wearing a faded orange jumpsuit, white cotton socks,
and white paper slippers. A county corrections officer pushed his wheelchair
into the interview room.

"That chair feel strange? I'm Conservation Officer Service, DNR. We
have a lot to talk about."

Buckshow rolled his eyes. "Fuck you, toy cop; I got arraigned on a chickenshit drug beef yesterday."

"You can look forward to more from us."

"For drugs?"

"Where's your attorney?"

"The wop? I sent his ass packing. Couldn't even get me bail, what kind
of bullshit is *that*?"

If true, and for whatever reason, this might be a lucky break for Tavolacci. "And now here you sit."

"Ain't nothing the likes of you can do to me."

"We took about two hundred pieces of evidence out of your house that suggests differently. Deer skulls and mounts, turkey fans, wolf pelts; you're a regular killing machine."

"I got nothing to say until I have representation."

"That's your right of course."

The interview room had been chosen with care. It shared a two-way mirror with the next room. Which side was mirror and which side you could see through was electronically controlled from the other room. Buckshow could see into the other room but not vice versa.

Service let the action take place as a door opened and Deputy Warden Hass Remington brought a handcuffed Tyrene "T-Rex" Talent into the room and gave him a chair.

Buckshow was as still as prey until T-Rex looked at the window. Buckshow lurched in his wheelchair. "What is *this*?"

"What is *what*?"

"Over there," Buckshow said, turning his head away. "That . . . thing."

"No idea who he is. Our business is here in this room."

"I *know* that guy."

"What guy?"

"In the next room; are you not paying attention here?"

Service glanced at T-Rex. "Sorry, no same-sex conjugal visits allowed in this jail."

Buckshow hissed, "I ain't one of them people. I'm normal."

Service said, "Yah; we saw that at your house."

Buckshow reddened, and Service told him, "We need to get down to business."

"What business?"

"Your poaching business."

"Weren't no business. Hunting's my avocation. Is that word too big for you? It means hobby."

"It also means minor occupation, and because you're allegedly medically disabled and have no primary occupation, prima facie, which makes it your primary occupation."

He noticed Buckshow was perspiring heavily. "Is it too hot in here for you?"

"I have medical conditions."

"Care to specify?"

The man shook his head, was now watching T-Rex and nothing else. "What do you want?"

"I want you to tell me about the animals you took."

"I do not possess an eidetic memory."

"No problem. We'll go through every item one at a time."

"Why is that *man* in there?" Buckshow asked again, his voice cracking.

"I don't know, and I don't care. Can we stay on topic? I have other things to do today."

"That's a very, very bad man in that room."

Service glanced at T-Rex. "He looks perfectly normal to me."

"Oh no, oh no, you are *wrong*. Not that one."

"What about the animals?"

Buckshow was talking to him, but his eyes were fixed on T-Rex, who was looking at the mirror on his side. "Is that man in this jail?"

"I don't know. Want me to ask?"

"Yes."

Service went next door so Buckshow could see him. The black man nodded, grinned, and held out a fist for the CO to bump.

"They're getting him ready for in-processing."

"You know him?" the prisoner asked.

"I've never seen him before this morning."

"What was all the doo-dap bullshit?"

"You must be seeing things."

"I know what I'm seeing. I'm not blind."

"Your sniping proves that."

"What do I have to do to make all this go away?"

"All this is not going away. You're in serious trouble, and you need to face it."

"I didn't mean go away forever, I meant go away today, this morning, go away now. Is there something I can sign?"

"We've taken the liberty of writing a statement for you. If you prefer, you can write your own. Otherwise, read the one here and, if you agree, sign it."

"What's it say?"

"It says that you killed all the animals listed in evidence in the appended report and that you acted alone. Is that an accurate summary?"

"Yes; give me a damn pen."

"First you have to read the statement and the attachment."

"Okay."

Service gave him the evidence list and the statement. The prisoner's attention remained next door.

"The report's on your table, not in that other room."

Buckshow held out his hand for a pen.

Service placed his digital recorder on the table. "Do you swear that you voluntarily sign this statement of your own volition and without coercion?"

"Yah, yah; give me a pen."

The man scribbled his signature and stood up.

Service said, "My God, it's a miracle. You can walk!"

"Up yours. I want out."

"What about your wheelchair? You might suffer a relapse."

"Are you deaf? I'm done here. I want back in my cell."

Service buzzed for a guard to take the prisoner, who paused momentarily at the door. "What's the fine for all this crap?"

"Our charges? No idea, except they won't be cheap. Restitution on one deer is a thousand. But if I were you, I'd worry more about the jail time the drug charges are likely to carry. Hundreds of plants suggests more than personal use."

"I use it only for medical reasons."

"Good luck with that."

"Weed is legal. We voted it in statewide a year ago."

"I heard something about that." He wasn't sure if the statement would hold up, but with Buckshow in jail and not out on bail, it didn't really matter. They had more than enough evidence, and when the season was over, he would have to sit down and write the complaint and request warrants on charges specified.

Claims he had fired Sandy. True, or had Sandy walked? The latter, he hoped.

CHAPTER 48

Rock, Delta County

MONDAY, NOVEMBER 30

Service fetched Allerdyce from Friday's house and they headed out. No real plan in mind other than to just drive aimlessly until something caught their attention. Right after a stop for coffee in Gwinn, they saw a doe carcass in a field, an orange tag in its jaw. Service got out and fetched the tag. The name was Dux Goldmanenmooi. He called Station Twenty in Lansing and ran the name, which came back to an address on Jokkola Street in Rock. "Let's go see this fella, then call it a day and a season."

"You gone write fella just t'row 'way bones?"

"We're going to have a little talk about littering and illegal disposal and see what other doors pop open."

"Youse's daddy woulda leff 'at t'ing right dere."

"I'm not him. Times change. The paper trail reigns."

• • •

Dux Goldmanenmooi (they learned it was pronounced Ghoul-de-moy) was in his twenties, on the gaunt side, dull-eyed, gold earrings, standard goatee of young men of his generation's age.

It took awhile to get the name straight, and finally Service asked, "You hunt this year?"

"Yah, sure."

"Get a deer?"

"Was fork horn, I think."

Thinks? "Where at?"

"Over by the river; you know, the Escanaba, up where the Sawmill Creek dumps in. Is there a problem, sir?"

"I was hoping you could tell me," Service told him.

"No, sir, no problem I know of."

"We found a carcass dumped on state land. That's illegal disposal, littering."

"Wasn't me put nothing nowhere."

"You don't even know where I'm talking about."

"I mean to say, I din't dump no deer carcass nowheres."

"It's got your tag on it. How do you think it got there?"

"Lefty, I guess."

"Lefty?"

"Lawrence Hugelyn, but everybody just calls him Lefty, eh."

"Hugelyn lives here in Rock?"

"No; he's up M-35 east of McFarland."

Service explained where they had found the carcass.

"There you go. That's not two, three miles from Lefty's place," Goldma-nenmooi said.

"You took the deer to him for processing?"

"Didn't have to; he come and got it. My work schedule's kinda crazy right now. Thing is, I don't got no meat back yet and it's been two weeks."

"Who do you work for?"

"Metz Propane, here in Rock."

"No game processors here in Rock?"

"There used to be an old fart, but he's up with the droolers in the Jaco-betti Home in Marquette now. Lefty does this for fun and for some of the meat. Don't cost me nothing, not even gas, and I'm all over that, sayin'."

"Do me a favor," Service said. "Don't call Lefty. If you do, I'm going to figure you're lying to me and up to something, in which case we will be back."

"No, sir; I won't call him."

• • •

Hugelyn lived in a dilapidated farmhouse with a broken-down barn and a row of low buildings that might once have housed poultry. Even in the cold, the entire area stank. There were cats everywhere—all colors, all sizes, most of them carrying on, hissing and growling, crying and cater-wauling. Service pounded the door while Limpy made a quick tour of the grounds.

The man who answered the door had gray hair in a bushy ponytail. He wore an unbuttoned, faded yellow plaid shirt over bare skin. It looked like he'd thrown on the shirt to come to the door. His jeans were unzipped and unsnapped. He had a neck tattoo of a large buck deer. "Sir," the barefoot man greeted him.

"Mr. Hugelyn?"

"Lefty."

"Do you process deer, Lefty?"

"No, sir, I do not. I used to but not anymore."

"A friend of yours says differently."

"He's mistaken."

"He says you pick up deer and process them for some of the meat as payment."

"I don't know why somebody would say that, sir. What's this all about?"

Three or four cats scooted in and two came out. The man seemed oblivious to them.

A tall, naked woman with unkempt hair came into view in the kitchen behind him and said, "Lawrence, where *are* your manners? Let that officer come inside. You're lettin' them damn cats in and all the heat out; you know I hate your stinky old cats, and heat costs us money. Please come in, Mr. DNR. Excuse Larry. Like, his mind is elsewhere at the moment, ya know?"

Hugelyn stepped aside and Service walked in. The place was filthy and smelled sulfureous.

"Did he come to pick up meat?" the woman asked Lefty.

Hugelyn made a growling sound. "There ain't no meat."

"There *ain't*?" the woman said. She seemed to ponder this and finally said, very slowly, "Right, no meat. Now I remember. That was my last boyfriend, the one with the—"

Hugelyn cut her off. "Put some clothes on. You look like a tramp."

"You know I don't like clothes, Lefty. You know that. Nude's nice, am I right, Mr. DNR?"

Oh boy. "Yes, ma'am, nude can be nice."

"Was real nice when you come a knockin' on the door, cause our bed was a-rockin' and donchyouse knows I was sittin' atop Larry at that very moment. See, Larry, this nice officer thinks I have a fine body, don't you, sir?"

"I do, ma'am, yes." She did indeed.

"Stop looking at my woman," Lefty said. "She ain't no public show."

"Tell me about meat processing," Service said to the man.

"Nothing to tell. She's just confused. You heard her."

"You hunt?"

"Both of us do, don't we, Star?" Lefty looked back at the woman.

"Sure, we both hunt," she said, taking one small step forward.

"Any luck?"

"Up till you knocked on the door, Lawrence was gettin' real lucky, weren't you, Larry?"

"Shut up, Star."

Service was at a loss for words.

"Don't be no sourpuss, Larry. We do it all the time. What's one teensy interruption?"

"One too damn many," Lefty complained.

Service suddenly felt invisible as they began to go back and forth at each other.

"I told you not to go so slow," she said. "I don't mind a break. In fact, it'll just make it better when we get back to it."

"Shut your mouth, Star. You like being interrupted?"

"It's just you and me, no biggie. Been my old boyfriend, I'da minded a whole lot."

"What the hell is wrong with *you*?"

"Wrong with *me*?" The woman stepped closer. "I shot a six-point," she said, "just the other day."

"Where is it?" Service asked.

"Or was it an eight-point? I can't remember what Larry told me to say to the DNRs."

"Larry *tells* you what you shot?"

"Don't listen to her."

"It's the man's job," Star said.

Oh boy. "Did Larry say what he shot?"

"Well he was right on the verge with me, when you come knocking."

"Deer, I mean."

"Honestly," she said, "I just don't remember. I sort of remember yesterday, and we were, you know, getting it on all afternoon. I just pushed all that stuff right out of my head, and I guess it ain't come back yet."

"She's not right in the head," Hugelyn offered. "Her dipstick don't reach oil."

The woman said caustically, "Your dipstick don't reach much neither."

"She seems all right to me," Service said. This was a very, very approximate statement of reality.

"You're blinded by her tits and stuff."

"Hardly."

The kitchen door opened and Allerdyce looked inside. He chortled and said, "Looking good, girlie."

Star said, "Why thank you, sir."

Limpy said hoarsely. "Shed outten back got an open door. You need take look, Sonny."

Hugelyn followed them, chirping. "You cannot just come onto my property."

Service stopped and faced the man. "We're on a complaint, Lefty, and if the door to your shed is open, then anything we can see inside can be used by us. You processed a deer and didn't give the client any meat. You tossed the carcass on state land."

"It's fuckin' biodegradable, man."

"It's also illegal for you to put it there."

"Where the fuck my 'pose to put 'em?"

"Them? You have more than one?"

"I got the ones Star and me shot."

"Let's see those, and your driver's license too."

Allerdyce pointed at the shed.

"I didn't know I couldn't dump deer on state land. Of course I'll clean it up, sir. An honest mistake."

"No need. It's in the back of my truck. I thought you said you don't process game?"

"Cool, thanks." Hugelyn ignored the question.

Service shone his Surefire into the shed and saw three deer hanging and some parts on a dirt floor. "What's this in here? Is there a light?"

"You need a warrant."

"You're not listening to me, Lefty. The door's wide open. All rights to privacy are null and void when the door is open."

"I never leave no doors open."

Allerdyce said, "Youse leave da kitchen door wide open when youse follow us out 'ere."

Service went into the shed. "Get a light on in here, Lefty, and do it now."

"There ain't one."

"You don't want to go down that road, Lefty. Find the light, partner." Lights came on almost immediately. Three buck heads on the floor; three legless deer hanging, not yet butchered; two more carcasses on the dirt floor, seven or eight feet back.

"Yours or customers?"

The man held up his hands. "Okay, okay. Star and me, we're a little tight on money. This gets us meat. Even poor folk gotta eat."

"You got paperwork? If you process, you have to keep a log. You don't need a state license, like a taxidermist, but you do need a log so we can look at it when we come around."

"I got their tags is all."

"I don't see any tags on any of these deer."

"Don't got to be. I'm processing 'em, right?"

"Wrong."

Service asked, "Who shot these?"

"No idea," Hugelyn said.

Service took Dux Goldmanenmooi's cell phone number out of his pocket and tapped it in.

The man answered, "Yes?"

"We're at your friend Lefty's. He denies cutting meat, says you don't have a deal with him."

"Oh?" Dux said.

"Did you shoot the deer we found, Dux? Don't lie. This is your chance."

"No, sir. I gave my license to Lefty. I don't got no time to hunt this fall, and I need the meat."

"You loaned your license to him?"

Service held the cell phone out so Hugelyn could hear. "Yes, sir, and I ain't the only one does it, neither'."

Allerdyce was examining various deer carcasses. "Dere's more deer back 'ere in dark, Sonny."

"Check them."

"No more bullshitting, Hugelyn. We have been dog-paddling in shit for two damn weeks and we're sick of it. I want the truth, and I want it now."

"Yes, all right, I admit it. I shot everything here and the one you found. Star don't hunt. Hell, she don't even cook. I gotta do almost everything around this pigsty."

"You use other people's licenses and give them most of the meat?"

"When I have time, but not until the season's over. Otherwise, I have to hunt."

"Dere's nice ten-point hid under tarp in back," Allerdyce announced from the darkness.

"Please don't take that. It's the only nice buck this season."

Service got the woman's ID and ran both the man and her through the truck's computer. Neither had ever bought a license, and neither had priors. Just one more example of the secret, underground violating that went down everywhere and nobody spoke of. Service passed on writing tickets but took Lefty's rifle and all the untagged deer they could find and left the man with a receipt for seized property. "I'll be writing a complaint, and a warrant will be issued and then a ticket."

"What we 'pose to eat?" Hugelyn asked.

Allerdyce said, "Youse got bloody cats everywhere. Coyotes like eat dose."

"That's disgusting. It's a crime to mistreat animals."

Service went back to the house and the woman asked him, "Am I going to jail?"

"No, ma'am, not right now, but the law says an illegal deer carries mandatory jail time."

Star said, "Well, I wish you would hurry and do whatever you got to do, 'cause I'm sick of eating damn venison." She arched an eyebrow. "Can a girl, you know, like poke her way out of the pokey?"

"No," Service said.

"There's a first time for everything," the woman said. "Call me the eternal optimist."

The partners got back into the Silverado, and Service looked at his watch. "An hour past legal shooting."

"Don't mean nothing," Allerdyce said. "We ain't in Kalamazoo no more."

"Kalamazoo?"

"You know dat flick wit Judy Garland and her dog, Tokyo?"

Service started laughing.

"You t'ink we set record for seized deers?"

"No idea. Does it feel like a record to you?"

"Not even close for me," the old man said deadpan, and Service stared at him.

"In da old days, Sonny; in old days, not no more."

ACT 5: SEASON IN THE BOOKS

Everything stinks till it's finished.

—Dr. Seuss, *Green Eggs and Ham*

CHAPTER 49

Lansing, Ingham County

THURSDAY, DECEMBER 3, 2009

Grady Service was on the fifth floor of the Mason Building in central Lansing, in Chief Eddie Waco's office. The DNR's chief legal counsel, a dork named Stone, was with him. The summons had come yesterday as a text. "My office, 10:00, 12/3/09. Chief Waco. Bring truck, badge, all state-issued weapons."

He had a pretty good idea of what was ahead, but not why. Something to do with Tavolacci, or T-Rex and Buckshow? The season had been long and complex, and he wasn't sure that without his notes he could even remember some of the mountain of crap they had collided with.

He drove the Silverado, and Allerdyce followed in his personal truck.

"You gettin' canned or somepin?" the old violator asked as they got ready to leave.

"We'll see."

"Ain't no way treat people, send some note on demm phone t'ing."

• • •

The chief's secretary/assistant met him in the lobby and rode up with him in the elevator.

The chief pointed at a chair.

"No thank you, sir. Firing squads shoot standing men," Service said. "I work on my feet, not on my ass."

Chief Waco said, "I talked to Special Agent Neutre. She says you are one hell of a fine officer. A *great* officer. Do you have any idea why you are here?"

"I'm guessing it's not for a medal."

"This is not the time for your lame jokes," his boss and friend said. "You employed a felon as a partner for the entire deer season."

"I consider him an unpaid consultant. He knows more about this business than most of us."

"Nevertheless, the governor has just learned about this and is beside himself. He wants all state law enforcement personnel to live and serve in an exemplary manner. He has ordered you suspended without pay for an indefinite period, at least into spring, at which time there will be a formal hearing regarding your future."

"You're onboard with this crap, Eddie?"

"Chain of command, Grady. You know that."

"Yes, sir, I do. Understood, sir."

"Got anything to say for yourself?"

"I'd do it again. Have you looked at what we accomplished this season?"

"Means are not justified by ends, Grady."

"Whatever, sir. Are we done here? This place has always made it hard for me to breathe."

"Badge, ID, firearms, keys, gear."

Service put his badge and the other items on the chief's desk. "Everything else is in the truck down in the lot."

"This isn't over," the chief said.

"Easy for you to say, sitting here in your office. Can I go?"

"You're dismissed." Service stood, gave a crisp military salute, pivoted, and departed with no further words. He felt all eyes on him as he passed through office rows and desks, and only as he got into the elevator with tears in his eyes did he hear it. Is that applause? Not loud, but definitely hands clapping ever so quietly.

"Jesus, *they're all* glad *I'm gone?*" he thought, stepped into the elevator, and punched the button to take him down to the ground. It felt like stepping out of an aircraft, only this time he didn't feel silk on his back or see it overhead, only the void ahead and unexpected reality rushing up to meet him.

CHAPTER 50

Slippery Creek Camp

THURSDAY, DECEMBER 24

Christmas Eve, fresh snow falling, the house filled with pleasant scents, presents under a tall, tricked-out tree. Friends and family in close: Tuesday and Shigun; Karylanne and Maridly; his friend Treebone and his wife, Kalina; Allerdyce; Newf and Cat. Plentiful libations for all; piles and mounds of food and sweets.

"Why do Indi'ns got a white Santy Claus?" Maridly asked Allerdyce.

"Onaccount injuns ain't all dat bright, girlie."

"That's *mean*."

Allerdyce shrugged, rubbed Shigun's shoulder, turned to Service.

"Smokin' lamp lit?"

"Porch."

Treebone said, "Me makes three."

Outside in the falling snow, Tree said, "You haven't said shit about the suspension."

"What's to say? Is what it is."

"McKower told me you went in and wrote all your complaints and reports for deer season."

"Had to be done."

"Not by you it didn't."

"My cases, my paperwork."

"I would have told them to fuck off."

"No you wouldn't. You're just like me."

"Yah?"

"Pink inside."

"That's lame."

"Whatever."

"I thinked up pome," Allerdyce announced.

"God save us," Treebone said.

"God got nuttin' do wiff dis. Here goes: Dere's skinny fine line 'tween what calls laws and calls sins, and even when youse lose, sometimes youse win." The old man looked at the other men. "Look me. I go prison, now all youse pipples frien's now. Youse know, oot der my worl' pipples say, even whin youse know youse gone die, it ain't right to not make no fight."

"That's something my old man used to say," Service said, smiling. He slowly raised one of his massive fists in a gesture of defiance and Tree fist-bumped him, as did the old violator.

"Wah!" Limpy Allerdyce said.

AUTHOR'S NOTE

Enter the Clown. It's Time for a Jig and an Accounting

Had this been an Elizabethan production filled with pithy iambic pentameter, we would now be to the point in the festivities where the cast clown would hop out on stage to entertain you with a jig, some songs, jokes, and clever repartee. But here I am, minus the dance, songs, and jokes. However, I do have a few observations to share about the cases Grady Service ran into in that very strange deer season of 2009.

This book's title is a term coined by a good friend of mine, a detective, and I think it fits the cases herein because this sort of obsession takes on an infinite number of forms and cuts across all so-called socioeconomic classes. DNR officers often make the distinction between real hunters and mere shooters.

The thing about major cases is that they can take a long while (sometimes years) to be fully adjudicated, so here I thought I'd finish by letting you know how the cases in this story turned out, to the extent that the public records will allow.

Case 8-1: Shooter Peter "Froggy" Basquell and Driver Belko Vaunt both got ninety days in jail. One year later, in 2010, they were arrested again for jacking deer at night. Parmenter Cair remains in federal prison on racketeering charges growing out of cigarette sales. His girlfriend got one year as an accomplice but was released after nine months. She now resides somewhere in northwestern Missouri. The federal government took Cair's scenic home on the bluff and sold it.

Knezevich, the Croatian, paid the agreed-to fine, had his hunting privileges revoked, did no time in jail, and has not been seen in the U.P. since. But every Christmas he sends to Service a Christmas card with a cartoon of Santa Claus standing beside a red pickup truck.

Noble Chern (alias Chernobyl to Wisconsin wardens) also got some jail time in Michigan and remains a hopeless mess. His fines and restitution remain unpaid. He still doesn't have a current driver's license. He traded his TV for a deer mount, nothing comparable to what once hung on his wall.

The two Henny Hills were investigated for animal cruelty (feeding kittens to coyotes), but no case was ever made because there was not enough solid evidence. Senior died in 2010. Junior still insists he has two kinds of diabetes and remains in the family trailer.

Arletta Ingalls and Penfold Pymn were both indicted by the Feds after Michigan nailed them for major poaching. The local court inexplicably returned the fancy kill rifle to the woman. Both had a larger role in the cigarette trade than Service recognized in the course of pursuing his case. Pymn eventually confessed to setting the two garage fires and got extra time in jail for those. Ingalls spent six months in jail and is now the subject of a deep IRS investigation, and more charges are pending with regard to Coppish and the hunt-for-pay scheme. Ingalls hires the best lawyers, who resist every legal move, drawing the cases out toward eternity or infinity. The pies-for-dogs business is no longer in operation.

Convicted firebug Teddy Coppish was charged as an accomplice in the garage fires and went back to jail for another year. It turned out that Teddy mentored Pymn on setting the garage fires. The night of the Slippery Creek blaze, Coppish set four other fires to pull fire coverage away from Service's camp. Other pending charges include the hunt-for-profit scam he and Arletta Ingalls ran on Coppish's land.

Jerzy Urbanik, who shot the gigantic sixteen-point buck while Limpy Allerdyce nearly had to deliver the couple's fourth child in the truck, was caught jacklighting in far eastern Marquette County by CO Angie Paul the very next summer. He was ticketed for shining with a loaded firearm in possession.

The Peaveyhouse clan all got felony time for stolen ATVs and the fish-and-game charges. Junco Peaveyhouse, the son who worked at a stop-and-rob and sold off-the-books state hunting and fishing licenses for a profit, went to jail for one year, same as his father.

Harry Pattinson and his crowd of landowners are currently vocal public boosters of the DNR. Privately they still think wolves were a large part of their deer de-population, but since Service's arrest of Jesper Buckshow, they at least pause before going into their old spiels.

The Tavolacci family crew was charged with eleven illegal deer, paid restitution and fines, and lost hunting privileges for three years. Since they never bothered to purchase licenses in the past, it seems unlikely that license revocations have curtailed hunting in subsequent seasons.

Sandy Tavolacci filed suit against Grady Service, alleging unprofessional activity and interference with his client. The judge dismissed the case as frivolous.

The big crew of ATV drivers all paid their fines. The three illegal handguns taken that night were condemned by the court and later sold at state auction.

Gray Eyes was charged with seven illegal deer, paid restitution and fines of more than $11,000, and lost his hunting privileges for three years. All the others in camp turned on him and fingered him as the shooter. Those with illegal fish were fined and paid up.

Jesper Buckshow was convicted of a number of drug charges and went to prison for three years. The Feds retain a lien on the house, which stands empty. Restitution for 174 deer, wolves, and turkeys came to $115,000, which was pled down from $130,000. It's still not been paid. Sally Palovar was not charged for anything and willingly helped the prosecution against her husband. She did not have to testify and, after the trial, moved to North Dakota.

Eight ball Lawrence "Lefty" Hugelyn was charged with multiple illegal deer but disappeared by the time Service filed his complaint and got the arrest warrant from the prosecutor. His kooky girlfriend, Star, moved on. Nobody knows where she went, or what happened to all of Lefty's near-feral cats.

No clue what happened to the daffy professor and his filmmaking cinema verité crew. No charges were ever brought by Service. It just wasn't important enough, given all the real and serious cases he was dealing with at the time.

All the deer, bear, turkeys, and wolves shot by the people in this story remain dead, and that's the brutal fact of poaching. Restitution doesn't bring back the dead. *Illegally* killing such animals amounts to nothing less than stealing something precious that belongs to all of us.

Limpy Allerdyce pretty much hangs with Grady Service and Friday all the time now and is adored by both Shigun and Maridly, not to mention Newf and Cat.

Tuesday Friday was speechless for two days after learning about Grady's money. There is an unspoken agreement that they will get married. When is an entirely different question.

When I was a young man, deer season was a happy, even festive occasion in Rudyard, the Upper Peninsula community where I went to high school. This was because the firearm opener was an official school holiday. My dad didn't hunt, but we got the day off, and that alone gave me positive vibes about hunting. Back then, in the late '50s and early '60s, the entire state deer herd was smaller than the annual harvest of deer is in the state today. Back then only bucks could be shot, and of course a big buck tended to give a hunter bragging rights for the year. Hunters had their local cedar swamp deer camps and repaired to the camps to stalk their prey. There were no store-bought tower blinds, no baits, no food plots, just lone hunters on two feet with a bow, rifle, or shotgun, hoping for enough snow to track moving and wounded animals.

The story of Grady's hearing in the spring of 2010 is for a future telling.

Be safe in the woods and streams, and as a pal of mine says, "Shot and a beer!" But not if you're gonna be driving.

—Joseph Heywood
Alberta and Portage, Michigan

ABOUT THE AUTHOR

Joseph Heywood is the author of *The Snowfly, Covered Waters, The Berkut, Taxi Dancer, The Domino Conspiracy*, the nine previous Grady Service Mysteries, two short story collections, *Hard Ground: Woods Cop Stories, and Harder Ground*. And the Lute Bapcat Mysteries *Red Jacket* and *Mountains of the Misbegotten*. The Woods Cop novels feature Grady Service, a contemporary conservation officer in the Upper Peninsula for Michigan's Department of Natural Resources. The other series focuses on Lute Bapcat, a Rough Rider turned Michigan game warden in the 1910s. Heywood's mystery series have earned the author cult status among lovers of the outdoors, law enforcement officials, and mystery devotees. Heywood lives half the year in the U.P. at Alberta (not Canada, eh) and spends winters Below the Bridge—in Portage, Michigan. Visit the author at JosephHeywood.com and check his blog: joeroads.com.